Debbie Dee was born and raised on a dairy farm in Northwest Ohio. She taught middle school language arts and reading for thirty-five years. Upon retirement, she promised herself that she would write and publish a historical romance book based upon the Civil War era. Her favorite book, *Gone with the Wind*, made a lasting impression on her when she read it as a young adult. She completed her promise and wrote a trilogy following McKenna and Captain Sloane throughout the Civil War and Reconstruction era.

Deb married her high school sweetheart forty years ago and is the proud mother of two sons and daughters-in-law. She currently lives in Dahlonega, Georgia.

McKenna's Crossing is dedicated to my loving father-in-law, Bompa Towns.

We have shared the love of Civil War history and the passion of written expression for forty-seven years and never once did he express skepticism during my writing, even when I doubted myself...

I will miss you and our magical colloquies.

Debbie Dee

McKenna's Crossing

AUSTIN MACAULEY PUBLISHERS™

LONDON * CAMBRIDGE * NEW YORK * SHARJAH

Ordering Information
Quantity sales: Special discounts are available on quantity purchases by corporations, associations, and others. For details, contact the publisher at the address below.

Publisher's Cataloging-in-Publication data
Dee, Debbie
McKenna's Crossing

ISBN 9781647502676 (Paperback)
ISBN 9781647502669 (Hardback)
ISBN 9781647502683 (ePub e-book)

Library of Congress Control Number: 2021902696

www.austinmacauley.com/us

First Published (2021)
Austin Macauley Publishers LLC
40 Wall Street, 33rd Floor, Suite 3302
New York, NY 10005
USA

mail-usa@austinmacauley.com
+1 (646) 5125767

Thank you to Austin Macauley Publishers who were willing to give my book a chance of publication.

Prologue

1838 – England

The classical portico and dome of the University College, London, welcomed all who entered its doors. It had recently been granted the authority to submit non-British students for degree examinations—and that had enticed two young Americans, Harper Reed and William Orson, to study at the prestigious college and adjacent hospital. Little did Harper know that his adventurous choice to travel and study medicine in England would forever change his life.

"William, my friend, I am going to marry that nurse I met yesterday," exclaimed Harper to his best friend, William, as they walked the white-tiled floor to their patients in the small dispensary on George Street in Euston Square.

"Harper, everyone says that when they meet Maribelle Wells for the very first time. She is a beautiful woman, I will not argue with you. But that doesn't mean you are going to be the lucky young doctor who will win her hand in marriage. After all, a lot of other young doctors have tried before you, but I hear her strict father scared them all off," replied William with a grin.

"Will, you and I have been classmates for a long time—all the way through medical school—and you know once I set my mind on something, I will achieve it. I'm telling you that I am going to marry that sweet young nurse if it is the last thing I do!"

"Well then, it may be the last thing you do if the rumors are true. I hear her father sleeps with a rifle by the bed and hides a shotgun in the parlor. You may want to reconsider the value of your life, dear friend," stated William before he approached his next patient's bed. "Besides, you are an American. Maribelle's father may not want his daughter to marry anyone but a proper titled Englishman. They adhere to the class system in the UK—still in place from the middle ages."

Harper looked at his friend and acknowledged Will's last comment with a crinkling of his brow. He shook his head and Will's statement from his mind for the moment as he walked to his young patient lying before him. The small girl had a badly bruised arm and a severe cut from a fall. Poor thing, she had just turned six years old and had a tree-climbing accident during her birthday party! He was glad that he had been working when her hysterical young mother brought her to the hospital. His quick actions had stopped the arterial bleeding and, so far, any infection. He had spent quite a bit of time stitching the wee thing's arm, since the cut had been visibly opened to the muscle.

Harper glanced down at the sleeping child. She was a pretty little girl and always so cheerful. Harper bent his tall frame at the waist, gently touched her shoulder, and called her name. She began to squirm from her slumber when he began to undo the wrapping of her bandages.

"Hello, Doctor Reed, I was sleeping," stated the child in a heavy-eyed voice while hugging her teddy bear.

"Hello to you, my dear little Ella. How are you feeling today?"

"I feel lonely," replied the child with a pout upon her face. She carefully scooted up and exaggerated her frown even more.

"Now, why do you feel lonely today?" asked Harper as he sat upon the edge of her bed.

"Well, I need to go home. Whiskers is all by himself and I need to take care of him."

"Who is Whiskers, dear?" asked Harper with a smile.

"He is my kitty. He is missing me, I just know it. Can I go home today, Doctor Reed? My arm doesn't hurt anymore. I have been here a very long time, and I miss my kitty."

"Ella, let me take a closer look at your arm. Would that be all right with you?"

"Yes, sir!" shouted Ella as she immediately stuck her arm out for Harper to inspect. He checked her bruising and her stitches that almost ran the length of her forearm.

"Ella, yes, you have been here nearly eight days. I do believe that you could go home today, but you must promise me something."

"Oh, I am very good at making promises," she said as she attempted to scoot up even more in bed with her good arm.

"Well, if you promise not to climb any more trees, I might let your mother take you home today. And if you promise to let your mother clean this arm in the morning and before bedtime, I will let you go home as soon as your mother and I have talked. Would you like that?"

"Oh, I would like that very much, and so would Teddy Bear," replied Ella with a smile from ear to ear.

"Well then, I will get a nurse to put on some more medicine and rewrap this arm for you with a new bandage. When your mother arrives, I will speak with her about you going home today. But you must keep your promise and allow your mother to do what she needs to do so that your arm will heal. I do not want a pretty little thing like you to have an ugly scar on her arm."

"I can do that, I promise. Can I come back and show Whiskers to you?" asked Ella with a pleading tone in her voice.

"I would like that very much. I would like to meet Whiskers. I will be back to check on you in a bit. You rest now and keep that arm laying up on this pillow. Close your eyes and hug your teddy, sweetie."

"Yes, sir."

"All right then." Harper gently slid off the bed and tucked the covers under Ella's chin. When he finished, he turned and saw Will standing behind him, leaning against the door frame with a half-smile.

"What are you looking at?" asked Harper with a tilt to his head as he walked toward his friend.

"I am looking at a young doctor who will become a legend one day. You will be a good father—you are wonderful with children," said Will as he clasped Harper on the shoulder. "Hell, you are wonderful with all of your patients, no matter who they are or how old they are."

"Well, thank you, Will. I hope that I will always feel as devoted to my profession as I do now. And for your information, I intend to be a father one day, Will. And I know just the woman who will be the mother of my children!" replied Harper with a grin upon his face and a wink. "Come now, let's finish seeing our patients. We still have a lot more of them to see, and I intend to be finished by supper."

"Remember what I said, Harper. Maribelle's father may not allow his daughter to marry an American. I don't want you to get your hopes up."

"Well, I am a firm believer that things happen for a reason. If she wants to marry me, she will, regardless of her father's approval," Harper determinedly replied as he walked slightly ahead of his friend.

Yes, I suppose things happen for a reason, but I know how obstinate and stubborn you can be, Harper Reed. Time will tell on this, Will thought to himself.

***

Charleston, South Carolina

1841

Harper sat across from Maribelle's bed with his unshaven face between his sweaty palms. Why in hell did he feel so helpless? Why had he gone on those house calls? Even though she wasn't due for six more weeks, he should have stayed home. *My God,* he thought to himself, *I have delivered over a hundred babies and I know that babies can come early. How could I have misjudged this?* His heart was breaking, and yet there was nothing he could do but wait. His sweet Maribelle lay so still. He watched her shallow breathing and prayed that she would wake from her unresponsiveness. He finally straightened his tired body, sat back in the wing chair, and stretched his long legs. He hadn't slept in two days, nor had he eaten. He just would not leave her side. He tilted his head back and closed his eyes. He allowed his mind to reflect upon the past three years of their passionate journey together.

He had kept his promise to his friend, Will. He did indeed ask Maribelle's father for her hand in marriage, only to be forced from the Wells home and threatened to never return. He remembered the day they decided to run away from England and get married. They were young and rebellious; they were so in love with each other that they did not think of the consequences of elopement.

She was his everything; he was her everything; they were soulmates. He could still remember Maribelle stomping her petite foot and placing her hands on her hips when she exclaimed, "To hell with marrying a titled Englishman. I will marry for love, not for land or social standing. Father will just have to accept my decision!"

Oh, she had a temper and a sassy mouth, thought Harper as he rubbed his aching neck. They had followed their hearts and eloped to America. No regrets and no going back. For the past three years, they had been deliriously in love. He remembered the exact moment when Maribelle had skipped down the stairs of their Charleston home with her announcement of her first pregnancy. They were jubilant. Their joy crumbled, however, when she delivered an unexpected early stillbirth during her twenty-sixth week of pregnancy. Their baby boy had not gotten the proper oxygen exchange through Maribelle's placenta. That was a horrid time, but they got through it and accepted it as God's will. Another year passed and God blessed them with a second pregnancy, and again she delivered a second stillbirth—a little girl at thirty-four weeks. The heartache, despair, and hopelessness overwhelmed both of their spirits. They gave up trying to conceive for fear of a third death.

Time passed and God blessed them a third time. They both had felt that Maribelle's pregnancy was a miracle. She had been extra cautious for eight months and took care not to overdo things. They had been so afraid to plan for their baby's future, due to the loss of the previous two. Maribelle knew that their neighbor, Sally Connell, would be delivering her first baby soon, and she knew that Sally was scared and nervous. She convinced Harper to ride out to the Connell plantation and check on her. She assured him that she would be fine.

If only I had stayed home. My sweet Maribelle, he thought, *always thinking of someone else before herself. God had other plans for us.*

Maribelle had delivered a baby girl hours ago. The baby was doing fine. She was beautiful, just like her mother. All had gone well, except for the fact that Harper had not been there to deliver the babe himself. Maribelle had gone into early labor and Harper was miles away delivering someone else's child.

Why, God, would you allow my two babies to perish and grant me the blessing of a third child, only to have me helping another woman other than my own wife? Where is your grace and mercy? Why, Lord, would you now take away the mother of my child? I see her weakening condition. I know what will ultimately happen. Why, Lord, after all we have been through? Please do not take my Maribelle, not now. I cannot raise a child by myself—I do not know how.

A throaty, hoarse sound broke Harper's thoughts. He heard a slight whisper and looked at Maribelle. She had her eyes open—those beautiful blue eyes of hers were looking at him. He quickly rose and knelt beside her, holding her small hands in his.

"Harper?"

"Yes, my love, I am here," he said with the all too familiar lump in his throat from hours of weeping.

"Harper, take care of our little girl. Be a good father," whispered Maribelle with effort.

"I will, my love. I will raise her with gentleness and kindness."

"Promise me, Harper, promise me that you will."

"I will, my love. Stay with me, dear, stay with me and keep talking to me," Harper said with tears in his eyes.

"I am so tired, my love. Promise me to cherish her."

"I will, my love. What shall we call her?" asked Harper pleadingly. Maribelle looked at the ceiling and smiled for what seemed an eternity. When she looked back at Harper, she said, "McKenna. We shall call her McKenna. Put her in my arms. I want to hold her."

Harper immediately rose, walked to the cradle, and picked up the sleeping bundle. He gently laid the babe upon Maribelle's chest, helping to hold the child.

"She is beautiful, isn't she, Harper?"

"Yes, my love, she is beautiful."

"McKenna Reed will be strong, just like her father," whispered Maribelle with very little strength left.

"She will be a beautiful woman, just like her mother. She will be full of kindness and compassion. She will learn to ride and shoot. She will be the envy of every other girl in the county! Oh, Maribelle, she will be a beauty for sure. What do you think, my dear, shall we get her a pony?" asked Harper.

Maribelle didn't answer Harper's last question. She passed that very moment. Harper Reed took his infant daughter and placed her gently into the cradle. He then crawled upon the bed and held his beloved Maribelle in his arms and wept, until he eventually cried himself to sleep.

Chapter 1

Charleston, South Carolina – 1860

"McKenna Reed, you had best get yourself off that stallion and to the breakfast table! You know your papa hates to be kept waitin' for his early mornin' breakfast. Go on now; you hurry yourself up," shouted Zadie from the summer kitchen doorway as McKenna trotted past.

I don't know why I decided to cook all this apple butter today, Zadie thought to herself as she wiped the sweat from her brow. *It sure is hot for October.* She shook her head. *That girl is gonna get in trouble if she doesn't hurry up! Lord, help that girl to be on time for anything when she is on that horse.*

That powerful, strapping stallion was McKenna's best friend. She had nurtured it from the minute it was delivered by her father. She'd raised him from a suckling, to a weanling, to a yearling, and had trained the stallion to ride fast and long. McKenna could ride as well or better than any man or soldier in Charleston County. Many a day, she would be on Solomon—as she'd named him—from sun up to sunset.

She had a natural gentleness and respect for all animals, including her other best friend, Knox. McKenna had delivered him from his mother going on five years ago. That dog was attached to her hip, and when he wasn't beside her, he knew where she was. No one dared approach McKenna with intent to harm her; Knox would kill them first. Pity the poor man who tried to get close to her with either of her animal companions by her side. Many men had tried to court her, but they had failed. McKenna's father, Harper Reed, guarded the girl with fortitude, brawn, and Southern pride.

Zadie knew it would have to be a special man to extract McKenna from her father. The right man would come along; the good Lord would see to it.

McKenna had just approached the house when she heard Zadie's warning. Having never known her mother, McKenna considered Zadie the next best thing, and over the years, McKenna had come to love the woman as if she were kin. McKenna had thrown societal protocol to the wind; she didn't care if Zadie was a colored woman; McKenna loved her as a mother. Harper encouraged his daughter's relationship with Zadie. Skin color did not matter to Harper; he only wanted his daughter to be loved by a mother figure, and Zadie filled that position. He raised her with the grand Southern etiquette Maribelle would have taught her. He also taught McKenna how to ride, shoot, and use her archery skills to hunt anything in air or on land.

Harper was a prominent physician and surgeon for Charleston, Berkeley, and Dorchester counties. He had attended the Medical College of South Carolina and had taken his opportunity for a private education quite seriously. He knew he had been lucky to receive a college education and have a chance to better himself. Thus, he was determined that McKenna would be highly educated as well.

She had attended Miss Murden's Seminary for Young Ladies in Charleston and attended Harper Reed's school of shooting, horsemanship, and archery to complete her nineteen years of Charlestonian life thus far. Of course, McKenna would have much preferred to stay at home with her animals rather than Seminary School, but she completed her studies as requested by her father.

"I'm coming, Zadie. I will be right there," McKenna shouted over her shoulder. She quickly unbridled Solomon and put him to pasture. *I should have put on my riding habit instead of my day dress*, she thought to herself as she hurried to the house. The mist of rain she'd encountered on her ride would certainly ruin the crêpe de Chine silk. *Oh well, Zadie will fix it*, she thought. And Zadie wouldn't tell McKenna's father she'd already been riding this morning. If her father found out the dress he'd bought for her in Biddeford, Maine, had water spots on it as a result of her carelessness, she would be in for a scolding.

She was to meet an acquaintance of her father's today, and her dress attire should show proper care. Ah, yes, this acquaintance would probably be another medical doctor who would like to convince her to attend medical school.

Oh, Papa, I just want to buy, breed, and train the best horses in this country. I would much rather attend veterinarian school than medical school.

Well, wouldn't that be something—attending veterinarian school with only three hundred and ninety-two veterinarian doctors on hand. If only Papa would read Dr. James Mease's writings on the need for horse doctors, McKenna thought to herself.

The rain was starting to increase as she made her way to the iconic colonnades of the main house. She dearly loved it and the influence her grandparents had borrowed from Charles Bulfinch and Thomas Jefferson in building it. Her home had character, and its walls had seen so much happiness, as well as its share of sorrows.

It was unfortunate that this very same home was where her paternal grandparents had died at an early age. An unexplained fire caused smoke damage to their lungs while they slept. Her beautiful mother died in the room next to McKenna's, as well as her older brother and sister in previous stillbirths. *Perhaps the future will provide happiness in this house once again,* she thought as she walked into the dining room.

"Good morning, Papa! I trust you slept well last evening." McKenna quickly seated herself at the elaborate dining room table.

"Don't you 'good morning, Papa' me, McKenna-girl. I have been waiting over twenty minutes for you to share my breakfast. Where in God's name have you been?" he asked with a half-smile.

"I was brushing Solomon."

"Why were you doing that this morn?"

"Um, because that is what one does to a horse after the horse has been ridden hard. That is what Harper Reed's equestrian school taught me," she said with a smile in the corner of her mouth.

"McKenna, watch that sass of yours. You are as cute as a button, but that beauty doesn't work on me. Although I like your spunk, I have patients to attend to this morning. I have Doctor Orson coming here soon to meet with you and discuss some possible plans.

"I do not want my daughter out in the rain with that horse of hers and spoiling the day dress I ordered from Maine. Didn't think I would notice?" He winked.

"I am sorry, sir; I always take Solomon out for his early morning ride. I should have left earlier, hmm?" She winked back.

"McKenna, you need to be alert when you ride. Even though you ride on our land, the talk of South Carolina secession has stirred up a lot of tempers and quick-angered actions. It would be best if you ride closer to home."

"Papa, I have Knox with me and my guns and bow. I will be fine. You don't think any Union soldiers would dare come onto our land this far from the bay, do you?"

"Never know, my dear, but look in front, behind, and sideways at all times. Remember, that damn horse of yours can't talk to you, and that dog can't warn you of trouble."

"That is where you are wrong, Papa. They can warn me, and they do. Knox and Solomon will always take care of me. Now then, what are these possible future plans all about?"

"Let's finish our breakfast, and I will tell you after we eat," stated her father with a detectable amount of anxiety in his voice.

"I am very hungry this morning, Papa, and I will be glad to talk with you after we eat," stated McKenna hesitantly as she slathered fresh butter onto her sweet bread. *What are you up to now? Is this another one of your schemes to convince me to go to medical school?* she thought.

Chapter 2

"Captain Sloane, sir, we have a problem. The ship will take longer than we thought for cleaning and repair."

"How much longer, Pepper?" asked the captain as he walked from his quarters to the ship's galley.

"A week, maybe more, sir," answered his first-mate, following behind.

"A week as in seven days or a week as in five days, Pepper?"

"Captain, sir, I am just relaying what the shipwright told me. He thought the repairs may be delayed due to the tension here in Charleston with the talk of secession."

"Pepper, I am not interested in what these Charlestonians may or may not do with their secession. I, sir, need to make haste for England and return my goods back to my buyers."

"Captain Sloane, I understand, sir, but we can't set sail if we have nothing to set sail in. I will do my best to hasten the shipwright."

"See that you do, Pepper. As always, I extend my gratitude." Captain Parker Sloane shook his first-mate's hand, abruptly turned, and took the steps two at a time down into the galley. There before him stood a short, stocky woman stirring two black kettles.

"Sally, I have a request for you." The captain came from behind and gently pressed a kiss upon her cheek.

"Aye, my fine captain, and what exactly would you be requestin' from ol' Sally this morn'?"

"I have a hankering for your clam chowder. Is it possible to have some chowder this evening for supper?"

"Parker, I would be glad to cook up some of my mouth-waterin' chowder. You knew I would say yes before you even asked, didn't you?"

Parker leaned over Sally and gave her a hug.

"Yes, my dear, I did. I look forward to supper tonight. I will be back shortly; I have to bring Lyla home. Come and walk with me upstairs. It is a good day for some sunshine to fall upon that pretty face of yours."

Together, Sally and Parker climbed the stairs to the main deck. Parker headed directly toward the docking bridge and Sally watched Parker head down toward the park. Memories flooded Sally's mind as she thought back to the day Parker's parents were lost at sea. He had been devastated when he had heard the news. Sally and her husband had worked with Parker on three of the five ships he had built, and he'd turned to them for the parental support he so desperately needed after his parents' deaths.

A few years later, Sally's husband had been struck dead by a loose mast beam. From that moment on, Sally and Parker had become closer than ever, forming an unbreakable bond.

She watched as he walked toward the park entrance. He was a handsome man. At six feet six inches, Parker Sloane was formidable. Sally remembered tying his shoulder-length hair while sailing. It was as black as a raven's chest and highlighted with bits of sunlit auburn. His eyes, oh, his eyes were captivating, and so much like his mother's. The piercing green with gold flecks within the irises enhanced the lighter shades in his hair.

As far as Sally was concerned, God had created the crème de la crème when he'd made Parker Sloane. She watched him bend down to pet his dog, Lyla. There had always been an unspoken conversation between them— caretaker and pet, teacher of respect and student of loyalty.

That dog was the last remaining connection to his parents. They had given Lyla to him when his first ship was christened, and Parker never went anywhere without that dog.

Sally turned her gaze to a group of young ladies seated on a nearby park bench. They seemed to be enjoying the weather underneath the shade of the willow trees. Their stares did not go unnoticed by Sally, though. It was almost comical to watch their mouths drop in awe as Parker walked past them with Lyla in tow.

Poor souls, she thought. *They would probably give anything to catch the attention of the handsome Captain Parker Sloane. Good luck, ladies… His heart was broken long ago by a selfish woman. His guard is up and his heart is sealed.*

Sally watched as Parker and Lyla returned to the ship's plank; she desperately prayed that one day, a young lady would be able to break down that guard and fill his heart with love again. She only hoped she would live long enough to witness it. Sally was in ill-health and she knew it; Parker didn't know, and there would be no reason to reveal her condition to him. *What he didn't know couldn't hurt him*, she thought to herself. At least, for the time being.

Chapter 3

"Absolutely not! Are you out of your mind? There is no way on God's green earth that I will agree to this, Papa!" McKenna half-stood and scooted her chair from the dining room table with such force that it toppled over. She immediately stood straight and paced before her father.

"McKenna, you have to agree," her father stated in a raised voice. "You have no other choice! Your safety is at stake! The way I see it, you have two options, my dear. Your first option is to attend medical school as I did, preferably out of South Carolina."

"No!"

"Well then, your second option is to leave the country, travel to England, and stay with my sister, your Aunt Olympia, until this secession nonsense blows over."

"No!" McKenna picked up her overturned chair and sat across the table from her father. "Papa, with all due respect, I simply cannot pick up and leave my home because you think there might be trouble here in the future."

"McKenna, there is talk of war. I do not want to have to worry about you if that war approaches here. I will be traveling and will be safe because I am a doctor available for any color of uniform that needs me. If or when this war begins, we may not even have a home left by its end."

"War? What war? Papa, how can you just send me off to England with no consideration of my thoughts or feelings?"

"Listen carefully, my dear. My concern for your safety is my top priority. John Calhoun and Preston Brooks are inflaming everyone's passion for secession. They are afraid that talk of emancipation of slaves will give the blacks the same rights as us. Everyone is thinking this would change our culture and our way of life. If Lincoln is elected and he has his way, all slaves could be free. Calhoun believes South Carolina Congress should not exclude slavery from Western territories, and that each state should have the right to choose if it will allow slavery. If plantation owners in South Carolina aren't able to have slaves, they would be forced to move their cotton and tobacco plantations to the Utah and Texas Territories, where neither product would grow well, but at least they would be able to keep their slaves and attempt to grow crops. McKenna, the people of South Carolina are so fired up that many of them do not want to move out west; they want to stay here with their crops and their slaves. Mississippi and Alabama have already sent delegates to the convention, and we have been advised to send South Carolina delegates as well. Again, the majority in South Carolina feel if we can't keep our slavery and our way of life, then we shall secede. If this comes to a vote in December, and if this overrides President Buchanan's thoughts, I want you far away from here."

"Papa, I can't just pick up and leave to live with Aunt Olympia. I barely know her. The last time I saw her was almost eight years ago, when I was just eleven years old. I barely remember my cousins. I barely remember Percy, the cook, and Tierney, the butler. If anyone were of interest to me, it would be Cooper, the stable master. After all, he is the best horseman in England, but that is beside the point!"

Her father reached across the table and enfolded McKenna's hands within his. "I know this is happening quickly, but heated tempers and the threat of war should not be taken lightly by anyone."

"Certainly, President Buchanan would never allow this country to split apart, would he?" asked McKenna.

"President Buchanan feels secession is illegal, but he does not believe the government has any right to prevent states from seceding. So, he really isn't pleasing anyone. We shall see on the twentieth of December when this comes to a vote. By then, you shall be gone, and I will not worry about your safety."

"I will not go to England without Solomon and Knox. I hope you have a ship that can set sail for England and accommodate my pets. Now, you know that most ships will not take small pets, let alone large animals, such as horses. And what about Zadie? Where will she go?"

"Daughter, do you understand that it is imperative for you to leave Charleston before December?"

"When would I be leaving?"

"Within the week."

"I will not be ready. How am I to be packed and ready to go and say good-bye to my friends and neighbors in so short a time?"

"You will simply get on that damn horse of yours, say your good-byes within a day, help Zadie pack you up, and help her pack as well. She will be going with you."

"Really, Papa? Really, Zadie is coming with me? She knew about this, didn't she? She knew all along?" McKenna asked, pointing her finger at her father.

"Yes, my dear, she knew. Of course, she would know. Who else would convince you to go if not me? Any other questions?"

"My animals?"

"We are working on this as I speak. They will accompany you to England."

McKenna scooted her chair back and folded her arms. She remained silent for a few moments before she looked into her father's eyes and finally spoke. "Well, I suppose I better start packing and sorting. I have a lot to do. How long will I be in England? Will I be able to visit? And why is Doctor Orson here?"

Harper stood and leaned over his headstrong daughter. He cleared his throat before he spoke his next words, slowly and firmly. "McKenna, start packing. No, you will not be visiting. You will stay there until it is safe to come home—however long that might be. Know that you will always be my little girl, and that I love you so deeply. I promised your mother to love you, cherish you, and protect you at all cost. I know I am making the right decision as your father. Doctor Orson is here because he may know a connection in London to help you further your medical training—veterinarian training, that is. He is going to give me a list of doctors I intend to write to on your behalf. I also asked him here for moral support… in case you refused to go," he said with a half-smile.

McKenna absorbed her father's words. The possibilities were endless. She could stay at her aunt's home, and Cooper would help her with the knowledge she needed outside of her medical books. But she was getting too far ahead of herself for now. McKenna rose from her chair, walked to her father, and gently placed a kiss upon his cheek. "Know that I love you and cherish you as well, Papa. You mean the world to me, and yes, I do understand everything you have told me. But how did you know I would take option two?"

"I know what you will think and do before you think it and do it, baby girl. Run along now and pack."

McKenna took her father's hands and squeezed them tightly. "Papa, I love you with my whole heart. I am sorry I raised my voice to you earlier. I just can't bear the thought of leaving my home and you, and everything I love."

"I understand your doubts and your fears, daughter. But I must keep you safe, and to do that, I must insist you leave here and head for safer ground."

McKenna embraced his hands and looked in his eyes. "I love you, Papa, and I will abide by your decision. I know you are doing what you think is best for me. I thank you for caring for my safety, and I hope Doctor Orson can help me pursue my dreams of animal medicine. With all due respect, Papa, you followed your dream of medicine, and now I would like to follow mine."

"I love you too, baby girl. I understand your passion for veterinarian medicine. We shall see what can be done to help you achieve your dream, whether in America or in England. Go on, now, head upstairs and start packing." McKenna nodded in understanding before she walked slowly from the table to the stairs.

Harper watched his daughter walk away with mixed emotions. He knew she carried the weight of the world on those small shoulders of hers. He understood her mind was reeling right now and could only empathize with her uncertain future. He methodically made his way into the parlor where his colleague waited.

"Well, did she agree?" asked Dr. Orson before placing his coffee cup on the table.

"She did. Thank you for coming, William, especially with such short notice."

"My pleasure. But I really must go, Harper. I have more meetings to attend to this morning. We shall talk again, soon." The two of them continued their walk to the front doors and bid each other their customary farewells—their old college handshake and slap upon the back.

As Harper watched his friend disappear down the drive in his carriage, his thoughts returned to his daughter. He knew how badly she wanted to attend a veterinary college, and England had the answer for that option. He had needed William there for support and for his knowledge of animal medicine in case McKenna started asking questions about school possibilities in England. Now that she had agreed to go, it was a matter of getting her there. Hopefully, his brother-in-law, Pepper, could help convince a certain captain to sail his beautiful daughter and her companions on his ship to England—within the week.

Chapter 4

The customary three knocks that Pepper rapped upon Captain Sloane's cabin door were gentle. However, Pepper knew the forthcoming conversation would be anything but.

"Enter," Parker's husky voice said from the other side of the thick mahogany door.

"Pardon the intrusion, Captain, but I have a situation to discuss with you, and it is important," stated Pepper as he carefully closed the captain's door. Pepper proceeded to sit down across from Parker, then quickly rose from his chair and began pacing.

"Pepper, for Christ's sake, man, we have been together far too long for you to be so skittish. What is so bloody important to take the color from your face? Sit your arse down and talk to me," Parker shouted as he laid his quill upon his desk.

Pepper knew he would be asking a lot of his long-time friend. He seated himself, leaned forward, and braced both elbows upon his knees as he began to explain the entire situation to the captain. He finished his final sentence with a swallow of offered bourbon.

"That's it. That's what needs to be done, sir," stated Pepper with a final hiccup.

"Pepper, you only hiccup when you are nervous. Are you mad, man? There is no way in hell I will take a lady, her pets, and a black woman on my ship. Either you drank too much before you came here, or you will need a drink when I am done beating you to a pulp." The captain laughed.

"Captain, I am asking for me. This is not a joking matter. I have been sailing with you close to ten years. I have never deserted you or broken your trust, have I?"

"No, you have not. Where is this conversation going?"

"The States are in a bad way. The Southern states want to keep their slaves because they feel it is their choice to do so. The North feels slavery is wrong, and no man should be chained to another. Soon, the South may split from the North, and there could be an all-out war—brother fighting against brother or cousin against cousin."

"And how exactly does this involve me?" asked the captain as he leaned backed in his chair and intertwined his unusually large fingers.

"Well, it doesn't, exactly," murmured Pepper.

"It sure as hell does if I must transport a pampered, spoiled brat from Charleston to Olympia's home in England."

"Easy, Parker. That spoiled brat would be my niece—my brother-in-law Harper's daughter."

"I realize that. So, am I to understand that I should inconvenience myself thus, all because we have sailed together for nigh on ten years?"

"Yes, sir. That would be a fair understanding."

"The answer is no."

"Captain, I insist. This is my niece we are talking about."

"Since when did you pay attention to family?" asked Parker as he leaned forward, facing Pepper.

"When I found out that my darling sister died giving birth to her. I should have asked, inquired, or done more for Maribelle. I didn't know, sir. I just sailed the seas and had limited correspondence with my sisters."

"How old is the girl?"

"She would be about nineteen or twenty—she is no girl, sir."

"Name?"

"McKenna Reed."

"What in the hell kind of name is McKenna?"

"Don't know, sir. I believe she was named after my mother, taking her middle name. At any rate, that's what she's called. I take it that you will agree?"

"If this brat gives me one ounce of trouble, or the servant woman, or her animals—I will take out my anger on you! Understood? Better yet, obtain another ship for those damn animals; I do not have the room or proper ventilation for them on the *Constance*."

"Yes, sir, understood. Plan on the *Constance* to be ready the day after tomorrow. We will load everyone then," Pepper replied with a smile and a quick nod before he left the captain's quarters and returned to the upper deck, where he breathed a sigh of relief. He hated using his friendship as leverage, but he owed this to Harper and to Maribelle.

What he remembered of his sister Maribelle was simply sweetness and kindness. He had left his sister when she had needed him. He had put his career and his life's choices above hers. He should have been at home to support her. Or, at the very least, he should have stood up to his father and told him to let Maribelle marry her true love. Instead, he let his temper get the better of him and had abandoned them both. He'd left her with their father and his dictates.

Perhaps if he had remained in England, he could have eliminated the stress and tension from their father. Maybe, if he had stayed, Maribelle would not have run away from England in the first place. She could have remained in her homeland and been closer to a hospital. No matter how much time had passed, he owed Maribelle in his mind. He needed to give her daughter a chance to live life without tyranny from another human being or from an impending war. He owed his niece a chance at happiness and safety. Even though he had not yet met McKenna, maybe he could right his wrong of leaving Maribelle all those years ago by taking care of her daughter.

Parker stood in disbelief, scratching his head as Pepper left his cabin. How had he arranged to have the ship done in haste? If he didn't know better, he would think Pepper had this whole plan arranged from day one of dropping anchor in this godforsaken, mixed-up city. *Hell, Pepper and I are cut from the same cloth. I help my sister whenever I can. We are no different*, the captain thought as he poured himself another brandy.

Chapter 5

McKenna woke up to sunshine and the sweet sound of the cowbirds. She loved hearing the songs of the birds outside her window each morning. They seemed to congregate in the weeping willows and lazily trill their voices to anyone listening in the big house. She eagerly rose and attended to her morning chores and breakfast.

Well, she thought later while packing up her valise, *I might as well make the best of things right now. Papa is right. If it is not safe here, I need not place extra worry upon his shoulders.* But her mind was filled with other thoughts. What would England be like? Would she make any friends over there? Would her cousins remember her? At least she'd have Zadie. Would she be accepted? Would Cooper remember her?

When it was finally time for McKenna to go, long, continuous hugs and tears were exchanged between her and her stoic father. The final hug was given along with Harper's promise to write and update McKenna with Charleston news. Knox and Solomon were packed up and ready to go, in a manner of speaking. They were packed inside the barn with their breakfast bowls—the only way Harper could distract their attention from McKenna was to feed them. He had managed to put her pets on another ship. What McKenna didn't know wouldn't hurt her, he thought—for the present time, at least. Harper watched as the carriage took his daughter down the lane. He had wanted to take McKenna to the ship himself, but an emergency surgery had changed his schedule. He knew this was for the best, no matter how badly it hurt to see her go. God willing, they would meet again.

An hour later, the carriage pulled to a stop by the north side of the main shipping channel and loading area in Charleston Harbor. McKenna looked out upon the harbor and saw that Fort Sumter was busy with their twelve-pound Howitzer drills, cannon boring, while loading and unloading supplies to the soldiers on the island. Northern soldiers, to be precise. She watched the activities happening before her and shuddered. *Would there really be war? Would this beautiful city truly be involved in this so-called secession?* The idea of war within a country was just not possible. How could people be so opinionated to the point of secession or death? She and her father considered Zadie no more a slave than a bird. *Her blood is just as red as mine. Why do people put labels on skin color?*

McKenna gathered her thoughts and sighed as she watched the lapping waves brush up against the break wall. A sense of tranquility allowed her thoughts to travel back to her childhood. Zadie had been McKenna's primary caregiver since she was an infant, and she hadn't fully understood the system into which she'd been born until she grew older. She remembered her father continually telling his friends and neighbors that human beings who worked side by side could not help but form relationships.

She knew he genuinely cared for Zadie and admired her abilities to care for patients and herself. But McKenna also realized his admiration for Zadie was limited by a Southern power imbalance and the confines of the word "slavery."

Their neighbors and inner circle of friends were not as tolerant of blacks. McKenna remembered their disapproving facial expressions when they would visit for tea, and McKenna would ask Zadie to join them at the table. Three-fourths of Southern whites didn't even own slaves; of those who did, most owned twenty or fewer. So why was there such hate toward people of color in the South? Would the slave owner and the slave ever approach equality? That question had plagued McKenna's mind for as long as she could remember. Perhaps the same question plagued President Lincoln. Thank goodness, her father did not enforce the Slave Codes. Zadie may not be able to testify in a court of law or own a firearm, but she was not considered property by the Reed family. She was a person, and McKenna loved her.

Her thoughts were momentarily interrupted by her hat ribbons flapping against her chin. She began to rub her arms to ward off the chill from the west wind as she stepped onto the dock. She had been so deep in thought, she did not realize her hat ribbons had become untied. The wind had picked up, forcing her to hang on tightly to her velvet hat, which had been a gift from her father. She gave her father credit. He tried to keep up on the latest fashions merely to ensure that she was dressed in the most fashionable gowns and accessories.

Papa prefers gowns to riding habits. I would prefer a new Spencer repeating rifle, she chuckled to herself.

"McKenna, Lord's sake, girl, grab your ribbons before the wind takes your papa's hat into the sea!" shouted Zadie, interrupting McKenna from her thoughts.

"Oh, dear, my mind was elsewhere and not paying attention!" She quickly tied the ribbon into a knot, knowing full well it wouldn't hold with another gust of wind.

"You'd best pay attention now; we are ready to board the *Constance*," said Zadie as she hauled her own plump body onto the boardwalk ramp.

What sort of name was *Constance*? McKenna wondered. She had read once that captains named their ships after a conquest or a woman. Perhaps this captain had done the same thing. McKenna looked behind and noticed her animals had not followed behind in a separate wagon.

"Zadie, where are Solomon and Knox? Why didn't they follow in Papa's other wagons?"

"Now, listen to me, baby girl, your dog and your horse will be sent over to England on another ship. The captain said this ship was not large enough to accommodate a 'mollycoddled' young lady and her belongings," stated Zadie with a furrowed brow.

"Oh, he did, did he? Mollycoddled? He thinks I am spoiled and have too many belongings? That was part of the deal. We shall see about this."

"Aw now, McKenna, don't go and get yourself all riled up—he just used some fancy words, that's all," said Zadie with her hands on her hips.

It was too late for words of comfort. McKenna was so angry that she spun around and, had it not been for a post to grab on to, she would have fallen face first into the cold, salty waters of the Atlantic. She quickly caught her breath, let go of the post, and realized that the post wasn't letting go of her.

McKenna looked up into the most alluring, prepossessing green eyes she had ever seen. She could not move even if she had wanted to. Slowly, inch by inch, the post in front of her turned into the shape of a man. The sun became unshielded by the clouds, and McKenna now saw this towering form was indeed the chiseled statue of one of the most handsome men she had ever laid eyes on.

"Pardon my clumsiness, sir. I fear I turned too quickly and lost my balance. Had you not stopped me, I would have taken an early Atlantic bath today."

McKenna continued to look in those captivating eyes, waiting for any form of a cordial response.

"You should not be so clumsy, ma'am. Hopefully, you will have better footing and balance on my ship. I am Captain Parker Sloane, and I assume you are Miss McKenna Reed?"

Chapter 6

"Yes, I am McKenna Reed, and I do have very good balance and footing. I was just caught up in the moment of daydreaming and thinking about Charleston's future as I glanced out at Fort Sumter. I am sure you understand my unease with the talk of secession and all," she replied softly with a half-smile. She really wanted to scold him for calling her 'mollycoddled.'

"Well, Miss Reed, the only unease I am feeling right now is associated with the fact that I have to transport you all the way to England. Hell, you have already fallen and haven't yet stepped foot on board the *Constance*."

"Excuse me, Captain, are you always this hostile?" asked McKenna with a forced smile.

My God, she is exquisite, thought Parker. He had felt two small hands grab on to him for dear life. When he'd turned to see the owner of those hands, he had looked down onto a head of flaxen curls.

Too bad her little hat didn't fall into the sea. That would have been a sight. She would have probably jumped into the water—dress and all—just to save the damn thing. Then I would have had to think about jumping in to save her. From what he'd felt as he'd hung on to Miss Reed, she was small-waisted and bestowed with a full bosom that filled out her dress to perfection. She was not tall—barely reaching the top of his breastbone; with the face of an angel and the body of a goddess. This little package would be a treasure for any man. *Time will tell if she has the endurance and the intellect to survive outside of Charleston and its cosseted boundaries*, he thought to himself.

"Captain Parker, are you deaf or just plain rude?" asked McKenna as she tugged on his sleeve.

The small tug brought him back to the moment. Her upturned nose and those eyes were now looking down on him, even though she had to tilt her head back to meet his gaze.

"Pardon me, Miss Reed, I was caught up in the beauty of your hat. I was thinking what a shame it would have been for such an expensive item to have been blown into the brink of the sea wall."

"The brink?"

"The edge, Miss Reed. A brink means the edge of something. In your case, your hat almost went into the edge of the water. I would have thought that an educated lady, such as yourself, would know what a 'brink' is," explained the captain with a tinge of sarcasm.

"Captain Sloane, I will ignore that statement. I thank you for your assistance," replied McKenna with a controlled sigh and gritted teeth as she abruptly let go of the captain's arms and turned to make her way to the ship.

"Take care in walking, Miss Reed; those planks along the boardwalk can trip up a lady, and I would not want anything to happen to those fancy shoes of yours."

How did he see my shoes? He is a cad with a smile. Keep walking, don't look back, she told herself.

"Miss Reed, do not tarry. I want to lift sails within the hour. I am certain my crew will have your cabin ready," replied Parker with a mischievous look in his eyes.

That's it. Now he thinks he can order me about. Think again, Captain!

McKenna stopped, took a big breath, and slowly turned, facing the captain before she spoke. "I will be sure not to tarry, Captain Sloane. I assume everything on board your ship is in perfect working condition for me. Although, I do notice your absentee pennant is still flying. You most certainly will want to change that to indicate yourself as the flotilla commander." McKenna smiled smugly at Parker for a moment, then pivoted and continued walking toward the entrance steps of the ship, holding tightly onto her hat.

Parker's eyes followed McKenna's form as she approached the ramp to his ship. *I may just enjoy this little adventure to bonny England after all*, he thought. *The little chit knows what an absentee pennant is, let alone a flotilla commander? I wonder if this spoiled, albeit beautiful, southern belle knows what it is like to sail on a ship without the comforts of home for the next few weeks?*

"Be warned, fair maiden," he murmured under his breath, "I do not play fair."

Chapter 7

McKenna and Zadie were shown to their cabin immediately. McKenna had started to unpack her small valise when a knock sounded on her door.

"Who is it?" she asked, hoping it was not the captain. She was in no mood for more verbal sparring.

"Miss Reed, it is the first mate, Pepper."

McKenna walked to the door and slowly opened it. On the other side, she saw a man who almost took her breath away. She inhaled quickly and caught herself.

"I am so sorry, sir, but you startled me. You remind me of someone. I thought for a moment I had seen a ghost."

"Who would I be reminding you of, Miss Reed?"

"Oh, no one you would have known. How can I help you?" McKenna began to wonder what was going through the first mate's mind. He stood there staring at her—or rather, through her, and she found herself staring right back at him. She noticed the birthmark on the left side of his jaw. A tiny, star-shaped mark just like the one that had adorned her mother's face.

"Miss Reed, dinner will be served at 5:00 p.m. The captain wanted me to let you know. He has requested your presence at his table for all meals, beginning this evening. Your servant is also requested."

"Requested? Does the captain normally go about making requests? Or is it beneath his manners to politely ask his guests to join him at his table for dinner, Mr. Pepper?"

"Pepper, ma'am, just Pepper. Yes, he does request because he is the captain of this ship, and he expects his requests to be honored."

"Well, then, we shall honor them tonight, sir. Zadie, who is not my servant, and I will be at His Excellency's table at 5:00 p.m. Please inform him of that. But Mr. Pepper, ah, Pepper, where is his table located?"

"Next to his quarters, ma'am. The captain wanted a separate dining room for meals to be served. Some of his guests have been very important and influential throughout Europe. When he designed this ship, he felt that meals should be shared at a table rather than over a crate in the galley. He and his invited guests take all of their meals there."

"Ah, I see, sir. I must admit I have never seen a ship so large or so grand as this one. It is quite beautiful."

"It should be. The captain built it himself. He is one of the finest shipwrights in England. If truth be told, he is the best in Europe. He is so busy building ships and sailing them, he hasn't much time for anything else. His skills are sought after in Europe and his reputation has spread to America, as well. In fact, that is why the captain was in Charleston," Pepper casually added.

"Why in Charleston, sir?"

"Well, the Southerners wanted to see for themselves how robust his ships actually are. There are many Charlestonians who are packing up their belongings and moving to Europe until your present political arguments have been settled. There are also some mighty fine horse breeders in this part of the country, and certain families of wealth want to take their horses to England and Ireland and begin breeding over there."

"I see," said McKenna. Now this was a conversation she could have with Captain Sloane. "Well, Pepper, I too enjoy riding and training horses. I have a horse that was supposed to come with me on this trip."

"Yes, ma'am. I met your father at the pub a few days ago, and we began talking about the ship and the transporting of your horse. He told me you are quite an excellent rider and have a keen eye for breeding good horses."

"Well, thank you for sharing Papa's conversation with me. Yes, I do like horses, and perhaps one day, I will be able to train and breed my own horses in England! There was one man over there whom I would trust with my life and with my stallion. But I haven't seen him in over eight years, since I last visited, so I do not even know if he is still there."

"Who would that be, Miss Reed?"

"They call him Cooper; I do not know his given name or his surname. But he is one exceptional trainer."

Pepper nodded. "I think I may have heard of him... Well, Miss Reed, I had best be on my way. I will see you at dinner tonight. Let me know if you need anything else."

"Thank you, Pepper. You have been very kind to me."

Pepper gave a slight bow and turned away. McKenna watched him walk toward the steps. There was something in the way he looked; his eyes reminded her of her mother's—at least from what she'd seen in the photos her father had given her. But that birthmark was just uncanny.

"Zadie, did you notice anything unusual about that man?" she asked as she closed the door and returned to her valise.

"Can't say that I did," she answered with a brief nod of her head. Zadie watched McKenna shrug her shoulders from the corner of her eye and forced back a smile as they continued unpacking.

You'll find out soon enough, child, soon enough, Zadie thought to herself.

Dinner would be served in an hour and McKenna wanted to tidy up her cabin before then. But she simply could not get that birthmark out of her mind. What were the odds of meeting another person bearing the same birthmark as her mother?

Chapter 8

"Captain Sloane, I am sure Zadie and Pepper will agree with me when I say dinner was delicious," McKenna said with sincerity as she looked at Captain Sloane, who was seated across the dining room table from her.

Parker returned her look with a curious smile. McKenna dabbed her mouth with her napkin and continued speaking. "Captain Sloane, your *table d'hôte* and the manners that accompanied this meal tonight were superb. Zadie and I were very hungry since we had left so early this morning, and your kind invitation, or should I say request, was much appreciated. I fear I overate in your presence—please excuse my hearty appetite this evening. Where shall we eat our meals from now on?" McKenna slowly raised her wineglass to her lips while suppressing a sassy smile.

"Thank you, Miss Reed, for your appreciative words and your compliments of my table. However, a table set for guests and a meal to be shared at a specific time is merely just that—a meal to be shared at the table. You do not have to try to impress me with your Charlestonian language—as in a *table d'hôte*. This is the dining cabin, for Christ's sake, and this is where I eat. This is where you will eat, as well, for the duration of our voyage. Savvy, Miss Reed?"

"Savvy, Captain Sloane," replied McKenna with a rising temper. "Captain Sloane, I appreciate that you are taking me to England. I have never met you until today, and I must say that your manners are in dire need of improvement. I was only giving you a compliment on your table. Most men do not set a table as well as you did, nor do they have the courses prepared and presented as elegantly as you have. If you can't respond to a compliment, sir, then I shall stop giving them. Perhaps you would like me to refrain from speaking to you at all!" McKenna began to rise from her chair, thinking she had won this round. "Now, if you will excuse me, I shall retire to my cabin and refrain from offering any more compliments. Zadie, are you ready to retire for the evening?"

McKenna rose from her seat and made her way toward the door without realizing Parker had risen from his own chair to intercept her retreat from the dining hall.

"Sit down, Miss Reed—now." McKenna slowly grabbed the arm of the nearest chair and gently sat down, spreading her gown before her. Parker stood before her with hands on hips and legs braced.

"You can take your haughty airs and discard them into the sea. Your thanks and appreciation were ignored, madam. What you really meant to say is that you were astonished to find I have table manners equal to yours. Or, do you think because I sail in the waters for my living, I do not understand or comprehend the simplest terms for a dinner at a predestined time?"

"Captain, I don't believe Miss Reed meant any harm. She is probably tired from the journey. After all, it has been a long day, sir," stated Pepper with apprehension. Pepper knew Sloane would not tolerate arrogance from anyone on board, least of all from a petite thing like McKenna. The captain acknowledged Pepper's interruption before he continued.

"My apologies, Miss Reed, for losing my patience. You must be weary from your busy day. I will remind you that your dinners will be served in the dining room from now on. Weary or not, it is an honor to take your meals with the captain of a ship." Parker remained standing in front of McKenna.

"An honor? Don't you mean *request*? Isn't that what you told Pepper earlier in the day? 'Miss Reed is requested to be at dinner at 5:00 p.m.' You, sir, have proven yourself to be a bigger cad than I thought possible. I was only complimenting you. You have a way of turning everything I say into a battle of wits. I only meant to thank you and did not mean to insult you, or your table manners, or your style of life upon the high seas. I will take my leave now and, hopefully, lessen your distress due to my presence."

"There you go again making unfounded statements. Miss Reed, you are a snob."

"Would you like me to tell you what I think you are?" asked McKenna with flushing cheeks.

"I will ignore that question. Pepper, would you please take Zadie back to her cabin? I would like to discuss my ship's procedure with Miss Reed. She'll be along shortly, I promise, Zadie. No harm will come to her."

"Yes, sir." Pepper scooted Zadie's chair from the table.

She rose and turned to leave, but not before leaning over and whispering into McKenna's ear, "Hush yourself up, baby girl. You have spouted off one too many times today. You need to stop getting so riled up, 'cause once you do, your temper gets the best of you, and you knows it."

"Wait a moment!" shouted McKenna. "I am ready to go as well. I really do believe we can discuss your ship's procedure tomorrow." She began to rise from her chair.

"Miss Reed, you keep that bottom of yours on that seat. If you so much as move before I return, you may be turned over my knee and given a proper spanking for your immature behavior," threatened Captain Parker.

"Spanking? You wouldn't dare. I have never been turned over anyone's knee. Of all the most incredulous ways to treat someone, you can claim top honors. I have done nothing to offend you, and you will not threaten me this way!"

"I just did," said Parker as he left his cabin with a harsh slam of the door.

"Zadie," Parker said, talking in hushed tones to both her and Pepper in the corridor, "I know she has been doted upon for a long time, but I am not the type of man who will treat her carefully. She will not put on airs on my ship. You had best tell her that."

"I will, Captain. But don't you dare lay a hand on McKenna, you hear?" Zadie said as she grabbed Parker's forearm.

"I will not harm the girl."

"Woman."

"Excuse me, Zadie, what did you just say?" asked Parker with a wink.

"I said, woman. I am pretty sure, Captain, you have noticed by now that she ain't no girl. Be patient with her; she has been through a lot, and this trip ain't easy for her."

"I will keep that in mind. Miss Reed will be along shortly, I promise."

Zadie squeezed Parker's arm one final time and turned to follow Pepper along the corridor toward her own cabin, ducking so she wouldn't hit her head on the I-beam.

"When are you going to tell her that you know me?" asked Pepper as he walked beside Zadie.

"Well, I surely didn't expect to see you here on this ship now, did I?" Zadie chuckled and asked, "When do you want me to tell her?"

"She looks just like Maribelle. Everything about her, from her golden hair to her tiny feet, reminds me of my sister."

"I know; I have seen her grow into a lovely young lady for the past nineteen years. But what in God's name is that captain doin' to her? She ain't got one haughty bone in her body. She would rather ride horses all day than eat fancy meals and clothe herself in fancy evenin' gowns. I don't know what has gotten into her to make her speak the way she did to Captain Sloane."

"Zadie, I think it is called 'love at first sight.' I believe your little Miss McKenna has met her match, and I believe Captain Sloane has also met his. She is a spitfire, isn't she?"

"Yes, she is. Oh, Pepper, I think you are right. She has never had a real courtin'. Not that her father didn't try. There was no man who caught her eye or could match her passion for life. McKenna has so much love to give; she just gots to learn how to give it. Pepper, I have much to tell you, and I am sure you have lots of questions for me. Can we please spend time together and get caught up between here and England?"

"We certainly can, my dear friend." The two of them continued their walk to the end of the corridor and seated themselves on a bench. Zadie had a feeling in her gut that the battle of wits about to ensue in the captain's quarters would last longer than a meager 'few minutes.' But who, she wondered, would win?

Chapter 9

Of all the nerve, McKenna thought. *If he thinks I am going to sit here and wait for his pompous arse to return, he is sorely mistaken.* McKenna noticed her half-filled wine glass from dinner remained on the table. She clutched her glass and took the final swallow of wine, unaware of the dining room door opening behind her.

"I see you know how to follow orders. That is a good thing, Miss Reed," Parker said as he slipped into his cabin and strolled to stand behind her.

"I will follow no orders given from you, sir. You are neither my father nor my protector. I will follow my own orders."

"As long as you are on my ship, you will follow my orders. Now, turn yourself around, and I will explain to you how things will be done while you are on board the *Constance*."

McKenna purposely turned slowly in her chair to face him. My God, he was beautiful. But he sorely needed a lesson in manners.

"Miss Reed," Parker said, "are you listening to me?" He seated himself in front of her and took hold of her chair—scooting it between his legs.

McKenna's eyes widened as she realized where she now sat. Door on the right, table on the left, and Captain Sloane in front of her—no possible escape. If only he would take those tree-trunk arms of his off her chair, she could scoot back a little. His breath smelled of the brandy and citrus rind he had drunk during supper. She could not help herself from inhaling his scent of musk and coconut. *Oh, my Lord, scoot back before you gaze into those green eyes of his and lose yourself.*

"Miss Reed?" asked Parker with a questioning look.

"Yes, Captain Sloane, I was just staring at the beauty of your face and wondering how a man as handsome as yourself could be so lacking in genteel language when addressing a lady." McKenna made sure she gave him a spacious smile and tilt of her head while toying with him. "I am sure you do not need to raise your voice to me in the future," she said as she delicately picked each of his fingers off her chair's armrests. "Please, continue, sir." She pressed her heels into the floor and scooted away from him. *Let's see how dear ol' Captain Sloane responds to intentional flirting.*

"Let me make this simple, Miss Reed," Parker began while slowly replacing each finger upon the armrests of McKenna's chair. "I am the captain of this ship. I have attended the best ship-building areas in London, precisely Millwall. This is the most advanced engineering experience England has to offer, especially at Cambridge, where I studied. You may be familiar with the Great Eastern steam ship of the 1850s. I studied about the construction of that ship and worked under the master builder, William Cubitt, who founded Cubitt Town." He paused to make sure McKenna was listening to him. "Now, if my experience and knowledge doesn't impress you, this will: I am a master builder and have been for five years. That is something, coming from a twenty-seven-year-old man.

"You see, Miss Reed, most men never achieve this title; the only way they do is to build their ships and have them inspected by other master builders and approved. I have built five ships, and I know exactly how to sail them, furnish them, and yes, even set a table for Charlestonian guests. So, you may take that cute little nose of yours and turn it back down when you are speaking to me. I am not beneath you—I am not one of your bloody slaves—I am Captain Parker Sloane, and you would do well to remember that. I demand respect from my passengers and will not tolerate those who are less inclined to give it. My rules are strict. None of my working crew members ever have a date with 'John Barleycorn,' nor do I hire on 'addlepated' workers."

"Good to know, Captain, because I do not drink nor have I ever been drunk. Are you finished?" asked McKenna while tapping her foot.

"For the moment, kitten." McKenna stiffened in her chair upon being called kitten.

"I am not your kitten, Captain Sloane. I am not a besotted young lady who crumbles at the mere sight of masculinity and muscles, such as yourself. I too admire education, and I attended a fine school for young ladies.

"You have done well for yourself, and I applaud your hard work and dedication to ship building. You achieved your dream of purpose. I want to achieve mine; I want to attend veterinarian school in England for horses. There are only three hundred and ninety-two current veterinarians, and I want to become the three hundred and ninety-third.

"I am impressed by what you have accomplished at such a young age—your ship building is as important to you as my horse breeding and training is to me. But you didn't even begin to ask what my interests were; you were too busy denouncing and disparaging my character. You saw a Southern girl and immediately presumed me to be pampered. Yes, I like nice gowns, hats, and shoes, but I'd rather own nicer riding habits, boots, and Spencer repeating rifles." Parker didn't flinch—he remained still and listened.

"My mother died while giving birth to me. I was raised without a mother, and my father did the best he could. So, I was required to learn proper etiquette; whereas, a young man may or may not ever acquire such knowledge, especially while sailing on the high seas. I learned to shoot and bow anything with legs or wings. I love the challenge of the hunt and the breeze in my face while riding my stallion, Solomon. If you had questioned why I wanted my horse with me, I would have told you. You were too busy making assumptions. I believe you thought me to be mollycoddled. You even called me a snob! Now then, are we *savvy*, Captain?" asked McKenna as she scooted her chair back.

"Yes, my dear, we are savvy. Well done. We certainly have stepped onto the wrong introductory pathway. Shall we begin anew?"

"Yes, I would like that very much, after you apologize for threatening to spank me."

"No apology will be offered, madam—that threat still stands. Stop scooting your chair back, Miss Reed. Your Southern accent and intent to soften my thoughts is all for naught. Your charm will not work on me, and by the way, your dress décolletage, although enticing, is too low. You will have every man on this ship ready to take a knife in the leg for one look at your bosom. I would suggest you wear more modest attire while on this voyage. You may use your charm on the shores of Charleston or the wharfs of England, but not on the deck of the *Constance*. Furthermore, I do not recall you asking about my education. You were too busy looking down upon my station as a captain. I believe you saw muscles and masculinity, as you put it. Madam, I applaud your dream; I hope you can use your love and knowledge of horses to your benefit. As for shooting and bowing, I would like to see your accuracy and your aim; I could arrange that event for the both of us," he said with a wink.

McKenna gave a firm scoot back and placed both hands upon her knees. "How dare you criticize my décolletage! What I choose to wear is my business. Perhaps you should deposit your eyes above my neck when speaking to me, sir. Any gentleman worth his salt would never discuss a lady's dress décor aloud—especially a man who just met said lady within a few hours' time!"

McKenna forcibly scooted her chair back once more and stood up. She walked toward the door and suddenly stopped. A large water pitcher sat on the table. She carefully picked it up with both hands, turned, and gave Parker a very mischievous look.

"Put it down, kitten," said Parker with a stern look. "I know what you are thinking; you had best consider the consequences."

"No," replied McKenna, as she braced the pitcher on her hip. "Offer me an apology, or end up with a wet head. I do not care about your so-called consequences!"

"Miss Reed, I am afraid I will be very displeased if I were to be soaked by that pitcher of ice water. Put it down, or this will lead to an unpleasant ending for you."

"For me? You big brute—more for you!" McKenna threw the pitcher quickly and accurately. The iced water-soaked Parker's head, face, and shirt completely. "There, Captain—that is the end of this conversation. Keep your comments to yourself about my décolletage, or next time, it will be the chamber pot on top of your head!"

"Hell and damnation, you bloodthirsty little chit." His jaw twitched, and his hands grasped his knees quite tightly. He rose to his full height, shaking the water from his hair.

"No name-calling, dear Captain; that is bad manners," McKenna replied as she quickly moved to put the small serving table between them. "Apparently, you are not as genteel as you think you are. Your master-builder teacher should have taught you manners while teaching you how to build a ship! My aim is quite accurate, don't you think? No lessons are needed on my part, sir!" Seeing a set of keys on the adjacent brandy table, McKenna leaned over, grabbed them, and ran out the door. She immediately locked Captain Sloane inside his own dining room and tucked the keys down her dress.

"Good night, Captain, sweet dreams," McKenna shouted, out of breath from her efforts.

"Sweet dreams to you, as well, kitten," he said from the other side of the door. "Remember, I have keys to every door on board. Be thinking about that tonight as you lay yourself down to sleep. I, too, enjoy a good hunt. I will find those keys, kitten."

His tone was saucy, earthy, deep, and captivating. *Oh, dear, I really did it this time. Now I have him mad at me. Will he really find these keys tonight?* she thought to herself. She would have to find a cunning place to hide them— or would she? The thought of him placing his hands on her caused an increased pulse. *What would it feel like to be held by those arms? Those hands? What would it feel like to be kissed by someone as handsome as him?* McKenna walked quickly down the corridor and entered her cabin. She locked the door and placed her forehead against the door.

He is just a man. Stop acting like a school girl.

"McKenna, is everything all right? Are you well, child? Captain Sloane didn't hurt you, did he?"

"Oh, Zadie, you startled me," McKenna said as she turned toward the familiar voice. "I didn't realize you were still up. What are you doing sitting over there in the dark?"

"I have candles lit. I am not in the dark, and I was waitin' for you. What are you up to? You look like you just stuck your hand in the beehive and got stung. Your face is flushed."

"Let's just say Captain Sloane and I had a small disagreement. Come now, let's get some sleep—I am tired and I know you are as well."

"All right, baby girl. Turn around and let me unbutton your dress and corset," said Zadie as she rose from her chair and walked toward McKenna.

"Thank you, Zadie; it has been a long day," she said as she twirled a golden strand of hair from a misplaced curl.

"Uh huh… sure, been a long day, baby girl. Don't you go hidin' nothin' from me. If that Captain hurt you, I needs to know."

"Zadie, nothing happened between the Captain and me. In fact, you would have been proud of me. I minded my manners and even offered the dear Captain some water when he became overheated."

"Overheated?"

"Yes, Zadie, he just needed to cool down a bit. I am sure he is feeling much better now." McKenna stepped out of her unbuttoned dress and into her nightdress. She tucked the stolen keys into her sleeve, pulled the covers back, and crawled into her bed. *Tonight*, she thought, *I may not get as much sleep as I need. I may have to sleep with one eye open—just in case dear old Captain Sloane comes to retrieve his keys.*

***

Parker sat back in his chair and heartily laughed. Miss Reed was not only beautiful, she was educated as well. If she thought she'd had the last word with that little tantrum of hers, she was sorely mistaken.

Beauty and brains combined into one little package is enticing, he thought. *I look forward to our next encounter, kitten.*

Chapter 10

The morning air misted upon McKenna's cheeks as she peered out onto the open sea. The smell was fresh, the colors of the horizon were exuberant, and the exhilaration of the new day was almost uncontrollable. Captain Sloane had not talked to her, nor had she seen much of him in the past two weeks. Dinners were taken at the dining table, but he was rarely there. Pepper had told Zadie that the captain was very busy on board and usually kept to himself.

Is he avoiding me on purpose? Mayhap I should try to find him and attempt a civil conversation. I miss seeing that handsome face. She chuckled to herself as she walked to the starboard side of the ship, watching the deckhands hard at work cleaning the deck. Distracted by all the activity, she took a wrong step, and caught her heel in the mast rope. The entanglement brought her to her knees with such force, the momentum caused her to fall forward, landing none too gently on her stomach and chin. The harsh impact of the fall took the breath from her as she lay sprawled out upon the deck. Her chin caught the worst of it and started to bleed rather heavily. McKenna tried to catch her breath, shake her head to ward off the fogginess that was encompassing her, and pull herself up. But she was so winded, she didn't have the strength to rise on her own. She resigned herself to fainting, but soon felt two strong arms encircling her waist, lifting her up and enveloping her against a chest of steel. She looked up into gorgeous green eyes, and for a moment, she sighed a sweet breath of relief before blackness overcame her.

"Damn it, Pepper, I told you to clear all roping to the side of the ship and lock-key the knots. Why in hell were there loose ropes? I did not want Miss Reed or any other passenger falling or becoming entangled." Parker carefully carried his precious little bundle to port side.

"Captain, it was my mistake, sir. I was portside, overseeing the deck cleaning, and had not supervised starboard yet. Honestly, Captain, I didn't see Miss Reed over here at all."

"Well, Pepper, she was, and now she has fainted on me. That is all I need—a woman who can't keep her balance and footing on my ship. For Christ's sake, this woman has tripped and fallen toward disaster each time I have seen her."

McKenna began to squirm in his arms as she slowly came to from her faint. The sun caught her golden locks and damn near radiated a metallic halo around her angelic face. Parker noticed a stray curl wrapped around a button on his cuff; trying not to squeeze her, he gingerly loosed it and watched it fall back into place.

The wind continued to blow her curled tendrils against his cheek, allowing Parker to inhale the scent from her hair. He recognized that smell from long ago. It was a mixture of peonies and wild orchids, the same aroma he used to smell on his mother's porch. His mind traveled back in time as he remembered his mother's love of flowers and her gardens. The sweet memory momentarily brought a smile upon his chiseled face, but was quickly diverted to the present as McKenna began to twist in his arms, forcing him to hold her head mere inches from his face. Her body emitted a fruity yet flowery jasmine scent—probably some fancy Charleston soap. He certainly didn't have anything of the like on board the *Constance*. God in heaven, she felt right within his arms. He could hold on to this little kitten for all eternity—not too heavy, not too light, just perfection.

"So lovely to have you back with us," Parker said with a hint of sarcasm as McKenna opened her appealing blue eyes.

"Captain Sloane, if you will kindly put me down, I will be more careful, and will not cause you any more trouble."

"Remember, kitten, you have nine lives—three have been used to ward off near disasters for you."

"Three?"

"One life for your near swim in the ocean, the second life for your temper tantrum with the pitcher of water, which, may I add, resulted in no punishment for you, and now, the third life for fainting and falling upon my deck. Stop twisting, kitten, I need to get a better look at that chin of yours. It is bleeding."

"How bad is it?" asked McKenna as she attempted to touch her chin with her gloved hand before Parker batted it away.

"Don't touch it until I take a closer look; it appears that you have a sliver of deck wood in your chin. I will need to pull that out."

"No, let Zadie pull it out. You may not be so gentle, and I know it is going to sting."

"My dear Miss Reed, I would never intentionally hurt you. Now, I am going to sit down with you on my lap. I want you to lean your head back and rest it on the rail. Pepper, reach into my vest pocket and get my tweezers. Go ahead and burn the tip of them for me. Do not be afraid, kitten."

"Oh, I am not afraid; I know you are sanitizing those tweezers before you come near my chin. Thank you for taking that precautionary step. I can probably pull the sliver out myself; if you will allow me off your lap, I will do just that."

In response to her request, the Captain merely tightened his arms around her. She knew the Captain was making a silent point—there was no way in hell he was going to release her.

"Sit still, damn it," he whispered against her ear.

McKenna watched as Pepper handed over the sanitized tweezers. The Captain braced his massive forearms on each side of her head, skin touching skin. He felt warm, and she felt incredibly safe. She allowed herself to stare at the sky; colors of cobalt, sapphire, and indigo formed layers of haze. She was completely relaxed and could even smell a musky scent from the captain. His burly forearms were resting on her bare chest. He was right; she should have worn a higher neckline today. His breath was warm upon her face while his free hand held her chin tightly. *Oh, I could stay in this position forever*, she thought—no worry, no fretting, no thinking, just enveloped within his arms—absolute heaven.

"Miss Reed, you can wake up now. The surgery is finished," the Captain laughed.

"Oh, I am so sorry; what did you say? You took the sliver out already? I was daydreaming, Captain, and wasn't even paying attention to what you were doing. It just felt so warm and comforting to be held within your arms; I lost myself in the moment." Good Lord, what had she just said? *No, no, no, do not for one minute admit you are comforted by the likes of him*, she thought to herself before blurting out, "I am sorry, sir, certainly, I will get up right away."

McKenna almost fell on her face again, trying to throw her entangled legs over the captain's knee. Again, he caught her and steadied her as she rose, placing his hands upon her waist.

"I meant to say that the warmth of the sun upon my face and the swaying of the ship just made me relax and appreciate the peacefulness of the open water. Thank you for taking care of my chin, Captain Sloane."

Parker looked at her intently. *So, the little kitten likes being held, does she? I could practically hear her purring when I was taking out that sliver*, he thought. He hadn't felt so protective of a female in a very long time. *Hell, what is this lady doing to me?* Parker's conscience was telling him to stay away from her and get her to England. He had more important things to do with his life than comfort and fall head over heels for a Charlestonian brat. *Ah, yes, she's all woman—Zadie is right; she just doesn't know it yet*. Perhaps his life could take a small diversion with Miss McKenna Reed.

"Captain, did you hear me? I said thank you, and I appreciate your help. You seem to have a knack for tuning out my conversations with you. I am beginning to think you do this on purpose!"

"Miss Reed, no man in his right mind would ever tune you out. I was thinking about something else, 'tis all. You are quite welcome for my assistance. I would wish that you be more careful, though, when walking on deck. Perhaps you have more appropriate shoes?"

"I do, sir. I will change into my chameleon shoes; they have very small heels. And I will also change into more appropriate clothing. You were right; my décolletage is too low for this sea adventure."

"Yes, it is. Thank goodness you presented yourself only to me and not some young pup, or else that splinter would still be in your chin. I would also suggest you be more careful and watch where you walk around the rigging. This could have been avoided."

"What did you just say? Are you out of your English mind? You can't possibly blame me for tripping over your tangled-up ropes. I didn't mean to do that."

She straightened as she considered those endless green pools of his. His hands remained on her waist, cinching her ever so slightly.

"Nonetheless, kitten, you did, and here you are. Maybe I should dunk you in the ocean to see if your temper can be cooled; a bit more water than a pitcher, wouldn't you say?"

"You wouldn't dare! Release me this instant!"

"I am sorry, madam; did I hear a please attached to your request?"

She sighed and hesitated. "Please, release me, Captain Sloane."

"Certainly, kitten."

Parker removed his hands from her waist so quickly, she almost fell backward. Once again, he held her arm within his grip.

"Stop calling me that. My name is McKenna, and I am not your kitten," McKenna howled as she started to walk away.

"We shall see about that. Six is now your lucky number, *kitten*."

McKenna continued walking without looking back at Captain Sloane. She didn't like how he had emphasized 'kitten.' *Of all the nerve. Why does he ruffle my feathers every time he comes near me?* she wondered. She decided her best action against him would be to stay the hell away from him. Zadie told her they had ten more days at sea, and then this little adventure would be over. *I can do it. Be polite, and do not engage in any conversation with this man. Be alert, and look in all directions, just as Papa taught. I can do this*, she thought. Or could she?

Chapter 11

McKenna's handmade lace shawl did not keep out the wind. She should have known better, but she was too lazy to go below deck and retrieve another wrap. She was so busy watching the sunset from the upper deck that she did not notice Pepper until he came to stand beside her.

"Evening, Miss Reed."

"Good evening, Mr. Pepper."

"Remember, ma'am, just Pepper."

"Yes, of course. Pepper, I have the strangest feeling I have met or seen you before. I do not want to be rude, but you remind me of someone. Have we ever met?"

"No, I don't recall meeting you before. Who would I be reminding you of, Miss Reed?"

"You remind me of my mother, Maribelle."

"Do I, now? In what way do I remind you of your mother?"

McKenna turned a bit from the railing to keep the wind from blowing her curls into her face. "You have a mark on your jaw, just as my mother did; in fact, it's the same shape. I find that to be very unusual. If you don't mind me asking, what is your real name?" McKenna waited for him to answer, but he didn't. When she repeated the question, he cleared his throat.

"My name is Thaddeus Wells."

McKenna stepped back and clung to the ship rails tightly. She felt that all too familiar gasp for breath when she had been pushed by a horse.

"Good God in heaven, did you say Wells?" McKenna asked.

"Yes, ma'am, I did."

"My mother's name was Maribelle Wells. How old are you, Pepper?"

"Miss Reed, before I answer you, why don't we find a place to sit? You look a bit flushed."

"I would rather stand right now. Please, answer my question. How old are you?"

"I am as old as your mother, dear girl. My last name is Wells, and your mother and I were born on the same day in the same home. Maribelle Wells was my twin sister."

"What did you say? Sir, you are telling me that my mother has a twin brother, and I am just now finding out about this? Are you certain? You are not playing a horrible trick on me, are you?"

"No, ma'am, I would never lower myself to that level."

"Why wasn't I ever told? Does my father know? Does Zadie know? Does everyone know except me?"

"Yes, I am her twin brother. Your father knows, and so does Zadie. In fact, I met with your father before we left. I arranged for your passage on this ship. Your Aunt Olympia is my older sister. Captain Sloane even knows because he boards his horses at your Aunt Olympia's stables."

This was too much for McKenna to absorb. "I have an uncle, and no one told me for the past nineteen years. Unbelievable! I have questions that need to be answered, Pepper. Was this trip prearranged? All that worry about secession, was it just a means to get me to England? Should I call you Pepper, Uncle Pepper, or Uncle Thaddeus? Why do you not use Thaddeus as your name?" McKenna was rambling and she knew it.

"Miss Reed, you have asked a lot of questions. We have much to discuss, and I am ready to talk if you are. I have waited a very long time to meet you, and now is as good as any time to have this conversation. Would you be so kind as to sit with me while I attempt to explain a part of your unknown history?"

"Certainly." McKenna was so taken aback that she nearly lost her breath. *Dear God in heaven, what else am I going to learn?*

Pepper and McKenna proceeded to sit on a small bench beside the stairs to the top deck, shielded from the wind.

"It would be nice if you would call me Uncle Pepper. I don't use Thaddeus because my father, your grandfather, had that name. I was named after him. I hate that man and everything he stands for. I do not want anything from him— especially his name. He wasn't a father to my sisters and me. He was a tyrant and a brute. I loved your mother and still love Olympia very much. Your mother and I were inseparable." Pepper leaned back and folded his hands in his lap.

"What happened to you and my mother?" McKenna asked as she turned toward Pepper, leaning in a bit closer to hear his words against the howl of the wind.

"Simply put, I chose to go to sea and make my way. Father didn't approve; he wanted me to attend law school in Oxford. Even though I had the intelligence to do so, I had the desire, at the time, to be on the open water. I've always had a fascination with ships and sailing. I met Captain Sloane years ago while he was master training. He had the skill and the knowledge to build a ship. I had the skill and knowledge to write contracts and financial duty papers. We worked together and became a team. We have been working together going on ten years now."

"So, how does my mother fit into your seafaring?"

"When I was ready to leave home and make my way on the high seas, my father threatened me. He said he would disown me if I left. Discussion after discussion with him did nothing but aggravate the situation. Maribelle did not want me to leave home. She knew Father would be livid and take his anger out on her and Olympia if I left. McKenna, there were times when your grandfather would lock your mother in her room and refuse her meals because she supported my ideas. Even though she didn't want me to leave, she encouraged me to choose my own career." Pepper sighed before continuing—the sadness was evident upon his face.

"Father was a cynical, sour man. If he couldn't be happy, then no one else would be, either. I would suppose your father talks very little of your maternal grandfather."

"He has never talked much about the Wells family at all. In fact, this is the first time I have ever heard more than a few words mentioned. As you can tell, I am quite beside myself. But please, continue," McKenna asked sincerely.

"Very well, my dear. I had fallen in love with a young lady, but my father didn't like her or her family. He said that 'her kind' was 'beneath us.' She disappeared, just like that. I knew in my heart he had sent her away from me— either through bribery or threat. That was the final insult for me. I decided to leave. The worst part was saying goodbye to your mother. She said she would never to speak to me again if I left. But Maribelle knew, deep in her heart, that

I had to go. Your mother would soon find out how powerful love could be. She met a certain American doctor who would become your father."

"What happened to the lady you loved? Did you ever see her again?"

"No, I never saw her again. My sisters even tried to discover her whereabouts, but without luck. So, I left the Wells' home and never looked back. I made my way with several good captains and learned the trials and tribulations of living upon the seas for just shy of twenty years. I took a few years off from the sea and attended law school. When I finally achieved my law degree, I built up legal offices along a few ports with partners I had met during school. Years ago, I attended to my practices when we docked, and I rotated my itinerary, so I could oversee my offices and clients. Now that I have gotten older, I have given many of my clients to my younger partners.

"I knew Maribelle had left England; before she left, we met in secret, and all was forgiven between us. I would write letters to her frequently and stop in and visit her whenever we docked—in secret. Father had threatened to take out his anger on Olympia if Maribelle and I ever communicated. We were afraid to take the risk, so our meetings were always hidden. I did not know she had died while giving birth to you until months later, when I received a letter from your Aunt Olympia. I just couldn't bring myself to return to the family home.

"I still continue to visit Olympia at her new home and often stay there for extended periods of time, but I never visit him—never him."

"Why didn't Papa tell me about you?" McKenna asked with creased brows.

"I warned your father to keep my existence secret even before you were born. If your grandfather found out that I still communicated with Maribelle, he would disown her quicker than hell's fury. He was angry when Maribelle ran away to marry an American doctor. You see, nobility still has its prestige. Your father wasn't good enough for his daughter. She was to stay and marry an arranged English suitor. Of course, your mother, being stubborn, wanted no part of any arrangement. She loved your father, and that was that. She left her father, her home, and bonny England.

"Your grandfather is a nobleman and owns a fortune of land in England and America. Since he also owns the largest printing company in England, he could have made your father's life miserable or possibly even destroyed his career if Father knew Maribelle had been secretly communicating with me."

"I do not understand. How would he have destroyed my father's medical career?"

"He would have written false and slanderous articles about your father, jeopardizing his good name in the medical field. Trust me, my dear, he would have gone to any length to hurt those who had defied him. In this case, Maribelle. I purposely kept no communication with him. He had no idea where I claimed residency. I knew if he ever threatened to destroy your father's finances or his good name in the Charleston medical field by slanderous publications, Harper would have the option to leave South Carolina for a while and move to one of the cities where I had established legal offices.

"For all practical purposes, I am dead to my father—your grandfather. When Maribelle left home, she was warned by your grandfather never to return. Only Olympia remained in England under his watch.

"Olympia worked with a veterinarian and breeder of race horses. She soon began to help care for wounded horses and learned the basics of breeding them for racing. Her passion for horses soon overtook her discontent with father. As years passed, Olympia became well known for her horses throughout England, Scotland, and Ireland. She moved away from father and established her own manor and stables. In fact, there are many in Europe who revere her name for her thoroughbreds. As far as I know, she has not spoken to Father since she left his house.

"I tried to protect your mother and ended up not being able to say a final good-bye to her. For that, I am deeply hurt and sorry to you, dear girl." Pepper grabbed both of McKenna's wrists and kissed the tops of her hands ever so gently.

"This is so much information to absorb. I have been caught up on nineteen years of life within the past hour of conversation. How in the world am I to process this?" asked McKenna with tears in her eyes. She slowly removed her hands from Pepper's and rubbed the back of her neck. She started to tremble and shake. The information was too much. She had missed an uncle her entire life, thus far. She had never even met her grandfather and probably never would. She felt as if her world was crumbling before she was even properly introduced to it.

"McKenna, are you all right?" asked Pepper as he tightened her shawl around her shoulders.

"I am shaken, to tell you the truth. I can't imagine living the way you did, all the while knowing you no longer had a home to return to."

"Oh, I had a home to return to, dear girl, just not a home with a father in it. He was angry, and he probably still is. He lost his twin children and was left with a broken heart. But he still had one child remaining at home. One would think he would have doted upon Olympia. Such was not the case. According to Olympia, she could not leave quick enough. He began drinking and remained housebound. Hell, he even quit riding, and he was an excellent horseman."

"Did you ever attempt to see him?"

"No, my dear. No amount of money in the world would ever tempt me to do that. Words were exchanged the night I left. He threatened to shoot me on sight if I ever stepped foot on his property again. If I may be more specific, I believe 'shoot to kill' were his exact words."

"Oh, dear God, I am so sorry to hear this. Fathers are not supposed to treat their children that way, especially their only son."

"You are absolutely right. In a perfect world, one would think that would not happen. But we do not live in a perfect world, and your grandfather was far from it."

"What ever became of my grandmother?" McKenna asked with a quivering voice.

"She died giving birth to your mother and me. She had delivered a stillbirth baby in a previous pregnancy. I suppose that just added fuel to the fire when the two of us wanted to leave home. He lost his wife to us, then he lost us."

"My God, just like my mother. She lost two children before me, then died giving birth to me. I am so sorry, Uncle. I would truly like to get caught up over the past nineteen years and welcome you into my heart! I haven't seen Aunt Olympia or her children in such a long time. I am afraid I won't recognize the lot of them! Father and I visited them when I was a little girl—almost ten years ago."

"Don't worry, my dear, they will recognize you. Now then, your aunt is an accomplished horsewoman, and she has a keen sense of medical treatment for them. I understand you wish to pursue a dream of your own, is that correct?"

"Yes, I do. When we visited Aunt Olympia's home, I helped her horse birth a foal, and from that moment on, I was fascinated with her animal medicine. I followed her and her veterinarian around like a pup. Uncle Pepper, what is the real reason that Papa wanted me out of South Carolina? Did he just want me to meet you?"

"McKenna-girl, your father is right in getting you away from the States. If war does break out, it will be odious. Families will be destroyed, and homes will be divided and diminished. It is best that you stay away from the uncivil hell that will inevitably break out."

"Do you really think there will be war?"

"I would bet my life on it."

"I hope Papa remains safe. I suppose he was right to send me to England. Although, I must say, I wish I was sailing on a different ship. Captain Sloane can be infuriating."

Pepper slapped his knee and began to laugh.

"Ah, he isn't so bad. In fact, perhaps you should try to initiate a conversation and get to know him. He is one of the best men I know."

"I thought about that; truly, I did. But every time I try to talk to him or approach him, I fall or stumble or lose my temper. I am beginning to think I am jinxed around him. However, I rather enjoy debating with him because I know he will lose his patience with me and walk away. So, in my mind, I win each round of verbal sparring with him," she giggled.

"No, McKenna, the Captain is allowing you to *think* you are winning. Parker Sloane's reputation is built upon strength, confidence, and good sense. He can be as vile as the next pirate, but also as benevolent and gentle as a nun. His massive size contains a massive amount of compassion toward his animals, especially his dog. Oh, my dear, you have yet to see what you are doing to our dear captain. I would encourage you to befriend him."

"Befriend him? I don't think so. And, as for what I am doing to him, I can tell you that he is befuddling my mind. One minute he is smiling at me, and the next minute he is threatening to turn me over his knee! The sooner I get away from Captain Sloane, the better off I shall be. He makes me so frustrated at times. Honestly, I can't carry on a conversation with him without getting myself into trouble or raising his temper."

"McKenna, let me give you a piece of advice about Captain Sloane. He will protect you with his life if you are his friend. He will help you in any way he can if he admires you and respects you. Don't be so hard on yourself, dear girl; I think you have inched your way into Sloane's heart in the few short weeks since you have met."

"Well, I am not so sure about that. He is always a bully to me, and he certainly has shown no admiration toward me. Of course, I probably wouldn't admire anyone who threw a pitcher of water on me, either!" McKenna laughed. "I take it you know about that?"

"Captain Sloane mentioned it to me," Pepper replied with a grunt.

"Uncle Pepper, I do have one last question for you."

"Certainly, my dear. What is it?"

"Why didn't Zadie ever talk to me about you? She is the closest thing to a mother that I have. I can't understand why she wouldn't confide in me. Especially about something as important as having an uncle."

"Do not blame her, McKenna. I made her promise not to tell you. I wanted to tell you. I could not nor will I ever trust your grandfather. I didn't want any complications in your life or in Harper's life. It was my decision, and she honored it."

"Well then, you and Zadie truly are friends. Most people go to their graves without a true friend, so feel blessed that Zadie has kept her promise all these years. I won't holler at her, rest assured."

"Well then, it is getting late. Lord, it feels good to finally introduce myself to you. I only look toward the future with you. You are a blessing I have been cheated out of for nineteen years, and I intend to make up for lost time."

"I intend to make up for those lost years as well. Good night, Uncle Pepper, and thank you for sharing."

She stood and kissed him on his stubbly cheek, then stepped down the stairs toward her cabin. When she entered her room, she found Zadie rocking in the rocking chair, holding her Bible.

"Did you have a good talk with Pepper?" Zadie asked with a hint of apprehension in her voice.

"Indeed, I did, Zadie. I learned all about him, my aunt, and grandfather. Would you like me to share what I learned? It may take a while, and I may leave out a few details, but you can certainly fill in the missing pieces, can't you? Or, am I interrupting you from reading that Bible of yours?"

"We got all night, child. I think ol' Zadie can help you along. Just don't be gettin' mad at me; my ol' heart couldn't take that kind of hurt. And don't be shamin' me for readin' my Bible. I made a promise to Pepper, and I've kept it all these years."

McKenna walked toward Zadie and knelt on her knees beside her, taking Zadie's hands in her own.

"Yes, you kept your promise to Uncle Pepper. You have been a loyal friend to him." McKenna laid her head on Zadie's lap and closed her eyes. Zadie stroked McKenna's head and kneaded her curls as she had done so often as a child. McKenna knew the love Zadie felt for her was indulgent, unselfish, and bountiful. Above all, Zadie was a woman of honor. She had kept a promise to a friend, no matter the cost, no matter the time span. She was a rare woman.

Yes, McKenna thought to herself, *whoever marries Zadie will be a very lucky man. Once I get to England, perhaps I will try and find a husband for Zadie. She has spent so many years caring for us, it is high time someone starts caring for her—in the form of a husband. She isn't getting any younger, and she needs to have that void filled. Maybe Aunt Olympia will be able to help—just maybe...*

Chapter 12

McKenna was standing at the rail of the ship, admiring the sunshine upon the water. Tomorrow, they would land in England, and she could hardly wait. The trip had been eventful and certainly full of acquired knowledge, but she was ready to step onto dry land. However, there was something about the breeze against her face and the smell of salt in the air that attracted her. Watching the rippling water gave her a sense of calm—of inner peace. She could understand why sailors enjoyed this lifestyle. *Water had a way of providing tranquility*, thought McKenna to herself, and it resembled a pool of diamonds when the sun shone upon it.

She remembered when her father would take her canoeing on the small pond behind their home. She loved those lazy afternoons spent fishing with him. He had taught her how to bait hooks for fish and skip rocks across the water. How she missed those days and those times with her father. She would miss him even more now that she would be in England. McKenna continued to lean against the rail, soaking in the sun. The sound of approaching footsteps had her turn to see Captain Sloane as he joined her at the rail.

"Well, well, well, Miss Reed, don't you look lovely this morning. May I add that yellow and blue are your colors to wear. The fabric of your dress matches your blue eyes with perfection. You will certainly be the envy of every English lady when we land. Your beauty radiates from every inch of your body, kitten, and I mean *every* inch."

"Well, Captain Sloane, I just adore waking up and seeing the glimmer of ocean water, smelling the salt of the sea, touching the moisture on the rail, tasting the dried coconut in coffee, and hearing the English rubbish spill from your mouth.

"Have a glorious day, sir." McKenna turned and thought to walk toward the other side of the ship just as Parker reached and clutched her forearm in his grasp.

"Now, you offend me, madam. Here I thought you would enjoy an early morning compliment. I meant no harm, kitten."

McKenna turned around so quickly that she ran straight into a chest of steel. She looked up into Parker's challenging eyes, which were filled with mischief. His arms once again encircled her to prevent her from swaying. He wasn't moving, and inevitably, that meant she wasn't going to, either.

"It seems, dear lady, that I am ever providing you with stability on this ship. How is it that you always stumble into me? I am beginning to think you do this on purpose. I am flattered, kitten, but if you really relish the thought of clinging to my chest, I could arrange better accommodation for that."

"You can wipe that smug look right off your face. If you said something sincerely, then it would be received with sincerity. But you said your compliment with mischief, and I can spot an insincerity a mile away. Perhaps you would like a lesson on etiquette, Captain?"

"I would be happy to listen to your lesson, Miss Reed."

"Where would you like to have your lesson? I imagine it will take me a while to saturate that brain of yours with the rights and wrongs of etiquette and manners."

"Careful, kitten, it may take all day and all *night*." He followed his statement with a wink that gave her much discomfort.

All right, Captain, let's confront this bantering between us like a game of chess. You need to be put in your place, and I need to checkmate your arrogant attitude.

"Shall we, Miss Reed?" Parker asked as he offered her his arm.

"You don't have to escort me, sir. I am quite capable of walking and sitting without falling. You will need to listen carefully to the conversation, Captain, as I will offer a certain amount of proper and improper strategies in my explanation—like playing a game of chess. I assume you know how to play chess?"

"My apologies, madam; I only offered to escort you to ensure you would not fall or trip. And, yes, I am quite familiar with the game of chess. Shall we sit just inside the door? I am sure we will have a cooler breeze there."

Parker led McKenna over to the carved mahogany bench, and together they sat side by side. A light breeze blew from the east, which provided sufficient comfort. *Damn*, Parker thought, *she is gleaming in the sunlight.* It took all his self-control not to run his fingers through her golden curls. Her hair was thick and wavy, falling nearly to her waist. He could imagine her lying upon a soft bed of sweet, English alfalfa with that golden mass surrounding her in a perfect halo. He wondered if she was really that humble or naive about her appearance. If she were, her total package would be more desirable. She would put the English ladies to shame. He couldn't abide the haughty bitches in court. They were too busy gossiping about others or ridding their husbands of coin.

"Captain, are you ready for your lesson? You seem to be preoccupied."

"Yes, I am preoccupied, kitten. I am more than preoccupied; I am mesmerized. Has no one ever told you how pretty you truly are? McKenna, you take my breath away."

"Thank you, sir, for your kind words, but Papa taught me to remain humble even when receiving compliments. I just thank God every day for what he has given me, and leave it at that. I try to do good for my neighbors and friends and not boast about what I have or complain about what I don't have. I enjoy life, Captain, and I like to be happy. I like to feel needed, and I like to make others happy. Now, can we continue with your lesson on etiquette?"

Her smile was impish. She needed to be kissed, and she needed to be kissed fiercely. *Let her play the teacher for now*, he thought; his turn would come, and the roles would be reversed. When that happened, he would certainly enjoy teaching and introducing her to the passions between a man and a woman. *Ah, yes, I would enjoy watching this kitten purr.*

"That's it, I am done. You are not listening, and I am finished talking to you."

McKenna began to rise but did not get far. Parker's arm encircled her waist, and he pulled her back down on her bench.

"May I remind you, madam, that I am captain of this ship, and I have eyes all over my head? I am looking at the sails, the wind direction, and the crew. You have my attention; please, continue. If my eyes wander, be assured I am only checking on the progression of my ship."

"Well then, all right. You can remove your hand from my waist. I will not blow away."

"Certainly, kitten. Please, introduce me to Charlestonian manners," Parker said while he slowly dropped his hand from her waist and rested it upon his knee.

"You had better be serious, Captain Sloane. No interruptions. Now, then, good manners are an accomplishment. Southerners feel that manners are a duty to take away rudeness. Some feel good manners for men are most important. Men will not be beastly if they have good manners. The South feels that good manners diminish possible altercations with words. They help one's pride remain humble, help one balance strength, and help to deal with all types and levels of fellow men without provocation. Are you still listening, Captain?"

"Yes, kitten, please continue. You have my full attention."

"Pride is the backbone of the South, sir. Bad manners are inexcusable. Every man should observe the rules of etiquette. There is a saying in South Charleston, Captain: 'Once a gentleman, always a gentleman. Once a pig, always a pig.' That has been embedded into the minds of every Southerner since birth. You see, kindness and politeness promote beauty in the man who possesses it and happiness in those who are around him. Any man who wishes to act as a gentleman should follow the code of rules which I have explained to you.

"Any man who wishes to be a Christian gentleman should follow the rules of etiquette and the Ten Commandments from God. Furthermore, there is an accepted rule in the South. Men should never be out of control; that means men should never allow themselves to get drunk."

"Well done, Miss Reed. I agree with you. There are gentlemen who try to follow the rules of etiquette, and then there are scoundrels. However, there are also terms for ladies that could be included in this conversation."

"Oh, really, and what would those terms be?"

"Much to my disdain, Miss Reed, there are basically two types of ladies—ladies of the day and ladies for the night. The latter is never permitted upon my ship. I have yet to discover either lady to be deprived of manners, but quite possibly neglectful of the sixth, ninth, and tenth commandments."

"You know your Bible, sir? I am impressed. So, I am to understand you have made the acquaintance of both ladies of the day and of the night?"

"That would be my business, Miss Reed; careful, do not pry because that would be most unladylike."

"You are quite right, sir. My apology. Do you favor any other books besides the Bible?"

"I admire Horace Greely, madam, as well as James Gordon Bennett. Now, Miss Reed, allow me to ask you a few questions, if I may. It would help me to understand your Southern etiquette."

"Certainly, ask away."

"Miss Reed, is Zadie one of your slaves?"

McKenna was so taken aback by his question, she nearly gasped. McKenna controlled her composure and continued. "No, she is not. She has black skin, but her blood is as red as mine and yours. She helped deliver me into this world and was there to comfort my mother as she was dying. Papa and I do not believe in slavery."

"That is a rare belief in South Carolina, I would imagine," stated Parker.

"Yes, I suppose it is. You see, he met Zadie at a hospital in Charleston. At the time, she was working there—cleaning and sterilizing instruments and doing the jobs that no one else wanted to do. But Papa saw she had a deep compassion for patients and possessed outstanding organizational skills. He eventually asked her if she would like to work at our home. He explained he needed someone to organize and oversee the cooking, cleaning, and gardening.

"He even suggested that she may be a future caretaker for his child one day. Papa told Zadie she would be paid like any of the other workers and would attend church with us. He even offered to teach her how to stitch a simple cut and share his knowledge of herbal medicines. She gladly accepted the position."

"How did your neighbors and friends feel about that?" asked Parker with a raised brow.

"Well, they were not pleased with Papa. They didn't feel Zadie should be treated like a member of our family, but he didn't care what others thought. Nor did I. I love her as a mother, and I know she loves me as a daughter. She has never married, and as far as I know, she has no children. I would like to change that, though. I am hoping I can find someone for Zadie in England; that would be the ultimate fulfillment for her! Don't you think, Captain?"

"Well, Miss Reed, let nature take its course. I am sure there would be someone in England for Zadie to meet. In fact, I think I know someone who would be perfect for her. Do you remember Cooper?"

"Oh, my Lord; yes, oh, yes, why didn't I think of that? Is he still in the stables? Oh, Captain, you just set my mind reeling. I would love to see Zadie happy and well taken care of for the rest of her life. She deserves much happiness."

"And what about you, kitten? Do you want to find your perfect match and be well taken care of?"

"Of course, I do. But I want to pursue my dreams. I do not want to be hastily married and soon beget a child just to see my dreams vanish. That may sound selfish, but I think you understand that feeling—especially since you wanted to become a master builder. I want to be loved from head to toe and inside out. That probably sounds silly, but I am a romantic at heart. I have so much love to share and so much to learn. Hopefully, the man who falls in love with me will share my dreams and my thoughts about love."

The silence was unnerving.

"Captain, forgive me for rambling. I am so sorry to have taken your time. Please, excuse me, and I will let you get back to your ship. I should not have gone on the way I did. I hope you understand Southern etiquette a bit better now."

"Stay seated, kitten. Tell me more."

"I beg your pardon?"

"Tell me about your horse Solomon and your dog. Tell me about your love of horses. I am most interested in hearing about your passions for horse breeding; I, too, am a horse breeder." Parker continued to gaze into McKenna's blue eyes. She politely coughed and placed a handkerchief delicately upon her lips.

Can one woman contain so much love for others? Are you really this perfect? Let's see how much you know about horses, thought Parker.

McKenna took the handkerchief from her mouth and continued, "Well, Solomon has been my horse for a long time. He is a registered thoroughbred. His papers show he is the product of a crossbreed between an English mare and an Arabian stallion. Thoroughbreds started being imported to the Americas in the 1730s, I believe, and are noted and respected for their intense speed and endurance in a fast canter. My father had some thoroughbreds sent home from England and a few mares, as well. Solomon was born on American soil, and I was there to watch his birth. He is a fast runner and keeps his head high for me. I have little use of the reins other than to steer. He is an excellent horse, and I love him dearly. Does that answer your question?"

"How often do you ride?"

"I ride him every morning and evening. Sometimes, I ride all day and trot back at sunset."

"Your father allows you to ride out alone?"

"Excuse me, Captain, but I ride on my land."

"Yes, but at the current time, your land is surrounded by Union soldiers who are a bit uneasy right now and trigger happy at anything that startles them. At any point in time, you could have been hit by a stray bullet."

"As I said before, I was quite safe on my own land, I assure you."

"I assure you that you were not. Why do you think your father sent you to England? Madam, you put yourself and your horse at risk. There were heated tempers around your land with live ammunition, and that combination is not a basis for safety."

"Well, I won't have to worry about that now, will I?"

"Someone should have placed constraints on you. So, I am to assume that a beautiful, golden-haired lady is riding alone throughout the countryside on her horse. Her only weapons are a gun, a bow, and a dog. That was foolishness in fine form."

"You haven't seen me ride or shoot or bow my arrow, and you certainly have never met Knox. Be glad, and be forewarned, Captain; you do not want to be on the wrong side of my dog's jaws."

"I assure you, lady, no matter the size of beast or dog, one bullet or one arrow can kill with accuracy. I do not have to tell you that. Or do I?"

"All right, Captain, you are doing it again. You are arguing with me and not attempting to understand my conversation. Do I continue or end this conversation?"

"Miss Reed, I am not trying to argue. I am just surprised your father would allow such a risk to his daughter. If you were my wife, you would never have attempted such riding without an escort."

"Well, that will be a cold day in hell, Captain. I would not become your wife, and even if I were, I would ride with or without your permission."

"Kitten, if you were my wife, there would be an understanding of what you could and could not do. Your life would be my utmost priority, and with that comes safety and common sense. You stated you wanted to be loved, inside and out; well, with that love comes protection and loyalty to one's possessions."

"Possessions? Is that what a wife would be to you?"

"In a manner of speaking, yes. I protect what is mine, and no one takes what belongs to me. I would protect the woman I love with my body, my soul, and my mind. If that included forbidding any perilous riding adventures, then I would enforce that rule—with or without her acceptance."

"Well, God's mercy to your future wife; however, your devotion sounds thoroughly romantic—a bit possessive, but romantic. Let me change the subject for the moment, sir. Have you ever been in love, Captain? Has there ever been a woman who captured your heart?"

What is the little minx up to now? he thought. Was there a tone of sincerity about her question, or an answer she was waiting to hear?

"There was one woman who almost stole my heart. But I realized she did not return the love I was giving her. She was stealing, or attempting to steal, my wealth."

"Oh, I am sorry to hear that. May I ask her name? What ever happened to her?"

"No need to be sorry, my dear. Savannah remains in London; I have not been in contact with her for quite some time. I learned a valuable lesson from her."

"And that would be?"

"If I am ever fortunate enough to find a woman who loves me as much as I love her, I will live and die a happy man. I learned that most women want money, status, nobility ranking, gems, and non-essential elements in life. What I was willing to give wasn't enough; she was greedy. She wanted the things in life that I did not."

"Captain Sloane, I admire what you are saying, and I thank you for sharing your thoughts with me. But remember, not all women are like that. Perhaps she was raised without the proper guidance, or she was raised in a home that exemplified greed and the aspirations that go along with it."

"You could be right, my dear. You see the good in a person, and that is a rare find." *What I wouldn't give to kiss those lips of yours right now. You are trying my nerves and my physical strength to the limits. You are too damn beautiful for your own good.*

"Captain, is that a compliment you just gave to me?" she asked as she leaned closer.

"Yes, kitten. What I really want to do is to kiss you and make sure you are real." He leaned in close, until he could feel the warmth of her breath upon his face.

"Well then, Captain, do not let me stop you. Go ahead and kiss me, and you shall see I am very real, indeed."

Parker could not believe what she had said. Christ, he'd just admitted he wanted to kiss her. This chit was breaking his resolve.

"Captain, what are you waiting for?" she asked tapping her foot a few times before she stood and walked around his knees. She delicately sat down on his lap and wrapped her arms around his neck.

What in the hell is she doing? Does she know she will get the kiss of her life? This little kitten is about to separate from the litter of safety and enter a snare from which there will be no going back, thought Parker.

"Miss Reed, I would like to instruct you on the art of kissing. Since you have probably never been kissed by a man, allow me to teach you."

"Captain, you are a cad. Teach me the art of kissing, please—English style, if you dare."

Parker put his hand behind her neck and leaned her head against the rail of the ship. He slowly took his other hand and tilted her chin up until she met his eyes. He ever so slightly put his lips to hers. Then, he placed soft little kisses against her forehead, her cheeks, her nose, her neck, and her ears, and finally sucked her bottom lip.

My God, this is heaven. McKenna couldn't breathe. *I am rendered useless within your power of seduction. Don't stop…*

Parker began to bite her lower lip, biting with intention to open her mouth, and when her mouth opened, his tongue went to work. He was like a breeze on the ship… soft, gentle, magical.

McKenna broke the kiss with an abrupt movement backward. She stared into those magical green eyes of his and saw the hint of sincerity tinged with pure pleasure.

"I hope I have not offended you, Miss Reed. Was my kiss too bold?" he asked huskily.

"Do not be silly—no offense taken. I asked you to kiss me, and now, Captain, let me teach you how I kiss—Charleston style." She sat straight and placed her hands on each side of his thick, curly hair, entwining her fingers around his head. She began to massage his scalp, his temples, and his cheekbones. His eyes instinctively closed from her gentle touch. She touched his lips with her fingers, seductively licking her index finger and inserting it into his mouth.

"Captain, dear, I am going to kiss you now. Open your eyes for a moment. I want to see your beautiful green eyes," she whispered seductively.

McKenna placed her lips upon his and gently bit his upper lip. She nipped and tucked her tongue between his lips in such a provocative manner that she could feel his heart racing. *Almost there, my dear Captain, almost there.* Finally, she pressed her hands tightly against each side of his temple and kissed him fervently. His groans of pleasure released from somewhere in the depths of his chest.

One more dangerous move to make, she thought. McKenna placed her chest against his, purposely, provocatively. *Almost there...* She moved her tongue in and out between his lips, mimicking the motion of lovemaking. She mesmerized the poor captain... he was weak... absorbed... no doubt dismantled...

McKenna released him and jumped up abruptly. "Next time, sir, do not attempt to think of me as a mere girl released from the nunnery. I do know how to kiss, and I am quite certain you enjoyed it. Checkmate."

She quickly traipsed away from the captain, knowing full well if she stopped, he would be there to counterattack with his next kissing lesson. She couldn't resist, though. She slowly turned back to the bench and met Sloane's eyes.

Oh, dear, she saw anger in those eyes—but mixed with admiration. Should she, or shouldn't she offer one more teasing word? She couldn't resist... "*Meow.*"

At that moment, the wind took her hair ribbon in a swift breeze, and McKenna flitted across the deck to catch it.

"I'll be damned. Checkmate, my dear little kitten?" he asked aloud. The little chit could entice and kiss and deliver a package of passion unlike any he had ever seen. Her checkmate statement was deliberate. She was toying with him and trying to teach him a lesson. *We shall see, my dear. You are entirely out of your league. I will let you have your moment of triumph. It shall not last long. Bloody hell... Meow.* He suppressed a smile as she sashayed from left to right, attempting to catch that damn ribbon. He watched her for a few more moments, then spoke across the light breeze.

"Well done, Miss Reed. I hope you enjoyed your game playing. Perhaps when we continue our conversation about your breeding aspirations—horse breeding, that is—you will be able to share an honest moment with me. You see, kitten, there is nothing more romantic than pure and honest seduction. Perhaps that should be your next lesson. My king was not captured, my dear, and you did not provide the threat of doing so. Checkmate is denied."

Parker rose quickly and snatched McKenna's ribbon as a gust of wind blew it his way. He walked toward her and carefully tied the silk ribbon around her wrist before he disappeared around the corner.

McKenna sighed. She wondered how her upper hand had turned on her, and how he had just made her feel so ignorant and foolish. What started out as a lesson to be taught had ended up as a lesson gone dreadfully sour! Once again, McKenna felt confused and inadequate. She had wanted to hurt him and show him she was no virgin—even though she was. How very dull-witted on her part. Now he thought of her as a simpleton. She should have stayed away. Her papa would be so embarrassed of her. She was so attracted to the man, but being with him day and night was a competition of wit and will. She just couldn't do this anymore. Her head hung low and her shoulders slumped as she walked back toward her quarters, almost bumping into Pepper.

"McKenna, is something wrong?" he asked as he sidestepped her. "You almost bumped into me. Head up, dear girl, when walking on board. Come along, I will escort you to lunch."

"I am sorry, Uncle Pepper, I wasn't watching where I was going—again. I just made a fool of myself to Captain Sloane. I tried to be something I am not, just to impress him and wipe that smug smile off his face. But my plan backfired and I failed miserably. I really do not have an appetite, Uncle. Do not worry about lunch for me."

Pepper watched McKenna as she walked slowly toward her quarters and descended the entire length of stairs with her head hung low. She might as well have mopped the floor with that pouting lip of hers. Any moment now, the girl would be crying. What had happened? Did she try to ensnare the captain? Perhaps she had lost at her own game. Those who attempted to dupe Parker Sloane ultimately lost. If they didn't lose their wealth or pride, they lost their dignity, that was for bloody sure.

Chapter 13

"What did you do to McKenna?" asked Pepper as Parker strolled up next to him. "I just saw her. Her body is so slumped over, she can barely walk. Tell me you did not hurt her or disgrace her."

"You know better than that, Pepper. I will admit I am attracted to the little minx, but I would never physically hurt her or intentionally berate her—except in the case of teaching a lesson. She tried to checkmate my king and she lost. I taught her a lesson—English style."

"What kind of lesson? You played a game of chess with her?"

"In a manner of speaking, I played a game of chess with her. I taught her the kind of lesson where pride needs to be discovered prudently. The kitten got her claws trimmed, Pepper; nothing to alarm yourself over."

"Very well. I need to tell you that I had the *talk* with McKenna, sir. She now knows everything about my father and Maribelle."

"How did she take to that conversation?"

"As best as could be expected. She seemed to absorb everything. I told her about past emotions and current feelings toward her grandfather. Time will tell, sir."

"What do you mean by that?"

"Well, she was most annoyed that you knew about her family. She also felt she should have been told years ago, and I can't say I blame her."

"I would agree, Pepper. Family secrets never lead to any good outcome. Perhaps we should leave Miss Reed alone for a while. She has a lot to sort out and think about. We will dock within forty-eight hours, so she will have other thoughts to entertain in that pretty little head of hers."

"You are right, sir. That would also give you forty-eight hours to do some thinking for yourself. I have never known anyone to play chess with you and win." Pepper walked away from the captain, grinning. "I will see you shortly at lunch, sir." He tossed the words over his shoulder.

"What the hell? Pepper, she didn't win. Turn your arse around here; she didn't win. Pepper, damn it, I said she didn't win." Parker narrowed his eyes on his friend's form as he glided across the planks. Pepper didn't twitch, he didn't stop, he just kept walking away. However, just as he reached the stairs of the second deck, he turned and looked over his shoulder.

"Yes, sir, she did. A checkmate ensures that the king cannot escape. Miss Reed just ensured the same of you." Pepper smiled a bit, turned, and continued on.

Like hell, she did, thought Parker. He would drop her and Zadie off on the shores of England and be done with them. McKenna Reed's life was none of his concern. Not now—not ever—perhaps a remembrance of an enticing kiss and nothing more.

Chapter 14

The port they docked at was a mass of hovering, pushing, noisy, strolling people. The women were shopping along the crowded streets for their upcoming fall vegetables, decorative gourds, squash, cornucopia, and spices, while the men were comparing and analyzing the best wood to be bought for winter shutters.

There were brief fights and shoves amongst the shoppers and carriage drivers trying to secure space for loading. The crowds of shoppers had one thing on their minds—buy their goods and discard whomever got in their way.

Charleston is busy, McKenna thought to herself, *but I have never seen its streets filled with such rudeness*. McKenna stood at the ship's rail, overlooking the shopping frenzy for close to an hour when she saw Captain Sloane approaching from the rigging deck.

"Miss Reed, may I present the Port of London—the central economy of this country—to you."

McKenna side-stepped to the left and raised her chin to look at his eyes. "I had no idea how busy this port would be. Of course, I have not been here since I was a very young child, and at the time, I paid no heed to the inhabitants or their duties to their lifestyles."

"Madam, this is the busiest port in the world. These wharves extend along the Thames River for eleven miles, and they boast fifteen hundred cranes that handle sixty thousand ships per year. Yes, Miss Reed, it is indeed busy."

"Who built these docks? There are so many. How do you know which dock to pull your ship up to and sink anchor?"

Parker stepped closer to McKenna and pointed to his right. "The dock we will anchor to is called the Victoria Dock. It is only five years old. If you look to the right and left side of each dock, you will see walls that have been built to enclose the dock itself. This was done to protect cargoes from an unusually high rate of river piracy.

"If you will excuse me, I must navigate my ship into the portal area. Please, make sure your belongings are packed and ready to be brought up on deck. I will see to it that your carriage is here before you leave the ship. Is there anything else I can do for you, Miss Reed?"

"No, Captain, I am fine. I will ensure that our belongings are packed. I do want to tell you that I truly do appreciate the effort you took to deliver Zadie and me safely to England. Captain, I do not want to end this voyage on a fretful or strained tone. I do apologize if I lost my temper with you or if I offended your knowledge and expertise in any way."

"Well, Miss Reed, what a delightful appreciation you have shown. I do not want to end this voyage in a tense position, either. Apology accepted, madam."

Well, where is your apology? she thought. She waited and kept staring at his handsomely chiseled face. *So much for an attempt at peace; he has no intention of apologizing!* "I am sorry, sir, I did not hear you."

"I did not say a word, madam."

"I know you didn't—yet. How about you swallow that pride of yours, and offer an apology to me as well?"

"I have no apology to make, madam. My job was to deliver you to England, and I have completed that job successfully. I will see you safely to shore in a few moments."

Parker politely tipped his tricorn, turned, and began shouting orders at his crew. It was imperative that the bow remain unscathed from the docks. He had done this a hundred times, and yet, he still held his breath each time until they were perfectly docked.

"Captain Sloane?"

"Yes, Miss Reed?"

"Be sure to buy a new litter of pigs when you return to your home."

"Why in the devil would I do that?" *What is she up to now?* That little nose of hers was turning up toward him, and those eyes were revealing a mischievous act about to be unleashed.

"Well, Captain, if you buy a litter of pigs, they will feel right at home with you! One big pig can live and sleep with a collection of smaller pigs. You will be able to live together and share each other's same temperament, behavior, and most importantly, manners. Remember, once a gentleman, always a gentleman... once a pig, always a pig... You, sir, offered no apology nor are you inclined to do so; therefore, go wallow with the rest of the litter. Good day to you." McKenna forcefully gathered her skirts and began to turn toward her cabin, only to be stopped and turned by a firm grip on her elbow.

"By God, someone should have taught you how to control that sassy mouth of yours a long time ago. I swear you have been eating sour berries this morn. I will gladly teach you what is appropriate and what is not appropriate on this ship!" Parker called out to his first mate, who had just come up from below. "Pepper, sail ahead and drag the stern. Dock the *Constance* with three feet from the bow."

Parker scooped McKenna up in his arms quickly, not giving her time to prepare or to dislodge his strength.

"How dare you! Put me down this instant!"

"Oh, I intend to, my dear, as soon as I find a good spot to sit. Perhaps I should sit with an audience, or I could find solace in a more private teaching area. Which do you prefer?"

"What in God's name is wrong with you? I insist that you put me down! You have no right to carry me against my will. Captain Sloane, I will scream if you do not put me down this instant!"

"Scream away. You are on my ship, kitten."

Parker carried McKenna to the stairs, abruptly changed his tactic, and threw her over his shoulder.

"Captain Parker, you are by far the rudest man I have ever laid eyes on. You need to buy the entire pig farm to equate with your lack of genteelness. What have I possibly done to cause you to act in such a roguish manner?"

"Lady, you tend to speak without thinking. If you truly feel I need to live with pigs, I will show you how I handle pigs that are not yet trained. I will not have a spoiled, pampered brat tell me on my own ship that I need to live with pigs. I will not offer an apology because I did nothing to apologize for. You, on the other hand, are a brazen little chit who needs to have her bottom spanked. I see that your father did not take care of this when you were younger. I fully intend to make up for his lost efforts." Parker continued to carry her down into his quarters and used his foot to pull the dressing bench out from beneath the desk. He sat down and flipped McKenna onto her stomach and over his knee in one swift movement.

"Madam, I will be glad to teach you some English manners, which you are sorely in need of." He lifted layer upon layer of petticoats until her chemise came into view. "Now, Miss Reed, how many spankings do you think you deserve?"

"I hate you. You are a despicable creature. You are a bully and have no right to spank me. I will tell my father about this."

"He will thank me."

"He will shoot you—if I don't do so first."

"I doubt that, madam." Parker raised his hand and gave a harsh swat to McKenna's bottom.

"Ouch, stop it, damn you—that hurt."

"So did your words."

"I am sorry, then; I am sorry I hurt your feelings."

"Excuse me, madam. I didn't hear you."

"Go to the devil, Captain Sloane. You did too hear me. I offered my apology; take it or leave it."

"I shall take it with one more to grow on."

Swat two met McKenna's bottom with a bit more strength. Her bottom was the most perfectly molded little ass he had ever felt. He should be doing something else besides spanking that perfection.

"Oh, my Lord, that hurts! Stop it this instant. I mean it; that really hurts."

Parker rolled McKenna off his lap and onto the floor.

"This is not finished, Captain Pig!" She looked up at Parker, her expression mutinous.

Obviously, the little chit doesn't know when to keep her mouth closed, he thought. "No, madam, it is not." Once again, he scooped her up into the air and tossed her over his knee, none too gently. McKenna tried to scream but couldn't manage to do so. Parker swatted McKenna for the third time, dealing a strong spank to her already tender bottom.

"Ouch, enough, Captain! You are causing tears. Truly, you are."

"Madam, I can do this all day. I hardly doubt your bottom can withstand many more spankings. Perhaps I should pull your chemise off and spank you like a young child—bare bottomed? That is certainly what you are imitating; maybe then you would learn to keep that pretty mouth of yours shut."

"You are a brute. Unhand me, Captain Sloane. Is this what they taught you in your schooling? You have made your point, and my bottom is sore; it really is."

The quiver in McKenna's voice caused Parker to stop. He turned her over in one swift move, bent, and captured her mouth with his. McKenna responded to his kiss with unconstrained passion. Parker took full advantage of her eagerness and kissed her deeply. Just when McKenna thought she had melted his temper, he abruptly ended the kiss and deposited her roughly onto the floor. Her chest was rising with each breath, her hair was out of place, and she looked a disheveled mess—a beautiful, disheveled mess. Parker stood to his full height of over six feet. When he spoke, he resumed his authoritative voice, showing no compassion.

"Miss Reed, I learned a long time ago when to talk and when not to talk. I learned when to use gentle words rather than hurtful words. I learned to offer thanks wholeheartedly. Most importantly, I learned to avoid apologies because I learned not to create situations that warranted them. You, madam, have a lot to learn. You throw hurtful words when things do not go your way. You look like a woman and act like a child. I sincerely hope you treat your horses better than you do your peers. Good luck in England; you shall need it. I offer my apologies for a sore bottom—nothing more."

Parker walked to the stairs without offering her a hand up. Slowly, though, he stopped and turned.

"I believe you once turned to me and said, 'checkmate.' I now turn to you and say, checkmate, madam; game over."

Parker slowly turned, leaving McKenna on the floor with her skirts in disarray.

Oh, my Lord. What is wrong with me? Why in God's name did I talk to him in that tone? Pigs? For heaven's sake. The sooner I am away from you, Parker Sloane, the better. My life will be much easier without you, she thought to herself as she rose from the floor and straightened her skirts. She would not see him again anytime soon, and that was bloody comforting. Or was it? She wouldn't be able to see those beautiful green eyes of his again. Where would he go? Would he meet another lady and forget about her? Did she want him to forget her?

McKenna Reed, stop acting so silly. Pull yourself together and leave Captain Sloane at the Port of London. Forget about him once and for all!

Chapter 15

McKenna could barely remain seated in one position on the boardwalk bench, where they awaited the carriage arranged by Captain Pig, before her bottom would beg for a new position. Sloane had spanked her hard. Well, she was done with Captain Parker Sloane, and good riddance to him! McKenna's humiliation soon melted into pity. Beggary, destitution, and penury were the first thoughts McKenna had as she viewed the east side of the Port of London. If this was the busiest port in the world, then shame on London for allowing such filth and despair to fill its streets. Dirty, stagnant water filled the rain barrels. Moldy bread had been tossed to the ducks in the channel. McKenna felt sorry for the poor ducks, hoping they would not get sick from bad bread. The air was damp and had a putrid smell consisting of rotten food and animal waste mixed together. Overall, this port was disgusting, and its inhabitants didn't appear to be faring much better.

When their carriage arrived, McKenna carefully observed her close surroundings with Zadie and Uncle Pepper as they walked toward it. She slowly and methodically looked over her shoulder to see Captain Sloane standing against the rail of the *Constance*. He raised his hand and tipped his tricorn hat in a gesture of good-bye. A slight smile appeared at the corners of his mouth, but his firm jaw prevented that smile from enveloping his devilishly handsome profile.

Well, if that is how you want to say good-bye, so be it. You can just stand there and watch me leave. McKenna turned her attention back to the carriage and the journey ahead. *Perhaps I should have given him a hug good-bye? Lord knows I wanted to. Well, what's done is done, and now he can be on his way.*

Parker watched McKenna Reed stroll to her carriage. *I will see you again, kitten. When you least suspect my presence, I will be there to hold you within my arms again and provide the stability you need. We are far from discontinuing this relationship, little one.*

The carriage ride to Oxford proved to be an enjoyable one. The colors of late summer were providing McKenna with an unimaginable display of golds, magentas, browns, and violets. The countryside was beautiful. She wished Solomon was here at that very moment to ride. Knox would love to run through the hilly grass and drink from the bubbling creeks. This was paradise. Perhaps this was even prettier than Charleston. Goodness sakes, she never thought anything would ever compare to Charleston's beauty. McKenna was so immersed in the landscape that she lost track of time. When the carriage stopped, she looked to her fellow passengers and noticed they were both asleep.

"Zadie, Uncle Pepper, wake up. We are here! We are finally here! Hurry, pull yourselves together. We are at Aunt Olympia's home!"

"Lord's sake, baby girl, calm down. Let ol' Zadie wake up her tired bones and stretch. I am getting older, you know—not any younger."

"Uncle Pepper, please help Zadie down from the carriage. I can't wait to see my aunt and all my cousins. Look, they are waiting for us!"

"Yes, ma'am, they are waiting. Do you remember their names?"

"I think so. Quaid is the oldest, then Livingston, Caleb, and Magnolia—she is the youngest. Tierney is the butler, Percy is the cook, and Cooper is the stable master. Oh, my goodness, they will have all grown up. Magnolia was just a baby when I last saw her. There she is; there is Aunt Olympia."

A tall, pretty woman came strolling from the front door of the English Tudor home. Her honey-colored hair resembled McKenna's mother's hair. But it was the smile and the eyes that took McKenna's breath away.

"Uncle Pepper, she looks like Mother—like Mother looked in the picture on Papa's desk."

"Yes, dear, she does a bit. Pia is taller than your mother was and her hair a bit darker. Her mannerisms are like your mother's, though. Her smile is just like Maribelle's."

Olympia emerged onto the tiled walkway approaching the carriage stop.

"Aunt Olympia," yelled McKenna as she jumped from the carriage. "Is it really you? Are you really standing here before me? I can't believe I am here in England."

"Yes, my dear, it is me." Olympia stretched out her arms and said, "Come, child, and give your aunt a proper hug. I have missed you, dear. Eight years is too long—almost sinfully so. My, do you look like your mother! You are beautiful, my dear. Look at your golden hair—just like your mother's. How I have waited for you to come running up this walkway to greet me." Pia hugged McKenna tightly and kissed her forehead. She then turned to the carriage and sucked in a breath. "Oh, my Lord, Zadie. Tears will be bursting soon if I do not get control of my emotions. Come and give me one of your hugs—perhaps two, for old time's sake."

"Olympia, I have missed you, my dear friend. You look lovely as ever, and I thank you for your kindness in allowing us to stay with you in your home." Tears fell from Zadie's big brown eyes.

"No, Zadie, it is you who do me the honor of staying here. I have missed you, my friend." The two women hugged each other tightly, absorbing the moment.

"Damn it all, what about me?"

McKenna, Olympia, and Zadie turned to the stopped carriage. There was Pepper, standing in the middle of multiple bags, his arms outstretched.

"Pepper, my dear brother, thank you for delivering and joining in this reunion. You know how much I enjoy seeing you. I will not contribute to any more ego than you already have, baby brother. Come, give me a hug!"

Pepper went to Olympia, swept her off her feet, and twirled her around. "I have missed you, dear sister."

"And I have missed you! I assume your trip was eventful?" asked Pia with a soft voice.

"That is one way of putting it," said Pepper as he lowered Olympia back on her feet and tossed a smile to Zadie.

"Oh, am I about to be filled in on exactly how eventful this voyage was?" Olympia looked at all three of them, her intense gaze settling on McKenna. "McKenna, dear, whatever is wrong? You keep shifting your feet as though your toes are on fire."

"No, Aunt Pia, my feet are not troubling me. I am just stiff and sore from the journey."

"More like her bottom is sore from the journey," whispered Pepper in her ear.

Zadie and Pepper exchanged what McKenna could only assume were knowing grins. Oh, how embarrassing. Did they both know what had happened between her and Captain Sloane?

Luckily, McKenna was saved from having to respond to any more of her aunt's inquiries by the approach of her cousin, Magnolia.

"Maggie, oh my goodness, is it really you?" McKenna sidestepped Olympia and ran toward her young cousin.

The moment her niece was out of earshot, Olympia turned to Zadie and Pepper with hands on her hips.

"All right, you two, what is going on with McKenna?" Olympia asked, tapping her foot.

"Let's just say she met Parker, and things didn't go well for her. Her sassy mouth got her into trouble—a bit of sitting trouble. Her discomfort will pass in a day or so."

"Pepper, what do you mean, 'sitting trouble'? Am I to assume that our little niece was taught a lesson across the knee?"

"Yes, sister, you would assume correctly!"

Pepper grabbed Zadie's and Pia's hands, and together they walked toward the house.

Dear Lord, thought Olympia, *Parker may have met his match with little McKenna. Someone needs to stand up to that hunk of masculinity, though. He is too handsome for his own good and too obstinate, as well.* This could prove to be an interesting journey for little Miss McKenna. Olympia wondered how Parker and her niece would react when they met again. Perhaps she could arrange for a party or assembly of guests.

"Pia, I know you, and you're designing something in that clever mind of yours. Out with it; what are you up to?" Pepper demanded as they walked.

"Oh, never you mind, brother. Come on, Zadie, let's go into the house and have some tea and scones. Pepper, come along, and stop looking at me as though I just robbed from a candy jar."

"I'm not worried about the robbing; I am worried about what or who may be in that candy jar."

"Never you mind," Pia repeated. She strolled into the foyer and quickly dislodged her scheming for the moment. She was more interested in sipping on a cup of tea. After all, she did her best planning with a cup of tea.

Chapter 16

That evening, the entire family sat around the formal dining table at the manor house. McKenna was delighted to be sharing her meal with family. She listened as Caleb talked about his schooling, and Livingston described his riding skills and hunting sessions. She had learned that Quaid was away on business but would be returning soon. Although the food was delicious, she barely ate, finding it much more interesting to learn all about her family.

"Cousin McKenna," said Caleb with a serious tone to his voice, "can you explain to me what this secession is all about back in the States?"

"We just keep hearing about your country possibly splitting apart, and it doesn't seem possible that your president would want that to occur," Livingston added.

"Well, boys, you are absolutely correct. President Buchanan doesn't want any type of war within the country, but it may be out of his control now. If Abraham Lincoln is elected as our next president, there could be a very strong division among the northern and southern states. According to the newspaper, the General Assembly called for a convention of the people of South Carolina to draw up an Ordinance of Secession. That means a paper or document stating that they want to leave the union and form their own government. I imagine they are working on this document as I speak. Papa had a hunch this would be happening."

"Why do people want to fight their own kind? Some of those people could be fighting their own relatives."

"You are right again, Caleb. Let me give you a history lesson. Do you mind, Aunt Olympia?"

"Go right ahead, my dear; I want to try to understand this secession ordeal, as well."

"Well, pass that pie around, and fill up your milk glasses; it may take a while to explain the mess we have found ourselves in."

The apple pie was indeed passed around, its scent wafting across the table, especially the nutmeg and cinnamon. It had been a long time since McKenna had sat at a table full of relatives, enjoying a glass of milk and homemade apple pie—the opportunity had not presented itself in Charleston. She slowly ate and savored half of her slice of pie before she gently laid her fork down. She politely dabbed her mouth with one of Aunt Olympia's crocheted napkins and pushed her chair slightly away from the table.

"All right, now that I have a full tummy, let me try to explain secession to all of you. In 1815, President James Madison wanted more building on the coastal areas to keep our defenses strong. Charleston Harbor was selected as a location for one of these forts to be built, and it was named Fort Sumter. Well, the Main Shipping Channel, the builder, decided to build Fort Sumter as a five-sided island."

"That is called a pentagon," chirped Livingston.

"Correct, cousin. The fort can mount one hundred and thirty-five guns and has space for six hundred and fifty soldiers. They said it would be ninety percent finished by December—in just a few weeks. But now that the General Assembly has called for an Ordinance of Secession, the fort has stopped all work."

"But why did they stop? What does secession have to do with this, Cousin McKenna?"

"Good question, Caleb. They stopped building the fort because the South does not want the Northern states to be able to use it. If there is a war, the South does not want that fort with all those guns to be pointing toward Charleston." McKenna turned to her uncle. "Uncle Pepper, can you help me with this explanation, please?"

"Yes, I believe I can, my dear. The Southern states feel that slaves are property, not people. They feel they should have no rights of their own. They are not allowed to defend themselves in a fight, they cannot carry a weapon, and they are not allowed to learn how to read and write. If they break these codes or rules, they are punished, killed, or even worse—sold off."

"What does that mean?" asked Caleb.

"That means being separated from their immediate families, their parents, or their brothers and sisters. Sometimes, they will sell a girl or boy to get money. Sometimes, they will sell a wife or a husband as a punishment. It is an evil idea. You see, there are those in the South who view slavery as a necessity.

But less than a quarter of white Southerners own slaves. Usually, the plantation or farm has twenty or fewer slaves. The Northern folks who are against slavery call themselves abolitionists. Escaped slaves have run and escaped to the Northern states and have told what happened to them while living in the South. The Northern folks do not think it is right to keep people as property. In fact, there was a book published about ten years ago called *Uncle Tom's Cabin.* In this book, Harriet Beecher Stowe writes about what happened to Uncle Tom while he was a slave. The book was so popular that it sold over three hundred thousand copies in the first year! Many people believe the book helped to start this fuss over slavery, and there are those who feel it may have started this whole secession and war idea."

Maggie sat up straight and impatiently interjected, "This isn't right, Mama. Uncle Pepper, tell us more."

"Well, South Carolina supports individual states' rights. For example, Caleb, suppose you want to plant corn in your field. You should be able to decide for yourself if you want to plant corn or any other crop. South Carolina believes they should be able to have slaves if they want. No one should be able to tell them if they can or can't have slaves. They do not think that one law or one government should tell them what they can or can't have, or, in the example I just gave, what they can or can't plant. Understand so far?"

"Yes, sir. But what is wrong with that? I should be able to plant whatever I want."

"Yes, Caleb, you should be able to plant your choice of crop. But should you be able to control another human being's life? Many South Carolinians fear that if Abraham Lincoln takes the presidential oath, he may try to free the slaves one day, even though Lincoln keeps saying he only wants to restore the Union.

"There is a man named John Calhoun, and he feels the states should decide for themselves if they should allow slavery. He does not feel that any one person, including the president, should even think about making a slavery law for everyone to abide by. In your example, you may hire and pay others to help you harvest the corn. A fair day's wage for a fair day's work, right? Well, Calhoun feels the black slaves should be expected to work the fields. They should not be paid but rather be a slave or a piece of property to the plantation owner. They should have to harvest your corn because you told them to do so. There would be no asking, no choice, and no payment.

"When the South realized Lincoln may be our next president, they started organizing conventions and large meetings because they were afraid that some members of Congress would stop slavery from expanding. Missouri and Alabama have already sent delegates to the convention and have advised South Carolina to do the same. Sometime in December, South Carolina will vote whether to stay in the United States or to secede and form a new government with the other states and create new laws.

"If what I heard is true, South Carolina, Mississippi, Florida, Alabama, Georgia, Louisiana, and Texas will secede right away after Lincoln takes office. I know I have given you a lot of information, but it is important to understand the basis for the division among people back in the states," stated Pepper with a sincere smile upon his face.

"Is Zadie a slave, Cousin McKenna?" asked Maggie.

"Perhaps I should have Zadie answer that for you," replied McKenna, as she looked at Zadie with a sigh and smile.

"Lord's sake, McKenna, you sure done put me on the spot. Maggie, child, let ol' Zadie try answerin' that question by askin' you some questions."

"This sounds like a game!" Maggie's eleven-year-old smile radiated her youthfulness across the table.

"What color is my skin, child?"

"Umm, it is brown."

"Is it the same color as yours?"

"No, ma'am. Yours is browner."

"Well, some folks do not like the color of skin like mine. Some folks thinks that people with my brown skin are not human bein's. They think we should be owned, like a pet. They think we should be treated different."

"But God made all colors of people, Zadie. The Bible says God made all kinds of animals and people. Remember when he told all the animals to go in his big ark?"

"Out of the mouths of babes," Aunt Olympia said while sipping her wine.

"You is right, child; God made everyone. But there are some people who do not like anyone with brown skin. So, the people with light skin started treatin' the people with brown skin like pets. They locked them up in pens, fed them like a dog, not like a person. Am I makin' sense, child?"

"Yes, you are. Momma says it is not nice to be mean to others. The Bible says to treat your neighbor as yourself."

"Well, Miss Maggie, if everyone thought the way you think, we would not have had the arguments and the hurt feelin's we have had for so long. If everyone followed the Ten Commandments, we'd all be better off."

Zadie looked at those seated around the table while they nodded in acknowledgment.

"Maggie, dear, let me help Zadie explain," McKenna interrupted. "Zadie has been like a mother to me ever since I can remember. She has browner skin than I do. I have never thought of her as anything else. Your mother is sitting next to you. My mother died and went to the angels in heaven. Zadie's skin color did not matter to our family. But unfortunately, not everyone thinks like we do.

"There will always be mean people who say and do mean things to others. One day, when they pass on and go to heaven, they must answer the very same question you asked—only they must answer to God. He will remind them what was written in the Bible."

"Then I hope he has a lot of beds," said Maggie.

"Why would you say such a thing, child?" asked McKenna.

"Because when I am naughty and I don't remember the rules in the Bible, I have to go to bed and stay there until I think about things and say I'm sorry. I don't even get my supper on time!" The entire table was humbled.

"If only everyone could view life through the eyes of a child," whispered Olympia.

"Perhaps we should have Maggie meet Mr. Calhoun and share her thoughts with him, or better yet, the child should address the Southern conventions that are attracting so many hot-headed delegates," Pepper added.

"Honestly, Pepper, a child?" asked Olympia.

"Well, she has displayed more sense than most adults, now, hasn't she?"

"Well," continued McKenna, "we shall see what happens within the next few weeks. Maybe this secession talk will blow over, and nothing will come of it. Or the South may decide to tear away from the United States and make its own laws and country. Time will tell. We are very happy to be here with all of you. Let's just pray that Papa remains safe while he works for the army, no matter what color of uniform he tends to. He promised to write and keep us informed of all activities back home.

"In the meantime, let's finish the last scraps of pie. Then, I will be glad to lay my head down upon a bed tonight that isn't rocking with the sea." Her ensuing yawn was an indicator that she should retire for the evening.

"I would like to add a final comment to this evening's discussion, if I may," said Aunt Olympia as she laid her napkin upon the table. "England has had a different set of rules than the Americas on the issue of slavery. The Slavery Abolition Act of 1833 was an Act of Parliament of the United Kingdom and it abolished slavery in the British Empire. Those high, social-standing families received compensation for allowing their slaves—or their business assets, as they called them—to go free. We do not recognize slavery here. Our colored friends walk in the same circles of business as we do. We entertain, socialize, manage businesses, and work together. We have been able to overcome the slavery issue for twenty-seven years now, and it has been successful thus far—especially in this area of the country that supports such a large shipping industry."

"I wasn't aware of the Abolition Act, Aunt Pia. It is comforting to know that England abolished slavery for the greater good—no matter the color of skin. One can only hope that one day, Americans will be able to do the same," stated McKenna. "Now, if you will all excuse me, I am ready to seek some rest."

"Wait, Cousin McKenna, please. I have a question for you—just one more question," pleaded Livingston.

"All right, dear, what is your final question for the evening?" asked McKenna as she placed her elbows on the table and folded her hands, smiling at Livingston.

"Cousin McKenna, was it fun to be on a ship?" he asked.

"Let's just say it had its moments. Some good, some bad. But I promise I will tell you all about my shipping adventure tomorrow. I am too tired right now. Good-night, everyone." McKenna scooted from the table and stood beside Aunt Pia. She squeezed her aunt's shoulders and gently placed a kiss upon her cheek.

"Aunt Olympia, thank you again for allowing me to stay with you. Uncle Pepper, would you take me down to the stables in the morning? I want to see Cooper."

"Sure thing. See you at breakfast."

"What time is breakfast?" she asked, subduing another yawn.

"Daybreak—don't be late. This isn't the captain's ship anymore, my dear. Breakfast is served and expected to be eaten in a reasonable amount of time. Dishes are cleaned up and put away quickly."

McKenna nodded her understanding and walked toward the grand staircase leading to the second floor.

You are so right, Uncle; this isn't the captain's ship anymore. I wonder what that skunk Captain Sloane is up to right now.

Was he alone or was he being entertained by his 'ladies of the night'? Would she ever see him again?

Why does my heart still flutter at the thought of him? I daresay I miss him— his smell, his strength, his eyes, his… oh, my goodness, his kisses. Will I ever be kissed like that again?

Chapter 17

"Good morning, Uncle Pepper, you are late." McKenna looked up and greeted her uncle as he squeezed her shoulders at the breakfast table before seating himself. "The sun has been up for an hour now!" she added with a smile.

"Did you save me any of Percy's biscuits, or did you manage to eat them all, McKenna-girl?"

"Oh, no, I have only eaten two; besides, Percy has more in the oven. I am so excited to get to the stables, I can hardly sit here and eat. Do hurry, Uncle; I can't wait much longer."

"McKenna, allow your old uncle to have his breakfast and to enjoy it. This is the first land breakfast we have had in quite a while, and it tastes a lot better on land than eating breakfast on the rocking *Constance*."

McKenna couldn't agree more, although Captain Sloane's meals were delicious. *I wonder if he thinks of me—just a bit. I still smell him. I can still feel his arms around me. I can still feel his breath upon my cheek when he took out my splinter. I can still—*

"McKenna, are you listening? Please pass the syrup. These thick pancakes taste better when they are coated in Percy's homemade syrup. I trust you slept well last night?" Pepper asked, taking the crystal container from McKenna's hand.

"Oh, I did sleep well; thank you, Uncle. I was more tired than I thought I was! It is good being back here. By the way, thank you, Uncle Pepper. If I didn't say it before, I am saying it now. Thank you for making my transportation arrangements."

"You are welcome, dear girl. Thank you for allowing me the opportunity to reunite with you after all these years. I suppose some young ladies would have turned their noses up at a long-lost uncle."

"Well then, it would be their loss, now, wouldn't it? Are you just about finished? I can hardly wait to see Cooper," asked McKenna as she rapidly tapped her boot upon the tiled floor.

"Yes, dear, let me finish my coffee and a few more bites. By the way, I have a big surprise for you down at the barn. In fact, I have two surprises for you."

"Really? I love surprises. Give me a hint, please."

"My dear niece, I want to, but I'd rather see the look of surprise on your face, instead."

Pepper finished his few remaining bites of pancake, and together, they walked toward the stables. The crisp morning air was refreshing, almost welcoming, as the pair walked down the stone steps.

As she reached the door, McKenna placed her hand upon the barn latch just as it opened from the opposite direction. As McKenna's eyes adjusted to the shadows, she saw before her a tall black man who was stooped in the shoulders, crowned with bits of gray hair, and wearing wrinkled facial skin from hours spent in the sun. His eyes were brown—so brown, they rivaled the color of molasses just tapped from a tree.

Ever so slowly, a smile began to creep across the man's face as he stared intensely at McKenna. Suddenly, a memory from the past rushed through her as she recognized that smile.

"Sweet Mary, Mother of Jesus. Cooper, is that you?"

McKenna could not have stopped herself even if she had wanted to. She skipped to Cooper and was instantly tossed into the morning air by those powerful arms of his. After spinning her around several times, Cooper set McKenna down on her feet.

"Lord's sake, no female has a right to be as pretty as you are. You've grown up, child. Please tell ol' Cooper you still ride as well as you used to."

"Of course, I do. I went to the Harper Reed school of riding. I love to ride, and I did so every day back home. By the way, I had another teacher before I was even old enough to reach the stirrups. Do you remember who that was?" asked McKenna with a saucy smile.

"Well, missy, why don't you refresh my memory?" Cooper replied, rubbing his beard stubble.

"It was the Cooper School of Horsemanship. Do you know it?"

"I have heard of it. Was it a good school? Was your teacher good?"

"He was the best. He put me in a saddle when my head barely reached the stirrups. He was so sure I could handle a horse, he gave me free rein, as well!" McKenna squealed.

"Were you frightened? That sounds very young to sit a horse."

"Oh, no, I wasn't scared—well, maybe at first—but then I learned how to talk to the horse and let him know I could be trusted. This teacher told me that a horse knows when its rider is nervous. He also taught me that horse and rider must respect each other, no matter what."

"Sounds like good advice to me. Is this teacher still around?"

"Why, yes, he is! In fact, I have missed him so much that I am going to give him a big hug and kiss," replied McKenna with a hearty giggle.

"Ah, no, no, McKenna-girl. You know I don't like that huggin' and kissin' nonsense. I was just havin' fun with you; you know ol' Cooper favors you. Just don't get silly on me, now."

"Oh, Cooper, it is so good to see you. When can we ride? Just like old times."

"How about right now?"

"I would love to, but I'll have to borrow a horse. Is Sammy still here?"

"Why are you going to ride Sammy? Ride your own horse."

She shook her head and sighed. "Solomon is back in Charleston because that pompous captain wouldn't let me bring him on the same ship as me."

"Unless these old eyes are deceivin' me, Solomon is in the third stall down," Cooper said with a serious tone.

"What? You must be mistaken; he didn't sail with us." McKenna looked at Uncle Pepper, then Cooper.

Both men had impish looks upon their faces, with a sign of humor peeking through their eyes.

"Uncle Pepper, what is going on here?"

"McKenna, stop your questions, and go saddle up Solomon," barked Pepper.

McKenna turned and began to walk briskly toward the stalls. She passed the first stall and the second, and then she saw him. There he was, standing in majestic form in the third stall, just as Cooper had said.

"Solomon, oh my goodness, you *are* here! How I have missed you!" she uttered as she walked toward his stall latch.

The horse recognized her immediately. His snort and head toss told McKenna he had missed her as well. McKenna opened the lock and walked into the stall, hugging Solomon with every ounce of fervor she could muster. She stepped back and looked him over. He seemed to have survived the journey quite well. She rubbed his head and scratched under his neck—his favorite spot.

"Are you ready to ride, boy? We haven't ridden together in over two weeks. I will saddle you up; then we shall see what this English countryside is like. How about that?"

Cooper walked up next to McKenna with a half-saddled horse and leaned against the stall as he spoke. "McKenna, I am goin' to ride with you and refresh your memory of the land and its boundaries. It has been a while since you rode out here. I also want to see how you've progressed in the eight years since we last rode together."

"I would love your company, Cooper. I am almost finished here. You sure are getting slow in your old age. I thought for sure you would have your horse saddled by now," McKenna laughed. She mounted Solomon and let out an exaggerated, teasing sigh.

"You just watch that sass of yours, girl. I'm not as old as you think! Go on, now, you and Solomon head on out; I am just checkin' the girth," Cooper said as he bent over and pulled tightly on the right-side girth.

"I will wait for you, Cooper. Hurry it up," replied McKenna as she checked her own stirrups.

Cooper finished tightening his girth strap and mounted. Together, they left the barn and rode the property side by side, reminiscing along the way.

Zadie had prearranged packed lunches for them both, and at noon, they partook of fruit and sandwiches while they picnicked by the pond. The breeze was soft—just perfect for an open trail ride.

"Cooper, I have a question for you," said McKenna as she bit into her apple.

"Sure thing, ask away," he replied, taking a bite of his sandwich.

"Why did you put me on a horse when I was so young? I think about it now, and I was probably too little to sit a horse. I was only five years old, Cooper."

"That may be, but you were a natural. You weren't scared of nothin' and you handled any horse I put you on. It was almost like you could talk to the horses—somethin' I ain't seen before, especially in a girl child. I guess I watched you ride that first time and followed my gut. I knew you would be alright no matter what horse you rode."

"Really, Cooper? You had more faith in me than I did in myself," McKenna replied with a smile.

"I suppose I did. You forget what a pain in my side you were. You begged me every day to ride. You wouldn't even look at the damn ponies. Christ Almighty, you rode every horse in the stable, except for the thoroughbreds. And then, you were bound and determined to ride one of them if it was the last thing you did."

"And you finally gave in, didn't you?" McKenna asked as she leaned back against the tree.

"Yes, and I am glad that I did!"

The two of them continued sharing and remembering horse stories for a while longer as they intermittently gazed upon the pond. When they finished eating, they remounted and rode down by the south pond, stopping to water the horses. The breeze picked up, and the sun was starting to set as they headed back toward the north pond lane. McKenna sat back in the saddle and gave Solomon his reins—she simply could not help admiring the golden tones of the sky. Shades of oranges, coppers, and magentas layered the horizon. *It is breathtaking here*, she thought to herself.

Cooper's deep voice soon interrupted her tranquility, jerking her upright.

"McKenna," Cooper hollered loudly, "we need to head back in. Solomon needs a good brushing. He hasn't been brushed down since he arrived."

"Do we have to? I am enjoying this so much. Oh, Cooper, I had forgotten how beautiful the sky is."

"McKenna-girl, your horse's welfare is more important than the sky. We've been out all day, and your aunt will have my head if we are late for supper. I promise, we will come out many more times, but we have had enough for today. You hear?"

"Oh, all right. I'll race you!" She kicked Solomon, allowing him to canter all the way back to the barn. She easily beat Cooper and was off the horse by the time he trotted through the door.

"Careful, girl, make sure you know every rut and hole in the grass before you take off like that," he scolded as he dismounted. "One wrong turn and that horse's ankle could break. Now, you know I taught you to be cautious."

"Yes, sir, you did. But you also taught me to check the holes and ruts on the trot out. I did just that and knew exactly what to look for. You are just a sore loser.

"You got beat by a younger horse and a much younger rider. Better luck next time! Maybe you'll beat me tomorrow," she giggled.

"Hush up that mouth of yours and brush down Solomon. You are by far the prettiest young rider in England, but you best be careful and not boast about how good you think you are. There will be a rider out there who is better than you are. In fact, I know someone who could put you to shame."

"Oh, Cooper, don't you be crabby with me!" she teased. "Who is this person who could put me to shame? He was probably taught by you," she asked as she picked up Solomon's brush from the stall bag.

"He was."

"Oh, really? And who would this be?"

"You'll find out soon enough. When he comes here to ride, you will know."

"Cooper, honestly, just tell me. Who is it? Is he one of your older friends who needs help onto the mounting block?" McKenna tossed her curls off her shoulder as she brushed Solomon's underbelly and forelegs, trying not to laugh.

"You can wipe that smirk off your face young lady—he doesn't need help with anything. He is that good."

"Well, then, out with it. Who is this one-of-a-kind rider who doesn't need help with *anything*?" demanded McKenna with hands on both hips.

"Parker Sloane."

Chapter 18

McKenna almost dropped the brush. Parker Sloane's name repeated itself two more times in her mind. Of course, he would be a good rider; why wouldn't he? He boarded his horses here, and apparently, he'd worked with Cooper for quite a while. She should have guessed it would be him. There would come a day when she would show dear old Captain Sloane how well she could ride! She became flustered just thinking about the man. He was so damn handsome, and he was good at everything he touched. Just the sound of his name quickened her heart rate.

I wonder where he is this very moment, she thought to herself as she finished Solomon's brushing. *Is he thinking about me? He is probably halfway back to the Carolinas by now, and glad that I am off his ship. I was probably nothing more than a nuisance to him in his mind. I wish he would have said good-bye though, or at least walked me to the carriage. Maybe he thought I wasn't worth the walk.*

McKenna sighed as she looked out the barn doors at the setting sun. She smiled to herself as she remembered the feel of the mist upon her face when she had stood by the ship's railing during sunset.

I miss you Parker Sloane. Is it possible that you miss me, too?

***

I miss you, kitten, Parker thought to himself while he stood at the bow's railing of the *Constance*. *I wonder what kind of trouble you are causing now.* Parker chuckled as he grabbed a leather strip from his pocket and tied his hair away from his face.

I will see you again, Miss Reed; you can count on it. In fact, I will see you sooner than you think. Somehow, you have warmed my heart, little kitten. I don't know how in hell you accomplished it in so short of time, but you have.

Parker continued observing the last remnants of the same sunset that McKenna was watching that evening. He would look forward to observing the look of surprise on his kitten's face when she met him again. And meet again they would—he would bet his life upon it.

***

Supper at Aunt Pia's table that evening was lovely; conversations were engaging and laughter was seeping into each person's version of their storytelling. There was a lull at the table, and Aunt Olympia took advantage of the quietness. She quickly scooted her chair out from the table, stood, and tapped her glass with her fork.

"I have an announcement for you all. I am going to host a Harvest Ball, three weeks from tonight. We shall have a light buffet, a string orchestra, dancing, and of course a box auction to benefit the hospitals and medical needs that are required."

"How exciting," exclaimed McKenna, taking a sip of wine. "It sounds like a magical evening, Aunt Olympia! But please explain this box auction a bit more."

"Well, my dear, it is quite common here. Every young lady who attends the ball will bring a decorated box filled with desserts to the entry table. The lady will put her name on the box, so everyone will know who the box belongs to. All boxes will be displayed and throughout the early evening, each gentleman will write a numerical bid on the slip of parchment attached to the box of their choice. Tierney will continuously check the parchment papers to see how the bidding is going. One of my business partners will announce the five-minute mark before all bidding closes. When time is called, my partner will see who the highest bidder is and announce the winner's name of each box! Then, the winner and the young lady will be allowed to escape for a few moments to partake of the desserts within the box. Of course, all propriety will be observed. All of the money collected from the bids will be donated to the hospitals. Tierney's job will be to assure that each box has been bid upon."

"What a beautiful gesture, Aunt Olympia. I believe your Harvest Ball will be the event of the fall season." McKenna winked at Zadie.

"McKenna-girl, what was that wink for?" asked Zadie.

"Well, we had best begin gathering our fabric, ribbons, and thread—we have some sewing to do."

"What do you mean, 'we'?"

"Zadie, you have to have a nice dress to wear, and I intend to help you make one. You never know who will be there for you to dance with."

"That's right, Zadie. We all have to prepare for the evening, and that begins with dresses, food, cleaning, the guest list, and many more arrangements," Aunt Olympia said with a mischievous confidence as she sat back down.

"Aunt Olympia, will this guest list be large, or will you only be inviting your closest friends?"

"No, my dear McKenna, I will open this up to the entire county. After all, it is to benefit our hospitals. Now, let's finish our supper; then we can start planning for the ball once the dishes have been cleared."

***

Later that evening, while McKenna sat engrossed in her planning of the buffet menu, Pepper ushered Zadie over to the other side of the room.

"Zadie," he said, keeping his voice low, "be sure to tell Tierney to identify McKenna's box to Parker. He insists that he wants to be the highest bidder on her box. I have already explained everything to him, and he is most willing to go along with the plan."

"Pepper, how does he know about this ball?" Zadie asked.

"I sent word to Parker, and he agreed to partake in the evening's festivities."

"He's here?"

"Of course, he is here. He lives here. He has been in port for a while. McKenna thinks he left England, but he did not. He would like nothing more than to surprise the little southern belle. His exact words were, 'I highly anticipate the look on my kitten's face when the bidder's name is revealed.' He told me that he had some unfinished business to discuss with McKenna, and that evening would be the perfect time for it."

"Ah, Pepper, that captain is up to no good, and you know it."

"Zadie, I believe the captain is infatuated with McKenna, but he doesn't know it yet. With Cooper's help, we will plan some more impromptu meetings—horseback-style. I have something cooked up for you, as well. I think it is high time you and Cooper stop sharing sideways glances and have a normal conversation."

"Pepper Wells, you stay out of my business, you hear!"

"Zadie, I am making it my business to ensure that you are happy. That is what friends do for each other!" Pepper said before he placed a quick kiss upon Zadie's cheek. He then turned and walked toward McKenna to peek at her food list, but not before flashing one last wink at Zadie over his shoulder.

Chapter 19

The next few weeks were filled with a flurry of activity. Every member of Aunt Olympia's household had a job to do. Preparations were underway for the Harvest Ball, and with that came cleaning, dusting, floor washing, cooking, baking, linen washing, and gown designing. McKenna still rode Solomon each morning and helped Cooper clean the stalls. Pia even wanted the barns to be as clean as possible for the ball.

One morning while McKenna and Cooper were cleaning the barn floors, McKenna decided to gather her courage and ask Cooper some questions that had been plaguing her for a while.

"Cooper, may I ask you something?"

"Ask away."

"Have you ever married?"

"No."

"Have you ever been close to marriage?"

"Maybe."

"Did you ever want children?"

"No, my students were my children."

"Are you going to attend the Harvest Ball?"

"I reckon I may."

"Well, then, I feel that I will need to help you. First, you need a hair trim, and then we need to get you fitted for an evening suit."

"Hold your horses, girl; I don't need no hair trim or new suit. I will go exactly the way I look now," Cooper muttered as he brushed the floor with more power.

"All right, then. It would be a shame, though."

"Out with it. What are you cookin' up in that devilish mind of yours?" he asked as he leaned against his broom.

"Well, Zadie and I are sewing new gowns for the event. Zadie will look ravishing in her apricot-peach silk gown. I just thought you may want to attire yourself with a peach cummerbund or ascot."

"A peach what?"

"Oh, dear, you need more help than I thought. Look, Cooper, you are not brushing the hind end of a horse or scraping out dung from their hooves at the Ball. You will be eating and dancing with a lady of your choice—hopefully, Zadie. You will need to wear a suit and an ascot—a tie—around your neck. This is a formal ball. We also need to make sure that throughout the evening, you place a bid on Zadie's decorated box of sweets; and you are to bid only on that box. When the bidding is closed or done for the evening, the winning bidders are announced and they and the owner of the box get to sneak off together, open the box, and eat the treats."

"I know how this works. I've seen this bidding nonsense before," shouted Cooper as he stepped to the other side of the stall.

"Good, then I don't have to explain that part anymore. However, you have some lessons to learn, and we might as well start now."

"Girl, you are out of your pretty little mind if you think I am takin' lessons from you—about women, no less."

"What's the matter; are you afraid?"

"No, I ain't afraid. I just don't need 'em."

"Well, there's the proof right there, Cooper," McKenna exclaimed, shaking her head in admonition. "You don't need *them*, not 'em."

"Don't you get all high and mighty with me, young lady."

"Cooper, you have taught me everything you know about horses. Now, I shall return the favor and teach you what I know about women, manners, and etiquette."

"Eti—what?"

"Oh, dear. Well, if you are too scared to improve yourself to catch Zadie's eye, then you can spend your time with the mares. I will warn you, though, they do not dance well."

Cooper stood still with his hands in his pockets. The look he gave her reminded her of a child wishing for a treat that was out of reach.

"Oh, all right. If you are willin' to teach me, I am willin' to learn. You sure Zadie will be there?"

"As sure as I am standing here with you. Lessons will begin tomorrow morning, here in the barn," said McKenna as she put her broom away. She was proud of herself for conniving her way into Cooper's heart. She knew he had a soft spot for Zadie and yearned to spend time alone with her. This would be her way of helping Cooper after the countless hours he had spent helping her learn to ride.

"McKenna?" asked Cooper as she headed for the door.

"Yes?"

"What color is peach?" Cooper asked, looking vaguely panicked.

"Exactly as it sounds—the color of a freshly picked peach. Don't you worry, Cooper, I will make sure your ascot matches Zadie's dress. This will be a Harvest Ball to remember!"

"Humph, it sure as hell better be," chuckled Cooper to himself, as he watched McKenna's small form leave the barn.

***

McKenna spent every morning helping Cooper polish his manners. First, they would ride together and return to clean the stables. After they finished all their chores, they would practice their etiquette lessons, which also included dancing. In fact, they were in the middle of a waltz when Pepper happened to catch them during their practice.

"What the hell are you two doing? Do my eyes deceive me, or is ol' Cooper learning to dance? Well, I'll be damned," chuckled Pepper as he walked toward the pair.

"Get the hell out of here, Pepper. All I need is you watchin' me and laughin'," complained Cooper.

"Uncle Pepper, if you would like a refresher on how to dance, I would be happy to oblige," chimed in McKenna, batting her eyes mischievously.

"Hell no, not for me."

"Then, you may leave and don't come back until I tell you to," shouted McKenna with a stern look upon her face.

"Well, you kids have fun playing dress-up now, you hear? I have work to do, and it appears you have decided to put your chores on hold."

"Our chores are finished. If you want to learn how to dance, Uncle Pepper, then stay. If you are going to ridicule, then leave," McKenna scolded.

No one had to tell Pepper more than twice; he made a quick exit out and never peeked back inside.

"Cooper, has Uncle Pepper ever been married?" asked McKenna as they both calmed down and continued their waltz.

"No, his father saw to that."

"Yes, he told me a bit about that on the ship," McKenna said softly.

"He talked about Jenny with you?" asked Cooper in disbelief.

"Yes, one story led into another, and I just asked about his past. Can you explain why his father disliked Jenny?"

"Well, now, let's take a break and sit down on that bale of straw and I will try to tell you everything I know." McKenna allowed Cooper to lead her over toward the straw bale. They both sat down while Cooper wiped the sweat from his brow.

"Jenny was a beautiful redhead from the next county over; her family was of old nobility, or so I heard. Anyways, they met in college and fell in love real fast. Your grandfather thought her family was not good enough for Pepper, and he told Jenny to end the relationship. He threatened her the way he threatened everyone he didn't approve of."

"How's that?" asked McKenna with a tilt of her head.

"He threatened to go after her family. Well, the long and short of it is that Jenny never returned, and Pepper was devastated. When he found out that his father had meddled in his life, he became infuriated and moved away."

"Did Jenny ever try to contact Pepper?"

"I can't rightly say for sure. Pepper tried to find her, but never could."

"Why did Grandfather dislike the girl so much?"

"McKenna, he didn't just dislike Jenny. He hated her and her entire family."

"But why? What could she have possibly done to offend Grandfather?"

"She didn't do anything intentionally. She was simply born Jenny McTavish. She was Scottish, and your grandfather hated the Scots. I think he still thought we were back in the fifteenth century."

"That's a horrible story."

"Yes, it is, my dear. But that's what happened. The worst part is, I know that Pepper would have married the girl. But when she disappeared, he became a different person. A part of him disappeared, too. I think it broke his heart."

"It makes me sad, that a father would ruin the happiness of his only son," exclaimed McKenna, practically shaking in her disbelief.

"It ain't right, but it was a long time ago. I don't know if Pepper will ever get over it or forgive his father. That is up to him. Now then, let's get up to the house and see the list of chores Zadie has for us to do," said Cooper as he helped McKenna up and walked toward the barn door arm in arm. "By the way, thank you for helpin' me learn to dance. I am grateful."

"I know you are, Cooper. Thank you for helping me learn to ride all those years ago. I will always be grateful for you." McKenna stood on her tiptoes and placed a kiss upon Cooper's cheek.

"You go on up to the house. I will be there in a bit; I need to give Solomon some more feed," she said as she escorted Cooper toward the barn door and watched him walk away.

Oh dear, thought McKenna as she turned toward Solomon's stall*, how can I possibly help Uncle Pepper?* Clearly, Pepper's father hurt him deeply. *Perhaps I could ease the hurt after all these years. Wouldn't it be grand if Miss Jenny McTavish could be found? Is she alive or dead? Married or nay? Children or nay? I wish Uncle Pepper could meet his long-lost love once again—just like in the fairy tales. Is it impossible to find such a person after all these years?*

Chapter 20

The impossible soon became the possible for little Miss McKenna. She remembered that Pepper had mentioned a very dear friend named Samuel Weaver, who was practicing law in Oxford. So, she decided to travel there and talk with his former colleague. Upon meeting Mr. Weaver, he did indeed remember Jenny McTavish, because she had served as his children's governess for a brief period. Jenny had then left that position and finished her schooling, eventually becoming the headmistress for the Orphans and Widows' Estate Facility. Samuel Weaver gave McKenna directions to the facility, along with a hitched carriage—compliments of his and Pepper's friendship. There was no guarantee that Jenny was still there, but McKenna knew it was worth a try.

The carriage took McKenna about twenty miles north from Oxford to the Orphans and Widows' Estate Facility. It was quite impressive, situated on rolling hills with an iron-gated entrance. Whoever built the place had done so with elegance and integrity. When McKenna's carriage stopped, she exited and walked up the grand concrete entrance stairs and into the lobby. She identified herself and found out that Miss Jenny McTavish was indeed present and would be with her shortly. While waiting, McKenna looked out the ornately carved windows, admiring the many fountains adorning the gardens and grounds. *The architect of this facility was indeed a genius! I will have to find out who designed these gardens and let Aunt Pia know. Maybe, just maybe, one day she would have her own grand stables and this architect could create a tiered fountain in the shape of a horse! Now, wouldn't that be something to be admired!*

"Excuse me? Miss Reed?" asked a soft, feminine voice.

McKenna turned abruptly and nearly gasped. From the way Pepper and Cooper had described Jenny McTavish, she knew she must be beautiful, but she couldn't have imagined this. The statuesque woman gazing down at her with a glint of both shock and amazement in her twinkling blue eyes was like something out of a painting. She had never seen skin so white, nor hair so luxuriously red. "Miss McTavish?" she asked cautiously, hardly daring to believe it. "Miss Jenny McTavish?"

Jenny McTavish raised an inquisitive eyebrow. "Yes, that is my name. How can I help you?"

"Miss McTavish, I just recently arrived from the States, and am staying with my aunt," McKenna burst out eagerly. "I came here to ask you a favor. You don't know me, but you do know my uncle."

"Your uncle?" Miss McTavish shook her head. "I am afraid you are not making sense to me."

McKenna quickly switched tactics, supposing that she had better lead with information about the charity ball before she brought up long-lost love.

"My aunt is having a Harvest Ball in two weeks. We are having a dessert-box bidding auction. All proceeds will go toward purchasing supplies for the local hospitals, doctors, and nurses, and I thought you would like to attend. Perhaps our ball may be able to help your facility as well."

"Oh, my dear, that sounds incredibly wonderful and generous," Miss McTavish responded, looking flustered. "But I am still at a loss; how or why would a girl from the States come here to invite me to a ball?"

"Well, Miss McTavish, I'm inviting you because I want to make my uncle happy. You see, you know him—he was a friend of yours long ago." McKenna couldn't keep the mischievous smile off of her face.

"Well, now you have captured my curiosity. And what is the name of your uncle?"

"Thaddeus Wells, ma'am. I call him Uncle Pepper."

"Pepper." Jenny McTavish turned as white as a ghost. She clutched her chest and sunk into a nearby chaise.

"Miss McTavish, I did not mean to startle you," McKenna said quickly, though she was pleased to notice how much emotion just the sound of Pepper's name drew out of Jenny. "I only learned about you the other day. You see, it has been eight years since I was last in England. I didn't even know I had an Uncle Pepper until recently. I learned that my grandfather treated you unjustly, and I just learned about my grandfather from Pepper and Cooper, the stable master."

"Cooper? He is still around?" she asked in surprise.

"Oh yes, he is still around, and bossy as ever." McKenna laughed. "You see, that is why I am here. Not only is the ball for charity, but it would be a perfect time for you to see Uncle Pepper again. He has no idea I am here. If it is at all possible, could you or would you come to the ball? Is there anything that would prevent you from coming—like a husband? Oh dear, that was incredibly rude of me to ask." McKenna took a step back, covering her mouth with her hand in a believable semblance of embarrassment.

"Yes, it was rude of you to ask, Miss Reed, but you appear to be so genuine, I am afraid it is difficult to get angry." Jenny laughed and stood up. "Come, let's take a small walk to the pond." Jenny took McKenna's hand in hers, and together they walked toward the curve of the cemented walkway.

"Miss Reed, it has been a long time since I shared these thoughts with anyone," Jenny said as they strolled, her eyes beginning to adopt a faraway expression. "I will try my best to explain what happened to Pepper and me.

"You see, I was married—briefly. He caught a cold, and it turned into pneumonia. I lost my husband after just two years. I have no children of my own, although I view the orphans here as mine.

"But before I married, I met your Uncle Pepper. I loved Pepper with my whole heart. Our relationship progressed very quickly. It was passionate and breathtaking, the kind of love young girls read about in fairytales. But your grandfather put a stop to my fairytale romance.

"He resented the fact that I was Scottish; he was still harboring resentment from long ago, I suppose. He threatened to sully my family's good name, and to ruin my chance of any type of a governess position, if I ever saw your uncle again.

"He said I wasn't meant for Pepper and that no Scot would ever marry *his* son. So, he paid me off to disappear. I took his money and threw it into the river. I told my family what I had done, and they begged me to stay away from Pepper for fear of retaliation in an already heated English-Scottish countryside. I refused to give in to Pepper's father at first, but I couldn't take the risk of any damage to my hardworking parents. Eventually, Pepper's memory faded, and I fell in love with another man. We moved away and were happy together for two short years, but then he passed away. My family was so worried about your grandfather, they begged me not to change my name back to McTavish after my husband died, but I did so out of pride. The rest is history."

Both Jenny and McKenna came to the shore of the pond and stopped.

McKenna took both of Jenny's hands in hers and looked directly into her eyes. "Miss McTavish, my uncle never married. He never stopped thinking about you. After Grandfather threatened him, he left for the Americas. He eventually attended law school and finished his law degree. When Aunt Pia announced to the family her plans for a Harvest Ball, I decided that I would try to find you. I wanted to make Uncle Pepper happy. No one, not even Aunt Olympia, knows that I came to find you today."

"Oh, my Lord, Pia." Jenny covered her mouth with both hands, her eyes shining. "I haven't thought about her in years! She was my best friend while I was enamored with your uncle! How is she?"

"She is fine. She also left Grandfather's home long ago, and now owns an estate and stables on the other side of town. Would you please consider coming back with me and attending the ball? We could hide you and prepare everything you need. I will make sure Uncle Pepper bids on your box!"

Jenny pulled her hands from McKenna's and twirled her fingers nervously. "Oh, dear, I don't know. I haven't done anything this reckless in years. I have nothing to wear. I barely know you, and I don't know if Pepper will want to see me! I feel like a foolish young girl. How in the world did you find me?"

"I had help from Mr. Samuel Weaver, a friend of Uncle Pepper. He had remembered you and suggested I come to this facility to see if you were still here."

"Ah yes, I remember Sam," replied Jenny with a sigh. "I just don't know. This would be very reckless on my part, dear."

"Don't you worry about being reckless. The ball isn't for another two weeks. We have time to prepare a dress for you. As for Uncle Pepper, I am sure he would want to see you again. He tried searching for you, but he couldn't find you."

"He did?" Jenny whispered with a beam in her eyes.

"Yes, he did, according to Cooper," McKenna said triumphantly. *So, Jenny did still care.* "Cooper even said that Uncle Pepper had a broken heart when he lost you. So, you see, you must come back with me."

Jenny sighed and looked down. "There isn't a day that goes by that I haven't thought about Pepper. Does he still look ravishing?"

McKenna stifled a laugh. "Yes, ma'am, he does. You could see for yourself, if you will just agree to come home with me."

"The children and mothers here—I suppose my assistants would look after matters while I am gone."

"I am sure they would. I have an idea. When the ball is over, bring Uncle Pepper back here, and show him what you have accomplished. He would love to see your facility."

Jenny chewed on her bottom lip for just a moment, but then she threw her hands up and released a burst of laughter. "Oh, all right! You not only have incredible beauty, my dear, but you have the talent of persuasion. Will you wait for me to pack?"

"I will do better than that, Miss McTavish, I will help you pack!" McKenna exclaimed, trying to restrain herself from grabbing Jenny's hands and spinning around like two enlivened schoolgirls.

Chapter 21

"McKenna, what will be served as a light supper for the ball?" Olympia asked, standing on the other side of the massive dining room table with her hands on her hips. "I'm afraid that I have been so busy, I forgot to ask you about the menu selection."

"Aunt Olympia, I have everything under control. I thought we would serve a variety of foods, and I took the liberty of mimicking the menus used at Father's parties in Charleston. I thought we would serve fresh jellies and Percy's homemade biscuits, cheeses, sliced ham, fresh fruit—especially Percy's apples and spice sauce—nougats, small cakes, whiskey, bourbon, and mint juleps. See, I have my lists laid out on the table before me. What do you think?"

Pia walked behind McKenna and leaned her tall body over McKenna's shoulder to get a better look at the written list. "My dear, does Percy know how to make these juleps?"

"Well, she does now. Zadie helped her—Charleston-style. You see, in the South, mint is considered a symbol of hospitality. It is refreshing, and I think your English friends will enjoy it! I must say, though, more women drink this than men."

"McKenna, bless your heart! You have outdone yourself! We will use our amber Collins glasses; be sure to advise Percy on those, so she can get them cleaned. Now, what about drinks for the gentlemen, if they don't prefer the juleps? Ahh… if memory serves me correctly, your father sent over barrels of alcohol, but I am uncertain as to what they contain."

"I know exactly what he sent! There are two basic kinds of Southern whiskey: Kentucky bourbon and Tennessee whiskey. During the Revolution, the British ran blockades and prevented the colonies from getting sugar and molasses. So, they resorted to making their whiskey with corn.

"Kentucky bourbon is aged inside oak barrels for at least two years. Papa always had some on hand. Tennessee whiskey, on the other hand, is filtered through a maple charcoal barrel. Most men say that whiskey has a smoother flavor than bourbon, but no matter, the gentlemen in attendance will drink their personal preference, Aunt Pia. Do not worry; there will be enough for all to enjoy."

"Well, I am quite sure the choices you have made will be enjoyed by all of our guests. Oh, I am so thrilled to host this party; the excitement is oozing out of my chest. I can barely contain my exhilaration, McKenna-girl," Pia exclaimed as she squeezed McKenna's shoulders and placed a kiss upon her head.

"Oh, just wait, Aunt Pia; I have some news that I need to share with you, and this news will really have the excitement oozing out of you," McKenna said with a sly smile as she stood and faced her aunt.

Aunt Olympia narrowed her eyes. "What is it? What are you up to?"

"Well, I met Jenny McTavish yesterday," said McKenna calmly.

"You met who?" Aunt Olympia's hand covered her mouth as she sucked in a gulp of air and abruptly grabbed a chair and fell back into it. "Explain yourself, McKenna."

"Well, a while back, I asked Cooper if Uncle Pepper had ever married, and he informed me about the past history with Miss McTavish."

"Good Lord, child, what have you done?" Olympia demanded.

"I have done Uncle Pepper a favor," McKenna protested, folding her arms. *Why on earth is she getting snippy?* "I traveled to Jenny's workplace, which I must say is quite impressive. I introduced myself to her and explained your Harvest Ball and how it could also help her facility and needs through the donations taken in from the box bidding. After I explained everything to her, I asked her, or rather, convinced her to return with me, and she accepted."

"Convinced her to return? Here? She is here?" Olympia's eyes widened as she leaned forward.

"Yes, Aunt Pia, she returned with me. She is upstairs as we speak."

"Oh, my Lord, I haven't seen Jenny in so long. You have done the impossible, my dear niece. Lordy, Pepper will not know how to respond." Aunt Olympia pressed one shaking hand to her pale forehead.

"Well, he'd better respond by bidding on Jenny's box at the auction! Now, to answer your first question, she is with Zadie, sewing her dress for the ball as we speak. I know she is awaiting you with eagerness, Aunt Olympia. So, let's not waste another minute—let's go to the sewing room, and you can see Jenny for yourself. How does that sound?" McKenna reached out her hand to Pia, and Olympia grasped it within her own. She then slowly bowed her head and whispered a prayer of thanks.

As McKenna followed Pia up the stairs, she knew the next few minutes would be especially emotional for both Jenny and her aunt. Eight years was a long time for a friendship to be physically separated. *How wretched Grandfather must be*, she thought. Hopefully, Uncle Pepper and Miss McTavish would be able to rekindle their fondness for each other at the Harvest Ball.

"McKenna, I swear, child, you can tune out the world when you are deep in thought." McKenna heard Aunt Pia's impatient voice coming from the hallway outside the sewing room. "I have said your name three times now!"

"Oh, Aunt Pia, I am so sorry. Sometimes, I just get so lost in thought that I simply do not hear any conversation around me. I was just hoping that Uncle Pepper and Jenny would reunite, that is all."

"McKenna, you mean reunited in friendship, don't you?" Pia asked, panting slightly from the exertion of carrying her many skirts up the grand staircase. "Do not put the cart in front of the horse, so to speak. I mean, do not rush things. They have not seen each other in a very long time. I do not want you to get involved with what may or may not happen between them. You must remember, child, Pepper had his heart broken when he lost Jenny. If anything happens between them, it will be up to them—not us."

"I won't purposely put the cart in front of the horse, Aunt Olympia. But if I did, who's to say I couldn't train the horse to push the cart?" McKenna asked with a mischievous smile as she placed three knocks upon the door.

"Come on in, we been waitin' for you," said the voice from the other side. McKenna knew that was Zadie's way of telling her everything was ready for Jenny and Pia to rejoin.

McKenna slowly opened the door to the sewing room and saw Jenny and Zadie sitting at the table, heads bent over, absorbed in their work. She entered the room in front of Olympia and paused before she spoke. "Aunt Olympia, you remember Jenny McTavish, don't you? Jenny, you remember Pia?"

114

The door could not have opened any wider; the room could not have gotten any stuffier; the breaths of Pia and Jenny could not have been more labored as Pia gazed across the room at Jenny.

"Dear God, Jenny, I have missed you," Pia tearfully spoke as she walked toward Jenny with outstretched arms.

Jenny rose to return the forthcoming embrace. It was simple magic—a remarkable sight, and an emotional moment of mutual compassion between two friends.

"Pia, it has been so long, my dear friend," whispered Jenny as she hugged her tightly.

Tears flowed, arms clasped, and hugs remained for passing moments. McKenna wiped away her own tears as she asked, "Zadie, let's leave these two to catch up, shall we?" McKenna gently put her hand on the small of Zadie's back, helping her from her chair and escorting her from the sewing room.

Before she closed the door, McKenna looked back at both women. They were holding each other's hands and gently wiping each other's tears. It was a poignant moment for them both. McKenna unhurriedly closed the door and left the two friends to get reunified.

"McKenna-girl, you have done somethin' wonderful today," Zadie said as the two made their way toward the fitting room. "But you best be catchin' me up on how you just managed to do it. Pepper is gonna be mighty happy to see Miss Jenny after all these years."

"Oh, I know he will, Zadie. Probably about as happy as Cooper will be to see you all gussied up in your new apricot-colored dress!"

"McKenna, what you cookin' up in that head of yours?" asked Zadie as they stepped into the fitting room.

"I'm not cooking up anything!" McKenna protested with a mirthful laugh. "I just know that Cooper is going to love your dress at the ball, plain and simple! And, if he happens to ask you to dance…" She shrugged and pretended to waltz away, flashing Zadie a wink. "Now then, Zadie, we need to finish hemming both of our dresses. Then, we must get our whalebone corsets laced and the crinolines ready to go. Every Southern girl wants that small-waisted figure, Zadie, and that means me, too!"

"McKenna-girl, your waist is so tiny, you don't need to be wearin' no corset. You can't breathe in those things. The only thing it does is cause your bosom to heave, and we don't need that, neither; your bosom heaves enough by itself."

"Zadie, for heaven's sake, I am not a baby, nor am I a girl. I am a woman, and you know I prefer riding habits over crinolines. But the Harvest Ball is a very special occasion, and I would like to look and feel pretty, if just for one night. Is that so bad?" she asked sincerely.

"No, child, it ain't bad. But ol' Zadie will tell you a secret."

McKenna tilted her head at Zadie. "What do you want to tell me, Zadie?"

"You ain't pretty, baby girl. You are beautiful." Zadie pressed one finger to the center of McKenna's chest and smiled up at her. "You are *my* baby girl, and you have been beautiful since I pulled you from your mama's womb. God sprinkled beauty dust on your head the day you were born.

"He made you prettier than any other girl child I have ever seen. But you must remember to be beautiful to those around you, as well. You have your share of beauty, baby girl, and that is the honest-to-God truth. But you just make sure you are as kind to others as your momma was, and you will have an escort into heaven. Ol' Zadie knows this to be true." Zadie gently cupped McKenna's face within her large hands and placed a kiss upon her forehead.

"Oh, Zadie, I love you so much," McKenna acknowledged as she wrapped her in a tight hug. "Thank you for your kind words about my mother. I will do my best to be kind to others." She gently pulled away and began walking back and forth. "Now, speaking of corsets, we had best get to work and try those on. You will be wearing a corset and crinoline, as well.

"I want you to look your best for Cooper! Zadie, I know that ol' Cooper is excited to be all gussied up, and remember, he is doing it to impress you! I want you to brush up on those waltz steps, because I can assure you that you will be dancing all evening long! In fact, when we are done here, we will practice your waltz," said McKenna with a gleam in her eye.

"Aw, McKenna, you have done so much for me. You are tryin' real hard to make ol' Zadie look pretty, ain't ya?"

"Zadie, I do not have to try hard. You have a natural beauty, and I know one man who will be taken aback when he lays eyes on you. Just mark my words!" exclaimed McKenna as she grabbed Zadie's hands and twirled her around in circles. The laughter between the two of them continued for the next few minutes, filling the room with consummate bliss.

Chapter 22

Pepper had no idea that Jenny McTavish had been in Olympia's home for the past two weeks. So far, the surprise had not been spoiled. If everyone could get through the present day without spilling the beans, the end result for Pepper and Jenny would be splendid. Aunt Olympia entered the dining room and walked to the breakfast table with a mission in mind. Her smile was present, but she was focused, and everyone seated at the table knew it.

"All right, everyone, today is a big day for us. I would like all of you to eat a hearty breakfast, then we all have chores to attend to. I would like all the ladies to have their baths done before mid-day. Our Harvest Ball is almost upon us, and we still have last-minute errands to complete. Now then, let's say grace and eat our breakfast before it gets cold," said Olympia as she scooted her chair to the table. Everyone seated around the table knew to eat plentifully, because it would be a long time before the buffet would be served at the evening's ball. Caleb, Livingston, and Magnolia immediately went to work on eating their grits, while Cooper and Pepper focused on spreading massive amounts of butter onto their biscuits. McKenna, meanwhile, fidgeted in her seat, stealing anxious glances between Pepper and the ceiling separating the dining room from the sewing room where Jenny was hidden at the moment.

"Uncle Pepper," she said with some reservation, "you mentioned to me the other day that you had two surprises for me. I now know that Solomon was my first surprise, but did I fail to notice the second?"

"In fact, McKenna-girl, you did," replied Pepper with a twinkle in his eye. "I had to wait for your second surprise because he needed some sprucing up before seeing you. If you are willing to walk to the summer kitchen after breakfast, you will find your surprise there. In fact, it is waiting for you at this very moment."

"What on earth are you talking about?" McKenna pondered at his riddle. Suddenly, like a thunderbolt, it occurred to her that if Solomon were delivered, it was quite possible that Knox would be here as well. "Uncle Pepper, would you like to come with me?"

"No, dear, go on ahead; I haven't finished eating. I will be there soon."

The rest of the people sitting around the breakfast table all looked at McKenna with encouraging eyes. She knew at once it was Knox. McKenna jumped from her dining chair and ran to the summer kitchen. Along the way, she snatched up two more biscuits and a strip of Percy's bacon.

"Knox? Knox? Here, boy. Knox, where are you?" called McKenna as she rushed inside the door. She heard thudding in response and recognized the sound of her joyful pup wagging his tail. She looked to her left, and there he was. Knox ran toward McKenna with his ears up and all four legs bounding in synchrony. As McKenna and Knox collided, she tumbled backward, with Knox jumping on top of her waist, licking her face with fervor. McKenna hugged her beloved pet, while his wet, sloppy kisses mixed with her tears of joy.

"What a beautiful way to start my day!" she squealed as she petted her furry canine's head. She rolled away from Knox and gave him the two biscuits and bacon she had brought with her. She could not be happier. Her best friend was with her.

"Excuse me, Miss McKenna. You received a letter from your father," said Percy as she handed the letter to McKenna and continued to sweep the floor beside Knox. "By the way, I wish you would finish your breakfast. Your dress will begin to sag if you ain't eatin' enough."

"Oh, Percy, you know I love you and your cooking. I was just so excited to see Knox," McKenna defended herself, rubbing the underside of her dog's neck.

"Well, I know you are excited, but I got cleanin' to finish! Now, get this mangy mutt out of my kitchen and tell him to stop beggin' for scraps. I didn't want him up in the main kitchen because of all his fur. Just look at what I gots to clean up!"

"Percy, he wouldn't beg if you didn't give him scraps in the first place," McKenna teased as she rose and stood beside her.

"Well, who's to say I did or didn't?" harrumphed Percy, shifting her broom to her other hand and putting a stern fist on her hip. "That big hairy thing can go; I have work to do and extra fur to sweep up before Miss Pia's party."

McKenna laughed. "Thank you, Percy, for my letter and for keeping Knox a surprise for me. I know you love dogs; your secret is safe with me."

"Ah… Miss McKenna, you know ol' Percy would do anything for you. I love you like one of my own. Now, git, and take that ball of fur with you. He is slobberin' all over my floor," Percy retorted as she nudged her broom at McKenna and Knox.

"I love you, too. By the way, what color dress are you wearing to the ball? I bet Tierney would like to match whatever you are wearing!"

"McKenna-girl, don't you go and get any ideas cooked up in that head of yours. You just let ol' Percy and Tierney tend to our own business. I know you, girly—you have the imp in your look," Percy said, pointing her finger at McKenna.

"Yes, I do. I will make sure Tierney looks nice. I wish you would give me the color of your dress, though. You know that Aunt Olympia invites everyone in the county to her parties. I just want to make sure your dress stands out, that's all."

"Well, McKenna, there was a time, not so long ago, when I would never have dared to stand out, except in a black or white servin' dress."

"I know that, Percy, but those times are over. Your well-deserved freedom came over twenty-seven years ago! Aunt Pia and her neighbors all agree that people of color are independent and free. Sam Sharpe convinced the British government that there was no longer any middle ground between slavery and emancipation."

"Amen to Sam Sharpe! Oh, McKenna-child, I know all about the Slavery Abolition Act. I lived through it. But do not forget that it has been a struggle for the blacks and the whites to come together since then."

"Percy, I can't begin to imagine the struggles that you have endured. But I tell you here and now, I pray for the hostilities and possible war back home, and everywhere for that matter, to be resolved. I pray that the South can learn from England and eliminate slavery once and for all."

"I do, too, child. I do, too," Percy repeated as she brushed a stray curl from McKenna's temple. Together they hugged each other tightly, until McKenna broke from Percy's embrace and held both of her shoulders in a firm grip.

"Now then, nothing is going to ruin the Harvest Ball, Percy. Thank you again for keeping my dog a surprise!" McKenna gave Percy a final hug and commanded Knox to follow her toward the dining room.

"Pink," Percy hollered after McKenna as she walked.

McKenna spun around. "Excuse me?"

"You heard me, girly; I said pink."

McKenna grinned broadly as she realized what Percy meant, then flashed her a wink. Percy rolled her eyes but returned the wink along with a silent *thank you*.

McKenna returned to the breakfast table and opened her letter from home. The more she read, the more concerned she grew.

"McKenna, what is it? You are intent upon that letter," Aunt Pia said, finishing her last bite of pancake.

McKenna furrowed her brow as she scanned the letter again. "Father wrote to tell me that the General Assembly met and called for a convention of people from South Carolina to draw up an Ordinance of Secession. It looks as though they are serious about this movement and intend to follow through with it." McKenna slowly put the letter onto the table and rubbed the back of her neck.

"Well, dear, there isn't anything we can do about it here on the shores of England. Meeting together is one thing, agreeing to go to war is quite another. Allow some time to pass and see what happens," said Pia dismissively. McKenna bristled instantly but forced herself to accept that Pia was right. "Let's focus on the ball," Pia continued. "Now then, let's do a final dusting check. Oh, and, McKenna, be sure to save enough time after your bath to do your hair."

"Of course, but why are you reminding me?" she questioned as she took a bite from a lone biscuit left on the table.

"I just want you to look extra special tonight. It is my turn to show you off to my English friends here in Oxford and the rest of our county. I want my Southern Belle niece to shine tonight."

"Of course, Aunt Olympia. I will have Zadie help me with my hair; I promise," said McKenna, still distracted by the solemnity of her father's letter.

"McKenna, I promise we are all concerned with what is happening back in Charleston, but tonight's festivities are taking a more important place in my mind. I am not shrugging off your father's letter, but rather pointing out that they are merely drawing up paperwork for now. Again, there is nothing we can do about that."

McKenna sighed, folding the letter back up. "I fully understand, Aunt Pia. I know that you are all concerned, and I thank you. You are right, of course.

Let's worry about tonight—let's ensure this evening goes off without a hitch!" said McKenna with half-hearted enthusiasm as she followed her aunt from the room, allowing Knox to eat the crumbs on the floor she was purposely dropping.

Chapter 23

The musicians were playing, dresses were swirling, and aromas of smoked ham were filling the ballroom. The entire barrage of colors emitted a winsome, charming aura of generosity and prosperity. Aunt Pia's Harvest Ball was an elaborate affair and was proving to be a highly refined and successful event.

Cooper and Zadie were inseparable. They complemented each other in both their attire and choice of color. Cooper's ascot matched Zadie's apricot silk dress to perfection. McKenna was so glad they had sewn an extra ruffle on Zadie's hemline, because that hemline swayed and circled in perfection as Cooper spun Zadie during the waltz. Cooper had been a good dance student, and he was keeping his steps with the music just as she had taught him.

How wonderful, thought McKenna. *All is going well with them. Now, if that romance could just blossom, there would be another celebration in this grand house!*

***

The most magical moment of the evening occurred when Jenny McTavish appeared at the top of the grand staircase. The music had just stopped, and the next set was about to begin. McKenna and Uncle Pepper were refreshing their drinks when McKenna caught sight of Jenny on the stairs.

"Uncle Pepper, did I tell you how nice you look this evening? I must say, your emerald-green ascot is a perfect complement to your dinner jacket. In fact, I believe it will also match the dress of one of the ladies here this evening."

"A lady's dress? Who did you have in mind, my dear?" asked Pepper in blissful unawareness.

"Well, dear uncle, if you would kindly turn your head to your left and look up at the staircase, you will know who I am referring to," McKenna replied with a hint of a smile curling up her face.

"What the hell are you talking about?" he asked with a chuckle.

"Turn, please. Turn now," McKenna said, forcefully turning his shoulders with her tiny gloved hands.

Pepper turned his head and nearly dropped his drink. His gaze went to the top of the staircase, and his eyes went wide.

Jenny stood on the landing, clothed in an emerald-green taffeta gown. Layer upon layer of inverted pleats fell from her sparkling, topaz-encrusted belt. Her red hair was swept into a chignon and encircled with a tiny diamond tiara.

My God, she is a vision. McKenna smiled as she watched her uncle's reaction. Jenny's creamy skin and gray-tinted red hair glowed in the candlelight.

"McKenna, do my eyes deceive me? Is that... Jenny McTavish?" he asked as he leaned close to McKenna's left ear.

"Yes, Uncle, it is. But you may want to walk over there and escort her down the remaining stairs so she doesn't trip or fall."

He was so mesmerized that McKenna had to offer him a slight push in the direction of the grand staircase. "You may want to go *now*, Uncle Pepper!"

Pepper slowly walked to the stairs and began his ascent. When he was midway up the stairs, he stopped. His labored breathing was evident from the rise and fall of his shoulders; his deep voice could be heard even from where McKenna stood.

"Jenny... is it... truly you?" His voice was tinged with huskiness. The woman at the top of the landing bowed ever so carefully before rising to speak.

"Yes, it is me—Jenny," she said as she swallowed quickly to hold back the tears that were emerging.

Pepper was so overcome with emotion, he remained frozen on the mahogany step, staring at Jenny. For him, time stood temporarily still.

"Thaddeus..." whispered Jenny. She raised her arms up and folded her hands together, nervously winding her bangled bracelet around her gloved wrist.

"Lord in heaven, woman, you are a sight to behold. I never thought..." he said as he shook his head. "I never thought I would *ever* see you again. You are as stunning as the first day I laid eyes upon your blessed soul—so long ago." Pepper's voice was cracking. Tears were forming that he could no longer hold back. His right hand grabbed the stair railing tightly, and he began to loosen his ascot around his neck. All the while, he never took his eyes from Jenny. Slowly, Pepper climbed the remaining steps one at a time until there were only two steps between them.

"May I hold your hands?" he asked steadily. "I have dreamed of this moment so many times in my mind," he asked as he held both of his large hands out toward hers.

"You may hold my hands, Pepper." She nodded as she gently placed her small gloved hands in his. "I, too, have dreamt about the moment when I would see you again. You are just as striking as the first time I met you. You were my everything… and I have found you again. Oh, Pepper, I can't keep my tears from falling… I want to cry, but please know that my tears are tears of happiness," Jenny's voice shook. "I would not be here without the help of your niece. Pepper, I hope I didn't anger you for attending the Harvest Ball this evening, especially without any previous knowledge of my arrival."

"Anger me? My Lord, you could never anger me. Seeing you has just restored my faith, my dear."

Pepper formally bowed before Jenny and placed a kiss upon her gloved hand.

"Allow me to escort you down these stairs, madam," Pepper announced as he turned and offered his arm.

"Oh, I wish you would. I am shaking like a leaf and do not want to tumble down and make a spectacle of myself in front of Olympia's guests."

"I wouldn't let you fall, Jenny. I cannot explain the depth of joy in my heart right now."

"Say it again," Jenny whispered in Pepper's ear.

"Say what again, sweet?" Pepper asked with a tilt of his head.

"My name. Say my name again. I want to hear it from your lips."

"Jenny McTavish, please share this evening with me, and only me."

"I like hearing you say my name." She smiled as she squeezed his arm. "And yes, I will share this glorious evening with you, Pepper. I do not want another wasted moment between us. Would you promise me that?"

"I promise, my dear Jenny. We have a lot of conversation to share. We also have a lot of dancing to share, and we have the entire evening to do just that. You will not disappear from me again, I swear," he said as he wiped a stray tear from her cheek.

"And you will not disappear from me again, either!"

The moment was perfect for the couple who had been separated for nearly a decade. As though on cue, the musicians began playing as Pepper and Jenny descended the remaining stairs and made their way toward the marble floor to begin their waltzing set.

As Pepper passed McKenna, he mouthed a silent *thank you*. She blew him a kiss and mouthed a silent *you are welcome* back at her uncle. She knew in that very moment that the lost love between them would rekindle. It was meant to be—utterly magical for the both of them.

McKenna peered around the room and spotted Cooper and Zadie still dancing and smiling. Ah yes, she was proud of herself for connecting four people who should have come to their senses a long time ago and connected on their own.

Well done, she congratulated herself and offered a silent prayer of thanks to God before she finished her julep.

Chapter 24

McKenna strolled to the table holding the dessert boxes and noticed how many had been taken. Most of the couples—the women who had brought the boxes and the men who had won the bidding—had already escaped the festivities and were partaking of the goodies in isolated moonlit corners or under the garden trellises.

This is a perfect evening, she thought, searching for her box. *To think, I shall soon have a wonderful, romantic interlude with a mystery man!* Her thoughts were quickly interrupted by Tierney's shrill voice.

"Miss McKenna, your box has been purchased. You were so busy with Miss McTavish and Pepper that you missed your box called out at the auction. Now, you are to meet your bidder in the stable—near Solomon's stall."

"What? In a stable? In this dress? I think not," objected McKenna immediately, folding her arms and tapping her foot.

"That is what the bidder said. Now, hurry along. I think you will enjoy a breath of fresh air."

"Oh, you do, do you?" asked McKenna with a daring tone to her voice. "Oh, all right, Tierney, I will do as you say," she answered before stepping out into the fresh air.

"Oh, by the way, Tierney," she said, looking back, "I really like your pink handkerchief tucked into your dinner jacket. You look very handsome this evening."

"Thank you, Miss McKenna. Thank you for the note you slid under my door, you know, the one that told me the color of Percy's dress." He winked.

"Note? What note?" McKenna smiled innocently and continued on her way. *Percy and Tierney look like a match made in heaven with her pink dress and his pink kerchief! However, this corset is not heaven-made. Zadie was right; this corset is too tight.*

***

McKenna carefully stepped on each stone leading to the stable, taking caution not to ruin the hemline of her dress. She walked straight toward Solomon's stall and removed one glove.

"Hello, Solomon. How are you doing this fine evening? I should have brought you a carrot—shame on me, right, fella? Well, I am supposed to meet my *bidder*, but it appears Tierney was mistaken. I will, however, bid you goodnight, my fine stallion. I look forward to seeing you in the morning for our ride," she stated before giving one last pat to the animal's forehead. McKenna checked his water bowl to ensure he would be sustained throughout the night, then turned and headed back toward the house.

"Excuse me, ma'am, are you Miss McKenna Reed?" asked a voice from behind.

McKenna spun around. "Yes, I am. Who, may I inquire, is asking?"

"My name is Timothy," said the young boy, looking uncomfortable. "I was asked to escort you to the garden on the other side of the stable because this garden is too full."

"Oh, you were, were you?" McKenna raised an eyebrow. "And just who *asked* you to do this?"

"I am not allowed to tell, as he said it would ruin the surprise. But I am also to tell you that your Uncle Pepper approves."

McKenna contemplated returning to the house and finishing this charade immediately, but ultimately decided to follow Timothy. *Well, if Uncle Pepper approves, it must be all right.*

"Very well, Timothy, please lead the way."

The young lad led McKenna down the torch-lit garden path, where she spotted her box on the bench beside the fountain. McKenna sat down upon the bench and flattened out her skirts, absorbing the cool air against her skin.

"Hello, kitten."

McKenna's heart felt as if it had stopped beating. *How did he get invited to Aunt Pia's Harvest Ball? His name was not on the guest list.* She turned and saw Captain Sloane standing to her right, wearing a crimson jacket adorned with lace cuffs and a royal blue ascot. He was so strikingly dressed, he took her breath away.

"Please, allow me to open your box of sweets, kitten. I must admit, I have a sweet tooth and cannot wait to see what you have prepared," said Parker as he came to sit beside her on the bench. "Miss Reed, you are by far the loveliest lady in attendance this evening. I will even go one step further and say you will be the envy and the talk of the party for quite some time. What, you have nothing to say to me? McKenna Reed at a loss for words—impossible," he smirked.

"What are you doing here?" asked McKenna earnestly as she looked at Parker in disbelief.

"Well, I am here because I was invited." Parker's tone remained polite, but his face lit up with a slight grin.

"By whom?"

"Your Aunt Olympia and Uncle Pepper. What is the matter? Would you like me to leave?"

"That would be a very good idea. But I will make it easier for you; I will leave first."

McKenna rose and gathered her skirts at the same time that Parker grabbed her elbow and gently stopped her progression.

"No, kitten, you will not be leaving anytime soon. I bought your box, and I intend to share its contents with you. Now, sit down. I have missed you and want to visit with you."

"Missed me?" McKenna bellowed, her heart pounding in her throat. *Is this a cruel joke?* "You stood at the rail of your ship and watched me leave. You tipped your hat, and you never said good-bye. You, sir, were rude. You made it quite clear that you had nothing to say to me."

"Well then, kitten, let me make amends. Please, allow me to make it up to you. Sit down here beside me, please."

McKenna heard the captain, but she couldn't move. She could barely breathe. All of a sudden, her eyesight became blurred.

Chapter 25

"McKenna, what is wrong, sweet? You look a bit pale suddenly. Bloody hell, woman, you are not going to fall or throw a pitcher of water at me now, are you?"

McKenna gasped for air, shooting Parker a deathly glare. "Captain Sloane, stop teasing. I need your help. Truly, I need it now. I do not feel well."

"What is it that you need me to do?" Parker became slightly alarmed; sensing McKenna was no longer toying with his humor.

"Are you carrying a knife?" she asked.

"Pardon me, Miss Reed; did you say a knife?"

"Yes, I bloody well did say a knife, and you know it. Do you have a knife on your person or not?"

"Yes, I do. Why?"

"I need you to cut this corset off me. I can't breathe, and I am afraid I will either get sick and vomit all over you or I will simply faint. Please help me, Captain."

Parker immediately stood, turned McKenna around, and began to unbutton her dress. He had seen his fair share of ladies faint from wearing those confounded corsets.

"Why in hell do ladies continue to wear these things when they know it can damage their lungs and breathing? This just confirms my belief that women will go to any length to maintain their vanity," he growled.

"I suppose you are correct, Captain, but can we please discuss your beliefs later? Hurry and unbutton my dress and cut off this blasted thing."

"Yes, kitten. I am hurrying, but there are a lot of buttons, and my fingers are quite large." McKenna's snicker immediately turned into another gasp of air, as the sudden expansion of her lungs for a laugh provided too much strain on her already labored breathing. Still, she couldn't help finding the humor in

Parker's plight. *A man as proud and strong as Parker Sloane, defeated by buttons! It was almost too much.*

Parker knew it was only a matter of time before she would faint. He could tell by her shallow breathing that she was putting up a strong front.

"Almost there, kitten. Keep breathing. Damn it, can you hear me? Try to stand up straighter and keep breathing."

McKenna collapsed over the arm he was supporting her with as he tugged open the final button. Parker quickly cut the corset in half and lifted McKenna into his arms.

He ran to the back entrance of the summer kitchen as quickly as he could, knowing full well what this scene would look like to an observer. Thankfully, the only one in the kitchen was Olympia.

"Pia, Pia, help me with McKenna," Parker ordered wildly. "The lady's corset was too tight, and she asked me to cut it. I was almost done cutting it when she flopped like a seal and fainted."

Olympia shrieked at the sight of her niece in such a compromising position. "Dear God, Parker, put her on the counter. Turn her over onto her back. Gently now, while I get some cold water."

He turned her gently, crossing her arms over her chest. She looked like an angel. Her dress was unbuttoned, and her silk chemise was fully exposed to his eyes. Some of those golden curls had come undone from her pinned hair, and she resembled a forest fairy or a woodland nymph. *Ah, kitten*, he thought, *you are a sight.* A slight movement drew his attention to her hands. She was clenching tightly onto Parker's sleeve.

Parker sighed in relief as McKenna's eyes fluttered open, looking around in confusion. Her cheeks turned a dark pink as she realized the state of undress she was in, and who was staring at her.

"McKenna, you are in the kitchen with Captain Sloane and me. Good Lord, child, how tight did you lace this blasted thing?" Aunt Olympia was staring down at McKenna, obviously concerned.

Her party! She should be entertaining, not coddling me, McKenna thought guiltily. "Aunt Olympia, I am so sorry. Please attend to your guests. I do not want to ruin your evening. I am all right now. Please, there is no need to fuss over me."

"She's right, Pia," Parker agreed. "You go on ahead and tend to your guests. I will stay with Miss Reed until she is back on her feet again."

"For Christ's sake, Parker, look at her." Aunt Pia was aghast. "You can't stay here with her; look at how she is dressed—or should I say, undressed. If the wrong people see her in this state, McKenna's reputation will be ruined! McKenna, you do not need a corset, so I am going to take it off. Parker, turn around. McKenna, stand up slowly, and raise your arms. Now, as I remove this corset, tighten your chemise, then we will button your dress. Parker, do not peek."

"I would never attempt a peek." Parker flashed a quick wink at McKenna.

"Oh yes, you would, you skunk," she snapped. "Don't you dare turn around until I tell you to."

"Whatever you say, kitten," Parker replied with a sly smile.

"Stop calling me that. I am not, nor will I ever be, your kitten."

"McKenna, stand still, or I won't be able to button these buttons," Olympia demanded. "Who unbuttoned them to begin with? There must be three dozen of these tiny things!"

"I unbuttoned them all, Olympia," Parker interjected, still dutifully facing the wall. "Simply put, Miss Reed asked me to unbutton her dress and cut off her corset. She was having trouble breathing. Like I said, she fainted and I simply carried her here, and that is when I found you."

"I am so glad you did find me. I am also glad you could help McKenna. We are indebted to you once again, Captain. Isn't that right, dear?"

"I am not so sure I would use the word 'indebted,'" replied McKenna with a tinge of sarcasm, "but I do want to thank you, Captain. Once again, you rescued me. I suppose I only have five lives left now."

Parker tossed back his head and laughed. "I am glad you are alert and back to your happy self. I was intent on eating your desserts, but I see that will now have to be delayed."

"Nonsense," said Pia. "You two march right back out there and resume your conversation and desserts. After all, you were the highest bidder of the evening, Captain."

"He was? He was the highest bidder? Captain Sloane, you did that for me?" asked McKenna, taken aback by his generosity.

"No, Miss Reed, I did it for your box and for Pia's charity. Now, shall we resume our conversation and sweets? I have worked up quite an appetite carrying you to the kitchen."

"An *appetite*?" McKenna snapped. "Are you implying I was a heavy load for you to carry?"

"I am strong enough to carry you anytime, anywhere, kitten." Parker appeased her wounded pride instantly. "However, you gave me a fright, and due to that fright, I have grown hungry. Now then, let's walk back to the bench and have a look at what you prepared in your box. Shall we?"

"I shall see you both later," whispered Pia with a wink before she returned to her party, hiding McKenna's corset in the food pantry.

Parker extended his arm and McKenna clung to him snugly, still feeling a bit dizzy. Together, they traveled back to the bench where her box was still sitting and seated themselves.

"I should be thanking you instead of antagonizing you," McKenna said as soon as they were seated. "My thanks, Captain. I truly mean that."

What is she up to now? Parker wondered. A man could get lost in those sapphire eyes of hers. *Let's play out this evening and see how thankful you are prepared to be.* At least he could make sure her breathing was under control.

Damn corsets—whoever invented those things should be shot. Parker watched McKenna reach beside her and gather her box in her arms. She opened it slowly, revealing its contents to the intense gaze of Captain Sloane.

"As you can see, I have small vanilla cakes, raspberry truffles, and peach cobbler squares. I hope you like what I have prepared." She offered her box to him and he graciously accepted it in his large, calloused hands.

"Did you prepare this or did Percy?" he asked before he swallowed a truffle in one bite.

"I did!" McKenna replied indignantly. "I like to bake things, and I must admit I have a sweet tooth, as well." She smiled.

"Damn, kitten, I believe we have another thing in common besides horses and shooting," said Parker with a twinge of sarcasm.

"Well, that is all we will have in common for the time being." McKenna stood and faced Parker with both hands on her hips. She chewed on her bottom lip as she stared down at the now confused man, a thousand thoughts racing through her head. Perhaps bringing this up would be a mistake; but she had already made such a show of standing up and facing Parker, she knew he wouldn't let her return to the dessert box until she said what was on her mind. She took a deep, courageous breath and looked into his eyes.

"Is there something you want to say to me, kitten?" Parker asked quietly in between bites.

"Why didn't you say good-bye to me?" she asked.

Parker looked genuinely surprised. "I wasn't ready to do that, my dear. I am ashamed that I didn't. I suppose I couldn't."

"Are you toying with me, sir? Or are you serious?"

"Never more serious. I acted like a rogue, my dear. You have every right to be annoyed with me."

"But why?" McKenna whispered, her heart pounding. "I wasn't that much trouble."

Parker set the box to the side and stood before her, reaching out to grasp one delicate hand. "McKenna, I did not say good-bye because I didn't want to. I wanted to keep you on that ship and see you every day for the rest of my life. But I know life doesn't afford such luxury, especially my life. I work on the high seas, and you will be following your dream on land. So, the quicker the good-bye, the quicker my next day would begin. However rude that sounds, I thought I had made a wise decision."

McKenna fought to maintain her composure. Had he really just said he wanted to see her every day for the rest of his life? "Well then, sir, was it a wise decision, or are you willing to offer an apology for being so rude?"

"I am offering an acknowledgement that I may have hurt your feelings with my harshness. For that, I would rethink my actions."

McKenna yanked her hand from his. "Bloody hell, Captain! Offer the apology and stop acting high and mighty with me. We all make mistakes, sir; some make more mistakes than others. You were rude to me, and you just admitted it. At least offer an apology for your rudeness, and I will hold nothing over your head."

"Miss Reed, I am sorry if I offended you or hurt your feelings in any way. Please accept my apology," Parker responded instantly.

"Well, that wasn't so hard, now, was it?" McKenna smirked. "I accept your apology."

"Don't push it, kitten," Parker said with a raise of his eyebrows.

"Oh, for crying out loud, step off that pedestal you have perched yourself on. You are allowed to laugh when you are with me, sir." McKenna grabbed Parker's hand, flounced back to the bench, and lifted a pastry to his mouth. "I will not bite you; I was just teasing you."

I wish you would bite me, kitten. I wish you would do many other things to me, and maybe you will... in time. Parker could not draw his gaze away from her. Was there any imperfection on her being?

"Captain, are you listening? Once again, I ask, do you like my treats?"

"Yes, my dear, I daresay they are delicious. However, I have an urge to return inside and test my dancing steps. Would you like to accompany me?"

"Oh, yes, I would. I love to dance. I could dance and dance all night!" McKenna rose and began to twirl blissfully, her skirts fanning out like a ruffled bell. "Couldn't you just dance the night away, Captain Sloane?"

"Oh, I could think of other things to do all night long, kitten."

McKenna stopped mid-twirl and shot him an annoyed look. "You are impossible. Stop thinking such things in my presence."

Not a chance, my dear. I will always think of things to do all night long with you, Miss McKenna Reed. After all, I am a man with manly thoughts. The sooner you realize the benefits of what can be shared between a man and a woman, the sooner you will purr.

Chapter 26

McKenna and Parker entered the ballroom through the garden terrace doors just in time for the next dance. Parker took McKenna into his arms and joined in the waltz. He held her tightly and inhaled the heavenly aroma of lilac and rose that was permeating his sense of smell. This little lady had no idea the amount of beauty she radiated. The entire ballroom was staring at her; they were either entranced with her, or green with envy. He marveled how his hand could encompass her small waist quite easily. She fit perfectly against him and he damn well liked it.

The top of her golden-haired head touched the middle of his chest. Holy hell, he wanted her more than any other woman he had yet to meet. He would have her on his terms and in his time. He would teach Miss McKenna Reed the enjoyment of lovemaking, of conversation, of life in general. But he would bide his time. By all that was divine, he would have her, and never again would he let her go.

A small tug on his ascot brought his attention back to the lovely woman in his arms.

"Captain, did you hear me? I said that you are a very good dancer."

"Why, thank you, my dear. I think we make a perfect waltz couple."

Before McKenna could respond, Tierney came running across the room, dodging his way through the swirling dancers before coming to an abrupt stop in front of Parker and McKenna.

"Miss McKenna, come quick! Come quick! Solomon is in trouble; he is heavin', and he is havin' a hard time breathin'."

McKenna grabbed her friend's shoulder firmly. "Tierney, what do you mean? What in God's name is going on?"

"One of the guests must have given him their dessert box to eat, and now your horse is payin' the price. He don't look good, and he is sweatin' real hard.

Please, Miss McKenna, hurry, you gotta get to the stable." Tierney was still breathing heavily, and his fear showed in his wide-eyed expression.

"Tierney, you did the right thing by telling me. Now, go get Cooper, and tell him to meet me at Solomon's stall," McKenna ordered. "Captain, will you join me?"

"Take a breath, kitten." Parker picked up McKenna, slung her over his shoulder, and ran through the crowded ballroom and out onto the terrace, retracing their previous steps.

"For the love of God, what are you doing? Put me down this instant!" she yelled while pummeling Parker's broad shoulders.

"You will get to the stable quicker if I carry you; otherwise, you are going to tip-toe down the stairs in that dress of yours. We both know how efficient you are at tripping. Hush up and let me concentrate."

"This isn't over, sir."

"You are right, kitten, but first, let's make sure Solomon is all right. Horses can't digest too much sugar all at once," said Parker in between breaths.

"I am aware of that. Just hurry," encouraged McKenna as she folded her hands together.

"Almost there."

Parker set McKenna down as soon as they were outside Solomon's stall, and she immediately rushed to her prized stallion's side.

"It's all right, boy, let's see what you have done." McKenna felt the stomach of the horse and recognized the signs of bloating starting to form. Solomon was uneasy, and she sensed his alarm.

"Cousin McKenna, I am so sorry. It is entirely my fault. I was showing off Solomon to my girl, and I gave him a lot of treats," Caleb announced as he slowly entered the stall.

"Caleb, how many treats did you feed him?" McKenna demanded as she continued to feel Solomon's stomach.

"The whole box. I am so ashamed."

McKenna groaned. "A horse cannot eat too much sugar, Caleb. Solomon won't be able to digest his feed corn and barley properly with too much sugar. He can get a massive stomachache. Do you realize what you have done? This could produce poison, and too much poison could damage the gut. If this poison gets into the bloodstream, we must be careful that his hooves do not get inflamed. Oh, dear, Caleb, run to the house—and I do mean run—and get me as many potatoes, squash, and fish as you can carry. Hurry."

"Miss Reed," said Parker with concern, "let's rub the underside of Solomon's belly. You rub from this side, and I will rub from the other. Do not give him any water."

"Are you sure, Captain, no water?"

"Not now. You don't want the sugar to travel to the blood," replied Parker as he rubbed Solomon's underbelly. McKenna could not help noticing Parker's large hands tenderly massaging her horse in slow, circular motions.

"He's right, McKenna. No water; not now," Cooper said as he came to stand beside McKenna and began examining Solomon himself. He was gentle with his touch and avoided any type of belly probing. The three of them rubbed for what seemed like hours. Young Caleb came running back into Solomon's stall with a bag filled with McKenna's requests.

"Thank goodness, Caleb," said McKenna, relief flooding her face as she peered inside the bag. "Thank you for returning with what I asked for." She carefully gave Solomon a potato to eat, then a squash, then repeated the procedure while Parker and Cooper continued to massage Solomon's belly.

"Cousin McKenna, why are you feeding him that?" asked Caleb.

"Because these things have a lot of potassium in them, and that is what Solomon needs to break down all the sugar in his system. Think about how you feel when you eat too many of Percy's small cakes. You get a stomachache, right? Well, so do horses. I have to make that ache go away, so I feed him foods that will prevent the sugary things he ate from forming a big knot in his gut."

"When I eat too many cakes, Percy gives me a carrot to eat. That makes me feel better," Caleb responded, shifting nervously on his feet.

"Yes, of course, it does. The carrot breaks down the sugars from the cakes you ate and takes away your stomachache. This is doing the same thing."

McKenna had gotten three potatoes and three squashes into Solomon. She knew she had gotten to her horse in time. "Okay, boy, now comes your favorite treat. Eat as many of these fish filets as you can." McKenna reached into the bag and pulled out two filets, gently feeding them to her cherished companion.

McKenna's tension began to ease. It seemed like hours, but it was only a few minutes before Solomon's breathing returned to normal, and his sweating subsided. It appeared that her stallion would be fine.

"Caleb, you will stay here and keep an eye on Solomon for the rest of the evening. You will sleep here tonight, as well," said McKenna firmly.

"Sure thing. I feel so bad, and I am so sorry, Cousin McKenna."

"Oh, you will get your due reward. In the morning, I want this stall cleaned out to the bare ground and fresh straw put in. I would imagine you will not feel so 'sorry' once you've finished that chore."

"Why would you say that? Of course, I will."

McKenna smiled. "We will talk again after you scoop out his droppings. Believe me, there will be a lot, and the smell will be putrid."

Cooper and Parker laughed. They clasped each other on the shoulders and shook their heads as they left the stall together. The spectators who had gathered around to watch McKenna take care of Solomon soon wandered off. Tierney escorted Caleb's girl back to the house, and Caleb immediately began brushing down Solomon. McKenna caught up with Parker and Cooper, placing her hands on her hips while leaning against the barn door. All three of them stood in the cool air, breathing sighs of relief.

"I must say, kitten, that was impressive. You should follow that dream of yours. You are quite capable of handling yourself."

"Why, thank you, Captain. If you will excuse me, I need to wash my hands. I shall meet you inside by the juleps. I am truly thirsty."

McKenna picked up her skirts and began walking toward the house. She stopped abruptly and turned, nearly bumping into him, not realizing he had followed her.

"Captain, remember just exactly how capable I am of handling myself." She flashed a wink and a saucy smile toward Parker before she turned and resumed her walk.

"Remember how capable I can be as well, kitten. If you would like, I can transport you back to the ballroom the way you left—over my shoulder."

"My dear Captain, need I remind you that kittens cannot be turned upside down? You must carry them upright."

"Your wish is my command." With that, Parker scooped up McKenna and slowly strode to the house.

"You know, sir, I could stay like this all night," sighed McKenna without a hint of innocence, surprising Parker. "I feel safe within your arms—even though you can be a devilish rogue at times. Let me know if I become too heavy for you, though. I am sure this is a bit different from carrying ladies of the night."

"How so, kitten?"

"Why, Captain Sloane, need you ask? I have on more clothing than they would," she smiled slyly.

"I can remedy that," he replied in a husky voice with a wink.

"Captain Sloane, you take **far** too much liberty with your words when addressing me, especially since we just met a mere few months ago. I am beginning to think that you like this sparring between us," she said with a smile. "Now then, hurry up, I don't want to miss out on another minute of dancing with you."

"Your wish is my command, madam," replied Parker with a corner smile and a twinkle in his eye. Parker continued his stroll to the house with his pretty little bundle tucked within his arms. He had no intention of hurrying the moment. He felt content and needed. He had not felt this wave of fulfillment in a very long time. He was happy, and he bloody well liked the feeling.

Chapter 27

McKenna sat on the porch swing, feeling the morning sunshine upon her face. It was quiet this morning, and the perfect setting to think and reflect before riding Solomon. She took a sip of breakfast tea before she snuggled deeper into her shawl, warding off a slight chill.

It had been two days since the Harvest Ball. The monies raised for the hospitals and Miss McTavish's facility were overwhelming. Their guests had been extremely generous, and Aunt Pia could not have been happier. Cooper and Zadie were now attached to each other, in a manner of speaking. If Zadie was not in the stable, working with Cooper, then he would be in the garden, tending roses with Zadie. They were like two lovebirds. McKenna had hoped for so long that Zadie would find the man of her dreams to care for her and to love her. *She certainly deserves to find true love. Perhaps I should encourage Zadie to consider wedding vows!* That would have to be a carefully thought-out strategy. *If Zadie thought for one minute that I was encouraging her to wed, she would retreat from all conversation with me. Perhaps Cooper will have to take control of this budding romance. After all, I got them together... they can certainly figure it out from here.*

McKenna's thoughts turned to Uncle Pepper and Jenny McTavish. She had seen them off the day after the Ball. Jenny had taken McKenna's advice and traveled to the Orphans and Widows' Facility with Pepper to show him the building. He had not left her side since she had appeared on the grand staircase the night of the Ball. In fact, when McKenna had woken early the day after the ball, she had heard soft laughter from the hallway. When she peeked out her door, she had seen Uncle Pepper emerging from Miss McTavish's room. Had he spent the entire night in her room? That would be scandalous! That would be enticing! That would be a question for him to answer upon his return—if he would answer it. *He will... I will nag him until he gives in and tells me the truth*, she thought to herself as she chuckled.

Not only had Jenny invited Uncle Pepper to go back to her facility with her, he had also stayed for a while under the ruse of ensuring that all of her legal documents were in order. They assured Pia that they would return in a week or so.

Time will tell on that, thought McKenna as she pushed the swing with her slippered feet. She continued to sip on her tea, reflecting back to that handsome devil, Captain Sloane. She had danced with Captain Sloane until midnight. He had said his farewells and departed the same way he had entered— breathtakingly. She could still hear his booted stride upon the marble floor and his deep voice. If she smelled her wrists close enough, she could still sniff a twinge of musk and coconut from that ravishing swain. There wasn't one lady at the ball who had not appreciated his good looks. Honestly, no woman could take their eyes off Parker Sloane.

Is my infatuation turning into a deeper feeling?

Was she kidding herself? Would a man like that be interested in someone like her? What was she thinking? He would return to his ship and set sail indefinitely. He probably had a girl in every port. But something about his eyes and how he looked at her made her knees go weak.

Is it possible that he may feel the same way about me? Does he think about me like I am thinking about him? Am I falling in love with Captain Parker Sloane? Dare I hope he is falling in love with me? It is too soon to fall in love, isn't it? I only met the man a few months ago.

I wish Papa were here. He would know the answers that I seek. Why did he agree to become a war surgeon? I need him more than any patient will. I am his daughter and I am three thousand miles away!

A sudden burst of cold air took McKenna by surprise. Perhaps that was Mother Nature's way of telling her to get to the stable and exercise Solomon. McKenna returned her teacup to the kitchen and hung her shawl on the hall tree in exchange for a woolen coat.

***

McKenna had almost reached the stable when she heard laughter—a man and a woman's laughter. Who would be out this early? She followed the sound of voices and abruptly stopped when she came around a turn in the pathway. She quickly hid behind the giant oak and carefully peeked beyond the ancient tree's branches.

"Oh, Parker, I am so glad I was able to see you on such short notice. I am so sorry to have disturbed you from your busy morning, but I had to see you. I have missed you, my dear, and you know how much I love you. Please, do not hold my previous absence against me. If I had been in residence, I would have done everything in my power to see you. But for now, I must be on my way or I will be missed, and I cannot take the risk of being missed right now. When can we meet again?"

"I will contact you—same method, same time. You know I would meet you anywhere, anytime, and in any way that I physically could. I will escort you back to your horse, love. Hurry, though; there is a certain young lady here who likes to ride in the early morning. I cannot risk the chance that she would see you."

"Parker, it would cause no harm. I am sure she is a fine young lady."

"She is that, but I am not sure how trustworthy she would be. She has a habit of talking without thinking, and that would be absolute danger for us," said Parker.

"Well then, I shall be on my way. Give me a proper hug. Until we meet again, know that I love you."

"I love you as well, but we need a code, my dear. I need to know when you are in danger—especially now—so I can help you."

"Oh Parker, remember the saying that we were told as children while in the orchard?"

"I do. 'The best apples are red!' That is perfect. Well then, we will use that. Remember, we only use that code when we are in trouble. Now, go before you are seen." Parker lifted the woman and swung her up onto her horse in one smooth movement.

She abruptly turned and trotted away into the morning mist. Parker kept staring after her until all that remained were the melodies of the morning doves. McKenna watched Parker drop his waving hand and slowly turn toward the stable.

McKenna's knees almost gave way. She felt as though her heart had split in two. *I have been such a fool. All those words that came from his mouth were false. He no more cares for me than he would a bug—just to be swatted when in the way. The words, the kisses, the hugs, the compliments... not one bit of it was real.* Tears were forming in her eyes, and she could not stop them. *Why did I let my guard down and absorb all that foolishness? Why did I open my heart to him? He is no more than a cad. Well, he can just go to hell and stay there.*

Chapter 28

McKenna continued to walk to the stable. Thank goodness, she knew the way; her tears and sniffles were complicating her steps. She would ride Solomon long and hard, if only to release her betrayed emotions and heartbreak. She quickly curried and brushed Solomon's coat and saddled him, then mounted her best friend and leaned over to unlatch his cross ties. That is when she felt two strong arms encircle her waist. The next thing she knew, she was being pulled off Solomon. McKenna turned toward the owner of those arms just in time to be kissed. She pulled back from Parker's kiss and brought her knee up hard, right into his groin.

"What the bloody hell did you do that for?" Parker groaned, clutching himself. "You little wench. What in Christ's name is wrong with you?"

"Me? Nothing is wrong with me, you lying bastard!" McKenna spat. "Stay the hell away from me. Go find another victim to pursue and use your charms on. I am no longer interested in the likes of you!" She turned toward the stirrup, intending to mount quickly.

"Madam, you'd better have one hell of a good explanation for your actions just now. Turn around!"

"No!"

"McKenna, I will not ask again."

"Captain Pig, you will never ask me anything again, because I do not intend to see or speak to you ever again."

Parker grabbed McKenna by the shoulders and turned her around abruptly.

"Unhand me, you are hurting me. Let me go!"

"Not on your life, kitten. You are going nowhere until you tell me what has drawn your claws and that sassy mouth of yours so early this morning."

"Let me go, damn you; I mean it."

"You can fight me all you want; you have neither the strength nor the defensive knowledge to get away from me. You will be telling me what has ignited that temper of yours, and you will be telling me now, before I shake it out of you."

"Oh, so now you are going to shake me? Let me ask you a question, Captain Sloane; what brought you to the stable?"

"Come now, kitten, you know damn well I was here to see you. I was hoping we would enjoy a ride together."

McKenna let out a short, biting laugh. "Really, sir? You came here to see me? Just me?"

"Of course; you ride every morning. McKenna, what is it that you are asking me? Stop squirming and stand still."

"Let go of me," McKenna screamed.

Parker had had enough. He picked her up and threw her onto her back on the straw pile, straddled her, and held her arms down on each side of her head. He knew she was hiding information; he could bloody well sit here all day until she told him the reason for her anger.

"Are you ready to tell me what has put you in such a terrible temper this morning?"

"Go to hell," she hissed in response.

"Not without you, my dear. You have a foul mouth for a well-bred Southern girl. Your father would be ashamed. I suggest you begin talking before Cooper walks down here and sees you on your back with your riding skirt hiked up to your knees."

"Oh, my God, let me up, you big brute. He will. He will come soon, and I am in no position for his viewing."

"You are quite right, kitten. You are not in a good position at all. I will sit here until you tell me why you have acted so outrageously."

"How dare you say that to me! I am not the one who has lived a lie these past months."

"What in God's name are you talking about? I have told no lies to you."

"Oh, really? I asked you if you had ever been in love, and you said once before, but you were quick to end that sour relationship because she wanted your wealth rather than your love. You said her name was Savannah," McKenna shouted as she squirmed and tried to release her hands from Parker's grip.

"Yes, I did. What is your point?" he asked, applying more pressure to her wrists.

"My point is that you were just talking to her. On my way down to the barn, I heard you two talking. I was so utterly shocked, I hid behind the oak tree. She called you her 'love,' and you said you would meet her anytime, anywhere. Then, you said I was not trustworthy. My God, Parker, how could you say that about me? That is irony in fine form. I can't be trusted, but you can slither out of your hole and meet your mistress in the wee hours of the morning. I wish to God I had never laid eyes on you. Now, get the hell off me," she screamed as she thrashed against his hold.

Parker rose and pulled McKenna roughly to her feet. He didn't look at her or speak to her. He simply mounted Solomon, reached down, and pulled McKenna onto the saddle in front of him.

"Oh, this is grand. Now you are going to ride my horse without my permission and drag me along with you. You are just full of surprises, aren't you?"

"Stop talking."

"How dare you speak to me that way? If I had a gun, I would shoot you."

"I think not. If I had a rag, I would bind and gag that pretty mouth of yours. However, madam, it isn't so pretty now. You have thrown insults at me and untruths. Stay in the saddle and keep quiet. When we reach the south pond, I will explain everything to you. What I am about to tell you is only known by myself and your Uncle Pepper. I hope you can swallow that feisty pride of yours long enough to hear the truth and refrain from throwing another childish tantrum like the one you so eagerly just displayed."

"Let me down right now. I do not want to hear any more of your so-called truths."

McKenna attempted to pull up on Solomon's reins, but Parker was ready for her move. He tightened his grip on her waist so securely, she thought she would faint.

"Shut your mouth, McKenna, and I mean it. Not one more word from you. If you so much as utter a sigh, I will stop, dismount with you in my arms, and spank your bare bottom. Do not tempt me or anger me any more than you already have. When you listen to the real story of what you overheard, you will be faced with a monumental dilemma."

"Oh, and what would that dilemma consist of?"

"An apology—more importantly, how you will deliver it, and under what terms I will accept it."

"When hell freezes over," she whispered.

"What did you say?"

"I said nothing."

Parker knew with certainty what she had said. *However*, he thought, *let her keep adding kindling to the fire; it will only make her apology that much better.* He did not understand how she could have made the assumptions she had, based upon the conversation he and Madeline had earlier. If only Maddie could be here to witness this forthcoming explanation. Then again, he was glad she was well on her way home. If his tyrant of a brother-in-law laid a hand on his baby sister, the man would wish he were dead.

Chapter 29

Parker reined in Solomon, guiding him toward the willow trees by the pond's fishing cabin. It was an unusually warm day for this time of year. This would be a perfect place to have a private conversation; there was only one way into the clearing near the pond and one way out. The breeze was minimal; *a good thing*, Parker thought. That would provide less chance of conversation drifting in the wind. What he was about to share with McKenna was to be heard by no one else.

"Can I open my mouth now?" McKenna demanded.

"No. I prefer you not speak until I am finished with my explanation. However difficult that may be for you, it is what I am asking."

"Agreed."

That's unusual, thought Parker. *That was too easy.* Parker dismounted and pulled McKenna off the saddle with one arm.

"Sit down, McKenna."

"I prefer to stand."

"You have no choice in the matter." Parker kicked her feet right out from under her, holding onto one arm until she dropped firmly upon the ground. Her impact was not gentle. *Good*, he thought, *that was payback for the knee in my groin.*

"You can manhandle me all you want, Captain. It only proves how much of a pig you really are."

"I would advise you not to speak. You deserved that, kitten—my groin is still aching."

"Why don't you just see your mistress? I am sure she can remedy your ache. If you hurry, you can catch her."

"That's enough, you vicious little girl. I warned you not to speak." Parker removed his sash and, showing no benevolence, tied it around McKenna's mouth with a very tight knot.

"Now, that should keep your naïve thoughts to yourself. You really are an immature, spoiled, pampered, self-centered brat." Parker sat down on the ground across from McKenna. He grabbed both of her wrists and held them tightly in his hands.

The look in Parker's eyes captured McKenna's complete attention, and her stomach tightened. Oh, Lord… had she made a huge mistake? Her intuition told her she had.

"I was down at the stable this morning with a young lady. She is very beautiful, and I have loved her since she was born. Her name is Madeline Sloane, my baby sister. What you heard was a conversation between an older brother and his younger sister. I am completely protective of her, especially now. Shake your head if you understand so far."

McKenna immediately shook her head. She wanted the gag off her mouth so she could kiss him and apologize to him. What a fool she had been. He had been right to call her all those names. Oh, Lord, what had she done? What had she *not* done? She never gave him the chance to explain. He must hate her now. *Oh dear*, she thought, *I've really done it this time.*

"Madeline is in trouble. She became enamored with a young man from the east side of London, fell in love, and married him. This was all achieved while I was at sea. He is a medical doctor, and well-respected within his field. However, Maddie and Reney have had trouble conceiving children. Reney has given Maddie every medical remedy known to mankind to aid in conception. She managed to conceive, but only carried until her fourth month of pregnancy, then lost the babe. This has now happened three times. You may or may not understand the heartbreak and unstable emotional state those losses have caused my sister to experience. Maddie went to a very good friend—a doctor— and asked his opinion on the medicine Reney was giving her. The friend expressed his shock and disbelief and told her she was lucky she was not dead! The concoction Reney has fed her is lethal. Maddie meets with me because she is fearful that Reney is trying to dispose of her—to kill her. Why would he do that, you ask?

"Maddie received, as part of her dowry, an obscene amount of money from our grandparents. The money is entitled only to Madeline, but if she should pass away, the money is then rewarded to her eldest child. If she has no children, Reney stands to collect. There is a clause, however. This particular part of the dowry was not given to Maddie's husband as a wedding gift from the bride to the groom. This money was set aside for Madeline, to be used at the age of thirty years. It was a tradition from my grandmother—her grandmother—and so on.

"According to Maddie, Reney has become mean and short of patience. He has not hit her, but she feels such behavior is forthcoming. He is drinking a lot more these days; many nights, he does not return home until long after midnight. He has not taken my sister by force—sexually speaking. If he does, he will die; as God is my witness, the bastard will die.

"She meets me when she knows I am in port and gives me news of her situation. She knows I would protect her to the ends of the earth. She also knows that if Reney suspected her thoughts toward him, he would hurt her. He strangled her puppy when she miscarried the last babe, in a fit of rage. He threw her pearl necklace from our mother into the sea when she lost the babe before that. You see, it was Reney who caused the medical miscarriages. But he continues to pretend and place blame on Madeline—insisting that she lost all her babes because she is not destined for childbirth. It has only been until recently that Maddie concluded the medicine given to her by Reney's own hand caused the deaths of their unborn children. Again, she found this information out through her doctor friend.

"Now imagine, McKenna, if you can, in that small, naive mind of yours, that your own husband would plot such atrocities behind your back—at all costs—to inherit money that was not intended for him.

"Pepper has been doing some secret work for us. It appears my brother-in-law is deeply in debt. Rather than go to debtor's prison, Pepper feels he would rather dispose of my sister and any child to escape his fate. Desperate men make desperate actions when faced with imprisonment. Pepper's theory makes sense—he would then take the money and use it to pay off his debts.

"I am also careful of my personal financial situation. Reney asked to join my shipbuilding business. I put a stop to that idea immediately. He has not spoken to me since, and I fear he may take out his anger on Maddie. If he chooses to act in any violent manner, I want her out of that home and out of his life.

"I would have taken her away from him a long time ago, but the problem is, she loves him. She thinks that the alcohol is the cause of the trouble between them. Thus, we meet in secret for continued updates for the time being. I hate the man. In my mind he has purposely caused the miscarriages—and he should hang for that.

"Now, I am going to remove this gag from your mouth. You have five minutes to speak to me. I will then return you to the stable, and I will be gone from your life.

"You have shown me how superficial you can be. I understand what the situation looked like to you, but a well-bred lady would have inquired the appropriate way. I sure as hell did not expect you to behave the way you did. If the roles were reversed, I would have been angry as well. But I would have asked you to explain. You asked for no such explanation from me. You had me crucified before any chances of vindication were offered."

Parker removed the gag, none too gently, from McKenna's mouth. She looked at him with tear-filled eyes and took a deep breath.

"I can't begin to apologize enough times in five minutes. I am so sorry, Parker. You were right to call me those names. I deserved every one of them but one."

Parker raised his eyebrows, waiting for an explanation.

"I am not self-centered. I love to make others happy and to do good things for other people. If I acted self-centered in this situation, it is only because I thought you loved another lady and not me. I am falling in love with you. I may already be in love with you.

"When I saw you with her and heard you both profess your love for each other, I thought I had been a foolish pawn. I felt angry because I thought you had kicked me to the side for another.

"I am sorry; I should have asked you. Instead, my temper got the better of me, and I said hurtful things to you. Please, forgive me. I don't want you to walk away from me. I want you to stay with me and be a part of my life. How many minutes do I have left?" She was crying so hard, she began to suck in air between sniffles.

"Come here, kitten." Parker scooted her onto his lap and kissed her with every ounce of emotion he could muster. "I fell in love with you the minute you almost landed into the sea back in Charleston Harbor. Thank you for your apologies and for understanding my delicate situation with Madeline. I want you to understand that I value trustworthiness, and I wasn't sure if you could be trusted to remain quiet. It is not that I didn't trust you to understand; I didn't trust your temper."

"Rightfully so, as I adequately displayed. Please forgive me, and I understand if you leave. I would be heartbroken, but I would understand."

"Shh, kitten. I could no more walk away from you than I could go without water and food. You have entered my heart, and I do not want to live my life without you in it."

"Really, do you mean it? You will forgive me, then?"

"Yes, I will forgive you. However, there will be a punishment for you."

"What? A punishment? I said I was sorry."

"I know you did. But when a young lady knees a man in the groin, there must be a punishment issued. That could have been a life-threatening situation."

"You are teasing me. There will be no physical punishment. You would never hurt me intentionally."

"Ah, kitten, I would never hurt you intentionally. But I would deprive you of other advantages."

"Advantages?"

"For example, you like it when I kiss you around your ears, and your neck, and your…" Parker began kissing her in the exact areas of which he spoke. "Perhaps I will punish you by removing myself from you. No kisses, no hugs, no winks, no embraces, no contact."

"No… you can't." McKenna threw herself into him and forced him onto the ground. She quickly straddled him and placed her arms on each side of his head. "I don't want your punishments. I want your forgiveness. I will make it up to you."

"Really, kitten? How?"

"In any way you want—within reason." She smiled and kissed his neck, his ears, his chin, and his temples. She leaned back, took his hand, and brought it to her mouth to kiss each finger, slowly and provocatively.

Little did she know that she was providing Parker with an enticing view of her décolletage. He reversed their positions quickly, so she lay upon the ground with her arms pinned to her side.

"Punishment will now be delivered, my dear. There will be no more hugging or kissing from me. There will be no more embraces or winks."

"How long will the punishment last? I said I was sorry."

"Your punishment will end if you repeat what you said earlier. The part about falling in love with me."

"I meant it, Parker Sloane. I truly am falling in love with you. I think I already do love you. Please don't remove yourself from me. I need you."

McKenna's eyes filled with tears and her lower lip trembled. Parker pulled McKenna up and onto his lap again.

"Come here, kitten. That is what I wanted to hear. Your punishment is ended."

"Captain, I do not believe it ever started…"

"That gag is within reach; be quiet and kiss me."

Chapter 30

The Christmas holidays were approaching, and the air of festivity was heightening. McKenna only wished her father could be there with her. She had never had a Christmas without him. She wasn't sure how this holiday would be, and she wasn't sure if she could get through a Christmas Eve without her beloved father. Her thoughts led her to look outside the dining room window from her chair at the table. Large flakes of snow were falling everywhere. McKenna knew that there would be fewer times to go riding now that the ground was covered with icy sleet and snow, and the thought of that made her pretty smile frown a tad.

"Good morning, McKenna-girl!" exclaimed Uncle Pepper as he broke her focus and sat down to the breakfast table across from her.

"Good morning, Uncle. I must say, you are quite chipper this morning. I trust all is going well between you and Miss McTavish, since your return from her facility." McKenna threw a wink and tilt of her head at Pepper.

He sat back in his chair, rubbed his chin, and sighed. "McKenna, I owe you a heartfelt thank-you. If it weren't for you, I probably never would have renewed a relationship with her. For that, my dear, I will always be indebted to you." Pepper reached across the table, took McKenna's hand in his, and pressed a proper kiss upon it.

McKenna was humbled and filled with happiness for her uncle.

"Uncle Pepper, I have learned a lot of information about our family within the past few months. I am so glad you have entered my life. I only hope you can live your remaining days with Jenny—together. What does the future hold for you both, if I may ask without sounding too nosy?"

"Not at all my dear. Like I said, if it weren't for you, we would still be separated. McKenna girl, lean closer, I don't want my voice to carry and be overheard," smiled Pepper as he leaned across the table a bit further.

"Well, now you have my utmost attention. So… do tell!" McKenna squealed with excitement.

"McKenna, I have loved only one woman in my life and that is Jenny. I simply do not want to live another day without her. So, I am planning on asking her to become my wife."

"Oh, Uncle Pepper, that is just wonderful. I am so happy for you. When are you planning to ask this big question?" McKenna asked while tapping her tiny fingers on her uncle's sleeve.

"I am not sure, but it will be soon. Please, though, keep this between us for now. I haven't even mentioned anything to Cooper or to Parker or even Pia, for that matter. And you know as well as I do, once Pia finds out, she'll want to throw a big party and I am just not ready for all that fuss right now."

"Your secret is safe with me. I promise. Let's raise our juice glasses for a small toast," she suggested eagerly. And together, they clinked their crystal stemware.

"To Jenny and Uncle Pepper!" McKenna uttered with joy, raising so quickly she almost spilled.

"Here, here!" Pepper declared with a nod of his head and a gleam upon his face.

McKenna drank her juice and carefully placed her emptied glass upon the table. Clearing her throat, she quickly changed her voice to a more serious tone.

"Uncle Pepper, there is a matter that I would like to discuss with you."

"What is it, dear? Your look tells me this may be a serious conversation," he said as he buttered his bread and bit into the crust.

"I suppose it is. You see, I stumbled across Parker and a young lady in the woods by the stable. I thought Parker was sweet on me. I actually thought that he and I were both developing feelings for one another—that is, until I overheard him speaking with the lady."

"You thought the young lady was a mistress," he asked without blinking.

"Yes, I did," she admitted as she sighed and propped her elbows on the table.

"Oh, God, tell me that you didn't accuse him of being anything but a gentleman."

"Oh, I accused him of quite a bit. In fact, I said so many things that he finally put a gag in my mouth. When I finally heard the entire explanation of his sister's situation… well, I felt horribly foolish."

"I would imagine you did. Did he understand how you felt?" he asked while he continued chewing.

"Yes, and we have since resolved everything. I just wanted to inform you that I know of the seriousness of Madeline's situation and am here to help should you ever need it."

"McKenna-girl, you have entered into a whirlwind since you have arrived, haven't you?"

"Yes, I have. In fact—"

"Good morning, dear brother and darling niece!" Aunt Olympia shouted as she happily strode into the dining room holding a letter. She leaned over McKenna's chair and gave her a quick kiss on the cheek before she laid the letter next to McKenna's plate.

"I am sorry to interrupt your conversation, but I just received this letter from your father, dear."

"Oh, thank you Aunt Pia." McKenna quickly opened the letter and read it aloud.

"My dearest McKenna,

All is well with me. I am not at home very much, as I am busy attending my rounds in the county and at the hospitals. I have agreed to serve as an army surgeon, should this country go to war. I must say, this decision made the possibility of war that much closer, but you knew that I would accept the position if I were offered it.

I am not sure if I had previously told you that the General Assembly met and asked for the people of South Carolina to draw up an Ordinance of Secession. Forgive me, daughter, if this is already old news to you. The newspapers here are filled with so many repetitive opinions, exaggerations, and blatant untruths every day, that it is hard to concentrate on the factual happenings.

Major Robert Anderson is now in command at Fort Moultrie on Sullivan's Island. He is a graduate from the United States Military Academy and a top artillery officer. The Secretary of War has given instructions to Anderson that any attack or attempt to take Sumter will be regarded as an act of war. Rumor has it that Anderson will move from Moultrie to Sumter, and if that happens, the conflict may begin earlier than we thought. Rumor also has it that at least a half-dozen more states will soon secede.

With that being said, my darling daughter, I am so glad that you are in England. You are safer there than anywhere back in the States. I shudder at what this impending war will do to our country. I cannot be with you on Christmas, and I know this holiday is your favorite. But my dearest, please carry on traditions with Pia, Pepper, and the rest of the family. I love you and will pray for you and will think of you on Christmas Eve while I am attending church service here in Charleston. Your safety is my utmost concern. I also fear that my letters will soon be censored; God only knows where this country is headed.

I leave you with my love and my very best wishes for a safe and happy holiday with your Aunt Pia and the rest of the family. By now, you have met your long-lost Uncle Pepper, and for that, I still owe you a personal explanation. That will come in time.

Much love,
Papa.

P.S. Please be sure to share my letters with Captain Sloane—he needs to be kept aware of conditions back here in the States, to ensure safety to his shipping business."

McKenna put the letter down on her gold-plated charger. She quietly bowed her head and wept. She had lost her mother and now she may lose her father to a foe that was out of her control. "How will I face my favorite holiday without Father?" she asked herself aloud, in between tearful gulps of air. The slight touches of palms upon her shoulders reminded her that she was supported by her family—and she was not alone. The sound of the closing door, moments later, revealed to McKenna that Aunt Pia and Uncle Pepper had graciously left her alone.

Good, she thought, *I need to talk to God… after I finish a good cry, and I'd rather cry alone. Besides, they don't understand what I am feeling—they will be surrounded by **their** family on Christmas. Lord, please keep him safe— that is all I ask—please keep Papa safe.*

Chapter 31

Christmas was observed and celebrated with as much enthusiasm as McKenna could muster. Aunt Pia had decorated her home with an outstanding display of greenery, ribbons, sparkling ornaments, and pinecone-adorned trees. McKenna gave an earnest effort and followed their traditions, and at times enjoyed herself. After morning church, multiple gifts were exchanged by all and the deliciously prepared meals were enjoyed throughout the festive day and into the late afternoon.

Uncle Pepper, Jenny McTavish, Zadie, and Cooper had the novelty of sharing their first Christmas together. Both couples were besotted with each other and the ladies beamed like school girls, especially when the women each opened their gift of a picture locket—a surprise that both Pepper and Cooper had worked on for quite some time.

Captain Sloane had joined the family on Christmas Eve and Christmas Day as well, and McKenna was enchanted by his presence. They found time to take a stroll to the stable where Parker had planned a lantern picnic. As unembellished as it may have been, it was exactly what McKenna needed. Parker had asked Harper to share a tradition that McKenna and her father would have done in Charleston. It was his suggestion that led Parker to share the Nativity Story from the Bible—both he and McKenna taking turns reading scripture aloud.

Of course, Parker hung his clump of mistletoe above his head several times during the reading, and McKenna eagerly fulfilled the kissing ritual, each kiss lasting a bit longer than the previous. Parker's gift to McKenna not only included a planned picnic and shared tradition, but he also surprised her with a new leather saddle, engraved with her first name.

"Parker, this gift is magnificent! I had no idea you would do something for me, and especially as grand as this," she said as she laid the saddle upon her lap.

"I would do anything for you, kitten, remember that," Parker said with a sultry tone, watching McKenna as she admired the quality of leather and her inlaid name.

"Parker, why did you engrave only my first name?"

"I will finish the engraving in the future, my dear," replied Parker as he took the saddle from her lap and hung it on the post.

"Well, I thank you, sir. No one will mistake my saddle with McKenna Reed on it!" She smiled.

"Kitten, that saddle will not be engraved with Reed," Parker said as he helped McKenna to her feet.

"Oh, and just what name will you finish it with? McKenna-Girl, McKenna R, or McKenna kitten?" she retorted, laughing out loud.

"Sloane. It will be engraved as McKenna Sloane. Now, come here, stop talking, and kiss me."

"Sloane… that sounds nice," McKenna whispered as she stood as close to Parker as physically possible. "Parker?"

"Yes," Parker replied in a husky voice, kissing the nape of McKenna's neck.

"Merry Christmas and thank you, from the bottom of my heart," she shakily uttered as his kisses neared her ear.

"Merry Christmas, kitten, and you are most certainly welcome," he replied in between kisses.

"Parker, I have a gift for you to open as well. But we must stop kissing for the moment," she said as she pushed away from his embrace, chuckling at his school-boy pout.

McKenna slowly pulled a fetching gold-wrapped package from her skirt pocket and handed it to Parker.

"Kitten, I was not expecting you to get me a gift," he said as he gingerly took the wrapped package from her tiny hand.

"Stop talking and open it," she ordered with a gentle smile.

"You are beginning to sound like me," he muttered as he carefully undid the ribbon and opened the wrapping. His breath was taken away when he saw a captivating carved mahogany frame with a portrait of the *Constance* and its name engraved.

"My God, kitten, how in Christ's name did you do this?" Parker asked in awe. He was visibly shaken by its beauty.

"The same way you engraved and purchased my saddle. I knew what I wanted to do for you and I did it. Do you like it?" she asked sheepishly.

"No, kitten. I do not like it at all. I love it! And I love you for this kind gesture," he shouted as he picked her up and twirled her in a circle. "You have truly touched my heart, little one. In fact, you have warmed my heart and I have learned to love again.

"For that, I will always be grateful to you." Parker's eyes never left hers as he slowly placed her on her feet. He smiled and lowered his head to meet her partly opened lips with his own.

"I think that I have fallen in love with you, Captain Parker Sloane," she softly said in between kisses as she placed her hands under his jacket lapels.

"That is good to know," he responded with a groan.

"Parker, well… do you think… that you have fallen in love with me, yet?"

"No," he answered too firmly and too quickly.

"No?" she questioned warily with a sigh, attempting to take a step back.

"I don't think, I *know* that I have fallen in love with you," he responded by closing his hands tighter upon her waist.

"Oh, Parker, you have made me the happiest girl on earth this very moment!" she squealed as she danced on her tiptoes.

"Kitten, I will not compromise your virtue, as badly as I want to, but I do I intend to kiss you until you faint away." Parker smiled as he cupped her face in his large hands. He scooped her up and gently sat down on a bale of straw with her upon his lap.

They remained in each other's embrace for the rest of the evening, neither one willing to retreat back to the house and join the rest of the family. They had found their Christmas happiness—together.

***

The snow that fell the following days turned the landscape into a sparkly, sugar-coated terrain. McKenna certainly missed her father, but she kept busy, even joining in some snowball-throwing contests with her cousins the following week. McKenna had also learned of her aunt's annual New Year's Eve Masquerade Party during her morning ride with Cooper. Cooper and McKenna both knew that one of Pia's parties meant another lengthy list of chores to do for the household. But that would keep her mind busy, and the busier she was here, the less she would think of Charleston and her father.

Daylight was just beginning to start the new day as McKenna sleepily descended the stairs toward the kitchen. She had promised Zadie that she would help her in the kitchen, and being such a quick learner, Zadie was now feeling confident enough to let go of 'her' kitchen, so to speak, and allow McKenna to prepare some meals on her own, with limited help. Zadie knew if McKenna was ever able to cook as well as she sat a horse, then her baby girl would be quite a catch for some lucky gent! Of course, Zadie was rooting for Captain Sloane to be the man to steal McKenna's heart, and the quickest way to a man's heart was through food—or so her mama used to say long, long ago.

The morning sun had just finished peeking through the cloud cover when McKenna placed her first loaf of freshly baked bread upon the table. As she turned to admire the sunrise, she noticed a carriage coming up the drive. This carriage was unlike anything she had ever seen. The harness on the horses displayed a crest of some sort. McKenna had never seen anything so elaborate, not even on the streets of Charleston where the wealthy lived.

Who owns such a carriage? McKenna stared in awe. Aunt Pia had just come into the kitchen on her way to the sewing room when McKenna drew her attention to the carriage outside. Immediately, Pia's shoulders dropped and she stood still and straight.

"Aunt Pia, what is it? Who does that carriage belong to?"

"I am not sure, but I have an idea, and this is one time I hope I am wrong."

"Why? Who is in there? Someone you know?" asked McKenna as she continued to stretch her neck around Pia's frame and attempt a peek at the passenger inside.

"Someone I would prefer not to know and not to see again. Where is Parker?"

"Parker? I would imagine he is in the stables with Cooper; a horse needed a new shoe, and Parker agreed to help this morning."

"McKenna, dear, run to the stables, and tell Parker he may have a guest here. Her carriage is painted black and purple. Tell him those exact words. Run along now and tell him."

McKenna quickly brushed the loose flour from her hands and ran to the stable. She found Parker bent over the rear hoof of one of the horses, picking it clean. Cooper was busy shaping the new shoe that would soon be put on.

"Captain Sloane, I have a message for you. It is quite urgent," McKenna said, completely out of breath.

"Well, good morning, kitten. Catch your breath and then tell me the message. Kitten, who is it from?" Parker asked, returning his eyes back to his horse's hoof.

"It is from Aunt Pia. She said to tell you a carriage has pulled into our drive. She told me to tell you that it is painted black and purple."

"Repeat that message again." Parker dropped the hoof, turned, and looked at McKenna with a concerned expression upon his face.

McKenna repeated the message and noticed that Cooper had come around to face her as well.

"What does it mean? Who is in that carriage, Parker?" she asked.

"Someone who should not be here. Never you mind—she won't be here long if I can help it." Parker strode to the stable door. He didn't look happy and he certainly didn't look interested in whoever chose to visit.

"Cooper, what is going on? Is something happening that I don't know about?" McKenna demanded as Parker vanished out the door.

"It already happened years ago, when the lady in that carriage broke Parker's heart," whispered Cooper, looking just as shaken as Parker had. "If she is here, she is here for one reason—money. Parker wants nothing to do with her and I imagine he will tell her so directly."

"I think I know who she may be."

"Stay away from her, McKenna. She is trouble with a capital 'T.' If she gets one look at you, she will make Parker's life a living hell. She will be filled with hate and jealousy, knowing that he only has eyes for you. Keep Knox by your side while she is here. She is not to be trusted, nor is her entourage to be trusted. I know Olympia will not allow her to stay. Please, for your own good, do as I ask and stay hidden inside the barn. I mean it, McKenna, stay out of sight from that woman," Cooper said with a very forceful tone as he stomped his boots, attempting to knock off dried mud.

"For goodness' sake, Cooper, she can't open the heavens and demand it to rain. She is only a woman, no different than I," McKenna said as she stood closer to Cooper, urging him to look at her.

Cooper placed both hands in a fairly tight grip on each of McKenna's shoulders before he spoke again.

"She can and will open the heavens upon whomever she dislikes. She is a woman, but she is different from you, my dear. She does not nor will she ever come close to your kind perfection."

"Oh my, Coop, you are going to make me blush," she smiled. "What is her name?"

"I would prefer you not know," Cooper answered firmly.

"Parker has already shared some information with me about a woman who broke his heart; he wanted love, and she wanted money. I am assuming the woman who is about to step out of that carriage is named Savannah. Is that a correct assumption?"

"It is," replied Cooper as he nervously removed his hat and swung it against his knee to remove its dust with undisguised force.

***

Damn it to hell. What is she doing here? Parker asked himself as he trudged up the walkway, kicking the stones that dared lay in his way.

She had left without so much as a good-bye all those years ago. She could go back to wherever she came from, for all he cared. Parker walked up the stone walkway and under the portico toward the front of the house. His unwelcomed guest must have spotted him because she waved through the coach window as soon as it stopped.

"Parker, my dear Parker, it is so very good to see you," Savannah shouted as she extended her velvet gloved hand for him to kiss. Parker ignored her hand and allowed her coachman to help her down the carriage steps.

"Parker, I have never known you to be rude. Please, do not start now," she chastised as she stood in front of him and looked up into his eyes.

"Why are you here?" he asked curtly, showing no emotion.

"What? No, 'Hello, Savannah? I have missed you, my dear! How are you? What a surprise!'" she said with an impudent tone to her voice.

"Pick up your skirts and sit your arse back inside that coach. You are not welcome here. I have nothing to say to you, nor do I want to hear anything from those lying lips of yours. How will that do for a greeting?" Parker replied with venom, his jaw twitching while he scanned his uninvited guest from head to toe with obvious disgust.

"Really, my dear captain, I would have thought the days at sea would have softened your feelings toward me. You disappoint me, Parker."

"Not as much as you disappointed me." His comment hit its mark. Tears were beginning to form in her eyes.

I wonder if those are real tears or pretend tears. You always were good at performing.

"Savannah, whatever are you doing here?" asked Olympia, breaking the tension between the two as she came down the front steps to the hitching post, holding her skirts up high.

"Olympia, how good to see you. I was on my way to the docks when I thought I would make a surprise visit at your home. It has been so long since I last saw you. I was hoping Captain Sloane would be in port, and much to my surprise, he is!" squealed Savannah, a feigned smile accompanying her words. Recognizing her devious tone and her attempt to dry her theatrical tears, Olympia knew she was up to no good. Savannah was on a mission and that meant trouble.

"Well, we are quite busy today. You will have to excuse us, as we are in preparation for tomorrow evening's festivities."

"Ah, yes, you still have the New Year's Eve Masquerade Party, do you not?"

"What do you want, Savannah?" Parker interrupted abruptly as he crossed his arms over his chest and locked his legs shoulder-width apart, as though he were bracing for a battle.

"Parker Sloane, don't you dare take that tone with me. Honestly, I just wanted to stop in and say hello. I wanted to inform you that I will be attending your party tomorrow. Now, I bet you are surprised to hear that, aren't you?" Savannah asked with a sneer upon her face.

Something is wrong here, thought Parker. *Why in hell would she want to attend?*

"I do not have you on the guest list, Savannah," said Olympia with a stern voice and an even sterner look upon her brow.

"Oh, you probably do not. But I am coming with a doctor you have invited. I believe you know him, Parker. A certain Reney Carlson?"

Parker saw red. He felt awash in hate, hurt, betrayal, aversion, abhorrence, detestation, and rage—seven years' worth all at once. He immediately grabbed Savannah by the elbow, turned, and dragged her up the stairs toward the grand foyer.

"My God, Parker, stop. I can't keep up with you, and I will trip," Savannah yelped as she half walked, half skipped up the stairs.

"That's not my problem. Pick your damn silk skirts up and keep up with me, then. You are good at running."

"Parker, I am so sorry about how we said good-bye all those years ago," she managed to shout as she hung onto her skirts and her hat.

"You don't know what the word 'sorry' means. You left. You didn't say good-bye. Compassion is not in your character description." Parker reached the front door and flung Savannah into the foyer, then grabbed her shoulders and forced her onto the settee while kicking the door partially shut behind him.

"Now, you will be telling me the real reason you are here. Why in hell are you attending the New Year's Eve party with Reney? You know damn well he is married to my sister. Start talking, Savannah, and I mean now!" Parker grabbed her chin and forced her to look up at him.

"I will not answer anything until you take your hands off me and offer me a drink of cold water."

"I will get you nothing. I offered everything I had seven years ago, but that was not enough for you." Parker placed his dirty, booted foot upon the settee as he removed his hand from her chin. "Start talking," he ordered as he bent with elbow on knee, a few inches from Savannah's trembling face.

"Parker, I am here for a good reason. You must believe me," she pleaded as she tentatively placed her trembling hand upon his knee. She immediately changed her posture and the tone of her voice. He could see sincerity written all over her face. *What is she up to? A minute ago, she played the English bitch to perfection. Now, she has withdrawn her claws and speaks with a civil tongue. Something is wrong,* he thought.

"Parker, you must suspect that Reney has been seeing another lady for quite some time. Do not pretend you don't know that Reney and Madeline are having difficulties in their marriage."

"I know Reney is up to no good. If you were a wise woman, you would stay the hell away from him. But then again, he is everything you want, isn't he? He is well-known, he has nice things, and most importantly, he is, or he was, wealthy," Parker replied while pushing her hand off his knee as though it were diseased.

"Stop it, Parker. After I left you and ran off with the lawyer, I realized I had made a serious mistake. I didn't know he was married. I didn't know he sired four children! There was no way on God's green earth that I was going to be saddled with a husband and four brats—especially not mine. The only reason he professed his love for me was so I would become a replacement mother and maidservant for his children after he annulled his marriage!

"Parker, the man played me for a fool. I had already left you, and I was too proud to come crawling back in the hopes you would take me back into your arms and marry me."

"You were correct; you would have crawled for nothing," Parker replied coldly.

"Parker, I remained alone for a long while. When I began seeing Reney, I did not know he was married. He never told me, and that is the truth! Honestly, I did not know. When he finally told me that he was in the process of getting his marriage annulled, I decided to end the courtship, for fear of going through what I had previously encountered. For all I knew, Reney could have had four children as well."

"Apparently you did not end the relationship. Do not lie to me, Savannah! You just told Pia you'll be attending her party tomorrow night with my sister's husband. Is it a challenge for you to break apart a marriage? Do you enjoy causing hurt and harm to the other spouse? I swear to God, Savannah, if you were a man, I would be tempted to lay my fist into your face and knock you out cold!"

"Stop shouting and listen to me! I am sorry about our past, and I regret my actions. But I am here to prevent another hurt—if you will just give me the chance to explain," Savannah shakily said as she adjusted her bonnet straps.

"Go on," ordered Parker without blinking.

"I made a surprise visit to Reney's office, thinking I would give him a second chance. When I arrived, he was furious that I would come there without telling him. At first, I couldn't understand why he would be so upset. One would have thought he'd be ecstatic that I would even reconsider a relationship with him. In retrospect, I realize I had given him no time to sabotage his office, to make it look as if he had already discontinued the marriage. He had pictures of Maddie all over the room. Only then did I realize he was still married—and he was wed to your sister! I immediately told him our relationship was over."

"How kind of you," Parker grunted as he lowered his boot and kicked the entrance door closed.

"Stop the sarcasm, Parker. I am being honest. He used me to get to you. That is why I am here. He deliberately wants to hurt you and shame you tomorrow evening. He wants me to accompany him throughout the evening. He plans to tell anyone who will listen that your sister is incapable of conceiving a child. He plans on admitting her into an asylum for the mentally ill because she is so depressed."

"The hell he will. He has verbally abused her and has probably physically abused her as well."

"I am not sure about that. Evidently, he asked you to consider him as a partner in your shipbuilding. Is that correct?"

"Yes, he did, and I immediately declined."

"Well, that made him boiling mad, and he wants to pay you back—he's out for vengeance."

"What does that have to do with you? Why are you here? Why were you so bitchy outside?"

"I had to be. I had to pretend we are still at odds. I didn't want anyone else to know the real reason I am here."

"Real reason? My patience is growing thin, Savannah." Parker gritted his teeth as he stood still, facing her with an apathetic and sober facial expression.

"Parker, I hurt you, and I know that. I want to make it up to you, and the only way I know how is to prevent Maddie from getting hurt. My God, I adore her; I always have. I can't imagine how it must feel to endure repeated miscarriages. For all I know, he may be behind her miscarriages as well! He is a monster! Madeline is your sister, and I owe you and her the decency of alerting you to Reney's scheme. I do not want him to disgrace her; she has done nothing wrong."

"Go on…" Parker uttered with contempt written all over his face.

"Reney, on the other hand, has been mean to me. He has hit me. He has threatened to rape me if I refuse to assist him in this ruse he has planned. If you want witnesses, for God's sake, go get Pepper, Pia, and Cooper, and I will repeat to them, what I have just told you."

"You don't have to. They have already heard. Come on in, you three."

167

The three of them walked through the adjoining veranda door with accusing eyes and wary expressions, never taking their eyes from Savannah. Their memories of Savannah were as bitter as Parker's.

"What is Reney's plan, exactly?" Parker asked.

"He purposely had me drive the painted carriage. He knew the reason behind the choice of purple and black—the colors of a bruise, like your bruised heart from me. I had probably mentioned the colors to him long ago, and he used it in his plan. He wants to attend the party, Parker.

"When the party begins to break for dinner, Reney plans to introduce me as a very dear friend that he has had during Madeline's mental instability. Don't you see? He will portray himself as the husband who has tried everything to please his wife in her quest for a child. Then, he will sadly announce that Maddie is an unstable wife who should be committed, so she won't harm herself.

"Of course, we know that Maddie would never harm herself, but he will tell all of Pia's guests that her behavior of late is questionable. He wants to hurt you, Parker. You denied him a business proposition, and he is desperate to pay back everyone who has loaned him money. He owes a lot of people a lot of money!" Savannah cleared her throat and readjusted her gloves before continuing.

"He even plans to concoct a story about me. He will tell everyone that I stopped Madeline from jumping out the second-story window. He will portray her as quite capable of killing herself, and I will be a hero. He knows our history—mine and yours—and he wants to bury the dagger into your heart because he knows I rejected you. And now, you have rejected him. Reney does not do well with rejection. I also think that there is a very real chance that Reney may kill Maddie. If he can convince people that she is capable of throwing herself to her death, then I would not put it past his heinous mind to actually push her from their tower window. I do not know if he would go through with it, but I do believe he would consider it—especially as of late. He is a different man than you knew, Parker. He is malicious, spiteful, hateful, and capable of nefarious crimes."

Savannah took a big breath before she continued, "There, Parker, I have told you everything I know. His plan is built upon pure vengeance. I must admit that I think there is more to this deep-seated vengeance, but that is only a hunch. He is after something."

"You have told me everything, Savannah? Aren't you keeping an important detail out of your story?"

Pia, Pepper, and Cooper exchanged looks.

"What's in it for you?" Parker spat viciously. "What did he promise you?" He bent over and grabbed Savannah's chin once again. "Look me in the eye, Savannah, and tell me the truth!"

"Parker, I am to do exactly as I did when I drove up. My coachman will attest to it. He is really Reney's steward and he is in on this scheme as well. In fact, I am so glad you dragged me into the house, so the coachman could not hear me reveal the real story. By the way, you were a bit rough, but that added more believability, I suppose. I am to flirt with you tomorrow evening. I am to work my charms on you, and bring you to your knees, because Reney believes that you may still have a soft spot for me. I am to…"

"You are to break me," Parker interrupted. "You are to persuade me to hire Reney on in my business to save Maddie from Reney and his public embarrassment of her that he intends to display tomorrow evening. Am I correct?"

"Yes; Reney is counting on it."

"And if you succeed in this charade?"

"He will pay me, and I will go back to London and live with my father. He is ill in health. He doesn't have long to live, Parker. That is the absolute truth."

"Is there any other kind of truth? What happens if you don't succeed?"

"He promised he would punish Madeline. You must believe me; I do not want anything to happen to Maddie. Please believe me, Parker," Savannah pleaded with tears in her eyes as she gently kneaded her forearm.

"What is wrong with your arm? You have been rubbing it since you arrived," Parker asked warily.

"It's nothing. It is just a bit sore," replied Savannah as she held her arm in her lap.

Parker knew there was something wrong—Savannah's grimace did not go away. If there was one thing he remembered about her, it was that she did not deal well with pain.

"Show me your arm, Savannah."

"No, Parker, that won't be necessary."

"Either show me, or I will show myself."

Savannah carefully rolled up the lacy, double-tiered puff sleeve to her elbow, exposing a horribly bruised forearm.

"My God, did he do this? These bruises have been here a while, Savannah. Your entire forearm is discolored," Parker shouted in disbelief while he examined the mottled skin.

"It is actually better than it was. Remember, I know what he is capable of. Parker, there is one more component to this story. Reney locked Maddie in the west wing yesterday. I know this because I snuck her bread and stew last evening. She is not mentally unstable, but her spirit is breaking. When I told her I was coming to see you today, she asked me to bury whatever hatchet I had with you and to travel here and explain this whole story to you. She knew you might question and doubt me, so she gave me a note to give to you. It has been sealed, and I didn't break it. No one forced her to write to you, because I was the only one in the room when she wrote it. Reney does not know of the note's existence." Savannah dug around in her reticule, pulled out an envelope, and held it out to Parker.

Parker unflinchingly took the note from her hand and broke open the seal. It was the seal of the *Constance*. No one else had it; it was used only in their private correspondence.

Parker,

Remember at the stable when you told me anywhere, anytime, anyway? Well, I am calling you on that promise. Savannah is telling the truth. She has just shared with you what she shared with me last evening. Arrange a plan and rescue me from this demon. Remember, the best apples are red.

Parker read the note aloud, all but the last sentence. Parker paced back and forth a few moments before he turned toward Savannah and spoke directly to her, showing no benevolence.

"I want you to return to Reney. I want you to convince him that we are having drinks and sandwiches one hour before the party formally begins—for favored guests only. Inform Reney that I want both of you to attend the party early. I also want you to tell Reney that I will be taking him aside to discuss a business proposal. Can you do that?"

"Yes, I can do that. Parker, what will you say to him? You are not really going to offer him a job or a partnership, are you?"

"If it comes to that, I will have to, for Maddie's sake."

"All right, Parker, I will do as you say. But now, I must be going back. I told Reney I would be home before dark, and it will be close to that by the time I get there," Savannah answered as she rose and lightly touched Parker's chest.

"Parker, I am sorry. I hope this will help you to forgive me for my past actions. I know I hurt you deeply, and I am truly shamefaced and contrite. I can't dwell on what might have been between us, but I can certainly prevent your sister from getting hurt. Reney thinks you still carry feelings for me. It's plain to see that isn't true, but he certainly underestimated how much I would be willing to put aside our history for the sake of your sister. I hope this works."

"We shall see, won't we? Until tomorrow evening."

"Parker, you must pretend that you are enchanted with me when we step outside. The coachman will most assuredly report back to Reney that I broke your resolve."

"I can do that," said Parker as he opened the door for Savannah.

He followed Savannah out of the house and gently escorted her to the coach.

"Driver, take the lady home," Parker directed, then gently placed a kiss upon Savannah's cheek before helping her onto her carriage step.

"If what you have told me is true, I thank you for—for Maddie's sake," Parker whispered into her ear.

Parker closed the door and nodded at the coachman. He remained stationary and watched the carriage hastened down the lane. It had just left their view when Pia, Pepper, and Cooper began to barrage Parker with questions.

"Are you out of your blasted mind? What the hell are you up to?" Pepper asked.

"A business venture? With that gutter rat?" Cooper added in haste.

"This is the man who is abusing your sister! You can't possibly invite them here an hour early—we have no drinks or sandwiches scheduled for that time," Olympia hounded nervously while she paced back and forth.

Parker whistled, and the three of them stopped their talking.

"I am not out of my blasted mind, Pepper. I do have a plan, Cooper, and I damn well know there are no drinks and sandwiches an hour early. Why don't you three shut the hell up and trust me?"

Parker was hell-bent on giving Reney what he deserved. He strode back to the house and slammed the library door behind him before he poured himself a brandy. He sipped his drink and peered outside the window. He watched McKenna from the corner of his eye slowly approach the house with Knox trotting beside her. He would need to explain this situation to her. Lord, McKenna was the exact opposite from the manipulating woman who had just left—the woman who had broken his heart so badly, he vowed never to love again until the golden-haired beauty outside these doors had entered his life.

This ought to be one hell of a New Year's Eve, he thought as he poured a second drink. He wasn't sure which display of fireworks would be better—the ones in the sky or the ones that would occur during Pia's party. One thing he was sure of: they would both be explosive as hell, and if all went according to the plan he was forming in his mind, his baby sister would be out of harm's way and safe from the behemoth named Reney Carlson.

Chapter 32

Parker watched Reney with disgust as he stepped from his carriage, dressed as a Roman soldier. Reney tightened his costumed wrist bands and adjusted his sword before turning and helping Savannah from the carriage. Together, they walked up the illuminated stairs to Pia's Masquerade Ball, unaware of the unpleasantness and trouble they would soon encounter.

You bastard, you will fall hard this evening—harder than you can imagine. Go ahead and play the soldier for a while longer, you dimwitted peacock. You won't be wearing those kinds of clothes where you are going—which will be nothing short of debtor's prison if I can help it, Parker thought to himself, trying to hold back the anger that was boiling inside him.

Pia was the perfect hostess, greeting her guests with a contagious enthusiasm. However, as soon as she saw Reney and Savannah making their way up the walkway, her smile all but disappeared. She breathed deeply and forced herself to nod and extend a welcoming hand to them.

"Good evening, Reney and Savannah. My, oh my, your costumes are unique. Reney, you are a soldier, and Savannah, let me see, you appear to be dressed as a Greek Goddess. Are my assumptions correct?" asked Pia, stifling a gag.

"Oh, Pia, yes, we are dressed from the Roman era, and may I say that you have outdone yourself with the luminaries up the walk. Wouldn't you agree, Reney?" Savannah asked as she gently touched Pia's upper arm, trying to offer a silent gesture of kindness.

"Yes, you certainly have outdone yourself, Olympia, and we are exceptionally humbled to have been included in your early hour of hospitality," Reney announced with a haughty tone to his voice and a theatrical wink to Savannah.

Oh, you will be humbled all right, you bumbling halfwit, Pia thought.

"Well, I am glad that you could attend our gala a bit earlier than others," Pia continued, "Reney, it has been a long time since we have spoken. Now then, Savannah dear, since you have arrived so early, I could use an extra pair of hands. I know it sounds a bit forward to ask you to aid me in a last-minute preparation, but would you please be so kind as to help McKenna take some of the stemware out to the sun porch? I am afraid that time got away from us this afternoon, and we simply forgot to place the glasses out for our early guests. Would that be too much to ask of you, my dear?" Pia looked sweetly at Savannah.

"No, don't be silly, Pia. I would be glad to help McKenna. I have yet to meet the woman who finally stole Parker's heart. What is McKenna dressed as?"

"You can't miss her. She is dressed as a cat," Pia answered as she took Savannah by the elbow and graciously turned her toward the kitchen. "Please excuse your Greek Goddess for a moment, Reney; this won't take too long."

"Of course, Savannah is always *willing to help*. I will find myself a drink in the meantime," Reney replied back with detectable menace in his voice.

Savannah found her way into the kitchen, where she was immediately met by McKenna and Pepper stepping out from behind the closed door.

"You must be McKenna," Savannah said quietly as she walked toward her with an outstretched hand.

"And you must be Savannah," McKenna replied sarcastically, circling to the side of her and ignoring Savannah's hand of introduction.

"Savannah, you can stop the façade. McKenna knows why you are here. In fact, you will be leaving shortly," Pepper interjected.

McKenna moved closer to Savannah in an attempt to lower her voice. She looked straight into Savannah's eyes without flinching before she spoke. "Parker told me your story in its entirety. I only hope that you are sincere in your attempts to help Maddie escape any further harm from her brutish husband, Reney."

Savannah stood still with not so much as a tremble as she spoke. "McKenna, I am not sure what Parker has or has not told you about me. But I want you to know that I would never, ever hurt Madeline. She was a friend to me when I needed a friend the most. I broke Parker's heart long ago and I am sorry for that. I hope that you can give him the love that I never could. I was foolish, wrong, selfish, and self-absorbed. I made many mistakes—too many to name. But perhaps, I can remedy some of the hurt that I have caused." She paused. "What do you need me to do?" She looked at both Pepper and McKenna with tears in her eyes.

"I will answer your question, Savannah," Pepper replied, crossing his arms behind his back. Pepper carefully looked at Savannah from head to toe, slowly, methodically, purposely causing Savannah to tremble from his sinister gaze.

"In my eyes, you are a deceitful and hateful woman. You broke Parker's heart and damn near killed his spirit to ever love or trust another human being again. With that being said, you will leave this house immediately. And you will never return. Parker has given you some money to see you safely to London; the envelope of money is in your carriage. You mentioned that your father was ill.

"Somewhere, deep in Parker's soul, he has found empathy toward your misfortune. He is a better man than I am. At any rate, you will take his generous gift of money and ride to London, now. You will never make contact with any of us again. If you agree, you will not be implicated in any of Reney's plans. I have a document for you to sign describing exactly what I have just explained. Judge McCain is fully aware of your involvement and your attempt to help Maddie. However, if you ever cross this land again or attempt to intervene in Parker's or McKenna's affairs, or any of our affairs for that matter, you will be questioned by the authorities, and our pity toward you and your ill father will cease. And by God, he had better be as ill as you say he is. I would hope you would not lie about your father's health. Now then, do you understood everything I have told you?" Pepper asked as he handed Savannah the document and quill.

Savannah nodded as she knelt down to her knees and signed the document in her lap. She trembled and shook uncontrollably until McKenna raised her up by her shoulders. McKenna cleared her throat before she spoke—never taking her eyes from Savannah's heavily rouged face.

"There are no more words to be said here except... I pray that you find a man to love. I pray that you love him as much as I love Parker, and I pray that he will return his love to you as much as Parker has returned his love to me. Go on, now. Your carriage is waiting."

Savannah looked at McKenna and uttered a crestfallen 'thank you.' She then turned and followed Pepper through the rear kitchen door and quietly entered her carriage. Pepper shut the door firmly and motioned for the driver to ride on.

"I hope I never see that woman again," whispered McKenna as she joined him on the walkway.

"You and me both. What we did here, just now, was the right thing to do. We could have implicated Savannah, and I believe she knows that. That chapter in Parker's life is finally closed. Now, my dear, let's return to the party. There is one more guest that needs to be taken care of," Pepper grunted as he looked at McKenna with nothing short of anger in his eyes.

"Uncle Pepper, you need to soften your face and smile. Rage is written all over you!"

"Good, I hope my vexation is apparent the moment Reney gets cornered. It will feel good to have that river rat thrown into jail."

"Well, then, let's find Parker and see what he does to a 'rat,' shall we?" asked McKenna with a certain sense of nervousness.

"I know what I do to rats!" mumbled Pepper under his breath.

***

"You are out of your damn mind if you think for one blasted minute I will sign an annulment to Madeline. I don't care if you are her brother or not!" Reney yelled as he threw the quilled pen onto the floor of the library.

"By God, you will sign this annulment and you will do it now!" Parker shouted back, within inches of Reney's already reddened face. "You have drugged her, beaten her, and done God-knows-what-else. Hell, you treat your horses better than her, and that isn't saying much."

"I have a legal and binding contract of marriage and you can't do anything about that. Are you trying to bribe me, Parker? Is this what this shouting match is all about? You asked Savannah and me to come to this party early so you could meet with me behind closed doors? For what? I had hoped that we could become business partners in the shipping industry. Evidently, you had other preconceived notions. You, sir, can take your annulment parchment and go straight to hell. I won't sign."

"Are you sure about that, Carlson?" asked Parker with a calm voice as he strode to the doors and began turning the latch.

"Damn sure! I will not be signing anything this evening," Reney muttered as he shakily removed his Roman helmet from his sweaty head.

"Well then, I have a few more guests to invite into my library. Perhaps, you will change your mind." Parker opened the library doors and ushered in several neighbors, asking them to form a slight circle. One by one they filtered in—looking at Reney with disgust and shame.

"Gentlemen, I know it is a bit awkward for you to be ushered into my private library like this, but I need your help this evening. I promise you will not be detained for long. I would like to ask you all a very important question."

The gathered guests had looks of confusion upon their faces, but muttered soft acknowledgements aloud.

"But before I proceed, I want to make sure that you have your glasses filled with the finest imported brandy, all the way from Paris, complements of Reney Carlson."

Parker raised his glass to the men standing before him, waiting for their glasses to be filled as he leaned over and whispered in Reney's ear.

"I think this brandy is from Paris, isn't it, Carlson? At least, that is what your house servant told me when I took it."

"You dirty bastard, you mean when you stole it?" Reney's face turned a purplish shade of red. His knuckles clenched as he struggled to loosen his costumed chest plate.

"Took, stole, one in the same," laughed Parker before he continued.

"Now then, gentlemen, who here is owed money by Reney Carlson? Raise your hands, don't be embarrassed. It is a simple question—in fact, Mr. Carlson wants to do right by those who he is indebted to, and I have agreed to help him."

One man after another began to lift their hands. This continued until every man present had his hand up.

"Shout out the amount that Carlson owes you, if you are not too ashamed to say," Parker shouted over their murmuring voices.

The men did just that. Soon, Reney began to get weak-kneed and sat down. Cooper and Pepper came to stand on each side of him, blocking any attempt of escape that he may have thought to attempt.

"I ask all of you now, did he promise to pay you back within a certain time?" asked Parker, never flinching. "Well, times have been tough for Reney, but as sure as I am standing here before you, Reney intends to make good on his debts. In fact, I have asked Judge McCain to attend this gathering. Thus, he has taken the liberty of quickly totaling up the sum of monies owed by Reney Carlson, based upon what you all have just admitted."

Judge McCain stood in front of the fire and cleared his throat. "Gentlemen, I am a man of the law and you all know that. Therefore, I stand before you in an attempt to clear all debt owed before the new year begins. Reney Carlson, you owe every man in this room a sum of money. For most of these men, your debt is well over two or three years old. You have bribed, cheated, and stolen money from under their noses. I don't know why you lowered yourself to this level, but you have. I am telling you now, in good faith, that I am happy to know that you intend to pay them back!"

"I am telling you now to mind your own business. What I owe is between each man and me. Keep your nose out of it," shouted Reney as he swiped the table nervously.

"It is my business, Carlson. I make it my business. Do you have the money to pay each man what you owe? It is an easy answer—yes or no," asked the Judge.

"No, I don't have the money to pay anyone back. If this righteous bastard Sloane would have given me a job, like a decent brother-in-law should when a man is down on his luck, I wouldn't be in this mess," shouted Reney with a vengeful look in his eye toward Parker.

Parker snapped. He took two steps and held Reney within his grasp. He shook him hard enough for his eyeglasses to fall from his frightened face.

"You dirty, good-for-nothing weasel. You have cheated money out of every man in this room—probably more than I care to count. These men were your friends at one time. They trusted you as a doctor! You are down on your luck because you chose to be. You were a reputable doctor once. Whatever you have done with your finances is your business. I owe you nothing, you rotten scum. I am your brother-in-law only because you coerced Maddie in to marrying you." Parker emitted enough rage to make a grown man soil himself.

"Parker, let him go. Get a hold of yourself," Cooper whispered as he removed Parker's hands firmly from Reney's arms.

Reney's reserve broke. He shouted back at Parker, stepping back toward the fire, not caring that the entire room was listening to his rants.

"Your sister is mentally unstable. Hell, she can't even conceive a child. I have tried to help her with medicines, but she is so depressed that she even tried to jump from our bedroom and kill herself! Madeline is a demented and disturbed woman. Go get Savannah, she will tell you—she prevented Maddie from jumping just the other night!" Reney reached for a glass of brandy to calm his nerves. It never reached his lips. Parker strode toward Reney in two steps and shook him so hard that his costumed chest plate snapped in two.

"Savannah told me plenty. In fact, Maddie told me about the drugs you have been giving her. They are lethal—in fact, it may very well be your fault that she miscarried her babies. In my eyes, that is murder, and Judge McCain will be the one to determine that, you bastard. But you didn't stop there, did you? You locked Maddie in the West tower. She didn't jump and Savannah didn't have to stop her. You wanted her out of the way, didn't you?"

"Go to hell, Sloane. I have heard enough. I am leaving," he shouted back as he tore Parker's hands from his chest. His path was blocked by Cooper, Pepper, and Judge McCain, not to mention the rest of the guests. He didn't stand a snowball's chance in hell of leaving that library on his own accord. Parker sauntered toward Reney and stood in front of him once again, close enough for Reney to smell the Brandy on his breath. He looked intently into his brother-in-law's eyes before speaking with an uncanny assurance.

"No, you aren't going anywhere, Doctor Carlson. That may be the last time you hear yourself addressed as such. You owe these fine neighbors' money— a lot of money. You figured you would get it one of two ways; one being that I would hire you and you would eventually and honestly pay them back from your wages. But in that unscrupulous and scheming mind of yours, an honest day's wage would take too long to pay off your debts. So, you planned for Maddie to have an unfortunate fall to her death. If she died, you knew you would be able to collect the large amount of money that was left to her by our grandmother.

"The only other obstacle that prevented you from inheriting Maddie's money were children. Well, you took care of that as well, didn't you? You gave my sister lethal drugs and caused her miscarriages, you inferior mongrel. Tonight, you refused to sign an annulment, because an annulment would leave you penniless. Either way, your plan will not succeed because you were found out. And, where you are going, you won't need much money."

"Where is Savannah?" Reney hollered. "Did that lying bitch tell you this? Did she rat me out? So, help me God, I will beat her to an inch of her life when

I find her. The only good thing about that lewd slut is what lies between her legs, and even then, I've seen better."

Parker slowly smiled and turned toward those gathered in the library. Their dubious faces displayed disbelief as they cringed with cynic anger around Reney. There wasn't a man there who was sympathetic toward Reney and Parker knew it. Those gathered knew they would never be repaid the money owed. Any semblance of humanity in Reney was gone. His last outburst had just established the lengths he would go to save his own hate-filled, rancorous soul.

Parker spoke slowly and clearly as he turned around and looked into Reney's eyes. "Where is Savannah, you ask? She is gone, whoreson.

"You won't be able to hurt her anymore. I saw the bruises on her arms. You won't be seeing Savannah anytime soon, not where you are going." Parker had vengeance in his eyes. "Debtors' prison doesn't allow copulation. Your memories of the tavern harlots and harbor wantons you have entertained over the years, while married to my sweet sister, will have to suffice.

"Judge McCain, if you would be so kind as to remove this parasite from my home, I would be grateful to you. The sooner this low-life is behind bars, the happier I will be," Parker stated with a sigh.

"You son-of-a-bitch… you can't do this to me. I am a medical doctor. I know important people in high places!" Reney shouted as Pepper and Cooper encircled Reney's flailing arms, trying to pin them down to his side.

"You just lost your license to practice medicine, Carlson," interrupted the Judge. "And if I find enough evidence that your medicines caused Maddie's babies to perish, you will be tried for murder, you wretched scum. You are not fit to clean the horse shit from my boots. Now, shut your damn mouth. Be glad we don't go out the front door and parade your filthy carcass to all of the guests, including your fellow medical colleagues," Judge McCain declared as he stoically put his hat on and followed Pepper, Cooper, and their prisoner out of the house.

Parker faced the men before him and wiped the sweat that had formed from his brow. "Gentlemen, I am sorry that you had to witness that. And I am sorry that you may never be repaid the monies owed to you. But know this: that man will never cheat another unsuspecting individual again, least of all his friends and my sister. Go now, enjoy the evening; and together, we will welcome 1861 with a lightened heart. Raise your glasses with me to the new year approaching, especially enjoy the wine on Carlson's behalf," Parker said with a smirk.

"Here, here," the men replied as they drank from their glasses and slowly, one by one, left the library to rejoin the evening's festivities, but not before offering handshakes of gratitude and acknowledgement for Parker's honesty. Parker shook the last hand and sauntered from the library where he found McKenna drinking a glass of punch.

"Well, dearest, I assume that all went to plan, and you were able to remove Reney Carlson from this house and from your sight for a very long time?" she asked with sparkling eyes.

"You may assume so, kitten. And, I must say how absolutely stunning you look tonight in your costume, although I find it quite humorous."

"You do? Well, I must say it was an easy costume to sew. A couple of ears, a nose, some whiskers, and a long tail with a fury fabric. I think I make the perfect *kitten*, don't you?" she asked with an impish look.

"Kitten, I would expect nothing less from that creative mind of yours," Parker replied as he stuffed a small tart into his mouth.

"Oh, Parker, look in the foyer—it is Maddie!" exclaimed McKenna as she rubbed her eyes to ensure she wasn't seeing things.

Parker's eyes darted toward the foyer. There, in all her glory, stood his beautiful baby sister. She looked stunning in her rose-colored chiffon gown. Parker watched her converse with the guests as a perfect hostess should. There were sparkles in her eyes—something that had been gone for such a long time. *How happy she must be*, Parker thought, *knowing she will never live in fear of that leviathan again.* Minutes passed as he continued to watch Maddie greet and hug her longtime friends. She did indeed look like the baby sister he used to know from long ago—smiling, laughing, and enjoying herself as she damn well should.

Her happiness was long overdue, and he sure as hell was glad that she would not be under Reney's oppressive rule ever again. As he turned to back to McKenna, he caught the swish of a costumed tail faintly brush his pant leg. The owner of that tail was sashaying across the dance floor with Cooper, both of them trying desperately not to step on the tail. The sight before him caused him to beam from cheek to cheek. In fact, he laughed, and he laughed long and hard at the couple before him—one trying to lead the dance and one trying to follow—both giggling around their turns like young pups right out of college.

Yes, I have fallen in love with you, kitten. You have entered my heart, McKenna Reed, and I never thought I would allow another woman to do so. I knew the moment the wind nearly swiped your bonnet from those golden curls of yours that you had captured my soul. This will be a new start for all of us, here in England; I only hope the same for those back in America. Please, Lord, keep Harper safe, and let this war be over soon. Keep my kitten safe while I travel—she means the world to me.

***

Parker left in early February for his regular six-month shipping schedule. As badly as McKenna wanted to sail with him, she knew that she was needed here with Aunt Pia and Uncle Pepper, having to help with the chores and the running of the house and stables. But that did not make the winter months pass any quicker. When the ever-present snowfall finally ended, spring rains were welcomed for the soil and flowers; however, April and May news from Charleston was not so good. Harper kept McKenna informed with news from home through letters and collected newspaper articles. As soon as she received news from her father, McKenna would alert the household at the supper table. It was during one such evening that Pia sat down at the table with a letter in hand.

"McKenna, my dear, you have a letter from your father!" she exclaimed as she stretched her hand toward her niece.

"Thank you, Aunt Pia." McKenna quickly took the letter, opened the seal, and began to read aloud.

"My dearest McKenna,

I have much news to share with you, but it will be in abbreviated form, as I am writing this during a lull. The soldiers keep coming in to our army's makeshift medical tents—ten, twenty, even thirty per day. My knowledge is not challenged, but my state of mind has been. These are young men your age, fighting for their lives or simply asking to die when the pain becomes too much to bear. It saddens my heart, baby girl—I am so very glad that you are not here to witness this wreckage.

I had one soldier who recognized me. He was so badly disfigured that I had to take his word that he was who he said he was. If you remember the

Clydell family on the other side of the pond, then you would remember James, the oldest boy. He was pretty good with his horses. It was James who was lying in my tent, begging for morphine. I was taken aback that a boy from our neck of the woods was injured. It made the war seem much more real to me, I suppose. Allow me to backtrack—I apologize—I jumped ahead of myself. In early January, Mississippi, Florida, Alabama, Georgia, Louisiana, and Texas formed the Confederate States of America. It has happened, McKenna. Our country is now divided.

I was told that Fort Sumter withstood thirty-four hours of bombardment before it surrendered. Fortunately, no one was killed during the actual bombardment; but a private was killed during the one hundred-gun salute when a gun discharged prematurely. We had to list his name as the first to die, but we all know that he certainly will not be the last.

I have struggled long and hard about my decision to work for the army. I am needed, and I swore an oath. So, please support my choice to travel with the army and help save as many lives as I am able. It matters not to me the color of uniform they wear. Billy Yank blue or Johnny Reb gray—they both have red blood flowing through their veins.

Until my next letter…
I love you,
Papa"

McKenna sighed deeply as she laid the unfolded letter upon the table and read the attached newspaper article.

"Who has Fort Sumter now, Cousin McKenna?" asked Caleb while McKenna read.

"Well, the newspaper article says that Anderson left. Beauregard raised the Confederate flag, and… the Civil War officially began. So, Caleb, it looks like the South has control of Fort Sumter," McKenna said in a low voice.

"God help America," whispered Aunt Olympia, "let us pray for those soldiers."

"Amen to that," McKenna whispered back as she tucked her letter into the envelope and bowed her head for the supper prayer.

Chapter 33

Oxford's August heat stridently swathed Aunt Olympia's manor. The moisture in the air doubled due to the surplus of rain. The humidity was unbearable past noon, and the chances to ride Solomon were limited. Any riding had to be done early in the morning because both horse and rider would be bone-weary after three or four hours in the saddle during this abnormal weather.

Captain Sloane had been sailing since February, and McKenna would never again question the definition of the word 'melancholy.' She kept busy enough in the house, and, in addition to helping Zadie with the gardening, she also had her stable chores.

McKenna didn't mind; she wanted to work because it kept the longing for Parker from creeping into her mind. The letters Parker sent did not make up for her loneliness. She understood that Parker had shipments to deliver, which were scheduled long before they had met, but six months was a very long time, and McKenna missed her handsome captain. She missed his laugh and the way he twitched his nose when he was teasing her. She missed looking at him. Never before had it occurred to her how gentle a man's hands could be. No matter how large or calloused Parker's hands were, she longed for his gentle touch upon her shoulders and neck; she especially ached for the tender and placid touch of his fingers upon her chin just before he kissed her. She coveted and craved his smile, his smell, and his strength. The ache in her stomach, at times, was her undoing. If Aunt Pia only knew how many nights she sat by her window, passing the midnight hours away watching the moon because her loneliness would not allow her to sleep. It was plain and simple to McKenna: she was in love with Parker Sloane and missed him terribly, and there wasn't a damn thing she could do about it until he returned home. Soon, very soon, her captain would be home, and she had decided she would sail with him the next time. Even if he threw a fit, she would find a way to soften his heart and allow her to accompany him.

Olympia recognized her niece's loneliness and set out to keep McKenna busy by introducing her to Dr. Withers, a veterinarian who just happened to specialize in horse breeding. With his permission, McKenna began to assist him. Many of the horses Aunt Pia boarded on her farm belonged to other people. Although Pia had been buying and breeding thoroughbreds for the past ten years, she knew how high the interest was for fast horses back in the States, especially during the war. Thus, she enlisted Dr. Withers and his expertise to begin expanding breeding at her stables.

Dr. Withers asked McKenna to ride the horses and record their vitals. Charts were made and hung in each individual stall. Food, water, and supplement delivery were also charted, as well as weight. It was McKenna's responsibility to keep track of this information for each horse. She enjoyed learning from Dr. Withers, but more importantly, she enjoyed being given the job of riding them.

When Pia decided to sell some of her horses for the war effort back in the states, Dr. Withers determined which horses would be suitable, and they were then sent down to the docks and shipped.

It was a particularly hot day when McKenna returned to the stable from riding filled with eagerness. "Cooper, I have an idea. It would take some doing, but I feel it would be worth it."

"And what would this idea be about?" he asked while heaving hay into the troughs.

"Let's make a race track here. Rather than ride in the woods and meadows with the possibility of any one of these horses falling into a rut and breaking an ankle, let's build a smooth race track here. I can ride these horses each day, you can record their speeds, and we can document the sire's name and the dam's name. If we especially like the horse itself, we will know which breeder to contact for further personal purchases. Horse racing is a lucrative business, Cooper. Perhaps we could even enter one of our own horses into a race!"

"Whoa, McKenna, slow down. I think your idea of a race track is a good one. Horse racin' for profit would have to be discussed with Olympia, because we would have to learn a whole lot more about racin' and the care of race horses."

"Cooper, you know everything there is to know about riding horses."

"McKenna, ridin' a horse and racin' a horse are two different things. I ain't no expert with racin', and I don't think that's somethin' I'm interested in doin'. It is a dangerous sport, my girl."

"Is it any more dangerous than two people racing against each other out there in the meadow? At least with a track, we would be guaranteed of no ruts. Perhaps Aunt Pia would like to become involved in the horse racing business, who knows?"

"Let's talk about this later this evenin' with Pia. Let's see what she thinks. In the meantime, Shadow needs a good ride. He has not been ridden yet today."

"All right, Cooper, but will you promise to discuss this later?"

"I said I would, and I will. Now, get that horse saddled up and ride."

***

McKenna quickly saddled up Shadow and took him out along the northwest meadow, giving him nearly free reign. *My goodness*, she thought, *this horse can run.* Solomon could run just as fast… but then again, maybe not. *It is this breed,* she thought. *This horse was bred for endurance and speed, not for personal pleasure.* McKenna pulled up on the reins and allowed Shadow to trot down to the north pond.

"Okay, boy, let's step into this pond and cool off your feet. You can drink here, and I will get my weight off you for a bit."

"Isn't much weight to take off," a sly voice remarked.

McKenna spun around and saw a young man sitting astride a black stallion. He appeared to be her age, perhaps older, and quite stocky throughout the shoulders. His beard length indicated that he hadn't shaved in quite some time.

"Sir, you startled me. Who are you, and what are you doing here by the pond?"

"Is this private property, miss? Do I have to have permission from you to be here?" he asked with an impish smile.

"Permission from me? No. But you are riding on private property, and normally, one would go to the house and ask permission to ride on someone's land."

"Well, now, what are you going to do about that? Are you going to giddy-up and tell the owner of this farm? I don't see how that would happen. After all, that horse of yours looks tired."

"Not as tired as yours does. I'll tell you what; why don't you ride up to the house with me? Then you can ask permission to ride on this property. If the owner agrees, have at it. If the owner says no, I will escort you off with my tired horse."

"You are pretty saucy for a girl."

"You are pretty arrogant for a boy."

"I don't need permission to ride on my own land, miss."

"Oh, so now this is your land? And to whom would I be speaking?" she asked with hands on her hips.

"My name is Quaid Wells. Olympia Wells is my mother."

McKenna started to laugh. She didn't know whether to run up and pull Quaid off his horse and hug him or kick him in the shins.

"What's so funny? Did I say something to amuse you?" he asked as he trotted closer to McKenna.

"No, not at all. Allow me to mount Shadow, and I will ride up with you to the house."

"For a little thing, you sure do have a lot of sass."

"I have been told that before. Come on, I'll race you!" squealed McKenna as she turned her horse around. She kneed Shadow, and off he went, leaving Quaid Wells behind in the dust. McKenna was off Shadow and had him tethered by the time Quaid came cantering into view.

"My, oh my, this tired old horse put yours to shame, Mr. Wells. What took you so long?" McKenna chuckled as she walked into the foyer pulling her gloves off—one finger at a time.

"You never told me your name," said Quaid, as he quickly followed McKenna into the house.

"You never asked," she replied with a half turn.

Olympia came into view at that very moment and dropped the basket of flowers she had been carrying. "Oh, my Lord, it can't be! Quaid, is that really you?"

"Hello, Mother." Quaid stretched out his arms for his mother's embrace.

"Quaid, where did you come from? I didn't see you ride down the lane, and I was out by the rose fence."

"I came up and over by the north pond. It has been so long since I've seen the place, I wanted to ride past my favorite spot. That is where I happened upon this lovely creature."

"Well yes, dear, McKenna certainly is a lovely creature."

"McKenna?" he responded with a crunched wrinkle on his forehead.

"Why, yes, Cousin McKenna from Charleston, dear."

"Yes, Mother, I know where she is from. I just haven't seen her in a very long time," he muttered while he rubbed his chin.

McKenna was trying very hard to contain her laughter at Quaid's expense. He, on the other hand, was blushing.

"I want both of you to join me on the veranda for some lemonade and some of Percy's freshly baked tarts," Olympia said with a shrug of her shoulders. "Come along."

"Certainly, Aunt Pia. Quaid and I would love some lemonade and tarts," McKenna replied as she began to follow Olympia toward the porch. "Of course, the tarts are probably not as sour as the look on your face right now!" she whispered as she pulled Quaid's sleeve teasingly.

"You could have told me who you were," replied Quaid sternly, following so close behind her that he could smell the scent of jasmine in her hair.

"Again, you could have asked." McKenna left Quaid speechless as she walked ahead of him, opening the double doors leading to the sun porch.

"Are you coming, cousin?" McKenna asked tauntingly as she stopped and turned to look at Quaid.

"I will be right there, *cousin*," Quaid hollered back at her with a half-smile. He continued to watch McKenna as she sashayed onto the porch, plopping down in the oversized rocker. He couldn't help but notice how damn cute she was as she bit into her tart.

You sure did grow up to be a beauty, little cousin. I just might stay a little longer than I planned, now that I know that you are staying under the same roof as I am. This visit could prove to be riveting, to say the least.

Chapter 34

The days of October passed quickly at the Wells' Manor. Activity was buzzing everywhere, from the kitchen to the stable. This was a busy time inside the house, as the family began preparations for the fall months ahead. McKenna always thought that one could never really enjoy the current season because they were too busy preparing for the next one!

Parker had written several letters to McKenna informing her of his shipping whereabouts. As always, he reminded her how much he missed her, and what his intentions to do to her were once he returned. That was one strong characteristic of Parker; he did not mince words—he came straight to the point. She would often snuggle in her bed at night and reread the stack of letters he sent. Many a time McKenna would fall asleep with her letters spread about her only to wake the next morning and retrieve them from the floor. McKenna knew that Parker would be coming home soon, as long as the weather cooperated. Until then, she waited with mounting anticipation for the moment when she would once again be held within his arms. She desperately missed her Captain Sloane, and had to make a conscious effort not to show a loss of patience or manners in her aunt's home. She was starting to lose her patience with others and she knew it.

Uncle Pepper, on the other hand, after lengthy conversations, brightened McKenna's mood by successfully convincing Aunt Pia to build a race track; and what a fine track it was. Once word spread throughout the county that Olympia Wells was buying, breeding, and now racing horses, her stables were filling, and there was always a throng of buyers coming to and from the place.

Aunt Pia couldn't wait to have her incredibly loyal captain back home to manage the shipping of horses from England to the coastal harbors along the United States. The states needed horses, and if Pia could help deliver horses in the hopes of ending the war, she would.

Both ladies would soon get their wish for Captain Sloane's return, for he had sent word to Cooper that his ship had docked in the early morning hours. He would arrive before the evening meal if all went well with his business meetings. When Cooper told McKenna of the captain's approaching arrival plans, she simply could not focus on her tasks.

"McKenna, I would like you to stop cleaning those hooves, and take this new chestnut horse out to the track before the mid-afternoon sun gets too hot," Cooper finally said, catching McKenna daydreaming at work again. "Go easy with her, because she is anxious from the ride here. She may be jumpy, so be careful with her. I need you to tell me how she rides. Pia said she has a buyer for this horse, and he is willing to spend top-dollar."

"Well, that is wonderful news. What is her name?"

"Cinnamon."

"Well, Cinnamon, let's get acquainted on the track, shall we?"

McKenna put the lead rope on the mare and began walking her toward the starting line. She talked to Cinnamon in a soothing voice and gave her an apple along the way. However, McKenna noticed that Cinnamon seemed skittish and nervous. She checked the mare's girth and hooves and found nothing pinching or irritating.

Once she reached the track, she tied up her own hair and put on her cap. Then, she slowly and carefully mounted Cinnamon, anticipating the horse to bolt.

"All right, girl, let's see what you can do." McKenna gently nudged the horse into a slow trot. At every quarter mile, McKenna stopped Cinnamon and dismounted. She would then stand in front of the horse, slowly massage the head and neck area, and offer her a small carrot. As the horse began to calm, both she and McKenna took notice of the scenic meadows and the songs of the red-winged blackbirds. *This is a heavenly place to be*, McKenna thought, *no war, no battle, no hostility... just pure gratification between horse and rider.* She remounted and continued her pace around the track. They were rounding the last quarter-mile when someone shot off a gun.

Startled, Cinnamon bolted. McKenna barely managed to maintain her hold on the reins. *Damn, I should have worn gloves*, she scolded herself. She let the horse run. She had trained for this type of thing, and instead of fighting to force the horse to slow down, she crouched low over the animal's neck.

Time seemed to stand still. Never in her life had McKenna felt so exhilarated. Riding like the wind, feeling one with the horse beneath her, McKenna couldn't begin to describe how she felt in that exact moment. Cinnamon was sensational, and Sweet Mother of Jesus, could she run! She was not winded, nor was her breathing labored. McKenna had never seen another horse like her. Cinnamon began her second lap, and McKenna let her continue to run. Her canter was incredibly smooth; not favoring one side or the other.

***

"Cooper, where in hell did you get that horse?" asked an approaching rider.

Cooper turned, recognizing that voice, and saw Parker sitting astride his horse, his expression one of total amazement.

"Glad to have you back home, Captain Sloane!" exclaimed Cooper with an outstretched handshake to Parker. "Pia bought the horse. Ain't she a fine specimen?"

"I can't recall seeing such speed in an animal like that," Parker replied as he began to look around the area. "When did you build the track? My God, a lot sure has happened since I have left. Christ, I leave for six months and come home to an entirely new track and horses to boot. Coop, that horse is a fine specimen, but who's the rider?"

"The rider?"

"Yes, who's the rider? Whoever that is, he is doing an expert job of handling that horse, especially on the inside curves."

"You think so?"

"I know so."

"Well then, Captain, be sure to tell her."

"Her?"

"Yes, sir. Be sure to tell *McKenna* when she gets off that horse." Cooper laughed and slapped Parker on the knee, knowing full well that the Captain probably had the urge to kick him on his arse.

"McKenna? Why in the hell did you put her on that horse? She could bloody well break her neck, and you know it."

"I put her on that horse because she is the best rider here, and you bloody well know it! A minute ago, you admired the rider's skill, and now that you know it is McKenna, you are ready to wring her neck. Just watch her; she knows what she is doing. Hell, she ought to; I trained her."

"Cooper, by all that is holy, I ought to beat you to a pulp. How can you stand here and watch?"

"By all that is holy, *I* ought to wring *your* neck for not believing in me or my capabilities as a trainer. The day I tell you how to build a ship is the day you tell me how to train a horse and rider. Understood, pup?" Parker grimaced and rubbed his chin, knowing full well that Cooper was right.

"Understood. My apologies, Cooper. It just makes me nervous to watch her."

"Of course, it does. You have never seen her ride before. I am telling you, she could have done just as well ten years ago on a horse like that. She is that good. The only other rider who compares to her is you. Have a little faith in your 'kitten.'"

"The hell I will. She needs to be off that horse while she still has control. Pretty soon, that horse is going to run off the track, and when that happens, McKenna will not be able to stop her. The horse is not a trail horse; she is running from pure instinct from the gunshot. Once she figures out what freedom is, there is no telling what she may or may not do."

"McKenna will know when to rein her in, Parker. In fact, look at her now. She is slowin' down. McKenna knows how to transition carefully, so as not to injure the animal. I would say she handled Cinnamon quite well. In fact, I will lay odds that when she dismounts, she will come to me and demand that we buy more race horses."

"Now, why in God's name would she do that?"

"Well, it was her idea to put in the track, and Pia and I agreed to it. While you have been gone, McKenna thought that purchasin' race horses would be a lucrative venture, and it certainly has been! McKenna even wants to race horses for prize money."

"Over my dead body." Parker did not see the rider and horse trotting toward him from behind.

"Well, Captain Parker, I would prefer your body to be very much alive. But if you came home to scold me and chastise my ideas about horse racing, then you can just turn your stallion around and go back to your bloody *Constance*." McKenna rode right up to Parker, bringing Cinnamon neck to neck with his horse. "And one more thing, Captain. I missed you, and that was not a very nice way of saying hello. Shame on you for being so grouchy after six long months at sea. One would think you would be happy to see me, and even offer a proper hug and kiss."

McKenna dismounted and began to lead Cinnamon back to the stables before Parker could grab her for the kiss he had dreamed of giving her.

"Cooper, I am going to brush her down and give her some hay. Did you see this horse run? I gave her more lead on the inside turns than the outer turns. She favors her left side on the turn but balances out on the straightaway. She held her bit tightly, too tight for my liking, but I will work on this as we practice more. This is one marvelous animal. I am anxious to see who the buyer may be. I would be interested in breeding from this dam. Well, I'd better hurry. See you at supper. Oh, and by the way, Parker, lose your surly temper before you come to the table. I am hungry, and I don't want to lose my appetite sitting across from an irritable sea captain," she scolded as she walked to the stable. He could not help watch the sway of her hips in her riding habit, imagining how those hips would sway without clothing on.

"This conversation is not over, kitten. It *has* been a long six months," said Parker as he urged his horse forward, attempting to block her movement.

"Oh, you are right, Captain, this conversation is on hold. I have many bones to pick with you, and tonight is the perfect night for bone-picking; I can feel it. Now, get out of my way, and be prepared to answer any question I might have for you after supper."

"Oh, I will be ready, kitten. Just make sure you are ready to hear my answers," Parker answered as she sidestepped and led Cinnamon to the stable. Damn, he had missed her. What a foolish entrance he had made! Well, he would repair his mistake and have his little kitten purring by the end of the evening; he would make damn sure of that.

Chapter 35

Aunt Pia graciously held out a hand to the people sitting on either side of her at the evening meal. It was a rule in the Wells' home to hold hands while saying grace. Memories surfaced in McKenna's mind as she remembered putting her small hand into her father's larger one while saying grace back in Charleston. She would give anything to have her father sitting next to her now, but she knew it wasn't possible.

"Please, bow your heads," Olympia began. "Dear Lord, thank you for this meal and for those who have prepared it. Bless those who are seated at this table, and especially bless those who have traveled and are able to join us tonight. Thank you, Lord, for what you have given to us and for leading us to live in your way. In your Holy name we pray, Amen."

"Amen," repeated those seated at the table.

"Tell me about this new race track you have here and your newest addition of horses, Pia," asked Parker as he helped himself to a rather large serving of potatoes before he passed the bowl.

"Oh, Parker, I haven't felt this alive in years. I can't take credit for this, though; I am afraid the credit for the race track must go to McKenna!"

"Really? Now why doesn't that surprise me?" said Parker with a hint of sarcasm. He flashed McKenna a quick wink.

"Parker, I would love to go over the details with you and explain exactly what we have done to prepare for this new addition. How about tomorrow morning, you and I take a walk down to the track, and I will show you first-hand what we have done?"

"That's a wonderful idea, Pia. I look forward to being brought into the loop, so to speak."

"Well, Captain, had you been here, I would have shared my ideas and included you *in the loop*, so to speak, but you weren't here. So, I shared my thoughts with Cooper and Uncle Pepper before we approached Aunt Pia. I must say, it has been quite lucrative so far!" said McKenna as she licked the strawberry jam from her finger.

"Well, I am glad your plan has worked, my dear. I look forward to seeing and hearing about this track and its operation."

"Mother, who is this Doctor Withers I have been hearing about?" asked Quaid.

"Oh, Doctor Withers is an expert horse doctor and breeder. He has more knowledge in his little finger than all of us put together."

"You truly mean that?" Quaid asked warily while he dabbed the tablecloth of spilled gravy.

"Yes, Cousin Quaid, she does. In fact, I have been working with him, and I have learned a lot from him already," said McKenna between bites of her biscuit.

"So," asked Parker with a hint of skepticism, "where does this Withers man come from, Pia?"

"This Withers man is *Doctor* Withers, Parker, and he comes from Oxford. He is truly remarkable with horses and their breeding. In fact, he has taken McKenna under his wing, and I would imagine she will one day like to work with him full-time. Would that be a fair assumption, my dear?"

"It would be, Aunt Pia. I only hope he can teach me much more before he decides to retire." McKenna put her half-eaten biscuit back onto her plate and twirled her remaining food with her fork.

"What's wrong, kitten?" Parker feigned concern. "Not hungry? I see you are not eating much this evening."

"My mind is elsewhere, I guess. I am thinking about future conversations that need to be addressed this evening." McKenna gave Parker the sultriest look she could possibly manage. Not only was she toying with him, she had purposely worn a low-cut bodice to dinner to entice him, making sure she had sat directly across from him. *I wonder if he even notices my dress. He is more concerned about that darn race track than me.*

"McKenna, dearest, how old is this Doctor Withers?" Parker inquired.

"What's the matter, Captain? Are you jealous?" she paused before continuing, "I have been working with him every day from *morning 'til evening*," she answered with a tempting smile.

"Just answer the question, kitten," Parker commanded in a none-too-polite tone.

"I told you to stop calling me that." McKenna scrunched up her nose which made her all the cuter to Parker. He leaned back in his chair and boldly appraised McKenna's appearance, his gaze lingering on her partially-open dress bodice.

"McKenna, do you think the dress you are wearing is—?"

"Doctor Withers is Papa's age. There, now keep your thoughts to yourself. You are nothing more than an overgrown skunk, and you know it!" McKenna replied, unaware how far her voice had traveled.

"McKenna, whatever has gotten into you?" asked Pia with a startled voice.

"Excuse me, Aunt Pia. Captain Sloane was about to chastise me, and I stopped him before he could play his little game."

"My apologies, madam, if I have offended you, or you, Pia," Parker said quickly. "That was certainly not my intention. I was curious about this new doctor; nothing to worry about, I assure you."

"Aunt Pia, if it is all right with you, I would like to be excused for the evening," asked McKenna as she dabbed her mouth with her napkin.

"My dear, you have hardly touched your meal," Pia protested. "I know you must be hungry. At least eat a few more bites."

"Cousin, you do look a mite thin. You want to make sure you can fill out those dresses and riding habits, don't you? Personally, I like my women a bit fuller," Quaid added with a teasing smirk.

"Your women? Well, I am not one of your women!" McKenna snapped. "Have you looked in a mirror lately? Why don't you learn how to use a razor?"

Quaid bristled in response. "McKenna, one of these days, that sassy mouth of yours is going to get you thrown into a pool of water—just enough to cool you down. Wouldn't you agree, Captain Sloane? And I would enjoy being the one to do just that!"

"I couldn't agree more, Quaid. It seems to me that McKenna threw a pitcher of water at someone while sailing over here. Pepper, Zadie, do you remember that day?" Parker stared McKenna down with a winning smile.

Pepper laughed. "Sure do, Captain. McKenna got so riled up that she threw a pitcher of ice water onto the Captain," he announced, leaning over to snatch another biscuit for himself.

"Uncle Pepper, you can hush up, too. There is a pitcher on the side table over there, and I could easily douse you with it!" McKenna glared at him, then turned her look upon Quaid. "As for you, cousin, anytime you would like to race again, I will be sure to oblige. After all, I did beat you fairly."

"Careful," said Quaid with an impish smirk. "I will keep you to your promise, *cousin* dear. I owe you already for your little joke at my expense. I will repay the humor."

McKenna looked at Quaid with an expression that clearly said, 'not if you know what's good for you,' and replied, "Anytime you want to play, count me in."

"Looking forward to it," Quaid chuckled. *More than you know, little cousin.*

"As for you, Captain, when you are finished eating, I would like to talk with you about some matters that need to be addressed. However, I must first ask you if you have news from Charleston."

"Indeed, I do. In fact, I have news to share with all of you if you would be willing to listen."

Everyone seated at the table immediately agreed, stopped eating for the time being, and put their utensils down.

"All of you are fully aware that the United States is now at war, North against South. The North comprises Maine, New York, New Hampshire, Vermont, Connecticut, Rhode Island, Pennsylvania, New Jersey, Ohio, Indiana, Illinois, Kansas, Michigan, Wisconsin, Minnesota, Iowa, California, Nevada, and Oregon. The South comprises Alabama, Florida, Georgia, Louisiana, Mississippi, South Carolina, Texas, Arkansas, North Carolina, Tennessee, and Virginia.

"The border states include Delaware, Kentucky, Maryland, Missouri, and West Virginia. With that being said, you all need to understand what this war is encompassing. This has been a bloody war thus far, and too many soldiers on both sides have given their lives. You must understand that the North has manufacturing and access to cannon building and ammunition. The South has poor and rural farm boys, who are signing up for war just to protect their way of life and send money home to their folks."

"Captain Parker?" Caleb interrupted.

"Yes, Caleb?"

"When will this war end?"

"Only God knows the answer to that, Caleb. I would imagine that General Lee and President Lincoln never thought it would last this long. Miss Reed, until this war ends, any desire you may have of returning home is out of the question. I will certainly keep you apprised of any further news I receive."

"Thank you, Captain. I know I can't return home right now. But I would like to sail with you when you deliver horses."

"That may come to a stop for a while, too. You see, the North has blockaded the ports along Charleston's coastal areas. My docking rights may be unattainable for quite some time," Parker stated calmly.

"How long would that be? I would still like to deliver horses," asked Pia.

"That is understandable, Pia, but not safe. If I may, just who are you selling your horses to?"

"Anyone who will buy them," she answered in between sips of water.

"Pia, if you plan on selling horses to the Southern armies, I am afraid your shipments will never arrive—the Northern blockades will use your animals as they see fit."

"Aunt Pia, are you saying you would sell horses to the Northern soldiers as equally as you would to the soldiers in the South?" asked McKenna with a serious tone to her voice.

"I am saying that there are currently too many cross breeds in America. My buyers are seeking thoroughbreds due to their speed. I am not taking sides, McKenna. I just want to sell as many horses as I can. It matters not to me if my horses end up on Northern or Southern soil. I am a business woman and I will sell my horses to whomever needs them, or whomever has the money to pay for them," Pia said with assertive confidence as she placed her elbows on the table, almost offering a silent dare to those opposed.

"I see," answered McKenna with a hint of hesitancy.

"Correct me if I am wrong, but your father is working as an Army surgeon and his job is to provide comfort and his medical knowledge to any solider, regardless if that uniform is blue or gray. Now then, if my horses can help a soldier to live another day, transport an injured company officer, or deliver meals or supplies to those in need, then by God, I will sell them to whomever needs them. I am not drawing sides; I am trying to help both." Pia sighed a breath of acknowledgement before she scooted her chair away from the table.

"Pia, I would suggest you strengthen your horse business with neighboring counties in England and adjacent countries, at least for the time being. I can't guarantee what the conditions are for your horses once they arrive by sea. But I can guarantee the travel conditions if you sell to your local neighbors. I understand Ireland has some lucrative horse races near Balmoral. Who knows, you may foster another Diomed or Glencoe!" Parker encouraged.

"Wouldn't that be something? I will certainly give it some thought, Captain Sloane. You are right, of course; I would rather my horses be able to perform as they were bred for rather than suffer due to poor ship conditions, or even worse housing conditions in a war-torn land. I'd like to discuss this further with you, if I may, Parker. Perhaps we could set aside some time tomorrow? Now then, for the rest of you, I suggest you call it an evening, but not before we thank the captain for his news."

"My pleasure, Olympia. I hope further updates will continue from McKenna's father. But I would not be surprised if the mail slows down or even comes to a complete stop. Miss Reed, when you are ready for me, I shall make my way to the library." Parker smiled.

You are a devil, thought McKenna. The way he said *when you are ready for me* had caused several people at the dining table to raise their eyebrows. *If he thinks he has the last chess piece to play, he has another thing coming!* McKenna nodded and smiled at Parker, a warning look upon her face.

After the supper table was cleared and all the dirty dishes were taken to the kitchen for washing, the children and cousins departed and went to their rooms while the adults scurried to the porch for a late-night cigar.

When McKenna and Parker were the only two remaining at the table, she cleared her throat to get his attention while she scooted from the table and stood.

Parker looked up from petting Knox and asked, "Well, my dear, as I said, I will await you in the library. Is that a suitable place to 'bone-pick?'"

"Let's do our bone-picking in private. Let's go into Pia's office, where we can discuss things behind thick, wooden doors."

"I would love to be behind thick, wooden doors with you, kitten," he said in his husky voice as he pushed his chair in and approached McKenna.

"Don't get your hopes up, Captain. I have a lot of questions for you to answer," McKenna whispered a bit louder than usual, stretching her hands in front of her and onto Parker's chest in a weak attempt to stop Parker's progression.

"Well then, I will do my best to answer them very quickly, while the night is still young," he replied, clasping her hands in his with a mischievous look upon his face.

"Captain, your eyes are filled with lust. Don't you think for one second that you can sail on home, holler at me on the track, toy with me at supper, and then expect me to swoon all over you and ravenously kiss your very being!"

"Oh, I don't expect you to ravenously kiss me, kitten. I intend to ravenously kiss you. Here and now." Parker's lips were on McKenna's before she could utter a sound. His kiss was deep and demanding, passionate and lustful. McKenna knew she was entangled in Parker Sloane's hardiness and quite frankly, she didn't want to leave his muscled forearms, which were taking far too many liberties at the moment, caressing along her ribcage and lower breasts.

"Parker," she uttered between his kissing fervor, "we need to move to the office. Honestly, you are acting like a rutting pig."

"My apologies, my dear, six months is a very long time to be away from you." His last kiss was a bit possessive, knowing all too well he was reinforcing his previous statement.

Chapter 36

Parker followed McKenna into Pia's office and closed the massive office doors while McKenna lit the oil lamps. She strode to the large bay window and pressed her fingers against the cold pane.

"The chill in the air tells me that the snowflakes are already announcing their forthcoming presence, Captain. I fear that our winter snow is right around the corner." McKenna swayed to the far oval window to observe the colors of the sky. "I always liked this time of evening when I was a little girl," she said. "No more work for the day, and that meant time for relaxation and reading with Papa. Oh, how I miss him." A familiar lump started forming in her throat. *Good God, don't cry now, not in front of Parker. This is not the time to be emotional. I need to stand firm. Breathe*, she thought. *Big, deep breaths.*

"McKenna, what are the questions that you have been harboring?"

McKenna turned from the window and walked toward Parker. She came to a stop in front of him and looked up into his eyes. Her chest was rising and falling, indicating the anxiety slowly spreading over her entire body.

"Captain, what I am about to say is difficult and somewhat frightening for me," McKenna said with a slight tremble. She was rubbing her fingers quite rapidly, biting her lip, and clearing her throat all at the same time, showing Parker how badly her nerves were getting the better of her.

He took her tiny, trembling hands and gently raised them to his mouth, where he placed a kiss upon each one. "Kitten, tell me what's on your mind. Clearly, something is troubling you. What is it?" McKenna took a big breath before she spoke.

"Parker, I know that you were asked to bring me over to England. I also know that you did this as a favor for Uncle Pepper."

"Yes, that is correct. Go on…"

"Well, somewhere between Charleston and England, I became attracted to you. In fact, even though we verbally challenged each other, I looked forward to seeing you. I was rather sad on the days when I didn't get to see you. I would go out of my way to ensure that I did see you. Oh my, I am making a mess of this conversation. What I am trying to say is that somewhere between Charleston and England, I fell in love with you."

Parker didn't move.

"Say something, Parker… for Christ's sake, I just poured my heart out to you and now you stand as still as a statue holding my hands… oh dear Lord, you don't feel the same way, do you? Oh, my heavens, I have just told you that I loved you, but you can't return those feelings, can you?"

Parker's lips were on hers so fiercely that she didn't have time to think.

His hands pulled her tiny waist against his chest, easily spanning it with one hand while the other hand wrapped itself in McKenna's mass of golden curls. His kiss was demanding, all-knowing, filled with a possessive emotion that McKenna felt heating her entire body. Just when she was ready to succumb to her weak-kneed position, he pulled away from her and cupped her lovely face within his hands.

"Kitten, I am in love with you. I am not sure if I was ensnared by you on the dock when we first met or when I removed the sliver from your cute little chin. Regardless of the moment, you have captured my heart, kitten, and that is something that I am not ashamed to tell you. Do not be frightened, my love; I am in love with you as much as you are in love with me."

"Truly? You are not just saying this?" she asked with tears forming in her beautiful blue eyes.

"No, love, I would never 'just say' those words, not unless I truly meant them," Parker replied, not letting go of her chin. "I must admit that I wasn't very enthused to bring your dog and horse and a black woman over here, but now, I sure as hell am glad that I did. I had to medicate both animals just to get them to remain calm while on board, especially Knox. He was very anxious, according to my sailors. But I would not expect less. I know how frightened Lyla becomes when she sails with me."

"Lyla? Who is that?" McKenna asked while stepping back from Parker's embrace and slowly sitting down into an overstuffed settee.

"Kitten, she is the most beautiful dog you ever want to meet. I can't wait for Knox to meet my girl. Who knows, they may find an attraction just as we have."

"Well, Captain, you know they could become so attracted to each other that my South Carolina boy might just be tempted to copulate with your aristocratic English bitch. Wouldn't that be something? I bet the puppies would be adorable, though!" smiled McKenna.

"Puppies? Hell, no, Lyla does not need to mate with any oversexed dog and go through puppy birth. I would be afraid that the whole ordeal might kill her."

McKenna giggled and pulled Parker down upon the settee, next to her. "My dear captain, giving birth is natural. If my dog is attracted to your dog, we will just have to wait and see what occurs. But you certainly would not let that overbearing, pompous attitude of yours deprive Lyla of the passion of breeding now, would you?"

Parker clutched McKenna's wrist in his large, calloused hand. "McKenna, I would never deny anyone the opportunity to witness or experience the passions of breeding. However, I am not so sure that you or I are able to raise and train puppies if that opportunity presented itself to the both of us. For the time being, I will monitor my dog's actions, as I would encourage you to do as well. Next question?"

"Well, speaking of the 'passions of breeding,' would you like children one day?"

"I have never thought much about it."

"Well, think about it right now. What is your immediate response?"

"Would you?"

"Captain, you are avoiding my question." Parker leaned back and drew McKenna's wrist to his lips, softly placing kisses down the length of her forearm. "Yes, kitten, I want children someday. I want to love and hug them and watch them grow."

"How many children?"

"Well, little one, I need a wife first, don't you think?" Parker paused, staring intently at McKenna's beautiful face, before he asked his question. "Would you like children?"

"Play fair, Captain, this is my night for questions. But to answer you, yes, I would like children—lots of them."

"Bloody hell," Parker whispered under his breath as he smiled and looked away. How proud he would be to take McKenna as his wife and see her one day carrying his child. He was so lost in thought, he didn't hear McKenna's next questions.

"Parker, you are doing it again. Please pay attention and answer my question," she repeated herself as she tapped on his shoulder.

"I am sorry, my dear, what did you say?"

"I asked you if you had ever thought about marriage and children, and if you had, where would you settle down and live: England or America?"

"I never really thought about the location of a future home. I would have to give that question a great deal of thought. This is my home, and I might want to stay here and raise my family in England."

I would stay here with you, too, she thought. *Your eyes are the prettiest green I have ever seen. Our babies would be beautiful—a little of me and a little of you—oh my, they would be darling.*

"McKenna, where is that mind of yours? Now who is not listening to who?" he asked while nibbling on her loose hand she had laid upon her lap.

Parker asked the question so smoothly that McKenna answered without thinking.

"I was just thinking that our babies would be beautiful, absolutely gorgeous."

"Well, kitten, to have babies, we must be in the position to make them."

Parker watched the horror creep up on McKenna's blushing cheeks as she realized what she had just stated aloud. *I'm a lucky man to have her within my grasp*, he thought.

McKenna stood and walked toward the fireplace. She placed her hands in front of the fire, rubbing them together to ward off the chill in the room. She slowly turned and pressed a wrinkle from her skirt before she spoke.

"Parker, please forgive me. Sometimes, I speak without thinking. I am sorry if I was too audacious with my words."

Parker rose and stood before McKenna, wrapping his arms around the small of her back. "No forgiveness is necessary, my dear. There is nothing more I would like to do than to make babies with you. But being a gentleman, I see that I will have to take things slowly with you and not compromise your virtue until there is a formal proposal and engagement announced."

"I didn't mean I was asking you to marry me. Oh, no, I didn't mean that at all. The man is supposed to do that all on his own. Oh, I have made a mess of things. It is just that you are so handsome, and you like the things that I like, and sometimes, I just can't stop staring into those green eyes of yours, and—"

"Stop talking, kitten."

She obeyed. One of Parker's hands encircled her waist while he tilted her chin up with two fingers from the other.

"McKenna, you did not make a mess of anything. Your honesty is what I love most about you. You say things purely from the heart, my dear. You do not sugarcoat your words, and I love that quality."

"Captain Sloane, I am not finished asking my questions." Her words came out in barely a whisper.

"Yes, you are." Parker kissed McKenna fiercely. He had wanted to do this ever since he had returned to England's coast. He pulled away from her swollen lips and brushed a stray curl from her brow.

"When I saw you on that horse, I almost lost my head. I was afraid for you, afraid you would get hurt, or worse yet, get killed from an ill-fated accident from that horse's speed. I have wanted to hold you in my arms, and until now, I was not given the chance. Well-planned, kitten; this little meeting of ours was my golden opportunity."

"Parker?"

"Yes, kitten?"

"I missed you so much. I just want to be held in your arms. I feel safe when you hold me."

"I will hold you for all eternity, kitten. I will be here for you this evening and for all the evenings ahead of us."

"Promise?"

"Till the day I die."

"I look forward to spending many more days with you as well, getting to know you even better."

Parker chuckled to himself and lowered his mouth to hers in a sensuous kiss. *I enjoy spending many more days and* nights *with you as well, kitten*, he thought.

Chapter 37

"Gone? Gone where? What do you mean, you can't find her?" Parker shouted at Pia with such intensity that the whole stable yard could hear him.

"Parker, she received a letter from Charleston at breakfast, and it upset her so much that she ran to her room. I thought she just needed time to cry or deal with her homesickness, but it is nearly midafternoon and no one has seen her. She hasn't done any riding with the horses, and Knox and Solomon are both gone."

"What was in that letter, Pia?"

"I don't know. I suppose it may be up in her room yet. Let's go see."

"You go and search for that letter, Pia. I am going down to the docks. If I know McKenna as well as I think I do, she is bound to catch the next sailing vessel home."

"Oh, my Lord, she wouldn't do anything foolish, would she?" Pia's distress was evident in her face. Her ashen coloring was spreading down to her neck.

Parker placed both hands upon her shoulders and gave her a comforting squeeze.

"Hard telling what the chit would do when she gets something in her mind. Now listen carefully, Pia. When you have searched her room, saddle up, and bring Pepper, Cooper, and the boys with you. I don't want you riding alone to the docks."

"All right, I will see you there," said Pia, visibly shaken.

***

Parker hurried and saddled his horse. *Damn little fool*, he thought. Something must have happened to Harper, and McKenna was going home. He knew it had to be urgent, or she would have asked him to sail her home on the

Constance. What in bloody hell was she thinking? She could get into a lot of trouble alone at the docks. It was no place for a woman, especially a golden-haired beautiful woman. Hopefully, he could intervene and catch her before she left the harbor.

***

Pia took two steps at a time up the grand staircase toward McKenna's room, meeting Zadie along the way. Together, they frantically searched her room.

"Oh, Olympia, that stubborn girl is gonna git herself into trouble; I can just feel it in my bones!" said Zadie as she looked under the bed.

"Zadie, I hope this is one time when your bones are imagining their ailment. What would possess her to run like this? Certainly, she could have asked for our help."

"You know McKenna. When she gets a notion in her head, she runs with it, and there ain't no stoppin' her."

"I hope Parker can get to her before any trouble crosses her path. Where could she have put that blasted letter? Let's walk through her actions. She would get her valise and pack. Then she would tidy up and fix her hair. Zadie, look in her armoire, and I will look over by her hairbrush."

Pia frantically pushed aside the items littering McKenna's vanity, but had no luck. *Where did you lay that letter?* As she was about to give up hope, she spotted a corner of something white folded underneath a damp washcloth. "Look, Zadie!" She snatched it up and unfolded it, careful not to tear the wet parchment.

McKenna,

Your father has suffered a serious injury. He was accidentally shot in the back by a group of Charlestonian soldiers, then fell off his horse and hit his head quite hard. He survived the gunshot wound, but we are concerned that this fall may have damaged his brain. He has not regained consciousness since the incident. I would advise you to come home and see your Papa; time is of the essence.

Doctor Orson

"Oh, my Lord. She has run to the docks to go home. Parker was right. Zadie, what if she gets into trouble? You know what kind of thieves and filthy men congregate down there!"

Zadie took Pia by the elbows and grasped tightly. "Now you listen to me, Pia Wells. Our McKenna will be all right. She has that dog with her, she is on Solomon, and if I know her, she has her pistol tied to her thigh and her rifle in her saddlebag. She knows how to take care of herself. Shucks, she'll probably ride that horse right onto the gangplank of the nearest ship."

"You are not doing a very good job of convincing me," whispered Pia.

"Come on, now, you gather up the boys and ride down to the docks like Parker said. Go on, now. I'll stay here in case she comes home. If that happens, I will send word to you."

Pia tried to be calm, but Zadie knew she was a shaking mess.

"Go on, now—no time for tears, Olympia."

Once Pia left the room, Zadie kneeled by the bed and recited as many prayers as she could. *Dear Lord*, she thought, *allow my baby girl to remain safe and strong within your power. Please, Lord, do not let her lose her father. I fear she would not be able to take the loss of both parents.* Zadie silently rested her head on the edge of McKenna's bed and wept.

Chapter 38

Parker had reached the docks and was searching for any sign of his golden-haired beauty. *It's busy today*, he thought. *Where in hell is she?* Parker went into the shipping office and climbed the steps to the observation roof. He frantically scanned the scene before him. Mixed crowds of sailors and passengers were waiting for the shipments to be loaded; it was too difficult to distinguish any individual clearly. Those loading boxes were bumping into each other, while others waiting to board were juggling luggage in-between carriages and skittish horses. The noise of the crowds made it impossible for Parker to hear his kitten's familiar voice or for him to possibly shout her name if he spotted her. Parker began to sweat beads of desperation. What if something terrible had already happened to her? At least, she would have that damn dog with her, and he would protect her, hopefully. For now, Knox was the only comforting thought he could hang on to.

Look for Solomon, Parker thought. He scanned the open wharves. *Where was she?* Parker turned and looked toward the ticket office for American passages.

My God, that's it; she's there. She would be there, purchasing her passage ticket. Parker ran down the stairs, through the office, and across the cobbled streets to the American passage office. She was not there. His only recourse was to walk toward the docks and hope to God he could spot her. He spun around and left the ticket office.

As he walked the muddied path, he took a shortcut behind the adjacent building, and through the vacant loading office, avoiding the congestion of crowds ahead. His breath stopped short as he peered straight and into the empty room.

Before him stood McKenna, clutched within the arms of what appeared to be the devil himself. Her right cheek was reddened and marked by a handprint. Her bruising upper arms were tied tightly behind her. The riding jacket she had worn was torn from collar to sleeve. Her captor stood behind her with a knife held tightly to her creamy white throat. To his left was Knox, behind a makeshift wall of chairs. To his right was the second assailant, with his gun pointed at the dog's neck.

"Well, look what just walked in here, missy," sneered the man holding McKenna as his beady eyes roved over Parker. "Looks like some man wants to be a big hero."

"Get your filthy hands off me," shouted McKenna as she squirmed in her bindings. "You have no right to touch me, much less talk to me."

McKenna was so obviously angry that her labored breathing caused her breasts to rise and fall against the torn fabric. One quick move, and that fabric would wrest away from her chest, exposing bare breasts for all to view. Parker saw where her assailant's eyes were diverting, and he knew he was running out of time before the thug would indulge in the view presented before him. McKenna's attacker tightened the knife against her skin, causing a small trickle of blood to appear.

"You need to shut your mouth, pretty bitch. I admire your stubborn streak, but it will do you no good," half-whispered her assailant.

"You need to put that knife away," stated Parker calmly, never taking his eyes off McKenna's attacker. "It would seem that you chose the wrong lady to attack this morning. It would also appear that you are out of your element. In fact, you have no idea who you are dealing with."

"Well, now, why don't you just turn around, leave, and mind your own business? The little lady and I were just about to have some fun."

"That little lady is my business. You should have stayed in the gutter that you crawled out of this morning. Unfortunately, you won't be returning to it. Your miserable life will be ending soon."

"Is that right? I can tell ya' right now that my life ain't ready to end just yet. The little lady wouldn't give me what I wanted, so I figured I'd take it. When I am done with her, you can have my leftovers. The way I see things, mister, is that I'm holdin' the gun, and you ain't."

***

McKenna's heart pounded against her chest. It had been easy to be defiant toward her attacker when it was just her own life at stake, but now Parker was here, and the thought of that gun being pointed at his face made her blood run cold. *I have to do something*, she thought fiercely, and gathered every ounce of Southern charm she could into her voice, hoping it wouldn't betray her trembling. "I have an idea. Why don't you take that knife away from my throat? If you untie me, I will show you how a little lady such as myself can please a man like you—American-style. I bet you have never had an American woman kiss you before, have you?"

"You shut your mouth, my little beauty. I have more than kissing in mind."

"Kissing is a start, isn't it? I promise I will be soft and gentle with you. Whatever you would like me to do, I will do for you," replied McKenna with a forced smile.

The attacker pulled the knife away from McKenna's throat and slid the pointed end down her blouse. The material ripped slowly.

"This is a start, honey; now, why don't you show me how you kiss while I look at these American tits of yours."

McKenna's breasts were entirely exposed to the dirty hands of her attacker. He palmed her left breast and squeezed her nipple until she cried out. Then he put his mouth to her other breast and sucked, drawing another cry of alarm from McKenna.

"I can't kiss you with my hands tied," she said urgently. "I need at least one hand to hold your chin and my other hand... well, you know what that's going to hold."

Son of a bitch! What is she doing? Parker thought. *The little fool is going to get herself killed or raped.* Parker knew she wanted her hands free so she could grab that damn pistol tied to her leg. *How in holy hell am I going to get that gun away from Knox's head and that knife from McKenna's throat? Think, damn it...*

"What about your fella over there? Is he going to watch?" asked the man holding her.

"I'm not worried about him right now; I'm focusing on you. Untie my hands, and we shall begin. Oh, please tell your man to stop pointing his gun at my dog. I can't please you if I am worrying about Knox. I am quite sure you are more than ready to be pleased. No more words now... just action."

"You heard her. Walk away from the dog. Better yet, sit over here in this chair." McKenna's captor turned toward his partner as he spoke in a voice shaking with anticipation. He jerked his chin toward Parker. "Keep a gun on him. He is too big, and I don't trust him. If he makes one wrong move, kill him."

The second man walked warily toward Parker. He motioned for Parker to sit down in the chair.

"I think not. I prefer to stand," said Parker with a controlled level of hostility in his voice. He sized up his opponent and knew that one punch to his head would render him useless. In that instant, Parker saw Quaid and Pepper crouching outside, just to the right side of the building's window, and Cooper and Livingston standing on the left side of the window. *They are careless*, he thought, *the reflection of their pistols will shine in here*. But with any luck, those four would be able to assess the situation and act as one, regardless of any reflection.

The man holding McKenna untied her ropes and pressed her back against his chest. The tearing of material ignited Parker's temper. McKenna bent forward, intentionally pressing her bottom into her attacker. He leered and gathered the fabric around her hips in his fist, pulling her skirt up away from her legs, but that was what McKenna had been waiting for. In a flash, she wrenched the pistol from her leg and spun, and her attacker fell to the ground in bewilderment and pain as the butt of her pistol collided with the side of his head.

The second man was distracted by the chaos for just a moment, and that's all it took for Parker to lunge forward and seize his rifle, yanking it out of his hands and spinning it to point directly at his face. "You filthy swine," Parker hissed. "The only woman you will ever come near again will be the one in your dreams."

"My, my, Captain Sloane," McKenna said with rapid breathing. Her clothing was ripped and tattered and her golden hair was disheveled, but she was grinning wildly as she pointed her pistol at the lowlife who cowered on the ground before her. "I suppose you really do care about me after all." She warily walked toward her dog and removed the wall of chairs, allowing her best friend freedom from his makeshift containment.

"Don't be silly, kitten," whispered Parker with a hint of a smile in return as he glanced at her, one eye still on the second attacker. "You and I both know I care about you more than anything."

Parker noticed McKenna's feeble movements with Knox. As much as she tried to show her strength, she was losing her balance and strength from the rough treatment of her attacker.

Parker and McKenna quickly turned, weapons aimed, as Pia and the boys entered the office with the local authorities, who quickly assessed the scene and handcuffed McKenna's attackers.

"Oh, dear God, what did he do to her?" Pia looked at McKenna's battered body leaning heavily upon the abandoned desk. Her hand came to her mouth as if to stop a scream.

Parker gingerly gathered a semi-conscious McKenna into his arms and laid her on the table top that Cooper had righted into position. He checked her body from head to toe, acknowledging her winces of pains. Her jacket was cut in half. Her blouse was macerated, and her chemise was hanging from her body in tattered pieces of cotton. A handprint and teeth marks marred her breasts, and ugly bruises were beginning to form. Pia quickly laid her shawl over McKenna's exposed chest. Her throat was bleeding from a small puncture, and the top of her ribcage was deeply scratched. McKenna had fought her attacker before Parker had even arrived, according to the large bruise forming under her left ribcage.

Parker carefully ran his fingers through her hair, feeling for any cuts, when his fingers felt a lump behind her left ear. *This will be a good-sized bruise, from the feel of it*, Parker thought. No broken bones, though; her body would mend, but her mind and heart would take time to repair.

"My God, he didn't…?" asked Cooper.

"No, he didn't have time," said Parker. "Had we not arrived when we did, he would have completed his intention."

"How the hell did she get him to cut her ties?" asked Pepper.

"The little fool told him she would show him how an American woman kisses. The whole time she was plotting to reach down and grab that pistol of hers. She is damn lucky. The scum caught on to what she was up to just before she knocked him unconscious with the butt of her pistol."

"You mean to say, she knocked him out?" Cooper asked Parker with a questioning look upon his face. He scratched his head and rubbed his stubble. "Damn, I am not surprised she fought back."

"Nor am I. Still, I ought to kill him now," Quaid whispered with determination.

"We all should, but it wouldn't do any good. It is almost as though he knew she would be here. Your typical thief and scum do not mill around a vacant ticket office," replied Parker. "We will find out more once McKenna is rested and able to talk with us."

"Well, she won't be going anywhere on that horse for a while. And when she does, she remains on the property, and she rides with an escort," said Cooper confidently.

"Coop is right," stated Quaid. "She needs to be escorted by one of us at all times. This is one time that little Cousin McKenna will obey and accept the rules."

"We'll discuss this later; let's get her home," said Parker. "We have had enough excitement and fright for one day. Boys, make sure no one follows us home. I want to make sure there were no lookouts working for these thugs. Cooper, get the horses. Pepper, do what needs to be done with the authorities. Listen to what you may hear in that office. I am sure one of these pieces of scum will awaken shortly and blurt out whatever he can to save his own neck. Pia, stop pacing, and walk out with me. Let's wrap McKenna up in a rug. I will carry her over my shoulder as though I were carrying a large shipment. The less of a spectacle we make, the better."

"Parker, you'd better hope she doesn't wake up while you have her tossed over your shoulder."

"Pia, if that happens, that will be the least she has to worry about. I still owe her a scolding for running off the way she did. And believe me, it will come."

"Parker, you can't be serious! She thought her father was going to die! There is a letter back home that was given to McKenna. It indicated that her father had been shot. She was just trying to hurry home before he worsened or passed away. Please Parker, she was scared."

"Letter? Who wrote it? How did it get into McKenna's hands? Pia, what would have happened if I would not have found her? Just because she was scared was no reason to run off to the wharves by herself. You know that as well as I do."

"I know that, Parker. But sometimes, fear overtakes common sense. In this case, McKenna panicked and she ran. I am not so sure I wouldn't have done the same thing."

"Christ, Pia, I would hope you would not have done the same thing. She didn't think, she just ran. That choice was dangerous and it almost cost her life, not to mention her virtue."

"Let's talk about this when we get home, Parker. Please, for my sake, go easy on her. She has been through a lot." Pia continued walking to the tethered horses and helped Parker hoist his rolled package onto his horse. Once they were out of sight, he would unbind his little beauty and get her home and tend to her wounds. Once she was feeling better, they would have a talk. By God, this time she would be the one listening and he would be the one talking. Come hell or high water, she would listen, he would make sure of it.

Chapter 39

The day after McKenna's attack, she woke with a blurred memory. But as her family entered her bedroom and conversation continued, the past day's events with her assailants came back to her.

"McKenna, do you understand what I have just told you?" McKenna was not happy, as shown by the pout upon her face.

"You can't be serious! I can't ride Solomon without one of you riding with me? This is not acceptable! I won't abide by your rules, Parker Sloane!" she shouted as she threw a small pillow at him.

"You will abide by these rules, and these rules will remain in place until further notice. We were worried about you, and we all know what can happen at the docks. A young, pretty lady never walks down to the harbor without an escort or possibly two. We know about your father's letter because your Aunt Pia and Zadie found it. We all understand why you felt you needed to go home, but the way in which you left was entirely wrong and dangerous. You did not think of yourself, and you sure as hell didn't think of your dog."

"That's not fair, Parker. I would never do anything to harm Knox, and you know that—all of you do."

"Well, my dear, when I entered that abandoned ticket office, you were not in control of the situation. You had been slapped, hit, held at knifepoint, cut, mauled, and accosted by river scum. You were lucky. **And**, I might add, your dog was confined—no help to you!" Parker moved over to the side of her bed and sat in the wing chair. He leaned forward and looked directly into McKenna's eyes with a somber, stone-faced expression.

"Listen to me carefully, McKenna. Until we understand the reason these men attacked you, you will not ride alone on this property or anywhere else."

"You do not think this was a mere coincidence?" she asked.

"No, none of us do," Pepper answered. "In fact, I did some nosing around at the authorities' office. It appears that an older man had hired these thugs to follow you for quite some time. They have been riding out here to the manor and watching you."

"But why? Who are these men?" she asked nervously.

"We have their names, and they are nothing more than river scum. They were asked to scare you out of England and encourage you to return to America. The letter you received from your father was a fake. The man who held you at knifepoint admitted that to the authorities."

"Oh, thank God. I was so upset when I read the letter that I barely took a breath before I packed and left. I didn't mean to hurt or worry any of you. It was just frightening for me, and I wanted to get home to Papa. I thought he was going to die, and I was afraid I would never have the chance to say good-bye to him." Tears welled up in McKenna's eyes.

Pia walked to McKenna's bed and wrapped her in a comforting embrace. "McKenna, dear, you are home now, and you are safe. We all worried about you, and we worried about Harper, as well. We will find the underlying cause of this. Someone will talk—it is just a matter of time. Right now, you need your rest. You will listen to Parker, and you will heed his orders. Until we understand the motive involved, you are to remain under a vigilant eye. We all love you, and we will do everything in our power to protect you."

"Thank you, Aunt Pia. You know I love you and will honor your wishes."

"I know, dear, now lay your head down and rest. As for everyone else, say your good-byes to McKenna, and allow her to get some sleep." Pia gently kissed her on the brow and left the room.

One by one, the rest of the family followed her, each embracing McKenna tightly on the way out. Finally, Zadie sat down upon the bed and gently clasped McKenna to her bosom.

"Baby girl, I am so glad you are back home safe. Don't you ever do anythin' like this again. Next time somethin' goes wrong, you come and find ol' Zadie, and we will figure out what to do together. You hear?"

"I hear you, Zadie. I love you, and I am sorry I scared you." McKenna held on to Zadie for a moment longer before letting her go. Zadie placed a kiss upon her forehead and quietly left the room.

McKenna looked at Parker, the only person left in the room. *Oh, no, here comes the tongue-lashing*, McKenna thought. *I know I deserve it, but please do not be hard on me. I am too emotional, and I don't want to be a crybaby in front of you. Not now, not today.*

"Parker, I am sorry I ran off the way I did. I'm also glad you were there to rescue me. Please understand that I didn't consider the possible dangers, I just acted. And for that, I am sorry. Please, don't stay mad at me." McKenna reached up for a hug with both arms stretched open. Parker rose from the chair and sat on the edge of the bed, gathering McKenna against his chest.

"Kitten, I damn near lost my mind when I saw that knife pointed at your throat. It took every ounce of self-control I had not to tear that man in two. I had no weapon except my hands, and I had no reason to trust what he would do with that knife against your throat. Yes, I am infuriated that you would be so foolish. I thought you were smart enough to not run off alone, and I thought you would reach out to your family and ask for help, because that is what families do.

"But you and your stubborn pride and foolish thinking almost cost you your virtue and your life. Shame on you! You will follow the rules for the time being, do you understand me?"

"Yes, I do understand," sobbed McKenna. "Parker?"

"What?" he asked with an agitated tone to his voice.

"Please, hold me for a little while longer. I am scared, and I have nightmares of that man's hands on me."

"I will hold you, kitten, until you fall asleep."

"Please keep a light on."

"I will."

"Promise me you won't leave until I fall asleep?"

"I promise, kitten."

McKenna snuggled down into her quilted covers and held tightly on to Parker's hand. Her tiny fingers would never reveal to a stranger the strength and courage she truly had. He had been proud of her strategy to divert that knife away, but he would not tell her that now. That would have to wait for a very long time; she was not about to get any comment that remotely resembled a compliment.

He had a suspicion he knew who was behind this scandal, and he hoped to God he was wrong. However, if he were right, this house and those who lived in it would be faced with a whole new adversary. An adversary who would fight with fierce determination and relentless skill. This challenger would prove to be a worthy combatant. If Parker were right, this opponent would have nothing to lose. Those types of foes were always the most dangerous and the most formidable.

Chapter 40

The Thanksgiving and Christmas holidays gloriously passed at the Wells' Manor House. Once again, the spirit of the season had graced itself upon the family. The lighthearted New Year's Eve resolutions had been declared by the children, and thus far, many resolutions had already been broken. Pia chose not to entertain another New Year's Eve Ball, but rather enjoy a quiet evening with the family. The winter had proven to be mild in snowfall and temperature, making the days pass quickly. Spring of '62 was approaching, and McKenna could not believe she had been in England for so long. Soon, another year would pass, and 1863 would be knocking at the door.

The morning had passed quietly and McKenna had finished her chores rather quickly, so she decided to take a moment for herself and sit by her bedroom window—one of her favorite places. Her mind wandered as she peered over the rolling landscape. *When would the war end?* she asked herself. Would it be tomorrow, or even better, would it be tonight? Would Lee's soldiers and Grant's soldiers come to some form of agreement? Would President Lincoln end this killing soon? She wanted to go home and see her father and friends. Yet, here by the window, the calm of England had enveloped her in a feeling of tranquility. One would never know the atrocities of death continuing across the vast ocean in the States. The beauty of the undisturbed meadows continued to plague McKenna's mind as of late. She kept wondering what the view would now look like from her bedroom window in Charleston. Her papa had written that many plantation homes had been burned to the ground. Farms had been destroyed; cattle and crops were either stolen or eliminated. What would happen to the South? Would they recover? Would the North and South be united again?

President Lincoln must never get any sleep, she thought as she twirled the curtain window tassel between her fingers. *I need to include him in my prayers every night, because he certainly needs them. Everyone back home is probably praying for this horrible destruction to end. Poor Mr. Lincoln must wake up and go to sleep with one thing on his mind—war. I wonder if he looks out his bedroom window and shares the same thoughts that I do?*

Papa had said from the start that this would not be a short battle, she remembered. He felt this would be a lengthy and hostile war. This was proving true thus far.

Did we lose thousands of lives because one man's skin is darker than another's? The irony of war was that the blood that soaked into the ground was one color: red. And after the last shot was fired, those who died would never know the outcome. Blood was red no matter the color of the uniform. Surely there could have been a better way to remedy the concerns of the North and the South—besides war. Did those in congress actually try hard enough? Truly?

McKenna found herself curled up tightly against the window pane. She had no idea how long she had sat there, asking the same questions over and over to herself. A knock sounded on the door, causing McKenna to jump. Little Maggie slowly opened the door, peeking her head around its frame.

"Excuse me, Cousin McKenna, but Aunt Pia told me to fetch you. She wants a family meeting in the dining room."

"All right, Maggie, thank you so much for telling me. Come, give me a hug. I sure could use one today."

Maggie crawled up onto McKenna's lap, holding on tightly to her waist. She placed her small head onto McKenna's chest, half-sobbing, and whimpered, "I was scared when you left. I was so scared you wouldn't come back, and I wouldn't have anyone to read with anymore."

"Well, don't you worry, Maggie doll, I am here, and all is well. I just had a few cuts and bruises, and now I am as good as new. Tonight, I promise we will read some more stories together. How does that sound?"

"That sounds good. Can we sneak some cookies from Percy?"

"I will see what I can do, sweeting."

The cute child lightheartedly jumped off McKenna's lap and ran from the room, on to her next adventure. What a blessing Maggie was to this family.

Oh, your brothers will have their hands full, keeping track of you, Maggie doll! Every boy in the county will be sniffing at your mother's front door, just for a chance to see the beauty that you will transform into, McKenna thought, smiling to herself. *Well, I had best get downstairs and see what this family meeting is all about. Captain Sloane probably has more rules for me—more so-called punishments.*

McKenna walked downstairs, and as soon as she entered the dining room, the somber mood enveloping her family seemed to wash over her like a dismal wave. Even Cooper and Pepper appeared deep in thought. Parker quickly entered the room behind her and asked for everyone to be seated.

"Well, is this a convention of sorts? There is enough gloom in this room to ward off spirits for a full month! What on earth is wrong? I do not want any more gloom—I have had my fill," said McKenna with her hands upon her hips.

"McKenna, sit down, please," said Parker with a firm look upon his face. He quickly pulled out a chair for her, and she immediately seated herself.

"The information I am about to share with you all will be hard to accept," Pia stated, "but allow me to tell you what I've just learned. Parker, Pepper, and Cooper have been quite busy trying to find out who instigated McKenna's attack. Parker has found the answer he was searching for. In fact, Parker had guessed the name of the mystery person long ago, but he had to have proof. He has indeed acquired that proof this morning."

McKenna looked around the table and saw that no one had moved or even attempted a breath. The facial expressions of those seated around the table showed no sense of kindness or warmth. In fact, quite the opposite—their expressions were cold—showing contempt and anger.

"The man who paid those thieves to hurt you, McKenna, is known to us, but not to you," stated Pia in an unusually calm voice.

Suddenly, Pepper seemed unable to stifle his rage, and he was out of his chair so quickly that it toppled over. Cooper rose and placed his hand on Pepper's shoulder to help contain his anger.

"We will confront this, and it will be handled, Pepper. Get a hold of yourself," Parker muttered from his seat.

"The only way to handle this is with a bullet, and you know it, Parker," Pepper hissed.

"Pepper, I understand the cause of your anger. Allow me to explain to everyone here what you and Pia already know. Please, sit down; you are only causing more alarm, especially for McKenna." Pepper picked up his chair and sat down, giving a small wink to McKenna, as though his eyes were saying, 'things will work out.'

"Now then," Parker continued, "allow me to tell my story. I thought it was odd when Savannah reappeared a while ago. I kept asking myself why Reney would become such a monster to my sister, Madeline. He was in love with her when they met. I mean, they truly were in love with each other. I thought it was odd that Reney would become so indebted to others. He had plenty of funds from plenty of patients. He came from a long family line of prestigious medical doctors, and they had all acquired a substantial amount of wealth over the years. Furthermore, Reney was quite skilled with mathematics and investments. Things were not adding up in my mind. So, after Reney's death, I decided to go the prison and see if the guards and officials could supply any further information about Reney.

"They knew little more than I did, but they did encourage me to talk to another prisoner, who occupied the cell adjacent to Reney. I met this prisoner, who, by the way, was very, very ill. This prisoner told me not to think poorly of Reney. Reney had told the other prisoner that he was being blackmailed. He said that there was a man who wanted to hurt anyone associated with Pepper and Pia Wells.

"At first, Reney didn't believe his blackmailer's threats. Then, small accidents began to happen. I remember Maddie telling me she had been thrown from her horse during her first pregnancy. It turned out that the saddle had been embedded with barberry prickles. There was another instance when Maddie was pushed in the market square and fell down a flight of steps near the fountain. Reney began to put two and two together.

"He became distraught and began drinking more. The prisoner also told me that the mystery man began to demand money; in other words, he was blackmailing Reney to pay him what he asked for, because his attention now turned toward harming Maddie. Reney had shared that this man enjoyed watching him fall to his knees and resort to drinking. Reney became another man due to fear."

"Dear God, what kind of monster does this?" asked McKenna.

"The kind who would hurt, sabotage, weaken, and cripple the moral crux of another human being. When I asked the prisoner for the name of this man, he informed me he could not read or write, but Reney had written the man's name on his cell wall. When I left the prison, I hoped to return and speak to

Reney's cell mate at a future time. Unfortunately, the man passed away. I would later find out that Reney had helped the man as best as he could to keep him comfortable—even sharing his food. I have no reason to believe that this prisoner would have lied or fabricated this story.

"So, I decided to return to the prison, and with the guards' permission, I did enter the cell Reney had occupied. I saw the initials T. W. and possibly a third letter etched into the stone several times. With the latest events that had happened, I decided I would interrogate the thugs who attacked McKenna. The authorities allowed me to do so any way I saw fit. After several conversations and bloodied lips, they admitted that they had been paid to 'scare off the Reed girl.' They were told to follow McKenna daily, learn her schedule, and scare her back to America. They were even told that they would earn triple pay if they roughed up a man matching Pepper's description and frighten a woman by the name of Olympia Wells. The instructions given to the thugs included house burning, horse and food tampering, assault, and phony letter writing. But as luck was on my side, I finally got the name out of them."

"Well, what is the name of the man?" asked McKenna with uneasiness.

Pepper glanced at Pia, who nodded stonily. "Tell her," she said. "She deserves to know." Pepper's eyes met McKenna's, and his next words hung in the air between them, sending a chill down her spine.

"Our father—your grandfather," he said quietly. "Thaddeus Wells."

Chapter 41

An eerie blanket of silence covered the room. No one moved. No one spoke. No one dared share a look. The family waited for Pia and Pepper to initiate conversation. Finally, Parker broke the barrier of silence.

"Thaddeus Wells feels that he has a blood feud to settle. He has the devil in his heart, and a bitter quarrel to settle with his children."

"Why in God's name would Father want to hurt Madeline and Reney like that? What kind of man has he become?" asked Pia, visibly distraught.

"There is no God in your father's life now, Pia," said Parker.

"I do not think there has been any spiritual guidance for Thaddeus for quite some time," Parker continued with a determined tone to his voice. "If there were, and if he were a God-fearing Christian, we would not be having this conversation. He is bent on revenge, and he lives and breathes hatred for his children."

Parker sat down and rested his elbows on the table. "I wanted to seek proof before I presented the information I had to all of you. Pia, I see that you are upset, and I am sorry to cause you such distress. But I felt you would want your family to know who had caused harm to McKenna."

"Parker, you have my gratitude and my thanks. I have known for quite some time how devious my father could be. But I never thought in my wildest imagination that he would go to such extremes to exact revenge, especially against his own family."

"Pepper, if I were you, I would ride out and bring Jenny back to the house, with your permission, Pia. I do not trust your father at this point. If he was following McKenna and by chance happens to find out that Jenny is now in Pepper's life, then…" Parker stopped…

"Then Jenny's life could be in danger. Good God, I will kill him if he harms her," said Pepper menacingly.

"Pepper, you hush up with that kind of talk. We have children in here, and they are listening to your every word," pleaded Pia.

"That's all right, Mother," Livingston stood and shouted, "We are old enough to understand what has happened here. We won't let anything happen to Cousin McKenna or to Miss McTavish." He pounded both hands upon the table.

"There is no need to shout, dear. I know that you will protect your cousin and Miss McTavish, and I want you to be aware of the current dangers that surround this family.

"However, I do not believe there needs to be such extreme language. Now then, Livingston and Caleb, you are both excused; please take your sister with you. Allow the adults to come to terms with what we have learned."

Livingston and Caleb nodded and excused themselves from the table. They had shown much composure throughout this conversation, thought Parker. *They are a rare find—especially so young.* Parker was proud of the boys' character, and of their loyalty to Olympia and their family. *Hell, most boys their age would be thinking of ways to get out of doing chores or pulling pranks on their sister and neighbors. Not these two. They have heart and loyalty.* Olympia's next words quickly interrupted Parker's thoughts.

"Boys and Maggie, before you go, know that I love you dearly. I do not think your grandfather would hurt you. He may scare you or try a trick or two on you, but he wouldn't hurt you."

"He already has, Mother," said Livingston as he left the dining room.

"I agree with Livvy," said Caleb. "I think he would hurt us to hurt you. We must be extra careful and stay together. We cannot afford to ride out alone or to let our guard down. We will be all right, Mother. Good night."

"Good night, boys. I love you. Please keep an eye on Maggie."

"Absolutely. Come on, Magpie, let's do some reading. Your pick of books tonight. Or do you want to continue your chess lessons?" asked Caleb.

"Let's play chess. I want to be able to say checkmate to you soon!" Maggie hurried on ahead of the boys.

The door closed quietly behind them. McKenna squirmed in her seat and could remain quiet no longer.

"All right, now what are we to do? Should I go back home?" asked McKenna.

"Hell, no! You aren't going anywhere for a long time. Remember, kitten, you are under strict rules until further notice," said Parker.

"Don't you dare curse at me, Parker Sloane! I meant no harm by asking that question. No one here had a knife pointed at their throat, and no one here had their clothing ripped and torn from their body while their hands were painfully tied. No one here had to be mauled and scratched by a filthy, dirty, vulgar human being." Tears were streaming down McKenna's face, and she was shaking so hard, she dropped the napkin she had been squeezing. "I only asked because if I could make this situation easier for Aunt Pia and the rest of you, then I would. I meant no harm. I just wanted to offer my help." Pia rose and knelt beside McKenna's chair, taking both of her small hands into her own before speaking.

"McKenna, I can't imagine the fear you felt. And yes, none of us here had the horrible things done to us that you endured. We all admire you for your strength and the grit you showed that day in the office. Most girls would have fainted, but not you. You planned your next move against your attacker, with a weapon, no less! But for safety sake, please abide by the plan until we can find out more information. Can you understand that?" Pia looked at McKenna's small frame, admiring her spunk and her quick thinking that day in the abandoned office.

"I will follow the plan," McKenna replied in between sniffles. "I will not ride alone until things have been cleared. Now, if you will all excuse me, I am going to retire to my room. It has been a long day." No one made a sound, not even a breath as McKenna walked to the stairs.

"Parker?" asked Pia, watching McKenna climb the stairs slowly to the second floor.

"Yes, Pia?"

"My God, just look at her. She is vulnerable right now. You and I both know she is putting up a good front for everyone. But deep down, she is ready to fall apart. Your little McKenna showed bravery, but mark my words, she is crumbling inside. Please do not be harsh with her. She was only trying to offer a solution. I do not want to see her spirit broken. I want her to be her old self again. I just hope it's not too late."

"Oh, if I know McKenna, she'll be back to her old self in no time. She just needs to rest. But you are right. She is more scared than she will ever admit to any of us. She will be alright, Pia."

"I hope so, Parker," sighed Pia as she slumped back into her chair.

"She'll bounce back. I will see to it myself. In fact, I will follow up with her right now. I will return momentarily." Parker leaned down and placed a gentle kiss upon Pia's cheek, turned, and left the room. He took the stairs to the second floor two at a time. When he entered McKenna's room, he found that she was already asleep, still fully clothed, wrapped in a woolen blanket. He tiptoed over to her and tucked her blanket tightly around her chin. He would have loved to remove all her clothing and check on those bruises, but out of respect, he held back. Zadie would be there soon. She would see to McKenna's undressing. He leaned over his kitten and placed a tender kiss upon her forehead.

"Land's sake, Captain Sloane, I daresay you are head-over-heels in *love* with little Miss McKenna, aren't you?" asked Zadie with raised eyebrows and a smirk upon her face.

Parker quickly turned toward Zadie. "I didn't hear you come in. Hush, now. Don't you tell anyone how much I love this little kitten. It will be our secret," whispered Parker as he turned toward McKenna's sleeping form and placed a final kiss upon her cheek.

"Aw, now, Captain Sloane, I think this here lil' kitten is in love with you, too. She don't think I knows, but I do."

Parker rose to his full height, turned, and gave Zadie an enormous hug, lifting her right off the floor.

"Oh, my goodness, you are one powerful man. You be careful huggin' McKenna like that; you'll squeeze the air right out of that lil' thing," squealed Zadie as she laughed.

"Good night, Zadie. Thank you for being here with McKenna, and thank you for being here for me, as well. You are truly a special woman sent from the Good Lord himself."

Parker released Zadie's portly body to the floor, but not before he placed a sincere kiss upon her cheek. He glanced at McKenna one last time before he stepped from the room and closed the door. He leaned against the other side, crossed his arms, and closed his eyes.

Yes, Zadie, I am head-over-heels in love with little Miss McKenna. Parker smiled briefly for the first time that day and continued back down the stairs to resume the conversation with the others.

Chapter 42

Ever since the family meeting had taken place, everyone was on edge within Aunt Pia's home. Jenny had moved into the Wells' Manor while—taking an indefinite leave of absence from the Widows and Orphans' Facility to ensure her safety and well-being. *Pepper probably didn't give her any choice*, thought McKenna. *He could be just as demanding as Captain Sloane!*

How she wished she could ride Solomon and be free of worry over the antics of Thaddeus Wells. Months had passed since her attack, and there had not been one occurrence or misdeed to cause provocation or incitement. When she rode Solomon, McKenna was accompanied by her cousins or Cooper. Parker and Pepper had spent the last few weeks down at the harbor, inspecting their shipments and cargo and ensuring that all orders were delivered on time.

McKenna filled her mornings with riding, stable cleaning, and horse grooming. Her afternoons were spent working with Doctor Withers. He had given her several books on veterinary science to study. It was her hope to pass her entrance exam for veterinarian school in a year. Through it all, McKenna kept herself busy and her mind off of Thaddeus Wells. Doctor Withers had been delivering quite a few foals as of late, and McKenna absorbed every movement he made. She was fascinated by his work and could not get enough of what he did. In fact, she had been invited to assist the doctor when one of the horses had accidentally gotten caught in barbed wire. The prong of one of the wires had embedded itself deeply into the shoulder of a gelding.

Doctor Withers allowed her to make the incision and remove the wire. Though the surgery was tedious, she had proven herself to be quite proficient. Weeks passed, and she was soon assisting on daily surgeries. Whether she was helping to deliver a foal or performing any type of surgery, McKenna was certain now, more than ever, that she wanted to become a veterinarian. She continued reading her books, sometimes long past the midnight hour. Many an evening, Zadie would peek in on McKenna and remove her book from her sleeping hands. She was eager to learn, but it was more than that—her medical books took her mind off the clashing between the north and the south back home, and the worrisome thoughts of her personal safety that continued to plague her mind. She was getting tired of looking over her shoulder wherever she went.

Aunt Olympia announced one morning that she wanted to go into the city to sightsee and shop. The new fashions from Paris would soon be in Oxford's shops, and all the ladies from the county would be demanding their carriages be cleaned and ready to go for a look at the new arrivals. McKenna was not overly concerned about the fashions; she would rather attend a few horse racing events—anything to escape her 'escort prison,' as dictated by Captain Sloane.

Perhaps it was her quiet disposition that alerted her need for escape to Cooper one morning after she had just finished her ride with Cinnamon.

"McKenna, how would you like to attend a horse race with me and the boys?"

"Really, Cooper, do you mean it? I would love to go, absolutely love to. When? Where? What kind of racing?"

"Hold on, girl. Lordy, you ask way too many questions in one breath. The race is the Stockton Racecourse in Lancashire, about a half-day's ride from here. If we leave tomorrow, we'd have all Friday and Saturday to watch the races. There are breeders there who are willin' to buy and sell. Who knows, we may come back with a new purchase! The boys will come with us and Aunt Pia will attend. What do you say, McKenna-girl?"

"I say yes! Oh, yes! I can hardly wait! Thank you, Cooper, for inviting me! I must admit that I am bored beyond sin and would relish a good day's ride in the saddle."

"Well then, it's settled. We will leave tomorrow mornin' after breakfast. You finish here, then start your packin'."

McKenna couldn't remember the last time she had been this excited. She could hardly control the giddiness that she was feeling right about now. This little excursion was exactly what she needed!

***

The next morning was filled with excitement as McKenna was readying Solomon. The air was a bit cool, just perfect for a day's ride in the saddle.

"McKenna, tighten up your girth; your saddle is leaning to the left. You know better than that," hollered Cooper. McKenna flinched at Cooper's order and desperately tried to control her sass when she replied to him.

"I was going to, Cooper; I just hadn't had a chance yet. Solomon loves to suck in his breath when I put on his girth and make his stomach smaller than it really is. I think he does it just to aggravate me."

"Be that as it may, by now, he knows the routine. Let's go, Wells family; I plan to be at the races by mid-afternoon. Caleb, Quaid, and Livingston, I trust you are fully loaded and ready to ride?"

"Yes, sir, fully loaded and ready to ride," Quaid answered, saluting and diverting a wink to McKenna.

McKenna knew what 'fully loaded' meant. All their guns were loaded and ready to be fired. Well, it was better to be safe than sorry. McKenna was just glad Parker and Pepper wasn't there to say no to her travel plans with Cooper. If they were around, McKenna would not get three feet off the front porch. The two of them had made it quite clear that McKenna could only ride on the property, no farther than the South pond and never without an escort. That was what her life had been recently. Short rides, escorted rides, no time to be alone, and certainly no chance to canter Solomon and ride across the open fields. If they ever found out that she was traveling all the way to Lancashire, even though she was escorted, there would be hell to pay.

Well, I just won't tell him, and I know the others will keep still. Besides, I am fully armed. What Captain Sloane doesn't know won't hurt him!

Besides, there was a traveling convoy of other Englishmen and women on their way to the race. Stockton was an attractive race for serious horse purchases, and if she knew Cooper as well as she thought she did, she would bet money they would return with a newly purchased racehorse. That in and of itself, was worth the trip and any risk along the way.

"Let's ride," yelled Cooper from the front of the pack.

This was what McKenna lived for—riding along the countryside and soaking up the fresh air and warm sunshine. Along the way, the group stopped briefly to water the horses and enjoy a small lunch that Zadie had packed. Zadie and Jenny had stayed behind with Maggie and some of the hired hands. They weren't much for riding, and Maggie had a friend visiting from Cambridge. Parker and Pepper were to return in a couple of days, but McKenna would be back before then.

Cooper and the group reached Lancashire that afternoon and checked into the boardinghouse with no trouble. The streets were filled with horse breeders trying to make deals and scheme for the top-notch penny of a sale. The track itself was incredible. McKenna had seen plenty of horse sales in her life, but nothing quite like this. Pia was so excited, she was downright giddy. The boys were shocked at the strength of some of the track horses. Cooper, on the other hand, seemed to take it all in stride. He had attended far too many races to be hoodwinked by any breeder who looked his way. Cooper knew what to buy and how much to spend, and that was that. He took McKenna for a walk and gave her tips about the breeds and their former owners. Many of the owners there were temporary ones. They bought and sold for the sheer pleasure of making money. Cooper, on the other hand, bought for the pleasure of enjoying the ownership of a beautiful animal.

When Thursday's afternoon had ended, Pia and her entourage were enjoying their supper at the boardinghouse. The cook had made beef and vegetable suet pudding, fish pies, and cheese mash. The extra-special dessert was ginger cake, and everyone in the dining room devoured a piece along with a steaming cup of coffee. The day had been wonderful thought McKenna as she looked over the patrons enjoying their dinner. She felt refreshed and actually, a bit tired.

McKenna ate until she could eat no more. Shortly after, Pia and McKenna decided that sleep would soon overtake them and decided to turn in for the night. The men and boys remained behind, enjoying tankards of ale.

The next morning, McKenna woke to the smells of bacon, scones, coffee, and ham. Her stomach growled, and she quickly donned her brown velvet riding habit, boots, and gloves. Cooper was at the bottom of the stairs and glanced up when she began to descend.

"Please tell me, McKenna, that you have your pistol strapped to your leg like I taught you."

"Yes, sir, I do. Do you really think there will be trouble for me here? It has been so long since the attack; I think *Mr. Monster* has all but given up vengeance for a while," she said sarcastically. Cooper walked up to McKenna on the last step, nearly touching nose to nose.

"Wipe that smirk off your face. Lesson one: never let your guard down. Lesson two: vengeance is ongoing. Lesson three: the way you look, the horses will come in second place today for a viewing."

"What on earth do you mean by that?" asked McKenna as she bent down to glance into the mirror on the adjacent wall, wondering if she had missed a button or two.

"McKenna-girl, you stay by my side or by the boys at all times. Your beauty far outmatches any horse here—that's what I meant. Most people here will think I am your stable hand, and they will try to sweet talk you and charm me. That's what I mean. When you walk by, the buyers here will not be lookin' at horses, they will be lookin' at you. You don't need to gawk in that mirror any longer—you look fine."

"I am not gawking! Now then, let them think what they want. It will be a wonderful day, and I am ready to see some fine horse racing. Nothing and no one is going to ruin this day for me. This is the first time I have been out and away from the house in such a long time. I am looking forward to this. I promise, I will stay beside you or the boys. Now, please let's eat some of that delicious breakfast that I keep smelling," said McKenna as she inserted her arm through Cooper's bent elbow and towed him alongside of her. "Come on Cooper, I promise, I will stick to you like glue," she said with a whisper and a wink.

"You'd better. If anything happens to you, I am as good as a dead man!" he whispered back.

"You can't be serious. No one in our family would harm you," McKenna said as she came to an abrupt stop.

"Oh, there would be one person you seemed to forget, now didn't ya?" Cooper asked with a tilt of his head.

"Oh, him," McKenna uttered with the coloring draining from her face.

"Yes, McKenna-girl. Captain Sloane would be none-too-happy with me if anything happened to you out here. You just remember that this little trip will be our little secret, you hear?" Cooper asked as he tapped her hand.

"My lips are sealed!" she whispered back with a brilliant smile that darn near brought Cooper to his knees. *You are a beauty, McKenna-girl. I will have to have eyes all over my head today just to protect you*, he thought to himself.

The day proved to be eventful. Cooper had his eye on a stallion and was tempted to buy him—for a lower price than what was being asked by an old friend and breeder.

"I will give you five hundred dollars for that stallion, Roscoe Woods, and not a penny more." Cooper would not barter with anyone there, even an old friend.

McKenna watched Cooper carefully. He knew everything there was to know about buying horses.

"He is worth more than five hundred, and you know it, you old goat! Coop, why don't you mount the horse yourself, and see how he runs? Then you will know why I need more than five hundred for this fine piece of horseflesh," Roscoe replied.

"I can't ride like I used to, damn it, and you know it."

"I can, Cooper," declared McKenna as she stepped between the two men.

"No way in hell. First of all, *you-know-who* doesn't know you are here! And, if he ever found out that I had you test a horse for purchase, he'd throttle me. I'm not talkin' a small trot to the end of the street, I'm talkin' a full gallop around that track—and that in itself is almost a mile away—not to mention a two-mile track. I can't escort you on that and you know it! Neither can the boys."

"Well, *you-know-who* is not here to find out, and the boys are two stalls down. If I get into trouble, I will whistle, and you know that I can whistle. Just mount up and follow me over to the track. Oh, for heaven's sake, Cooper, you know I can ride better than the boys and probably better than most of these men gathered here today. If I say this horse is worth the money, then buy him. If not, move on to your next choice. Now, hold my jacket," commanded McKenna as she handed Cooper her jacket.

"I don't know about this, McKenna. I just don't know if I should let you ride."

"Cooper, I will be on and off this horse quickly. I will only take one lap. I will know within that lap if this horse is worth the money."

"All right. But this is our secret. Understood? Parker doesn't need to know."

"Fair enough," she said with a smile. "We have a lot of secrets adding up, Cooper. I may have to cash in on some of these secrets!" Cooper just nodded at her and gave her a half-smile, knowing full well that he would regret the day he made secrets with this bundle of sass.

Cooper checked the bridle and bit, all the while second guessing his decision in allowing McKenna to ride. It wasn't that she couldn't handle the horse, he just didn't want her to become a target for any stray bullet. What if the mystery man followed them? His heart was telling her to ride, but his head was having second thoughts.

"Cooper, are you listening? Would you please shorten the stirrups by one hole, and tighten the girth on the right side, please? I am leaning. And would you stuff a few carrots in the saddle bag?"

Cooper grunted and did as she asked. When he was satisfied, he stepped back.

"One lap, McKenna-girl, that's all you get. Do you understand?" asked Cooper as she began to walk toward the track.

"Yes sir, one lap," McKenna replied over her shoulder while stroking the stallion's neck.

"Cooper, where is McKenna going on that horse?" asked Quaid rather loudly as he and Caleb and Livingston came to stand beside Cooper.

"She is gonna give that horse a test run and see if he's worth the $500 that Roscoe thinks he's worth."

"Well, you had better hope that Parker and Uncle Pepper don't find out about this," Caleb muttered under his breath, but loudly enough to be heard by all.

"They ain't gonna find out, now are they? Mount up on Roscoe's horses and ride out to the track with her. I want all three of you to position yourselves around it. If McKenna gets into trouble, she'll whistle at you. Understood? Roscoe and I will ride out and stay by the opening gate."

"Come on, boy, let's see what you got," McKenna said to the horse. "Let's go for an easy trot, and then we will pick up the pace when we get on the track. My, you are a very handsome and tall boy; how about a carrot to entice you to behave for me?" McKenna reached into the saddle bag and pulled out a carrot. She stopped and dismounted, all the while talking to the stallion, feeding him the carrot, and stroking his forehead. She allowed him to smell the perfume on the inside of her wrist while he chewed. Papa had taught her that horses pick up scents fairly quick and respond favorably to them. Lavender oils and perfume seemed to intrigue horses, almost making them calmer and a bit more trusting, according to Papa. Since she always wore lavender, it was second nature to put her wrist under the horse's nose, just like old times back home. When she felt comfortable with his eye movement and breathing, she remounted and nudged his side for a slow trot. She carefully entered the track and picked up the pace. McKenna gave the horse his lead and allowed him into a full canter as she reached the quarter-mile mark.

Roscoe and Cooper leaned upon their mounts and watched McKenna ride in awe.

"Hot damn, that girl can ride. Who the hell is she, Coop?"

"Christ Almighty, lower your voice!"

"Well, who is she?"

"She is Pia's niece. McKenna is Maribelle's daughter."

"Holy shit! Maribelle Wells, I should have guessed. She looks just like her, doesn't she? She sure is a beauty, Coop, and I ain't talkin' about the horse, neither!"

"I know she is a beauty, you big oaf, but you don't need to go and flap your jaws and announce it to the whole crowd now, do ya?" Cooper asked in an irritable tone. "She is stayin' with us due to the war back in the States. Damn, she rides even better now than when I trained her years ago."

"I can see that. Hell, so can every other man here. Call her in, Coop, and buy the horse."

Cooper whistled to McKenna, and she slowed down to an easy trot as she approached the pair at the gate. Her cheeks were pink from the wind, and she was feeling exhilarated—truly exhilarated. McKenna reined in the stallion and started to dismount.

"Cooper," McKenna exclaimed, "you have to buy this horse. This is one amazing piece of horseflesh. Did you see him canter? Did you see how smoothly he ran?"

Strong arms encircled McKenna's waist from behind to help her down; however, those arms planted her firmly on the ground and spun her around with biting pressure on both shoulders.

"Yes, kitten; I did see how smoothly he ran. More importantly, I saw who was riding him. Would you care to explain to me why in bloody hell you were riding this horse?"

Chapter 43

"Parker, what are you doing here?" McKenna asked with a mounting feeling of unease and shock. Her eyes were ready to bulge out of her head. She knew she was in trouble, and she knew it was going to be big trouble.

"I might ask you the same thing," replied Parker with an authoritative tone, never releasing McKenna's shoulders.

"Oh, Parker, Cooper asked me to come with Aunt Pia and the boys. Everything is all right; truly, it is. Our mystery man has not bothered me in quite a few months. If I had to remain at the house, I just know I would have gone stir crazy. I have looked forward to this day; please, don't ruin it for me—not now. If you must holler at me, please do it later. I needed this trip and I needed this fresh air and sunshine. I need to ride just like you would need to sail if you had been dry-docked for six months. Please, don't be mad at me or Cooper or Pia. Cooper did it for me, just to get me out and away for a while."

"I told you to stay home, and only ride if you were escorted. You broke the rule, and you broke your promise."

"Come on now, Parker. She needed to get away. We are all here and we had our guard up the entire time. If you need to holler at someone, then holler at me. It was my idea to bring her here," Cooper said as he dismounted and walked toward the two of them.

"Oh, we will have a discussion, Cooper, you can count on that." Parker's jaw quivered as he looked Cooper in the eye. He was as close to punching a man as he had been in a very long time. The only thing saving Cooper's precious nose was Parker's friendship with the man. He dropped his hands from McKenna's and wiped the sweat from his neck. He slowly turned back to McKenna, backing her against her horse. The menacing look he had upon his face would have driven a grown man to tremble in his boots. But not McKenna. She stood her ground, chin up and eyes glaring right back at Parker. Parker studied that defiant look of hers before speaking.

"You were so busy riding this damn stallion that you didn't notice the men on those two chestnut geldings over to your right, now did you? The ones that are watching us right this moment. The same two riders who followed you out to the track. The same two riders who have rifles at their disposal and more than likely have pistols under their top coats. Did you notice them? Did you look at their faces? I believe you would have recognized them from the ticket office. Am I the *only* one who saw them suspiciously follow you out to the track? Christ almighty, I just arrived. And, I might add, I only arrived because I had to pry your whereabouts from Zadie!" Parker's tone was increasing by the second as he leaned closer. Soon, he would be shouting mere inches from McKenna's upturned nose.

"So, I have Cooper, Quaid, Livingston, and Caleb here protecting you, is that right? Let's see, where are the boys now? Oh, if my eyes are not deceiving me, I would say that they are taking a leisurely ride in the *opposite* direction with three young ladies! They sure as shit aren't protecting their cousin, now, are they?"

McKenna took a breath before she spoke.

"You know what you are? You are a brute. You only care about yourself and your goals. I am the one who went through that ordeal, and I realize I should have thought things through. But no matter where I'd gone, those men would have followed me. If they hadn't attacked me at the ticket office, it would have been somewhere else. You know that as well as I do. I have been rather mopey and sad lately, and I just wanted to ride and get outside of my 'prison' boundary. Cooper asked me to come, and my spirits have lifted— exceedingly so. Now, you arrive, and all you can do is to holler at me and tell me that I broke the rules. Well, you can take your rules and kiss my Charlestonian ass. I am tired of being your teeter-totter—you either fondle me or you scold me. I won't let you ruin this day, Parker Sloane, do you hear me?" asked McKenna with both hands on her hips.

"Are you finished?" Parker asked, not budging in his stance.

"Yes, I am. For now." McKenna didn't move. She was breathing so hard that the rise and fall of her breasts were causing her blouse buttons to strain.

"Good, so am I."

Parker bent and threw her over his shoulder and proceeded to walk to the boardinghouse. McKenna was mortified. How dare he embarrass her like this?

It was as though they were meeting on the dock in Charleston for the very first time, all over again.

"So help me God, Parker Sloane, put me down and allow me to walk of my own free will. I am not a doll to be tossed around. I mean it; put me down this instant."

"McKenna?" he asked with urgency.

"What?"

"Shut the hell up."

"Of all the outrageous and mean things to say to me. I will not shut up. You put me down now!"

"As you wish, kitten. I will cool that temper of yours down." And with that, Parker deposited her none-too-gently into the horses' water trough.

When McKenna realized where she had been dropped, her fury became unleashed. She wiped the water from her eyes before she screamed.

"You stinking son of a bitch. How dare you treat me like this! How could you do this to me? I was having such a good day. I haven't felt like this in a long time, and you had to come here and ruin it all, just because you think those two men on the geldings are the same two men who attacked me. I hope you are happy, Captain. You showed me just what kind of cad you really are. Why don't you just march your naval ass over to those men and find out who they are once and for all?"

"Watch your language, young lady, or you'll get your mouth washed out," said Parker as he leaned over the trough, offering no hand to aid in McKenna's exit from the water.

"Don't you come near me. Don't ever touch me again, Captain Sloane. I hate you, and I hate what you have done to me. You've embarrassed me, and you did it on purpose. I apologized for my rash behavior. That's right; I had to apologize for nearly being raped. But I did, so you wouldn't think ill of me. I was so ready and willing to give you my love that I would have climbed to hell and back for you, regardless of what I may have encountered along the way. You can go to hell and stay there, Captain Sloane. I want nothing more to do with you."

"Finished?"

"With you, Captain? I sure as hell am."

"You will do exactly as I say. Now, close that pretty mouth of yours and listen carefully. There are three men walking toward us, and the two from the geldings are behind you. Look over my shoulder. I am pretty sure they are fully armed. I want you to keep arguing and name-calling. I want these men to think you hate me and we are fighting."

"Oh, that won't be hard, Captain. I do… from the very depths of my soul. I see three men walking toward us, but I don't see any weapons. You must be as daft as you are mean. Like I said, Captain, do not touch me or talk to me ever again. I am through with you."

McKenna attempted to get out of the trough but slipped on her way back down, landing harshly on her already-bruised bottom. Parker immediately bent over to pick her up, as McKenna screamed and kicked in frustration.

"Stop kicking, you little hellcat. I am trying to help you," Parker said loudly, then whispered into McKenna's ear, "Give me the gun that you have strapped to your leg. Give it to me now, or I will take it myself."

"All right! Get your hands off me and put me down this instant. I can stand by myself."

"I think not," he said as he slipped the gun from her leg strap.

Parker let McKenna slip out of his arms, and once again, she slipped to the bottom of the trough.

"I hate you! You are doing this on purpose," shouted McKenna in frustration. Once more she stood, and this time, she got one leg out of the trough and onto the ground for balance. As soon as she lifted her other leg out, she turned, intending to slap Parker in the face.

She raised her palm, but Parker shoved her to the ground. She landed hard, breaking her fall with her hands. A gunshot rent the air, and she watched in horror as Parker's body jolted, and a red stain blossomed and grew on his shoulder area of his formerly pristine-white shirt.

"Parker!" she shouted.

He fell to the ground.

"Oh, no. Parker, can you hear me? Parker!" McKenna crawled to kneel beside him, holding his head gently in her lap.

McKenna took the gun from Parker's half-clenched fist and fired at the two attackers coming toward her on her left. She hit one of them in the leg before they both turned and hobbled off before they were barreled down by onlookers. She quickly turned and aimed at the three men who were now backing away. She took aim and hit the middle of the three above the knee cap. The other two abruptly gathered their partner and ran through the crowd. Rather than fire into the crowd, McKenna dropped her gun and turned her attention to the bleeding man laying upon her lap.

"McKenna, we have to get him out of here. Come on, now, help us get him up," said Cooper, rushing over to kneel beside her. They carefully picked him up and carried him into the boardinghouse.

My God, she thought, *what just happened?* She peered out the window and saw the chaos breaking out among the breeders, buyers, and spectators. Men were grabbing their guns; women were gathering their children and running for cover.

This is horrible, she thought. *Why would someone want to shoot Parker? Oh, dear Lord. Were they shooting at Parker? He was right the whole time! They were shooting at me! Oh Lord, I was in danger and he was the only one who saw it coming.*

McKenna turned toward Parker and grabbed his hands, sinking down beside his unconscious form on the foyer's settee. Within minutes, the others were at her side.

"Aunt Pia, Cooper, Uncle Pepper, will he be all right?" asked McKenna with tears in her eyes.

"We don't know, child. Quaid ran to find the doctor," Pia answered as she felt Parker's forehead.

"Looks like the bullet went clear through the shoulder," said Cooper as he inspected Parker's wound.

"Clear through? Well, that is better than being lodged inside his shoulder. Oh, dear, Quaid must hurry. He seems to be losing a lot of blood. Cooper, hand me that towel on the counter. I need to put some pressure on this wound to stop the bleeding," hollered McKenna.

Cooper quickly did as McKenna instructed. No sooner had McKenna placed the towel over the wound then she saw Quaid running through the boarding house door, visibly out of breath.

"Aunt Pia, the doc left. He was needed about an hour ago for a baby delivery. He is all the way out, about twenty miles."

All eyes turned to McKenna.

"All right, McKenna-girl, you have patched up a horse with Doc Withers, right?"

"Patched up a horse? Certainly, I have. But Parker is no horse, and I have never patched up a human being's gunshot wound. I have watched Doctor

Withers as he removed cysts or tumors from a horse, but that is the extent of it."

"Well, did you help him patch those up?" asked Cooper.

"Of course, I did. Why are you asking me these questions right now? We need to get Parker a doctor!"

"You are the closest thing we have to a doctor right now. Get your hands washed," Cooper ordered as he tore the shirt from Parker's chest.

"Cooper, you can't be serious. You think I know how to clean this wound and remove anything left of this bullet from Parker's shoulder? You are mad!"

"No, I am not mad. I am hurryin' against time. You know how to work on a horse; it ain't that much different from a man. You tell me what to do, and I will help you."

"Like hell, I will. I have never done this sort of thing on a human before, Cooper! You can't possibly expect me to. I simply can't do this!"

"First time for everything, girl. The longer you stand here and throw a fit, the less chance Parker has of survivin' that bullet wound. Now, are you goin' to help him, or not? He took the bullet that was meant for you. I saw him push you out of the way."

"Dear Lord, Cooper. He did tell me there were men who were following me, but I was so angry I wouldn't listen to him. I said such hurtful things to him. I thought he was being mean to me because I had disobeyed him. I accused him of horrid things, and I cursed at him and told him to go to hell. Oh, dear God, how will he ever forgive me now?" McKenna was on the verge of a breakdown.

"McKenna, the captain will forgive you. If he knew those men were following you, then he probably had a good reason to do what he did. Hell, I didn't even know you were being followed, and I was with you all day. Thank God Parker showed up when he did. Things played out for a reason, and now you can repay Parker by helping him. Go on now; wash your hands and clean up this wound before it gets infected. I will go and ask for a room and find a bed to put Parker on."

McKenna did as she was told. *Just pretend he is a horse. Better yet, think back and remember helping Papa all those times during his surgeries. Calm down*, she told herself as she looked at the cracked mirror on the wall. She could do it; she knew she could. *Say a prayer, and get the job done—that is what Papa use to say. All right*, she thought, *let's get this job done*.

"I need iodine," stated McKenna firmly as Parker was carried upstairs and laid upon the bed in a vacant bedroom. The family that had gathered looked at McKenna with empty facial expressions, offering no iodine. "All right, then, I need alcohol. Someone get me some alcohol," she commanded with undisguised irritation. A bottle of whiskey was offered by the landlord and promptly placed in McKenna's hands. She poured the whiskey over Parker's wound and her own hands. Then, she took a deep breath, willing herself desperately to stay calm.

Make Papa proud, she thought as she inspected the wound and assessed the bullet's damage.

You better survive this, you stubborn peacock, she thought desperately. *Because when you wake up, I have an abundance of apologizing to do… again.*

Chapter 44

Parker blinked, his eyes adjusting fuzzily to a watercolor array of blue, gray, and gold. He could see enough to tell that he was lying on a bed in a bare room.

What happened? Why am I here? I smell lavender—the smell of McKenna. Good God, what happened to her? Is she all right?

Parker felt pain in his upper left side. *Ah, yes, I remember now.* The bullet hit him with all the force of a cannonball. It had been a long time since he had felt pain like that. He vaguely remembered being shot like this while in the Royal Fleet. *Did I move quickly enough to save her?*

Parker threw off the coverlet and moved his right leg over to the side of the bed. That was the best he could do for now. He strained unsuccessfully to roll himself up into a sitting position. *Breathe, man. Take your time and breathe and haul your ass out of this bed.*

The door opened.

"Oh, no you don't. Parker Sloane, you stay still. You aren't going anywhere without my permission. Do you understand?"

"Thank God, you are all right. Come here, kitten; I need to see for myself that you are unharmed."

Parker stretched out his arm to McKenna, and she immediately took his hand and embraced him with a kiss.

"Parker, I am unharmed, thanks to you. I know you took the bullet that was meant for me. It was a clean shot, and it went through your upper shoulder. I cleaned out your wound and removed a few fragments. Now, you need to stay still for a few days, so the bleeding doesn't resume and infection doesn't set in."

"You operated on me?" Parker asked in disbelief.

"Well, in a manner of speaking, yes, I did. I had to. There was no one else around who could help you. Time was of the essence, and I had to stop the bleeding and clean the wound. I needed to ensure that infection would not set in. The only other doctor was called away before the shooting. Cooper was by my side the entire time, and together, we removed the fragments and patched you up."

"Did I hear my name?" Cooper rapped lightly on the open door and stepped into the room. He came over to stand beside Parker. "Good Lord, man, you gave us a fright. But I need to correct McKenna. There was no 'together.' McKenna is the one who cleaned you up. I just handed her the things she needed."

"I see. So, kitten, why did you operate on a man whom you hate? I believe I was cursed at, called ridiculous names, and even told to go to hell and stay there."

"Parker, I am so very sorry for the things I said. I had no idea you were protecting me. I thought you were being a brute and teaching me a lesson for attending the horse race. Please forgive me; I didn't mean those words." McKenna leaned over and kissed his hand over and over again.

"All is forgiven. I owe you my thanks for taking such fine care of me and, quite possibly, saving my life. Cooper, I appreciate your help, as well."

"None of us knew the severity of the problem, Parker. We did catch the men, and they are sittin' in jail."

"They are?" Parker winced as he tried to move back into the bed into a more comfortable position.

"Yes, sir. We asked the authorities if they could hold 'em in jail until you were able to have a good look at 'em and prove they were the ones who did the shootin'."

"Thank you, Cooper. That will certainly help me to heal faster!" Parker replied as he smiled through his pain.

"I feel responsible for your wound, Parker. If I hadn't brought her out here, none of this would have happened. I am truly sorry to both of you," said Cooper with a solemn expression.

Parker stared at the two of them before he spoke. "What's done is done. Nothing to be sorry about. Your intentions were good, dear friend, and I know that. When I am feeling better, we will sit down and go through the events. I want to make sure I leave no details out before I have a look at those men who shot me. Right now, my shoulder feels like it is on fire. Are you sure there is no sign of infection, kitten?"

"Why, no, I just changed the bandage this morning. Would you like me to check it?" McKenna asked so sweetly that it made Parker's pain level go down a few notches.

"No, I think that if you give me a kiss, though, it may help," Parker replied with a sly smile.

"Parker Sloane, you are impossible. Do not tease about infection. I am worried enough without your antics." McKenna took his hand from hers and carefully laid it upon the blanket before she leaned forward to check his bandage.

"McKenna, thank you for removing the bullet fragments." Parker looked into her eyes with such longing that McKenna's eyes began to tear.

"Thank you for taking the bullet for me." She kissed his forehead ever so gently before she leaned back and resumed her bandage peeking.

"I would have it no other way. Now stop talking and give me a proper 'thank you' kiss."

Chapter 45

Parker was ready to knock his attackers senseless. He had walked over to the jail after ten days of recovery, in the hopes of making a positive identification and quite possibly learning who had hired them to harm McKenna. He probably would have rendered them unconscious if Cooper and McKenna had not been standing beside him. After a verified identification, he repeatedly tried to get any form of an answer or a hint of a name. Finally, Parker decided to use a more deliberate attack.

"I know that you were here for a reason, and it sure as hell wasn't to buy horses. So, why don't you boys just spit out the truth? Tell me who sent you or who hired you and if your story checks out, I will not press charges against you. Now, you really can't say no to that, can you? Wouldn't you rather be home with your family than held up here behind bars?" Parker was hoping that one of the five would crumble. He was running out of time.

The tallest of the five got up from his bed and sauntered to the bars separating himself from Parker. He slowly clasped the cell door with each palm, pressing each finger around the metal rods. His yellowed teeth were on the verge of falling from the decayed gums that loosely held them in place. He sneered at Parker and gathered up his saliva. Parker reacted by backing up, knowing the man's intention of spitting on him.

"So, if I spit it out, what's in it for us? You gonna let us all go from this stinkin' jail?" the man asked, creasing his brows.

Parker approached the cell a bit closer, far enough away to dodge any spit that the man may still have in his mouth. "You tell me who hired you and I will leave your families alone. How does that sound? Let me see, you three against the wall are all married and you have young children. It would be a damn shame if anything happened to your children. More importantly, it would be a shame if your young wives were to be harmed, now wouldn't it?" Parker then walked to the far side of the cell and looked directly into the eyes of the two men who had attacked McKenna. "The way I see it, you can sit here in jail for the attempted murder of the young lady behind me. Or, you can spill your guts and tell me everything you know. Either way, I will find out the answers I need. Either from you or your family. It is up to you."

"You leave our wives alone; do you hear me?" shouted the man with loose teeth.

"Like you left mine alone? Or, should I do to your wives what you did to mine and what you would have done had I not shown up when I did? You are in no position to tell me what I can or can't do. You lost your bargaining power when you attacked her and nearly killed her. I will ask one more time and then I will press charges and leave. Your fate will lie with the judge, and based upon the witnesses who have already told what they saw, you don't stand a snowball's chance in hell of ever being on the other side of these bars again." Parker backed away from the cell one step at a time, never taking his eyes from the men on the other side. "It is your choice. Do any of you want to tell me who is behind this? This is your last chance."

"I'd rather die first," replied one of the men.

"Well then, I'll be sure to pass those words on to your wives. You had your chance."

Parker, Cooper, and McKenna gathered their belongings and walked toward the sheriff's door. "By the way," Parker said as he turned back toward the men, "you better eat a good meal tonight. Where you are going, the food won't be so tasty."

"You can't prove anything, you son of a bitch!" shouted the man from the bed.

"Well, the bullet that was taken from my shoulder says otherwise. Have a good sleep, gentleman. I will be sure to check on your families for you."

The three of them closed the door and walked back to the lodging house side by side.

"Parker, you really aren't going to hurt their families, are you?" asked Cooper.

"No, I don't even know for sure if they have families. I just said that to scare them. As you noticed, it didn't work."

"Well, no one around here knows them, so it tells me that wherever they come from, their boss has some sort of hold on them. They are facing a hanging for attempted murder and they still won't talk! I can't believe they didn't squeal," Cooper offered as he entered the lodging house and poured himself a hot cup of coffee.

"I thought they would talk, too. But tonight was not my lucky night. I'll try one more time in the morning. Let them sleep on it."

"Parker, you led them to believe that I was your wife," McKenna said with a tilt of her head.

"Yes, I did, kitten."

"I liked that. I mean, I liked being called your wife." She quickly turned and ran up the stairs to her bedroom.

"Well, I'll be damned," muttered Cooper. "I can't recall the last time McKenna had nothin' to say. I think she blushed and ran up those stairs, Parker."

"I think you are right, Cooper. I'll see you in the morning. Good night to you."

Parker took the stairs slowly, thinking over his conversation with those dimwitted men in the jail. He was sure one of them would spill his guts tomorrow morning. If luck was on his side, one of the five would be married and one of them would be worrying about spending the rest of his days behind bars. Hopefully, his scare tactics worked. As far as little Miss McKenna was concerned, he was in agreement with her. He liked saying the word 'wife' as well—especially when the word 'wife' dealt with McKenna Reed.

The three of them left Lancashire a few days later. Parker was healing nicely and gaining strength each day. He had asked the men in jail to identify their boss, but ultimately left without any more information than he had before. Since they had been held up in Lancashire much longer than expected, the three of them were eager to get home and celebrate the Christmas holiday with the rest of the family. Once the town doctor had ruled out any infection possibility, they saddled up and headed for home. They stopped along the way and purchased some gifts and supplies for Christmas, all while keeping their guard up.

Cooper, McKenna, and Parker made it home safely, with one day to spare before Christmas Eve. They all needed that extra day to recoup from their long journey and to wrap those last-minute gifts.

Pia and the family enjoyed another Christmas in grand, English style. Dinners, decorations, gift-giving, auctions, charity events, and church services were wrapped into one exquisite package. Olympia decided to host another masquerade ball on New Year's Eve, in an attempt to distract McKenna's mind from the shooting. The guest list would be heavily monitored. No one would enter the ball without an invitation in hand.

Zadie and the girls had been working around the clock to prepare for the festivity and grand celebration at the stroke of midnight. Pia had arranged for a light display to welcome in 1863. Perhaps this would be the year that the war in the States would cease, thought McKenna. She had not seen Papa in over two years, and she dearly missed him and revolted at the thought of passing through another year without the company of her father.

Parker had healed well. In fact, he had worked his body to its fullest extent to recoup the strength that had atrophied. *Good Lord*, thought McKenna, *that man has more muscles in one arm than most men do within their entire body!* McKenna flushed as she remembered the afternoons when she would sponge bathe Parker. Of course, that skunk had asked for a full-body sponge bath, but McKenna had declined. There would be very little scarring to mar that body of perfection. Time had moved on, and the family didn't dwell on the past attack or past shooting. Parker, Pepper, and Cooper had found out that the thugs responsible for the shooting were indeed hired by a man with the initials of T. W. Pia had informed everyone that there would be a family meeting and an overall discussion in a few weeks. The local sheriff and Pepper's colleagues had arranged a meeting with Mr. Wells. Apparently, Judge McCain received a letter for Mr. Wells through his office. Evidently, Mr. Wells had been bequeathed a rather large sum of money. Pepper knew his father would attend any meeting if there were money involved; especially if there was money that would be given to him.

McKenna had just finished kneading some dough in the kitchen when Zadie interrupted her reflections.

"McKenna-girl, where are you? I need help with these rugs."

"I am in the kitchen," hollered McKenna.

Zadie stomped into the kitchen with hands akimbo.

"Child, how long does it take to knead bread and sweep floors? I need help beatin' these rugs. Come on, now, and help ol' Zadie."

"I will be happy to. Let me get this bread rolled and put into the hearth. Come on, Zadie, you grab the other end, and it will take half the time."

"All right, slide on over," said Zadie as she began kneading the opposite end of the bread roll. "What are you thinkin' about, child? Your mind is somewhere else today."

"I haven't seen Papa in over two years. It is hard during the holidays because I miss him so."

"I know you do, darlin'. But we must wait and see how this ugly war turns out."

"But this war could continue several more years! I just don't know how much longer I can wait until I see Papa. Do you understand?"

"I do. I have experienced loss before."

"Who have you lost, Zadie?" asked McKenna as she grabbed Zadie's end of dough and placed the ring onto the hearth.

"I was a little girl when my momma was taken from me," Zadie said as she wiped the flour from her hands. "We were workin' on a farm, and there was a nice white man who lived down the road. He always brought me a peppermint stick when he came to the big house to visit. Well, one day this man came to the house and asked to see me.

"I was out playin' and was told to run to the big house. So, I did. The nice white man gave me a peppermint stick. I thanked him and returned to my house. When I walked in through the door, my mama was gone."

"Where was she?" asked McKenna with a concerned look upon her pretty face.

"The white man's servants had taken her, and I never saw her again. The only way I survived was by becoming the big house maid," Zadie responded sadly.

"Well, what happened to your father?"

"Never saw him again, neither. I imagine he was sold to another neighbor. My daddy was strong, tall, and built like a brick house. He would have been a good field hand, or the overseer's right-hand man." Zadie took a breath, trying to offer a smile of confidence to McKenna.

"Zadie, why didn't you ever share this with me? Was I so selfish that it never occurred to me to ask about your past?" McKenna asked.

"No, baby girl, you made my life worth livin'. When your momma died, I knew how you would feel growin' up without a mother. You were a newborn and would know no different. I was five years old when my mother was taken. The good Lord always says he won't give you more than you can handle, but he sure came close—'specially to a five-year-old little girl left with no momma and daddy."

"Were the people in the big house kind to you?"

"They sure were. Mister Brown was a medical doctor, and he is the one who taught me nursin'. He taught me to read and write and understand numbers. You see, the lady of the house could not bear children. So, in a way, I became their child. Imagine that—a black child in a white man's house. The cooks taught me to cook, and the gardener taught me to garden. I had the best of both worlds, except I could never forgive them for takin' my mother away from me and sendin' her to another house."

"Whatever happened to Mr. and Mrs. Brown?"

"They passed away."

"Did you ever find your parents?"

"No, I never did. My mama was only fourteen when she had me—just a baby herself. I worked in the hospital, and that is when I met your papa. He tried to help me locate my mother, but we had no idea where she had gone to."

"What about the nice white man down the road? Did she work for him?"

"Your father inquired about that. But the nice white man had died, and his servants had gone to other farms for work. 'Ventually, your Papa asked me to stay with him and your mother."

"Zadie, I never knew this. I only wish you would have shared this sorrow with me a long time ago. I am sorry I never stopped to ask you about your childhood. In some ways, I never thought of you as a nanny—just as my momma."

"McKenna-girl, I have always thought of you as my own. You are a blessin' to me and your papa. Your mama was the sweetest thing on this earth, and you are a spittin' image of her. There is no need for apologies, dear girl; you are God's gift to me."

"Zadie, you will never be a substitute mother. You are my real momma, as far as I'm concerned, and I will always think of you as such. I don't care what others might say about that. It is how I feel that is important."

"Come here and give me a proper hug. Ol' Zadie needs one, after this talk. I will always protect you, baby girl."

"And I you," whispered McKenna as she silently prayed to herself, *Thank you, God, for placing Zadie in my life. And thank you for allowing Papa to see the beauty embedded in Zadie's soul.*

Chapter 46

The masquerade ball was superb with the guests attired in various costumes and masks. Jenny had volunteered the older girls from the Widows and Orphans Facility to serve the sandwiches and punch, allowing them to enjoy a proper party while at the same time introducing them to societal etiquette. McKenna was costumed as a fairytale princess in a pink chiffon dress that Zadie had helped her create. She looked absolutely gorgeous, from her sparkling headpiece to her shiny shoes. It was the first time that she had truly felt safe and content in a long time. She had just moved to the veranda with a full plate of sandwiches when a voice startled her from behind.

"Halt, madam. I see that you are by yourself. This would be the perfect time to abduct you to my ship," ordered Parker, dressed as a dashing pirate, quickly unsheathed his sword and sidestepped her movement.

"Well, sir pirate, I would never run off with a man such as yourself. I have been told that pirates are grimy and crafty, and that they loot, pilfer, despoil, and violate…"

"Madam, I am offended. I would never steal from you… Then again, I would steal a kiss. I would never plunder from you. Then again, I would take hugs and kisses from you. I would never violate you, but I would gladly welcome you into my bed and share the passions of life with you, albeit willingly, of course."

"Of course, sir pirate, I see that we need to discuss your ideas a bit more. Perhaps you would steal me away to the other side of this veranda, plunder me into a pirate embrace, and then…"

"And then, my lady?" Parker asked with questioning eyes and dazzling smile.

"And then we could ride off to my magical kingdom and begin a few lessons on the passions of life." McKenna was purposely flirting with him and they both knew it.

"Aye, my lady, this pirate is prepared to do just that. Follow me, princess."

"I would follow you to the ends of the earth, Captain Pirate. Lead the way."

As Parker grasped her hand and led her off the veranda, McKenna noticed with a blush how blissful she felt even at this slight touch. She gently stroked the back of his hand with her thumb, willing him to understand how much she wanted him.

McKenna and Parker sought an easy escape from the veranda and into the rose garden. The evening air was cool, and the melodies of the musicians mixed with the aromas of the foods being served were heavenly. The guests were commenting how lovely the garden looked with the luminaries lining the inside perimeters. The overall view was magically resplendent.

Parker turned and lifted McKenna onto the stone pillar overlooking the fountain below.

"Captain Blackguard?" she asked with a tilt of her head as she straightened her gown.

"Yes, my fair princess?"

"I need you to do something for me. This is going to be a large request, but I need you to answer a question that has been bothering me for quite some time now."

"Aye, my lady, what is your question?" he asked as he placed a kiss upon her hand.

"Parker, ever since I met you, my heart has been in turmoil. One day I am mad at you, and the next day I ache for you in my heart. You make me so frustrated at times, but then you make me feel as if I am the only woman on this earth. I can't wait to see you in the mornings, and I can't wait until we can spend time together throughout the day. I love our verbal sparring—to a point. The day you were shot was horrid. I almost lost my mind. I was so upset, and when I was asked to operate on you, I was a complete mess…"

Parker quickly put his fingers to her lips. "Shh, kitten. Allow me to add my thoughts. I cannot wait to spend time with you, as well. I look forward to each day, knowing I can catch a glimpse of your beauty. When I was sailing the seas several months ago, I longed to be back on land, holding you in my arms. I took that bullet for you because I had to. I could not bear the thought of you receiving a gunshot wound. I believe I fell in love with you the moment I laid eyes on you and that damn silly hat of yours."

"Really? Oh, Parker, this is a difficult question for me to ask of you, but I must. Do you love me more than you loved Savannah?" she asked with pleading eyes while tentatively grabbing the lapels of his pirate costumed jacket.

"That wasn't love, kitten. I think I was infatuated with her, and because it was the first time I had those kinds of feelings for a woman, I was blind to common sense."

"Do you think we may have a chance at finding true love with each other?"

"I think we have already started that journey. Right now, though, I need for you to close those pretty lips, and allow me to kiss them fully and fiercely. Your lips need to be kissed, and they need to be kissed by someone who knows how to kiss," Parker answered with such intensity that McKenna's got goosebumps.

"Oh, and what makes you think that I don't know what it is like to be kissed?" she asked, pulling away.

"Do you? Do you know what it is liked to be kissed by a man who loves you? McKenna, you and I both know your kissing has been limited. But that is all right in my eyes, kitten—your lips belong to me, now."

"Parker, you make me sound like an inexperienced, naïve schoolgirl."

"A beautiful, inexperienced, naïve schoolgirl who cared more about her family and her goals than kissing the nearest Southern gentleman that hung around the barn. Am I correct in this statement?"

"Parker, just hush up and kiss me. Teach me what to do, and how to please a man," she commanded as she leaned back on the pillar, purposely supporting herself with her arms and pushing her bosom toward Parker's roving eyes.

"Kitten, I will never teach you how to please a man. I will only teach you how to please me." Parker lowered his mouth to hers and kissed her with urgency.

McKenna began to return his kiss and abruptly stopped, placing both hands upon his chest. "Parker, as much as I want to continue, we can't be here like this, doing this in the open. We are at the ball, and we need to act accordingly. Oh, my goodness, if Papa knew that I had snuck out to kiss a man—unescorted, no less—he would be ashamed of me."

"No, he wouldn't, because he probably did the same thing a time or two. But you are absolutely correct. Please forgive me for my forward advances. I am truly sorry, kitten. Allow me to escort you back inside. Would you like to dance with me, kitten?" he asked tenderly while he lifted her from the pillar, purposely holding her against his chest.

"Parker, are you always this well-mannered?" She was so close to his face that she could feel his exhaling breath graze her cheek. He smelled good—a mixture of musk and some sort of evergreen scent. She knew she could have stayed in this position forever, but she also knew that she needed to get back to the party.

"McKenna? Are you listening?" he asked as he tipped her chin to meet his gaze.

"Yes, yes I am. I'm sorry, Parker. You just smell so good, I wanted to remain close to you and inhale your scent. I am sorry—please continue."

"Thank you, fair princess, for your compliment," he said as he placed her on her feet and bowed. "Of course. My mother taught me well. I must admit though that the ladies do seem to like my manners and my charisma! I've been told that I have a most captivating smile."

"Ladies, as in more than one? You are still a skunk, Captain. The only lady that you need to captivate is standing right in front of you!" She smiled as she kicked him in the shin.

"Kitten, that little kick of yours was unnecessary," he said as he guided her through the arbor. "Now then, did I answer your questions to your satisfaction?" he asked as he gave her a pat on her bottom.

"Yes, and then some, dear pirate. Behave yourself and take your hand off my backside. People will see you!" she whispered as she pushed his hand off with her gloved hand.

"Never. This beautiful backside of yours belongs to me, and no one else. Remember that, kitten."

McKenna winked at Parker before she hooked her arm in his as they ventured back into the ball. Nothing could ruin this evening for McKenna; she was in complete bliss and rapture. If only Papa were here, she could confide in him, and tell him she may have found her future husband.

"Miss Reed? Miss McKenna Reed?"

McKenna's moment of bliss was interrupted by a deep, throaty voice repeating her name. As she looked up, she saw a very large, golden-haired man peering down at her. He was quite tall and huskily built. His hair looked like sunshine, with streaks of hazelnut running through its waves. He was a very handsome man, she realized with slight embarrassment. She gathered herself before she answered.

"Yes, I am McKenna Reed. And you are?"

"I am a friend of your father's. I was taken under his wing while he studied in England."

"Well, then, I am glad to make your acquaintance Mr....?"

"Rothberry. James Rothberry, Miss Reed. It is a pleasure." Mr. Rothberry took McKenna's gloved hand and placed an introductory kiss upon it.

"Tell me, Mr. Rothberry, how long were you able to work with my father?" she asked softly pulling her hand out from his embrace.

"I was only with him for six months, but the things he taught me were monumental."

"I am sure it was. My father is an exceptional medical doctor. Excuse my manners, Mr. Rothberry, this is Captain Parker Sloane," McKenna said elegantly, clutching onto Parker's forearm.

Parker stiffened, but he shook the man's hand. Something was amiss, but Parker could not pinpoint what it was. The look in Rothberry's eyes was not right, as if the man were issuing an unspoken challenge. Parker's gut told him that this man was dangerous and a threat to McKenna, but outwardly, Rothberry gave the impression that he was an exceptionally well-attired and attractive young medical doctor.

"Miss Reed, since I have to leave shortly, may I have one dance with you?" he asked with a fair amount of persistence.

That was sly, thought Parker. McKenna wouldn't be able to refuse a dance with someone who had worked with her father. What was he up to?

"Certainly, Mr. Rothberry. Just one dance. Excuse me, Parker," she uttered politely, tapping Parker's arm in a silent confirmation that it would be alright.

"Certainly, my dear. Enjoy yourself and dance with Mr. Rothberry." Parker stoically removed McKenna's arm from his and placed her gloved hand toward that of Rothberry's.

James took McKenna's elbow and guided her along the punch table, waiting for the musicians to begin the next set. Parker watched the two saunter away with a tense grimace upon his face. Something didn't feel right, but he couldn't place his suspicion.

"Parker, who the hell is that?" asked Cooper as he and Pepper came to stand beside him, biting into their chocolate-glazed cakes.

"He says his name is Rothberry—James Rothberry—and that he worked under Harper while he was in England, practicing medicine."

"Rothberry? I have never heard of that name," said Pepper. "Is he going to dance with McKenna?"

Before Parker could answer his question, a small scream was heard from behind. All three turned to see a small flame gaining strength on the punch table. The tablecloth soon caught on fire, forcing the guests to disperse.

Parker, Cooper, and Pepper quickly moved to douse the flame and reassure the guests that it was a simple accident of a turned candle. When all thought of danger was put aside, Parker turned his attention back to the dance floor.

"Bloody hell. Where is she? Where is McKenna?" Parker scanned the floor but could not find his golden-haired princess. Cooper and Pepper searched to the right and left of those resuming their waltz sets and could not find a pink chiffon dress. "Damn it, he took her. I knew he was up to no good. That fire was no accident. Coop and Pepper, seal off the entrances and exits. Get the boys."

***

Outside, McKenna was being forced off the veranda and led down to the stables in a most aggressive and hurried manner by her father's intern.

"Mr. Rothberry, I assure you that all is fine in the house. I do not need or want to step this far away. I will be going back now." McKenna attempted to stop and hold her ground, but Rothberry kept a firm grip upon her and pushed her along with him on the pathway.

"You won't be going anywhere, little lady, except with me." He didn't look at her or even attempt to ease his grip. Fear started to creep up McKenna's spine. This was not the same man she had met moments ago inside the house. Her gut was telling her to get away from him and soon.

"Take your hands off me. I have had enough of your charade. You did not work with my father, nor are you a doctor, are you? Who are you, really?" Again, she tried to stop.

"Stop talking, and keep moving," the man snapped through gritted teeth, forcibly guiding McKenna by the arm, applying more pressure.

As they approached the stable, he started walking toward Solomon's stall. McKenna came up with a hasty plan, formulating an escape in her mind. If she could get on Solomon, she would be able to escape. But Rothberry's question brought her back to her current situation.

"Missy, listen to me, damn it! I said, do you ride?" Rothberry gripped harder on her arm. "Answer me, damn it. It is not a hard question. Do you know how to ride a horse or don't you?" His face was so close to hers that she could smell remnants of alcohol on his breath. His teeth were yellowed and chipped. He was dirty and disgusting; she had to get away from this man and soon. His final pinch on her inner arm brought tears to her eyes.

"You are hurting me! Let go of my arm this minute!" she yelled while trying to dislodge Rothberry's grip. "Yes, I know how to ride. But I am just learning." She hoped her face would not betray her lie, although her tears of pain were real.

"Give me your hands." The man was as compassionate as a rock. He was on a mission and it appeared that he was in a hurry. Wherever they were headed was important and this man was in no mood to dawdle.

McKenna was brought to reality by his next question.

"Are you a simple-minded chit? I have asked two questions and you don't answer! Are you deaf? For the last time, give me your hands!"

"What for?" asked McKenna, putting her hands behind her back. She wasn't going to make his job easy.

"I said, give me your hands." Rothberry's voice sent chills down her spine. He grabbed her hands and securely tied them in front of her, knowing the rope was digging into her wrists.

"We are going to ride together, and you are going to keep that pretty mouth of yours shut."

He didn't give McKenna the chance to think on his words. No sooner had he spoken, he was in the saddle, leaning over and grabbing McKenna under each arm, lifting her off the ground, and planting her none too gently in front of him.

You are a fool, Mr. Rothberry, thought McKenna. She needed to convince him that she was fearful of riding—perhaps this would bide her some time until Parker and the others found her.

"Mr. Rothberry, this horse looks way too big and fast. Are you sure you can control him?" McKenna asked with feigned fright.

"You just hush up. We will make do. I will ride slowly; make it look like we are out for a moonlight ride, my dear. Do you understand me? If you so much as utter a scream, I will knock you unconscious. Do you understand me? There ain't no one around here; everyone is inside and no one knows where you are. I intend to keep it that way. Understood?"

"Yes, I understand. I will keep quiet," said McKenna, injecting a note of fear into her voice. *You are about to find out just how well I can sit my own horse, you overgrown fool!*

McKenna and Rothberry rounded the veranda when she started squirming in the saddle.

"Damn it, girl, sit still. You are going to end up falling and breaking both of our necks, you stupid bitch."

"Well, Mr. Rothberry, that is where you are wrong. I may be a bitch, at times, but I am not stupid!" With that, McKenna turned to her side, leaned back, and forced her elbow into Rothberry's ribs as hard as she could, attempting to undo his balance and knock him from the saddle. He wasn't prepared for her response, and her hit caused him to lean dangerously low from the left side of the saddle. McKenna quickly grabbed the reins and commanded Solomon to back up and rear up, ultimately causing Rothberry's pitiful hold on the saddle to give way.

Parker arrived just in time to grab Rothberry's slipping body and throw him to the ground. Although Rothberry was a bit stunned, he still attempted to fight back, but Parker's strength was no match for McKenna's would-be kidnapper. The more Rothberry struggled, the tighter Parker pressed his knees into his shoulders, rendering him useless.

"You have two seconds to start talking before I render you unconscious, you filthy bastard. Who are you, and who sent you to kidnap Miss Reed?"

"Go to hell, Englishman."

"Been there and back. Your turn to go." Parker hit the man across the face, bloodying Rothberry's nose. "The next hit will break your nose. I suggest you start talking."

The man looked at Parker in stubborn defiance.

"Captain, before you break his nose, I would like to talk to dear Mr. Rothberry." McKenna spoke over Parker's shoulder as she sat upon Solomon. "Mr. Rothberry, my gun is aimed at your private parts. It is my intention to shoot them off, so scum like you cannot reproduce. Which testicle would you like to lose first? The left one or the right one?"

"McKenna, put the gun down." Parker looked at McKenna with authority.

"Oh, you hush up; I intend to carry out my threats, and you know perfectly well that I will. I say what I mean!"

"Well then," Parker smiled as he looked from McKenna to the man beneath him. "I would start talking if I were you or resign yourself to remaining fatherless for the rest of your grimy life. She is an expert shot," advised Parker, changing his hold on Rothberry. "McKenna, just make sure you don't miss and hit me instead. I prefer to keep my manly parts intact!" Parker looked at McKenna with an intensity that she had not felt in a very long time. She noticed the muscles twitching in his neck. She knew he was playing along with her threat to Rothberry. But he also knew, she hoped, that she wouldn't back down. If push came to shove, she would shoot the man where he lay. She had to pity the poor man under Parker for the moment, though. Parker's weight would have taken the breath out of a smaller man a long time ago.

"All right, all right... both of you calm down," Rothberry muttered nervously. "Put your gun down, missy, and I will talk. Tell this giant to lighten up on his hold. I can't feel my arms!" Rothberry was scared witless, and he had a good reason to be. McKenna nudged Solomon a step closer and placed her rifle in her crook of her arm.

"Now, you hold on. There is no way in hell I am gonna be relieved of my man parts by a woman half my size! I swear I will talk, and I will tell you everything I know. You just put that gun down."

"Come now, Mr. Rothberry," McKenna smirked, still holding her gun steady. "You are on my property and my home. You will not be telling *me* what to do. I will be the one doing the telling. You lied to me, coaxed me from my home, and intended to kidnap and do God knows what else to me. Your time is up—left, or right?" McKenna repeated as she put the rifle scope to her eye.

"All right, all right... I am sorry ... I will talk. I don't know who wants you, but he wants you somethin' terrible. I was to pretend to be a friend of your father's. I knocked the candle over when I grabbed your elbow just before we went onto the dance floor. While everyone was worried about that little flame, my job was to get you to the barn, saddle up a horse and ride to the designated meeting place."

Parker shifted his weight off Rothberry and pulled him into a sitting position, tying him to the gate post.

McKenna stared at Rothberry for a bit. She couldn't tell if he was telling the truth or not. His body actions definitely told her he was nervous and ready to rat out his boss. But his eyes, there was something about his eyes—almost as though he was holding something back.

"Well, then, let's continue and ride to this 'designated' meeting place. I would like to meet this man who wants me 'somethin' terrible.' What do you say, Captain? Would you like to continue this adventure?" McKenna asked as she sidestepped Solomon toward the fence. She took her eyes off Rothberry briefly as she lowered her gun and holstered it back into its saddle case. "Well?" McKenna asked with a challenging look upon her face. "I am ready to meet this man!"

"No, kitten. This is too risky. I don't trust anything this scum says."

"Never fear, Captain, dear. I have a plan. Let's talk over there." McKenna pointed, dismounted, and walked to the small clearing with Parker following behind. Cooper, Pepper, and the boys were waiting for the two of them ready to act.

"I suppose you heard most of that conversation?" asked McKenna as she removed her costumed gloves from her hands, fully aware that her pink gloves were now dirtied and grimy.

"We heard enough to know that this man is working for someone else," Cooper replied, "and we need to find this man."

"We all do," chimed Pepper and the younger boys.

"But we need to think our way through this. One wrong move and you could be killed. I am not willing to let that happen," Cooper whispered softly, so as not to have his voice carry to the prisoner.

"Neither am I!" Parker reinforced, never taking his eyes off of McKenna. "I understand time is of the essence here, and now is the perfect opportunity to see who this mystery man is. We think our man is Thaddeus Wells. But still, there is something that isn't right. Think about it, boys; it was too easy for Rothberry to get McKenna out of the house. Had we not come when we did, they would have been long gone."

"Parker, you are right; time is of the essence," McKenna whispered. "We need to move now. Remember, this man is waiting for Rothberry and a woman to meet him. But I have an idea. Caleb needs to put on my costume—he needs to be me! Caleb, you are the closest to my size, and his boss will think you are me. Parker, put on Rothberry's clothes. His boss will think you are him and that you are delivering me. Please, there are enough of us to surround whomever is waiting. We know the area better than this mystery man does." McKenna was becoming impatient and it showed.

"At least we think we do. How can we be so sure that Rothberry will tell us the truth? How do we know he will tell us the right spot—where to meet this boss man of his?" asked Pepper with a skeptical tone to his voice.

"My gut is telling me he will. If he proves to be dishonest with us, I will return and carry out my threat that I made to him," McKenna whispered. "And believe me, he wants to remain intact, so to speak. Oh, for heaven's sake, time is wasting! There is only one way to find out if Rothberry's words will ring true."

"She is right, let's put an end to this once and for all." Cooper spoke with authority and yet his voice was tinged with hesitancy. He knew they could be riding into a trap, but that was a risk they would have to take. Albeit, a mighty big risk.

McKenna marched straight over to Rothberry, who was now trussed like a pig. She slowly bent down and looked him straight in the eyes. She didn't blink before she spoke, nor did she move. "Where is this meeting place? Remember, if you lie to me, I will ride back here and I will shoot off both your testicles and feed them to my dog. Do you understand?"

"I understand." Rothberry was terrified. "Take the road to the pond. Veer off to the right—there is a clearing there. He's waiting there."

Parker listened to the two of them as he removed and finished buttoning Rothberry's jacket, which he now wore.

"The clearing by the cattails?" McKenna asked suspiciously.

"I didn't see no cattails there, but there is a clearing there. I think there is a wood shed there—don't have no roof on it, but it is standing," Rothberry muttered back.

"Your boss better be there, or I'll be back for you. Be thinking about that while I'm gone," McKenna said as she stood up slowly and walked back to the others handing Caleb her pink veil and tiara and cloak. She helped Caleb cover his face with the veil and then waited while Parker finished buttoning his overcoat. He was on Solomon in no time and helped Caleb mount in front of him.

"Caleb, you must act like you are my prisoner. Give me your hands and I will tie them loosely. Remember, you need to act frightened. That means to keep your mouth closed." Parker tugged the ropes through a loose knot on the underside of Caleb's hands. Parker edged Solomon towards McKenna as he reached down and rubbed her cheek.

"Parker, I just want to meet this man and be done with this. Oh, I feel so foolish for falling for Rothberry's lies. I should have known better!"

"Kitten, you were played—simple as that. No one knew any better. Now, mount up. I know it will be difficult for you to ride and not speak, but do your best." Parker nudged Solomon ahead as he adjusted his hat to cover most of his face and then looked over his shoulder and saw that Cooper, Pepper, Quaid, and McKenna were mounted and were ready to ride. The stillness of the night was broken by the swishing of the wind. Fortunately, the sky was dark with minimal moonlight, better for the riders to stay unseen.

"Hey, you can't leave me here like this! I ain't got any clothes on except my long underwear and this pirate outfit! What the hell, cover me up for God's sake!" Rothberry was a mixture of fright and anger rolled into one. McKenna wasn't sure if he was trembling out of fear or humiliation or rage. One thing was for sure: he had better be telling the truth.

"Livy, you guard him with your life. Do you hear me?" Pepper said assertively. "I mean it; he'd better still be tied to this post when we return."

"He will be, Uncle Pepper. Trust me, he isn't going anywhere," Livingston said with assurance.

"See to it that he doesn't. Shoot if he tries anything, but don't kill him," hollered Cooper as he rode off with the others.

"I will. I am a good shot," Livingston replied, puffing his chest out like a peacock.

***

The caravan of riders was nearing the pond. Cooper, Pepper, Quaid, and McKenna split apart from Caleb and Parker and circled around the old shed. Caleb kept his head down and refused to speak. As they turned and headed for the shed, Parker noticed a lantern light. Parker could not quite make out the shapes behind the light, but someone or something was moving up there. As they drew closer, the pair could see what appeared to be three men on horseback. They were almost upon them when a voice questioned Parker.

"What took you so long?" asked one of the riders, his face hidden in the midnight fog.

"She gave me a bit of trouble. She had never ridden before and was skittish on this horse I stole."

"Well then, you fool, you have the wrong woman. The woman you were supposed to get can ride as good as any man," stated the second man.

"Well, she can't ride. Hell, I had to ride at a snail's pace the whole way here, the girl was so nervous."

A third man trotted his horse forward. "Lady, take off your hood. Did you hear, missy? Take off that hood. Rumor has it you are the most beautiful woman in England. I want to see if the rumors are true. ... Take off that hood now. ... Do not make me ride over there and do it for you."

Caleb slowly started to remove the hood. He could see Cooper, Pepper, and Quaid slowly approaching from behind. When he lifted the bulk of the hood from his head, he immediately took the pistol from the folds of the cloaked costume and aimed it at the closest rider to Solomon.

"Keep your hands in the air. If you so much as lower them one inch, I will shoot you dead," spoke Caleb through the veil with all the authority he could muster in his frightened body.

"You snotty whelp; get off that horse," snapped the rider, inching closer to Caleb. "You fool, you gonna let this slip of a girl hold a gun on me? Knock it out of her hand, or I will!"

"I think not," Parker replied as he raised and cocked his gun at the lone rider. "Look behind you. Look to your left and then to your right. You are on our property. You, sir, are the fool. Let go of your reins and keep your hands up."

The others quickly encircled the riders and took their weapons. All three were unmercifully shoved from their horses onto the ground and tied together.

Parker and Caleb dismounted, then strode to the trussed men and paced in front of them several times before speaking.

"We can do this the easy way or the hard way. Speak, and tell me everything I want to know, or refuse to speak to me, and I shall allow the lady, standing behind you, to shoot off your balls. We will then haul your rotten carcasses to jail. I might remind you that the woman you were supposed to kidnap is an excellent shot. She simply does not miss. What shall it be, gentlemen? Speak now or forever remain fatherless."

"Thank you for the lovely compliment," whispered McKenna as she came to stand beside Parker.

"Hush, kitten, and try to keep your face concealed," Parker muttered into McKenna's ear. He gently pulled McKenna's hat over her forehead as he walked closer to her would be assailants.

"Well, if you men are not willing to talk, you leave me no choice," said Parker as he motioned for McKenna to walk in front of the men—hearing the cock of the rifle.

"All right, mister, ain't no reason to be hasty. We will tell you what you want to know. Just leave our body parts in one piece."

"Well, gentlemen, that will depend upon the information you give. Let's begin with your names and who hired you." Parker kneeled before the men, balancing his gun upon his knee. "State your names."

"My name is Otto, next to him is Willie, and then Johnny. Look, mister, we are just doin' a job," answered Otto, who appeared to be the leader of this scruffy threesome.

"Well then, Otto, your partners here look to be pretty young. I would guess they are barely over the age of eighteen. Is that correct?" Parker asked, never flinching.

"Yes, sir. They are my younger brothers. We were hired to catch a certain lady, and that's all we were to do!" Otto was beginning to fall apart and Parker knew it.

"Well then, Otto, what were you supposed to do once you caught her?"

"We were supposed to take her into London and deliver her to someone else. A lady."

"Lady? Does this lady have a name?" asked Parker.

"Savannah," replied Otto.

Rage crept through Parker's skin. Why in hell would Savannah be involved in this mess? He had done everything to rid her from the family shy of sending her to jail. Christ, never in a million years would he have guessed she was mixed up in the attacks on McKenna. Dear God, how would Otto even know Savannah's name? He couldn't be lying. Parker looked at Pepper and Cooper while they silently motioned for Parker to join them.

266

"I smell a rat, Parker. There ain't no way in hell Savannah would be mixed up in this," Cooper said. "You saw how grateful she was when we sent her away—we could have sent her to jail and she knew it."

"I agree with Cooper." Pepper placed his hand on Cooper's shoulder before he continued, "Look, I am not buying Otto's story. I think the name Savannah is a diversion. These are not the sort of men Savannah would tangle with. Something isn't adding up, Parker. I just know it!"

"I know it isn't adding up, but I am out of ideas." Parker looked at all three of the young men tied together. He scratched his head and wondered what his next move would be. *Damn, Savannah better not be involved in this*, he thought to himself.

"Excuse me gentlemen, I have an idea. Allow me a few minutes alone with those three." McKenna smiled sweetly.

"No way in hell. Not now, not ever!" Parker shouted at her.

"Parker, let me talk to them. Sometimes a sweet lady's tone of voice can do more than a burly voice such as yours. Please, let me try," she asked as she laid her small hand in the crook of his arm.

"Parker, let her try. There is no harm in it," responded Quaid. "Besides, she may find out more—that young one tied up on the end looks like he is ready to wet himself. Let Cousin McKenna work her charm on him. I bet he will spill his guts. Just wait and see."

"I promise, you can all stand at the ready in case one of them attempts to thwart me. Let me talk to them." McKenna looked at the three men and nearly laughed. They looked like three overgrown children who had been caught with their hands in the cookie jar. They wanted to object but knew that they couldn't. She didn't dare tarry though; she knew she was on borrowed time with their patience, not to mention her own. McKenna mouthed a silent 'thank you' and took a big breath before she turned toward the three men tied together. She gently knelt down and sat directly across from them as she slowly removed her hood. She could tell by the intakes of breath that she had dazzled them.

"Gentlemen, do you have a sister?" she asked fetchingly.

"We do," answered the young man in the middle—Willie.

"Well then, Willie, how would you feel if someone had threatened and scared your sister? How would you feel about that?" asked McKenna as she smoothed her golden curls, knowingly enticing the three.

267

"I wouldn't like it. I'd want to kill him," Willie replied with a squint to his eyes.

McKenna nodded before she continued, "And, how about you, Johnny? How would you like it if your sister had been hit and assaulted by another man?" McKenna asked.

"I… ah… I wouldn't like it neither! I'd just as soon shoot the bastard," he replied haughtily.

"Those are some big words coming from one so young. But I believe you. And, Otto, I am sure you would be willing to hurt whomever laid a hand on your sister, too? Am I right?"

"Yes, ma'am, you are right." Otto could barely blink. McKenna knew they were all infatuated by her, especially Otto. "Well, I have been threatened and scared and hit and even assaulted. Let me assure you that I was embarrassed and humiliated that any man worth his salt would stoop so low as to tie me up and purposely hurt me." McKenna put her head down and wiped away an imaginary tear with her hand.

"Ma'am, don't cry. We weren't going to hurt you, none. We were just supposed to take you to someone else. Honest, I wouldn't hurt someone as pretty as you." Johnny looked like a lost pup, not knowing what to do next or what to say.

"I believe you, Johnny. But nonetheless, you three are here and you did hurt me. You took me away from my family and they must be worried sick! You had Rothberry grab my arm so tightly, that I am sure there are bruises as I speak. Then, you frightened me by telling me I would be going to London, and quite frankly, I don't even know anyone in London! How can you three say you weren't going to hurt me? What would happen to me once I reached London?" McKenna was playing her role so smoothly that the three young men began to squirm and look at each other. She knew she was chipping away at their resolve.

"Can you please tell me who wants to hurt me? I am from the States and I don't know anyone here except my aunt and uncle. Please, if this were you sister, wouldn't you want to know?" McKenna resorted to using her cloak to wipe her eyes. She even winced a bit as she rubbed her arm, hoping to show a definite indication of an injured arm.

"Tell her, Otto. Go on now, tell her. She doesn't deserve this. Either you tell her or I will!" Johnny was talking quickly, slurring his words, trying to breathe in between sentences. It was clear to McKenna that there was more information to be had.

"Tell me what? I am sure that you all know where you will be headed after this conversation. And it won't be back home. You see that man over there with a red scarf around his neck? He is a well-known lawyer around these parts, and his friends are even more powerful judges. If I am not mistaken, anyone who is involved with a kidnapping goes to jail for a very long time." McKenna paused and watched their jaws drop. "So, if you have anything to say to me, now would be the time to tell. Remember, if you are all in jail, you will not be seeing you sister for a very long time."

"Ma'am, some man wants you. He just told us to say the name Savannah. He said that the name Savannah would upset you," Willie burst out. "In fact, his exact words were 'when she hears the name Savannah, she will jump out of her skin.'"

"You are right, Willie, I almost did. You see, Savannah is a friend of mine, and she has no reason to hurt me." McKenna paused and looked at each man. They wouldn't return her look; in fact, they averted their gaze to the ground.

"Well, I suppose if you have nothing else to tell me, you might as well mount up and head to the nearest jail. I am sorry you won't be getting any supper tonight; I would imagine that the kitchen is closed. In fact, the next time I see you will probably be in court. I will have to tell the judge that all three of you were involved in my kidnapping. I sure hope that means jail time for you and not that awful 'h' word." McKenna continued to play her shaken role well as she placed her hand over her mouth.

"What's the 'h' word, ma'am?" asked Johnny with wide eyes.

"Johnny, 'h' stands for hanging," McKenna answered his question without emotion. "I hope what happened to me never happens to your sister. There was a time when I wanted to die because the pain was so hard to bear. And the worst part is, all three of you know something more to this story and you are not telling me. I will be sure to search up your sister when your trial is over, and I will tell her that you would not help me nor would you aid me in finding the monster behind this." The three men bowed their heads even lower in humiliation.

"Well then, if you have nothing more to say, I will see you in court." McKenna slowly stood up and adjusted her cloak.

"Wait!" shouted Otto. McKenna stopped in her tracks and looked Otto in the eye.

"There is a name that we are suppose let slip to you. His name is Thaddeus."

"Who is giving all these orders, Otto?" asked McKenna impatiently.

"I don't know. I just know that he said to drop two names to you— Savannah and Thaddeus. He said those names would rile everyone up. Even the man who took you, Rothberry, has never met the boss. All we know is that he lives around here and has a mighty vendetta against you and your family. That's the honest truth, ma'am. That is all we know." Otto looked at McKenna with such candor that she had to fight the urge to forget the whole thing, untie the lot of them, and kick them all the way home.

"Thank you, Otto, Willie, and Johnny. I appreciate your help. I will see what I can do to prevent you from ending your lives at the end of a rope. But I would also like to scold all three of you for a moment. You see, life is precious, no matter whose life it is. You were so willing to do a job for the sake of a few dollars, that you didn't even ask the 'why' or the 'how' or the 'reason' behind it. I hope this teaches you a lesson. I could be your sister and you could be in the exact same position as my friends behind me. They are just protecting me because they love me. I would hope you learn a lesson from this."

McKenna picked up her skirts and turned slowly back to the four men awaiting her return. She never looked over her shoulder. If she had, she would have seen Johnny sniffling from spilled tears.

"Well done, kitten," Parker said as he and the others guided McKenna a few yards away from the horses.

"You know, I truly meant what I said about their 'sister.' I hope they think about what they have done." McKenna rubbed the back of her neck and took a sip of water that Pepper offered.

"Kitten, it is time for you to go home. It is nearly sunrise and you are still in part of your blasted princess costume, for Christ's sake! You must be tired."

"I am tired, Parker. Please take me home now."

"Pepper, Cooper, and Quaid, I trust that you can handle things here and get these three back to jail where they belong. And don't forget Rothberry. I hope Livingston still has him in his sights. We'll talk about this in the morning, over breakfast and after a good night's sleep. Caleb, you did real good out here. You are a brave young man and you just proved it to us."

"Thank you, Captain, that means a lot to me. I'd do it again if I had to," puffed Caleb as he smiled at McKenna—feeling as tall as the Oak trees in the woods.

"Thank you, cousin, we could not have done this without you," McKenna added as she placed a soft kiss upon Caleb's cheek. "Go on now, and ride home with the *other* men, you must be tired! And, thank you, Caleb, from the bottom of my heart."

"Now then, kitten, let's get you home!" Parker wasted no time in scooping up his sleepy princess and riding back to the manor house. Along the way, McKenna tossed and turned in Parker's arms. Finally, she could take no more riding and pulled up on Solomon's reins herself.

"Parker, will those three young men hang for their part in the kidnapping? I mean, I told them that they might, but it would be awful if they lost their lives after they tried to help me." McKenna turned and looked up into Parker's eyes, one hand holding onto the saddle and the other holding on to his jacket lapel.

"That will be up to the judge, my dear. But I am sure that Pepper will speak on their behalf and save them from dangling at the end of the rope. Kidnapping is a major crime, kitten. Don't be too soft on those boys—they knew what they were getting into."

"Parker, I am not so sure they did. At any rate, I hope they have learned their lesson." McKenna snuggled deeper into Parker's chest and soon fell fast asleep. Once they arrived home, he carried his beauty to her bedroom and laid her gently upon her bed. Zadie and Pia followed behind, ready to strip her of her dirtied costume and tuck her under her covers.

"Captain, this is becomin' a habit—you carryin' McKenna up to bed and all. You need to stop doin' this. Now, go on downstairs and I will make you some of my pancakes. You must be awful hungry!" laughed Zadie.

"I suppose you are right. I have been carrying her up to bed recently. Thank you both for taking care of her. Now then, if you will excuse me, I am tired and hungry. A stack of your pancakes sounds perfect; however, they will taste better after some sleep and a bath. I want to wash the dirt off of me." Parker placed a kiss upon McKenna's forehead, left the room, and headed straight toward a room with a tub.

Several hours later found Parker, Cooper, and Pepper sitting around the kitchen table enjoying a very late breakfast of Zadie's pancakes. The stillness

271

was finally broken when Pepper shifted in his chair, tossing his fork onto his finished plate.

"Those three young men are behind bars, Parker. Rothberry is also behind bars."

"You mean to tell me that Livingston held guard on him that whole time?" Parker asked, looking up as he finished his last bite.

"Yes, he sure did. Although when we found him, Rothberry was still tied up, but the guard, as you said, was fast asleep!" chuckled Cooper.

"Well, I'll be damned. Though he stayed there the whole night with that thug. Good for him!"

"Parker, I know this day is half over, but I have to get something off my chest," Pepper said as he cleared his throat and sauntered to the window.

Parker looked at Cooper and they both shrugged, not knowing Pepper's intent.

"Go on, Pepper, what's on your mind?" Parker asked as he poured another cup of coffee.

"I believe it is time to meet with Thaddeus Wells. In fact, when I saw Judge McCain earlier, he told me that he still has a letter and the matter of 'money situation' to discuss with the old man. I don't know what is so important, but the judge was adamant that we make the attempt to see him. Since he will be in town to discuss this so-called letter with the judge, McCain says it is high time we put all the cards on the table and confront him." Pepper studied each face of the two friends seated before him. His words were absorbed by Cooper and Parker, and yet it was a few moments before either one responded.

"What exactly is this letter all about?" asked Cooper with a sigh.

"Don't know the details, but it must be important," Pepper answered as he returned to the table and poured himself a second cup of coffee.

"Pepper, will you be able to do this? Will you be able to look at your father, let alone talk to him? After all these years? After all the hurt and anger you have stored up?" asked Parker solemnly. "I have known you for a long time, so has Cooper. But I am not so sure that you or Pia will ever be ready to see him."

"Thank you, Parker, for your sincere words. But too much has happened. If he has anything to do with the attacks on McKenna, I need to know. It has been a long time since I have seen the bastard, but I will be able to face him. I have nothing to hide."

Chapter 47

One week had passed since Pia and Pepper had been informed that Judge McCain had arranged a meeting with their father. The Judge assured them that he had good reason to invite Thaddeus into his chambers and discuss a most important piece of information. The catch was, Thaddeus would be under the assumption that he would be talking privately to the judge in his chambers. Judge McCain, however, advised Pia and Pepper to remain hidden behind the secret bookshelf door, all the while listening to their conversation. When Pia and Pepper had shared this news with Cooper and Parker, disbelief overcame them both.

"Of all the harebrained ideas, you two take the topping to the cake. Eavesdrop? On your own father? Are you both out of your minds?" Parker asked. Cooper even shook his head in disbelief as they sat on the veranda.

"No, we are not out of our minds. We simply don't want to see him right away. In fact, it serves him right—we want to hear what he has to say without knowledge of our presence. There is nothing wrong with that!" Pia snapped back, almost spilling her glass of cider on the veranda swing.

"Nothing, except you don't even know what the Judge wants to discuss with Thaddeus. Maybe it will be something that you don't want or need to know!" Parker snapped back and got up from his chair so suddenly that it nearly toppled over.

"Parker, for heaven's sake, do you honestly believe our father could surprise us any more than he already has?" Pia asked the question so suddenly that it caught all of them off guard. She was stubborn and Parker knew it. She wasn't going to back down.

"Alright," Cooper added, "it is your business, not mine. Just don't come crying to me if you find out something that you wished you hadn't!"

"I assure you we won't come *cryin'* to either one of you. But…"

"We need a favor," interjected Pepper with a serious look.

"This doesn't sound good," muttered Cooper under his breath.

"We would like you both to join us. Please..." asked Pia, stopping her swing with her feet.

"You mean to say, you want us to eavesdrop with you?" asked Parker.

"That's exactly what we mean. And, if your answer is yes, we need to be going. The meeting is in an hour." Pepper smiled as he stood and straightened his hat.

"An hour? And you are just now telling us? This is beyond belief, even for you two." Parker took a few steps away and looked out upon the morning fields.

"You knew we wouldn't say 'no,' didn't you?" Cooper asked as he sat beside Pia on her swing. "For the love of God, are you sure you want to hear what the old man has to say?"

"Yes, and so does Pepper." Pia rose and straightened her skirt. "Now then, let's be going, I want to beat him there. We cannot be seen."

Pia and Pepper quickly left the veranda porch and walked down the path toward their waiting carriage. Cooper and Parker remained standing with a dumbfounded look upon their faces. "They had this planned all along!" Cooper said as they both turned and walked down the pathway steps.

"They sure as hell did. What's worse, they knew we'd come along, and they told us with little time to spare. We have been hoodwinked, my friend!" Parker just shook his head as he took his last step before jumping into the carriage. "Let's go, driver," Parker shouted as he thumped the door.

***

"Thank you for meeting me at my office today, Thaddeus. Now then, let's get down to business. As I said, I received a letter in which you were bequeathed a gift. A gift of money to be exact."

"Are you saying someone left me money, Judge?" Thaddeus asked again in disbelief as he sat across Judge McCain's ornately carved oak desk.

"Yes, Thaddeus, someone has bequeathed to you what appears to be a sum of money, according to this letter."

"Who wrote it, Judge?"

"Well, how about I read it to you?" Judge McCain opened the seal and began to read the letter aloud.

"Dear Thaddeus,

I write this letter to you, hoping you are in good health. We met long ago, during a horse auction event, and at the time, we were bidding on the same horse. You outbid me and bought the horse; I left empty-handed.

We met up at the local alehouse later that same day, and we shared conversation. We soon started attending yearly auctions together. Well, dear friend, during one auction, I was busy looking at the quarter horses, and you snuck away and bid on a Haflinger for me and ended up purchasing that horse for me that very afternoon. Thaddeus, that was the kindest thing anyone has ever done for me.

It has been ten years since we have seen each other. I stopped going to the auctions because my wife became ill. As time passed, she worsened, and eventually she passed away, but before she did, she made me promise that I would repay the kindness that you had extended to me long ago.

You are receiving a payment from me, Thaddeus. It is twice what you originally paid for the Haflinger that you purchased for me. I want you to take the money. I have no regrets giving it to you. You are a good man, Thaddeus, and you were a good friend to me all those years ago. I have since moved to Ireland to be with my sister and her family.

Your friend,
Alexander Longender"

Judge McCain quietly placed the letter upon his desk and held up the paper check to the light. "Well, Thaddeus, the check that is enclosed has been written out to you in the sum of three thousand dollars."

"What? He wrote a check to me for that amount? I bought that horse for less than half that. I never would have guessed he would have done such a thing," Thaddeus said in earnest.

"If truth be told, I would never have guessed that you would have done such a kind thing for a stranger. You are a crusty old bird, and kindness is typically not in your character description, now is it?" the Judge asked with sarcasm.

"Judge, you can just keep your opinions to yourself. I did what I did, and I never regretted it."

"Well then, be glad that you did, because you are now three thousand dollars richer." Judge McCain rose from his leather chair and around his desk. He placed the letter and the check into Thaddeus's hand.

"Thank you, Judge. I mean it."

"Don't thank me, I didn't do anything. I am just the deliverer. You are right, though; we should never regret the good things we do in life. You have no need to feel bad about this gift of money. What you did was good, Thaddeus." Judge McCain looked at Thaddeus and gave a half smile before he grabbed the arms of the chair and sat down directly across from him.

"On the other hand, I have done plenty of things I have regretted... How about you? Anything you've done that you ever regretted?" Judge McCain asked as he scooted his back against his chair, hoping that the four pairs of ears on the other side of the bookcase were prepared for what may be admitted.

"Well, if we are talking freely... I regret that I have not seen my son and daughter in over nineteen years. I regret that I forced my son's first love out of his life. I regret how I treated Maribelle, and now she's not here to accept any apology I would offer. Yes, I think about my children and the mistakes I made. I regret a lot where they are concerned."

"I suppose you do," nodded the judge with compassion.

"I haven't touched alcohol in over fifteen years because of those mistakes, Judge."

"You are off the bottle? That is good to know. Thaddeus, I must ask, have you tried to contact your children?" the Judge asked intently.

"I wouldn't know where to begin to locate Pepper. I often drive past Olympia's home on my way to horse auctions, but I have never stopped in. She would probably have me shot on sight or run off. I wish I could tell them that I have changed, Judge—I even go to church every Sunday now. I volunteer to feed the poor, and I give a percentage of my horse sales to the church."

"You do? What brought you back to church?" Thaddeus had the Judge's full attention, noting how he scooted forward and sat on the edge of his chair, intently listening.

"The reverend. I hated everybody and blamed everyone, including my own children, for the death of my wife. When my Maribelle left, I just got angrier. I said horrible things to my son and daughter and I know that now. I was too blinded by my own foolishness to admit it then. But I really would like to see them. In fact, I need to find them and soon. I need to make my apologies known to them both." Thaddeus shifted in his chair and loosened his tie a bit.

"Why the urgency?" asked the judge, tapping his fingers on his knees.

"I am dying, Judge. The doc has given me a couple years—maybe more—to live. I have a cancer in my lungs." The look on Thaddeus's face would have made a grown man cry. He was humbled. He had just admitted his faults, and now he was admitting that his life would soon be taken from him.

"I am sorry to hear this, Thaddeus." The Judge just looked at the man sitting across from him.

You have nothing more to lose, do you? My God, you are living on borrowed time and an empty heart.

"Do you have all of your legal papers up to date and ready to be processed in the event of your death?" the Judge asked as he grudgingly cleared his throat.

"I brought everything with me for you to read over. I was hoping that you would do this for me. I want to bequeath everything to my son and daughter and grandchildren. Isn't that funny, Judge? I have a granddaughter from Maribelle that I have never met. I understand she was in Lancashire at the horse auction recently. She must be a beauty if she looks anything like Maribelle." His eyes filled with tears as he blew his nose.

"I sure would like to meet her, as well as be reunited with all my grandchildren. I also understand Olympia's boys are excellent shots, and the little girl is a perfect likeness to my pretty Pia." Thaddeus finally stood and paced.

"Thaddeus, after everything that you have shared with me this morning, I have a question for you. If you could see Pepper and Pia, what would you say to them?"

"I would be scared as hell, but yes, I would like to see them. You know, I would ask both of them to find it in their hearts to forgive a foolish old drunk who thought more of himself than he did his own children. Hell, I don't even know if Pepper ever married. I chased off and threatened his only true love years ago. If my father had done that, I probably would have left, too. It was bad, Judge. I told Pepper I would shoot him if he ever came home again. I locked Pia in her room to keep her at home. My God, she probably hates me as much as Pepper does. Hell, he doesn't even go by his given name, and that is the worst hatred a son can own, I reckon."

"Thaddeus, sit down and get hold of yourself. You were a foolish old man, but the man I see in front of me isn't foolish anymore. I see a broken man that is willing to do whatever it takes to reunite with his family. There is nothing wrong in wanting to do that." Judge McCain was trying hard to swallow down that lump forming in his throat. Never in a million years would he have predicted this conversation between himself and Thaddeus Wells to be so woeful.

"I have prayed over and over again and asked God for forgiveness. The reverend told me to ask for God's forgiveness, then try to seek out my children, admit to my mistakes, and ask for their forgiveness. He has been there for me, Judge. He has cancer too, and can relate. Lately, he and I have had a lot of good conversations. He encourages me to pray to God, and I encourage him to keep hopeful."

"I didn't know about the reverend; I am sorry to hear this."

"Keep that to yourself, Judge, he doesn't want a lot of people to know."

"Anything that has been said will not leave these walls. Thaddeus, I have a proposition for you. I can arrange a meeting between you and your family—here—today. But you would have to be totally honest with me before I do that."

"What do you mean?" Thaddeus asked as he sat back down in his chair and faced the Judge, pouring a drink of water from the glass decanter.

"Thaddeus, I need to tell you that Harper and Maribelle's daughter has been in England for the past two years. She is staying with Pia until the war back in the States gets settled, and it is safe for her to go home. Since she has been here, she has been threatened, accosted, hit, held at gunpoint and knifepoint, kidnapped, and everything shy of being raped."

"Oh my God. What are you implying, Judge? Do you think I am behind this?"

"I am not implying anything now. I am telling you the men who have attacked McKenna have all pointed fingers back at you. They say you hired them to scare her back to the States."

"My God, Judge, I didn't even know she was here until the horse auction a few months back. The bartender, Charlie, told me that a blonde beauty had been at the auction, and she resembled Maribelle. That bartender and Maribelle had been childhood friends, and he would know the physical likeness as well as anyone. That is as far as it goes," replied Thaddeus, pounding his fist on his armchair.

"Thaddeus, calm down. All I am saying is that we all make mistakes in our lives. Some more severe than others. If you are truly remorseful, I would ask that you remain in town for the next hour while I see what I can do about rounding up your family. They may want to see you, or they may not. But isn't it worth a try?"

Thaddeus Wells didn't move. He didn't blink. He didn't even swallow. The emotions passed over his face as clearly as shadows spilling forth from the heavens. Judge McCain could only assume that the man before him felt decisively defeated. Yet, there was a calmness and an attempt at self-possession that was emerging from his eyes.

"Judge McCain, I would be very thankful for whatever you could arrange. I have made terrible mistakes throughout the course of my life. But I would hope that before I pass, I could remedy the wrongs I have caused. I am not demanding that they forgive me; I want to apologize to my children. As far as these men who say I have hired them, I know nothing about any of that."

"I will see what I can do. I understand your feelings and I will do my best to get this meeting under way. I must ask though, Thaddeus, do you have any enemies right now? Do you owe money to anyone? Have you gotten into an argument lately, one that stands out in your mind?"

"No, I do not owe money to anyone. I haven't had any arguments, but there is a neighbor of mine who wants to buy my property. His lawyer keeps sending me letters and I keep returning them. I am not interested in selling, but my neighbor doesn't seem to understand that. Recently, someone set a few small brush fires, but I haven't been able to catch the culprit. I am concerned though that one of these smaller fires could turn into a larger blaze. I'm guessing my fool neighbor had something to do with those fires. Shoot, I even got a brick thrown through my window a while back. It had a note tied around it that said, 'sell your land.' That is the extent of my enemies, as far as I know. I keep to myself these days, so I haven't riled anyone up." Thaddeus attempted a smile, but soon realized the Judge wasn't in the mood for a slight teasing. Something was on the Judge's mind and he was extremely stoic.

"What is this neighbor's name, Thaddeus?" the judge asked solemnly.

"All I know is that his first name is Ian. I have never talked with him." Thaddeus looked at the Judge, waiting for the next question.

"Does this Ian have a last name, Thaddeus?" the judge asked in a more interrogative tone.

"If he does, I don't know it. Like I said, I have never talked with the man."

"Then how do you know he was responsible for throwing the brick through your window?" Judge McCain asked cautiously.

"His lawyer let it slip."

"Well, I believe our conversation is done for now. Why don't you go down to the bakery, buy a few scones, and have a cup of tea? If I can arrange a meeting with your family, I will send word to you at the bakery. If I can't, I will still send word for you to return here, and we will take care of your legal matters. Are you willing to give your family a chance to see you?" Judge McCain rose from his chair and stood directly in front of Thaddeus.

"Judge, the Good Lord will forgive my sins. I just hope my family can forgive mine before I die. Thank you, Judge, for trying; it means a lot to me." Thaddeus could no longer hold his emotions intact. He slumped against the judge and briefly wept. When he pulled himself away, the judge shook him slightly.

"Thaddeus, you are doing the right thing," the Judge whispered. "Go on, now. I will send word either way."

Thaddeus nodded slowly and turned, glancing in the mirror to ensure he had properly aligned his hat before leaving.

Never have I seen more remorsefulness and self-condemnation than I have today. Contrition will surely deepen in Thaddeus Well's heart if forgiveness is not given.

Chapter 48

"You can come out now, all of you," ordered the Judge after Thaddeus had left his chambers.

"Well, I'll be damned," said Pepper, with a look of shock upon his face.

"I'm stunned," said Pia as she sunk into a chair, her face pale and ghostlike.

"I believe everyone needs to take a step back and reassess the conversation we have just heard. Pia and Pepper, are you willing to see your father?" asked Parker.

"I simply do not know. He is right; if we don't forgive him, we will go to hell. The Bible says so."

"He is not worth my going to hell," whispered Pepper. "What does shock me is that the name Ian was brought up. The only Ian I know around these parts is Jenny's father. You do not think that Ian McTavish would be behind all this, do you?"

"Pepper, I do not know," answered Judge McCain. "But I have been in this field of right versus wrong for most of my life as a judge. I can say I am pretty accurate in judging a person's character and integrity during a single conversation. I truly believe Thaddeus is telling us the truth. He would have no cause to lie to me, especially since he was unaware of your presence. You heard how he regretted his past actions. Before your father passes away, I believe you both need to remedy your situation, or at the very least, come to terms with him and allow him to offer his apologies… before it is too late. I fear that if you don't, you will regret it for the rest of your life. Please, think about this."

"Oh, Judge, I am so overwhelmed. I came to hear this monster admit to his hatred for Pepper and me, and about his desperate and violent actions against McKenna," whispered Pia, fighting back another round of tears.

"I came here to hate the bastard even more than I already did. But when I heard him state his mistakes about my past with Jenny, I had sympathy for the old man," Pepper stated as he pounded his fist upon the desk. "I am angry, and yet, I was moved by his words. And damn it, I didn't want to be moved by him. Not now!"

"Pepper, you are a man of the law, as am I." The Judge stared appraisingly down at the three uncertain family members. "This is not the first time you have heard this scenario. Pull yourself out of this and ask yourself what you would tell a client if they found themselves in this same situation." The Judge walked over to the window, waiting for Pepper's reply. Moments passed before Pepper cleared his throat and answered.

"I would tell them to seek the truth and find the answers they are searching for. I would tell my clients to avoid passing judgment until all details, questions, and facts have been disclosed."

"Well, then, there is your answer. I shall go down to the bakery and bring Thaddeus back to my chambers. In the meantime, gather your thoughts, your emotions, and most importantly, your ability to forgive. I would imagine Christ had to do the same in the Garden of Gethsemane before the soldiers approached. We do not want to have a Judas within our walls. This is a room of law and protection for all those who enter. You all know that as well as I do."

Chapter 49

The scene in Judge McCain's chambers was exasperating.

"I never wanted to speak to you again, old man," Pepper spat at his father. "In fact, I never thought I would be sitting across the desk from you, listening to you utter apologies, much less ask for forgiveness. I hated you for how you treated all of us. I hated you for driving Jenny away from me. I hated you so much that I used to pray for your death. God strike me dead if that isn't the truth." Pepper pushed the wing chair he was seated in forcefully away from the desk, as though he couldn't even bear the three feet of space in between himself and his father. He glared at the wall, refusing to make eye contact.

Pia stood up shakily and walked to the window. She looked out through the glass pane as she talked. "I never thought I was good enough for you. Maribelle was small and blonde and fairy-tale beautiful. I was the tomboy. I loved horses as much as you did and would sit in my bed at night, wishing you would take me along with you to the horse races and auctions. My God, you locked me in my room and didn't even offer me supper at times! You were a monster to both Pepper and me! When Maribelle and Pepper left, I wanted to die." Pia held her face in her hands and trembled.

Her sobs were becoming heavier, paired with labored breathing. Her face was etched in red, and her eyes spilled forth uncontrollable tears. It was a humbling, wretched, heart-rending sight. Parker walked behind Pia and gently placed his hands upon her shoulders. After a moment, she turned and walked to her father, bending down in front of him while holding on to the armrests of the chair.

"You are my father. There was a time when I loved you and thought you were the best and strongest father in the world. All I ever wanted to do was to be acknowledged by you for my horsemanship. I never received that acknowledgement. In fact, I received very little praise from you and a whole lot of negativity, instead. I need to forgive you, and I will admit it will be hard for me to do that. But if I am not willing to forgive you, then I go to hell, and I am not willing to go to hell for the likes of you."

She gathered her strength and continued on, never averting her eyes from Thaddeus.

"You do not know your grandchildren. You don't even know I was married and lost my husband in a tragic jumping accident. Very few people know this, but one would think a daughter could go to her father and seek comfort and refuge within his arms. I could not. I am glad you have found God again. But you need to find your family, and Judge McCain did share with us that you have limited time to do this. I only hope you are sincere in your words. I have damned you to hell and back a thousand times, and now I find myself struggling to believe you, much less forgive you. What made you turn to God? It surely wasn't guilt." Thaddeus reached for her hands, but she pulled away.

"Olympia, I am not sure what made me turn to God, or the exact moment I decided to put my trust and faith in him. Perhaps it was grace. I cannot honestly say. I do know I have hurt both of you deeply, and for that I am sorry. I am not demanding your forgiveness, but I am offering my apologies to you. Yes, I have a cancer in my lung, and I need to go to my grave with a clean heart. I know God will accept me into his kingdom because I have repented for the things I have done. I want to see your mother more than anything else in this world. Whatever I must do to see her, I will do. I know she will forgive me, and once that happens, I can live in peace and with her eternally. But I must come clean with myself before I can ever hope to see her again. As far as hurting Maribelle's daughter, I have no knowledge of this. I didn't even know her name till the judge spoke of it a while ago."

At that moment, Thaddeus began to lose control. He searched Pia's eyes, and suddenly, he began to cry.

"Pepper, come here," Pia said as she reached out her hand toward her brother.

Pepper walked over to Pia, grabbed her hand, and knelt beside her. He looked at his father's eyes long and hard before he spoke.

"I hated you for taking the love of my life away from me. I hated you with every ounce of my being. I pursued law, and often wondered how I could hurt you where it would count—your wealth. I want to believe that you have repented, and I want to believe that the tears in your eyes are genuine. But you must understand how difficult it is for us to rewrite our memories of the decades upon decades during which you treated us as no father should." Pepper finished his response and stood, only to find minutes of silence permeate the chambers. A slight breeze caused the chimes to ring, finally breaking the silence.

"Will you ever be able to forgive me?" asked Thaddeus, looking up remorsefully.

"I think we can, but it may take time to heal the wounds in our hearts, and time is something you are lacking." Pia stood and leaned against the desk, facing her father.

"I understand. But I want both of you to know I am leaving everything I own to the two of you. I want you to decide how to manage and finance my holdings and my wealth. I know you are racing horses, Pia. I would love to come and see your home. I would love to see your children—my grandchildren. Pepper, I wish I could tell Jenny how very sorry I am."

"You can, old man. You can meet her in person and tell her yourself. I found Jenny, with McKenna's help, and we have finally found our happiness and we did it without your approval." Pepper knew that was uncalled for him to say, but it felt good.

"What a foolish old man I was. I had foolish thoughts, as well. Again, I am so very sorry, Pepper. I wish I could turn back the clock and relive my life, but I can't. Perhaps Jenny will be able to forgive me one day. I know her father never will."

"Why do you say that?" asked Pepper defensively.

"He sent me a letter. He said he would destroy anything and anyone who was related to me. He wanted to hurt me as much as I had hurt his daughter. As God was his witness, he would have blood revenge upon me. Those were his exact words. You can even ask Amos, my trainer, as he read the same thing I did."

"What was your response and how did you know it was Jenny's father who sent it?" asked Pepper with renewed curiosity.

"I burned the letter. It was signed from Jenny's father."

Silence prevailed in the chambers before Thaddeus spoke again. "I have a question," he said in a hushed voice.

"What would that be?" asked Pia.

"You said McKenna helped you find Jenny."

"That is right," said Pepper.

"Oh, my God," said Thaddeus. He looked into Pepper and Pia's eyes.

"What? What is wrong now?" asked Pepper.

"You don't suppose Jenny's father is the man who has caused harm to McKenna?" Thaddeus asked, sitting up straight in his chair.

"Why would he cause harm to McKenna? She is the one who found Jenny and brought her back into Pepper's life," Pia questioned nervously.

"Yes, we all know that, but her father doesn't know that," answered Parker. "He doesn't know that Pepper and Jenny are together again. Simply put, he is out for blood revenge, as stated in his letter. He must have heard that McKenna is here and he knows that McKenna is the grand-daughter of Thaddeus Wells, not to mentions Pepper's niece! In his mind, he found a relative of Thaddeus— someone to hurt and seek revenge upon." Parker slammed his hand down on the desk before continuing. "Thaddeus, Jenny's father's name is Ian McTavish."

"Dear God in heaven, Ian?"

"Yes, his name is Ian McTavish and that is the only Ian I know," Pepper replied with a firm and final tone to his voice.

"I think we may have found our mystery man. It makes sense; he wanted to hurt McKenna the way his daughter had been hurt. All this time, we have been pointing fingers at you, Thaddeus, when we should have been looking in another direction," declared Parker as he walked behind Thaddeus and laid his hand upon Pepper's shoulder. "Cooper, you haven't said a word; what are you thinking?"

"I am thinking we should end our business here. I am thinking that Pepper and Pia need to do what their hearts are tellin' them to do. I am thinkin' that you and I need to get the hell home. McKenna is by herself with Zadie and I sure as hell don't like them bein' alone, especially with everything that has happened. The boys aren't home and enough has been said here today. Pepper and Pia, the rest is up to you." Cooper looked at the group before him. He slowly walked over to the judge and uttered his thanks and his good-bye.

"You comin'?" Cooper asked Parker over his shoulder.

"Right behind you, Coop. By the way, Judge, can you give Pia and Pepper a ride home?"

"Certainly, after we tie up loose ends here," he responded as he cordially shook Parker's hand.

"Thank you, Judge, for everything." Parker grabbed his hat and followed Cooper on out.

Thaddeus sighed and rested his hands in his lap before speaking. "I am sorry if my actions brought havoc upon my grand-daughter. I didn't know she was even here. I didn't even know her name. I should have guessed that Maribelle would have named her daughter McKenna."

"How would you possibly guess that? After all, it is an unusual name for a girl," asked Pepper.

"McKenna was your mother's middle name. She gave her baby a piece of herself."

"Well, I'll be damned. I never knew her middle name or much else about her because you never talked about her. You shared very little about our mother with us," Pepper responded as he leaned against the desk, folding his arms.

"Yes, I suppose I didn't share much about her. It hurt too much to talk about the woman I loved. But perhaps, I can fix that. I would like to tell you both about her if you give me the chance." Thaddeus lowered his head.

"Well, ladies and gentlemen, I feel the time has come to move on to the future," interrupted Judge McCain. "We know what has been sacrificed in the past, but are we willing to take the future and make the most out of it? The way I see it, apologies have been given, but it is up to you two to accept them and move on. If you continue to hold grudges, you are no better than he is. What say you both?"

"Judge, I need time to digest this," said Pia with a trembling voice.

"Time is something you don't have. Continue on with hatred in your heart or begin anew. You too, Pepper. Erase the hurt and hate from within and begin fresh. I am not saying it will be easy, but your life and your children's lives depend on your love and your ability to forgive."

"The Judge is right. I can forgive you, Father, and I want you back in my life, but I must take baby steps. I can't welcome you into my heart just yet. But I am willing to try. What about you, Pepper?"

Pepper met his father's eyes with wariness and suspicion. A flair of hope lit up the old man's expression. "I will try," said Pepper. "Expect nothing for the moment. But I will try."

"Thank you. Thank you both. I have a question for you, Pepper."

"What would that be?"

"Where did you get the name Pepper, and why do you go by that name?" his father asked cautiously.

"I hated the name Thaddeus. I thought of you every time I heard that word, and I wanted nothing from you—not even your name. Pepper is a nickname given to me by Captain Sloane."

"Captain, as in the English army?"

"Captain, as in the Royal English Fleet," corrected Pepper.

"I see," answered Thaddeus. "Well then, I guess that I have been put in my place by my son. Is there any higher honor in life, other than giving a son his father's name? Is there any higher dishonor in life other than a son rejecting that very name? We all know that our family certainly has a lot of healing to do within a limited amount of time. God willing, we will be able to overcome and once again, be a family."

Chapter 50

Time began to heal the misdeeds and hurt that Thaddeus Wells had caused. Pepper, Pia, and their father began increasing their time together, especially by including Pia's children on Sunday afternoon picnics. Thaddeus was thrilled to watch Quaid, Livingston, and Caleb shoot their targets, often joining them and taking aim himself. Maggie, being oblivious to past hurts, was resilient enough to welcome her new-found grandfather into her life, rarely leaving his side when he visited. Ah yes, Thaddeus was slowly being accepted by his children, and even more so welcomed by his grandchildren.

Jenny had been reintroduced to Thaddeus on a prearranged picnic with Parker, Pepper, and McKenna. Jenny insisted on a walk around the pond with Thaddeus, without the company of Pepper. Although Pepper reluctantly agreed, McKenna suspected that Jenny needed some private time for confessions and for forgiveness. When they finally rounded the other side of the pond, Thaddeus appeared to have a gleam in his eye. Pepper, of course, was insistent that he be made aware of their conversation, but to no avail. Jenny and Thaddeus decided that what had happened in the past would stay in the past.

Sweet Jenny, McKenna thought as she unpacked the picnic basket she had prepared for Parker and herself. She was so kind and so willing to forgive the actions of the past. Jenny had taken the bull by the horns, so to speak, and confronted Thaddeus herself with a private conversation.

McKenna, on the other hand, was not so lucky. She had met her grandfather by accident. There was no prearranged picnic, and there was certainly no aunt or uncle present for McKenna's informal debut to Thaddeus Wells. She remembered how startled Thaddeus was when he came upon her from behind, hearing curse words spewing from her mouth. She now giggled out loud as she thought what a sight that must have been when he first encountered her down by the pond. So caught up in her sentiments, she didn't hear Parker kneel behind her until he nuzzled upon her neck.

"Parker, you startled me!" she said with a gasp, almost dropping her wrapped sandwich.

"Pardon me, my dear, and where was that pretty little mind of yours?" he asked as he gently took the sandwich from her hand and began to unwrap it.

"I was just thinking about the first time that Thaddeus met me. It wasn't exactly the way I planned it to be," she giggled as she took the sandwich back, laying it gently on the blanket provided.

Parker laid down beside McKenna, propping one leg up while snatching a tart from the picnic basket. "Didn't he find you fishing? Right over there, wasn't it?"

McKenna laughed and pushed a stray curl from her face. "Yes, he did, and yes I saw you sneak that tart, Captain." McKenna sighed heavily, tilting her head back into the sunshine before continuing.

"I went down to the pond by the willow early in the morning to find that catfish that keeps evading me. I knew that if I got there early enough, I might still find him in a sleepy and unsuspecting mood." Parker chuckled as she spoke. "Anyway, he took my bait and I caught him on my line. But he certainly gave me a fight. And, of course, my patience wore thin and I said a few bad words… and that is when Thaddeus came from behind me and offered his help to reel him in."

"Correct me if I'm wrong, love, but you lost the bugger, didn't you?" asked Parker as he seductively moved his hand across McKenna's thigh.

"Yes, Captain, I did. And you can take your hand off my thigh." She softly slapped Parker's roving hand as she continued. "Well, I fell backwards, Thaddeus fell into the water, and my friendly catfish swam away. It was quite funny, until… until he looked at me."

"What happened, kitten? You never mentioned anything about this before." Parker sat up straight, his jaw twitching rapidly.

"Calm yourself, love. Nothing happened to me, except when Thaddeus looked at me, he almost fainted, if men truly ever faint. He said that he thought he had seen a ghost… he said he thought he was looking at his Maribelle."

"I would imagine a vision as lovely as you would send any man to his knees."

"No, Parker, only because I looked identical to my mother, a young woman he hadn't seen in years. I am about the same age as she was when she ran away from home with my father. Parker, he cried, and I know he felt embarrassed but I didn't know what to do. I didn't even know his name at the time. He introduced himself to me as Thaddeus Wells and I started to introduce myself to him, but he said my name before I did.

"That is when we decided to sit down and fill in all the missing pieces of my nineteen years and his absence as my grandfather. Parker, did you know that I was named after my grandmother?" she asked with a lovely smile upon her face.

"Yes, kitten, I did. He told Pia and she told me. Actually, I think it was endearing that your mother gave you a piece of your grandmother. Maribelle wanted your grandmother in your life, love."

"Yes, I suppose she did. At any rate, that is how we met. We sat by the pond until noon. And ever since then, we have shared quite a few conversations—nice conversations, I might add."

"Kitten, I am glad that you have had the opportunity to meet your grandfather. Hopefully, you shall share many more conversations with him, providing his health remains intact. Now then, have I told you today how much I love you?" Parker asked with sultry eyes.

"No, as a matter of fact, you have not, Captain Sloane, but you can tell me now," she murmured while she leaned forward and pressed her lips on his.

"Well then, allow me to tell you, kitten," he muttered under his breath.

"I would prefer you show me," McKenna whispered into his ear as they both laid back upon the picnic blanket, embraced in each other's arms.

***

This would be McKenna's third summer in England. Fortunately, she was busy riding horses, breaking horses, charting their physical traits and speed times, cleaning stalls, and cooking in the kitchen alongside Zadie.

She was beginning to feel sorry for herself, and she knew it. Pia noticed this, as well.

One evening, the family was seated around the table for the evening meal. The conversation was interesting, and the faces of those seated at the table were filled with satisfaction from the day's hard work.

"McKenna, you received a letter from your father today," said Pia, handing it over the table.

"Really?" McKenna snatched it and began unfolding it, her hands already beginning to shake. She always feared what words would be inside. "I haven't heard from him in over six months!"

"Well, don't dawdle, child," Pepper ordered. "What does it say?"

"My dearest McKenna,

I know it has been such a long time since I have written. The battles here in the States have become bloodier and deadlier. I have run out of bandages and iodine. There are days that I don't even have a clean shirt to wear. They are so stained from blood, I find it difficult to assume if they are white or pink. That sounds terrible, doesn't it, my dear? Here I am worried about clean clothes when young men are worried about surviving through the night.

When Lee marched outside of Sharpsburg, the Union corps came from the north and the fighting broke out. My God, I was there, child. I heard the cannon barrage for three hours!

The newspapers said that twenty-two hundred Union soldiers were taken down in less than twenty minutes. Twenty minutes, McKenna-girl! Where do you think all those wounded came? To our tent, and the sad part is, I had nowhere to put them. I am tired and hungry and yearn for a good night's sleep. But as duty calls, I took an oath to preserve life and I must stay strong to fulfill my oath. A few colleagues of mine have had their bellies full of death and injury and unsanitary conditions, so much so that they ran off. That leaves me in a horrid position. I find myself training young field nurses how to amputate—no formal training, mind you—just on the field service. Some of these girls are younger than you are! I am so damn glad you are away from this bloody conflict. Sometimes I have to take the shirts off the dead just to tear strips to have enough bandages. We are in such desperate need of supplies and there is nowhere to take them from.

I suppose you know that President Lincoln gave a speech and told the country about his Emancipation Proclamation, which will free the slaves. To me, that means more soldiers will enlist and that means more wounded and dead for me to tend to. I am tired, baby girl, so very tired.

Every farm, as far as the eye can see, has been used as a temporary hospital. Every field has been used as a tomb for the dead. When I was asked

292

to travel to Sharpsburg and direct the field surgery, I eagerly accepted. Dear God, the sight sickened me the first day. Fingers, toes, arms, legs, knees, elbows, noses, ears, and even parts of skulls were lying upon the floor.

What has happened to this country? What has happened to mankind's spirit? I can tell you—it has been burned and charred in the fires from the North to the South. The remaining ashes are the only remnants left of what was once the United States. Many of my colleagues feel that the next battle will determine the outcome of the war. No one, and I mean no one, knew it would last this long.

If the fighting continues into another state, we may have another round of needless amputations and deaths to deal with. I thank God that you do not have to witness the despair and extinction of what was once a beautiful country. I took an oath to save lives, but I had no idea how many lives would perish before my hands could even prevent death from arriving at the hospital's doors. Forgive my evident despair in my words; however small the attempt, it is therapeutic for me to share my thoughts.

I love you, baby girl,
Give my love to the family
Papa"

Chapter 51

McKenna folded the letter and inserted it back into the envelope. She silently scooted her chair from the dining room table and politely excused herself. She walked onto the veranda, hoping that the outside air would help her breathe. She was suffocating from helplessness.

"Dear God," she cried out in anger. "Tell me what to do. How can I help my father? My friends? The soldiers who are injured? Please guide me, Lord. I need to do something to help."

She knelt upon the ground, still holding on to her father's letter. Knox came and stood beside her and licked her neck, trying to comfort his owner. She wrapped her arms around her big dog and silently said the Lord's Prayer. Such was the scene presented to Parker as he watched through the window. That little wisp of a lady had more tenacity in her pinky finger than an entire sailing crew. He made no movement toward her, however. McKenna needed space right now—she needed her father, and there was no way to satisfy the latter. Pia joined Parker and sighed.

"If only I could transport Harper here," she whispered.

"You can't transport Harper here, but I can transport supplies to him," Parker said with an eagerness to his speech.

"Parker, you are right. We could send supplies to Harper! I will inform McKenna of this and she and I will go to the hospital tomorrow and see what we can secure. Bravo, dear Captain, what a wonderful idea! This will boost McKenna's spirits for sure," Pia said as she lightly clapped her hands together.

"She must work this out by herself. She knows we are all here for her. She fears the unknown, Pia."

"Of course, she fears the unknown; we all do. But it isn't the same, Parker. It is hard to work things out on your own. I know what it is like to do that without a father's presence. My father was footsteps away from me; her father is thousands of miles away. She knows that, and there isn't a thing she can do about it." Pia and Parker watched McKenna in silence for several minutes until Pia spoke.

"I have an idea, Parker. McKenna needs to get away for a bit. Take her to a new place to visit for the day. Take her to the hunting cottage. I will fix it up and prepare it for you both."

"Pia, she is not married. It would ruin her reputation if I did that."

"Well then, my dear Captain Sloane, do something about that. Ask her to marry you!" Pia turned to leave, but not before she said, "Oh for heaven's sake, what are you waiting for? You both love each other; just don't wait too long before you ask, Parker Sloane."

Christ Almighty, Pia is right. What am I waiting for? Parker thought. Bloody hell, that little blonde angel had wrapped him around her little finger. Pia knew it, Pepper knew it; hell, they all knew it. Tomorrow they would go riding, and he would approach the subject. What if she said no? Well, she wouldn't be given that choice. She would marry him, come hell or high water. Right?

McKenna remained on the veranda long after Pia had gone to bed. When Parker finally came to check on her, he smiled fondly at the sight before him. There was his beautiful little kitten, curled up alongside Knox, holding him in one hand and Patches in the other. Both owner and pets were breathing in undisturbed harmony. How Parker hated to disturb the trio, but once again, he scooped his lovely bundle and carried her sleeping form up the stairs and placed her upon her bed. He gently took the letter from her sleeve cuff and laid it upon her nightstand, then pulled the coverlet over her and removed her shoes. Parker whistled to Knox, who bounded into bed to sleep beside his beloved owner. Even Patches got a boost to McKenna's pillow and nestled himself beside the curve in McKenna's neck.

My poor kitten, I am so sorry that you must endure so much hurt. I will try my very best to lift your spirits tomorrow, if only for a day.

Chapter 52

Parker persuaded McKenna to go for a ride the following day. Solomon and Midnight trotted along the hillside paths and winding creeks, stopping briefly for a tuft of grass. McKenna was captivated by the summer snowflakes and the lilac foxgloves growing along the rock tops. The turquoise-blossomed spring gentians were dispersed wildly in the rye grass, forming a maze of vitality upon the countryside. She was so enthralled with the landscape and its beauty, she hopped off Solomon and gathered primroses and Jacob's ladder into a wild bouquet. She even made a boutonniere for Parker.

Oh, how I wish Father could see this beauty rather than the dismal frames of death and grief, she thought to herself as she inhaled the overwhelming fragrance. As they rode farther up the trail, Parker noticed that it was becoming dangerously narrow due to the past rains.

"McKenna, pay attention. The path is getting narrow and filled with hidden roots; you will fall into that creek if you and Solomon are not careful. Be alert!"

"What?" McKenna asked and turned so quickly that she did not see the rut Solomon walked into. Her balance was shaken and she was thrown sideways from the saddle, landing hard upon the trail's edge before rolling down the slope and into the creek.

"Oh, my God, the water is so cold," she screamed.

Parker immediately dismounted and carefully climbed down to the creek. *Damn careless girl*, he thought.

"Here, give me your hand, and I will haul you out of there." When she merely sat there, staring at him, he huffed and shouted again. "McKenna, give me your hand before you freeze to death. Now, kitten!"

"Oh, all right. You do not need to raise your voice!" McKenna pushed her feet into the dirt bank and reached toward Parker.

"That's it, kitten, almost got you."

"I almost have you, too!" McKenna clasped Parker's hand with both of hers and yanked hard.

Parker fell face forward into the water.

"Damn it, you did that on purpose, you little wench!" he sputtered as he resurfaced.

"Why, Captain, yes, I did, and it was well worth it! In fact, you look as if you need another dunking!" McKenna quickly jumped on his back and shoved his head and body under the surface before he threw her off. She swam back and forth in small circles, laughing and waiting for Parker to emerge. When he didn't reappear right away, McKenna stood and began waving her hands in nearby, hoping to find Parker's form.

Where did you go, you skunk? I know you dove down and swam away. I am not falling for your pranks, today.

"Parker, where are you? Answer me this instant, Parker Sloane! This isn't funny anymore, you are beginning to frighten me. I know you can hear me; this water isn't that deep. Parker, will you resurface, please?"

All of a sudden, McKenna felt her waist being grabbed and her body being tossed up into the air.

"Take a breath, kitten!" She heard the familiar masculine voice shout before she went under. When she emerged, she couldn't help laughing and coughing up water at the same time.

"Why, Captain Sloane, I believe you are laughing as well!" McKenna grinned.

"Yes, kitten, I believe I am. You have a little bit of mud on your cheek."

"Why don't you wipe it off, then?" she spoke before she realized what her words would induce.

"Why certainly, kitten. Hold your breath, again."

Under the water she went again. When she reappeared, she was held within Parker's embrace, feeling every muscle in that gorgeously formed chest of his.

"That's better, the mud is all gone, now!" he chuckled as he swirled in the water.

"Captain Sloane, you can hold me like this all day long."

"I am afraid if I do that, we shall both freeze to death. Your teeth and mine are chattering. Now then, little one, let's get out of this water and dry off while the sun is still shining."

"Five more minutes… please," she begged with a pout upon her face.

"No. You do not listen well." Parker scooped her up in his arms and walked up the creek bank.

"Remove your shoes, and I shall rub your feet," Parker ordered as he placed her softly on the ground.

"Aye aye, Captain. You remove yours, and I shall rub your feet, as well." McKenna smiled so widely that Parker kneeled in front of her, staring into her eyes.

"You would do that? What kind of woman are you?" he asked.

"The kind of woman who cares about your cold feet. Come on, now, kick them off."

Parker quickly removed his shoes and together they reclined in the sunshine amidst the flowers, safe in their own secluded piece of heaven, rubbing life back into each other's cold limbs.

"McKenna, we need to go home and get out of these wet clothes right now," Parker finally insisted. "We will catch cold."

"No, Captain, we don't need to go home. We can get out of them right now and hang them on the tree limbs to dry. What say you, Captain? Are you willing to be a bit adventurous?"

"You are a brazen chit." Parker could not help but admire the legs and feet he was rubbing. Although McKenna had small feet and delicate ankles, her calves were shapely. As he began to rub a bit higher toward her knees, he felt the toned legs beneath his touch. Years of riding and post trotting had formed these beautiful legs of hers. He could only imagine what her thighs looked like and what they would feel like under his hands. She was a beauty, and she didn't know it.

"Kitten, you are thinking what I am speaking. Unless, of course, you insist upon riding back home. I will do whatever you suggest." She had no idea the effect she was having on him. Her wet dress hung to every curve her body possessed. Her waist could be easily grabbed by his two hands, not to mention her breasts. They were all but spilling out from the strained buttons. All he would have to do is pop one of those buttons, and the rest would tear away easily.

"Captain. You are doing it again. You are not listening to me!" McKenna said as she scooted up and leaned against the tree.

"I am sorry, kitten, but you present such a vision here in front of me, it is all I can do to keep my hands off of you."

"Well then, I suggest you stop talking and start undressing. You can easily reach the branches of this tree and hang our clothing." McKenna froze a moment before she continued, "Help me out of these clothes, will you? I know you are quite good at unbuttoning buttons." She winked.

"You are too brazen for your own good, McKenna Reed. Allow me to get behind you and take a look at these buttons. I managed once before, if memory serves me correctly. I think I can manage a row of buttons again." Parker crawled behind McKenna and lifted her wet hair from her back.

"Do you remember that night clearly, Captain?" McKenna asked as she lay her head back against Parker's massive shoulder. "I was trying so hard to look nice and I was bound and determined to wear a corset and shrink my waist, just so I would catch your eye!"

"You didn't need a corset to catch my eye, kitten. You caught my eye long before that." Parker lowered his hands, crawled up on the bank and sat directly in front of McKenna. He gently held both of her hands in his and cleared his throat before he spoke again.

"McKenna, I have a question to ask you. In fact, this is probably the most important question I shall ever ask of you."

"Parker Sloane, what is wrong? You have gone from playful to serious in a matter of seconds. Have I done something to offend you? I am sorry if I shoved your head under water, is that it? Are you angry with me?" McKenna began to pull her hands from his grasp, but he wouldn't allow it.

"No, kitten, hush now and let me speak. I am not angry with you for playing in the water. It is exactly what you needed and it is why I brought you here in the first place.

"McKenna Reed, I want to ask you to marry me, and I can't think of a better way to do that than lying side by side in this glorious spot, both of us naked, peering at the sky above without a worry in the world for one spectacular moment. But that would not be proper." Parker was speaking so sincerely; her heart was beating out of control. She smoothed away a drip of water cascading down his cheek before she spoke.

"I can't think of anything more romantic. Sopping wet hair, muddied clothes, bare feet, and shivering bodies. How much closer to nature can we get?" McKenna asked seductively. Parker leaned forward and cupped her chin in his hand. He slowly kissed her upper lip, nibbling upon her lower lip, then prying both lips open with his tongue. His kiss was long and filled with a tinge of possessiveness. McKenna felt as though they were the only two beings upon God's green earth when he kissed her. She felt so natural in his hands and arms. She melted at his touch and looked forward to any contact.

"Kitten, how many times are you going to make me repeat my question?" Parker asked as he pulled McKenna from her thoughts. He bent to one knee. "McKenna Reed, will you marry me?"

"Why, Captain Sloane, I thought you would never ask. Of course, I will marry you." McKenna smiled and leaned forward to kiss her Captain.

"You are a bold bundle, McKenna Reed. We will have to come to some understanding between us," he teased, leaning back against the tree and wrapping his arm around his shivering kitten.

"Understanding? Whatever are you talking about?" she asked, slightly turning and looking directly into Parker's eyes.

"I am merely saying that you need a firm hand occasionally." Parker pulled her onto his lap.

"Well, so do you, Parker Sloane!" she exclaimed.

"Well, I'll be damned. You are telling me I need a firm hand?"

"I am telling you we both want and need each other, and if we can both help each other along the way to become better people, then we will be happily ever after. Don't you think? Now then, I have answered your question with a definite yes! I will marry you, Parker Sloane. Please stop talking and give me a proper English kiss." McKenna leaned back and closed her eyes.

"Kitten, open your eyes and look at me. A proper kiss you shall have, but I am afraid that is all you shall have, here in the middle of the woods. I am a gentleman and was raised a gentleman. I believe you once told me that, 'once a pig, always a pig.' Well, my sweet, I am no pig, and I will not take you and make you mine in every sense of the word upon the forest floor. As badly as I want to, I must act with decency and take both of us back home.

"When our time comes to consummate this marriage, kitten, know this: our time together will be perfect, uninterrupted, and filled with the utmost respect, love, and passion. I long to touch you, kiss you, taste you, and listen to that little heartbeat of yours when I make you Mrs. Parker Sloane in every way. Until then, Miss Reed, I respect you too much to have a tumble in the woods. Agreed, kitten?" He held her face in her hands and slowly massaged her jawline with his thumbs.

Dear God in heaven, I am ready to melt with the slightest touch of his hands upon my face. Lord have mercy when those roving hands of his touch my naked body.

"Agreed and thank you. I am a virgin, Parker. I was taught to save myself for my husband because it was the moral thing to do. I trust you, and I know that when I am with you, I will never have to worry. Please know that I respect you even though you rile my temper at times. I want to be happy with you and laugh with you. I want you to be happy with me, and more importantly, I want to have your children one day. I want to be McKenna Sloane in every way possible. I can wait, sir, until our wedding night, because it is the right thing to do."

"Then so be it. Now, turn just a bit and I will button the loose buttons by your lovely neck, and then we will be on our way home."

"Must we go right now? Can't we stay just a tad bit longer?" she asked with an obvious pout.

Parker smacked McKenna's bottom as he helped her stand. "No, we can't stay just a tad bit longer. You are cold, I am cold, and we have an hour's ride home."

"Ouch, Parker, you didn't have to do that! A swat on a wet dress hus! There you go again, bullying me just because you are bigger than me."

"McKenna, mount your horse, or that cute little bottom of yours will be facing up… with me on my horse. Your choice."

"You are a cad. Maybe I should rethink my answer to your proposal," she said as she stomped away from Parker.

"Not a chance, kitten. Now, get on your horse."

Parker winked at McKenna, and she knew she had better mount Solomon. Parker loved her, and she was glad of that. But she also knew he meant what he said and didn't always like to play. McKenna just smiled devilishly at Parker and mounted Solomon before he could carry out his threat. One day, she thought, she would throw him over the saddle and spank his bottom.

"Oh, Captain?" she asked provocatively.

"Yes, sweet?" he asked as he mounted and trotted Midnight next to Solomon.

"Lean on over here and give me a kiss."

"You are a saucy little woman," drawled Parker slyly, one eyebrow raised, but he turned his horse closer toward her. The impatient minx met him halfway and entwined her fingers in the fabric of his unbuttoned shit to pull him for a kiss. He inhaled sharply as he realized that her other hand had found its way between his legs.

"Just remember, Captain Sloane, what lies between your legs now belongs to me. If I ever hear of another woman touching or taking liberty with what is now mine, I shall have to make a eunuch out of you."

Parker immediately cupped a breast within his hand and said huskily, "If I ever hear of another man touching or taking liberty with what is now mine, I shall kill him." Parker grasped the nape of her neck and placed his lips upon hers with fervent possessiveness.

McKenna knew he would carry out his threat if the need ever arose, but rather than frightening her, it filled her with pleasure. *What is now mine*, she thought blissfully to herself as she let herself be consumed by his kiss.

Chapter 53

The fall of 1863 lulled everyone at the manor house into a sweet, hypnotic feeling of euphoria. The weather had been unseasonably glorious, and the flowers displayed their beauty along the hills, cliffs, and tranquil landscapes. The happy mood extended itself into the house, especially since Pia was successfully buying and selling more horses from Ireland these days.

Perhaps the most exciting event was the upcoming wedding of Zadie and Cooper. They had become inseparable since Pia's charity ball and auction. Everyone in the house knew that they had developed strong feelings for each other, but both Zadie and Coop had refrained from talking about their future together. Not that McKenna didn't try; she had pried and questioned at every chance, but Zadie would not lend any information her way. Even Pepper and Parker would attempt a conversation with Cooper, encouraging him to pop the question of marriage to Zadie. Cooper would simply tell them to mind their own damn business and stomp off. So, the Wells household simply resigned themselves to the fact that they would avoid any marriage conversation.

McKenna; however, decided to take matters into her own hands. She thought it was high time for the two of them to get married. All she needed was a bit of help from Parker, and that would be a bit difficult because he didn't like to meddle in other people's affairs.

"What did you just ask me, kitten?" Parker asked while bent over, picking out mud from Midnight's hooves in his stall.

"Oh, you heard me well enough, Parker Sloane! I said that Zadie and Coop need to have a romantic dinner, just the two of them. They work so hard around here that they never get a chance to be by themselves." McKenna looked at Parker's shapely behind as he bent over Midnight's hind legs, admiring his muscled upper thighs and his attractive bottom. Dear Lord in heaven, he had the nicest ass she had ever seen on a man. She continued staring a bit more before she caught herself, cleared her throat, and continued.

"Do you like what you see?" Parker asked with a smile, still bent over.

McKenna sighed and smiled. "Yes, I like what I see, but I didn't come down here to talk about your comely behind. Parker, behave yourself. Now then, I was thinking if we could provide a romantic setting, and if you could persuade Cooper to pop the question to Zadie, we may just pull off a romantic dinner with a marriage proposal to boot!" McKenna giggled and swirled herself in a circle, stopping just in time to see Parker looking down at her and scowling.

"I will do no such thing and neither will you. You just let them be. They have been doing just fine without your interference and I am sure that their conversations about their future, if they have had any, are none of our business. So, take that pretty little head of yours and concentrate on some of the chores that need to be done around here. Stop interfering, kitten." Parker swiped the tip of McKenna's nose with a finger before he turned and resumed cleaning out Midnight's hooves.

"Parker, that was mean," McKenna pouted as she stooped over beside Parker and looked him in the eye. "I was only trying to set the mood for a dinner between our dearest friends. Honestly, wouldn't you like to see the two of them get married?" McKenna rubbed his back, allowing her hand to drop lower upon his belt, moving down his lower back toward his tailbone.

"Careful, kitten. You are flirting with me and you know it. You can keep your little hand on the top of my ass, or you can slide it down and pat my ass. You will not change my mind about Cooper and Zadie. Leave them be and let them work out their own dinner! Did you ever consider that they may not want to marry?" Parker asked as he turned and pinned McKenna against the stall, placing both of his hands on each side of McKenna's golden-curled head.

"Well, no, that never crossed my mind. I just think they should be together, you know, in the same room and all."

"Oh, for Christ's sake! You mean to tell me that you think they should be sleeping together?" Parker roared with laughter while watching McKenna's face blush to a deepening red.

"You know what, Parker Sloane, just forget everything I just said. You are making fun of me and my words, just never you mind!" McKenna was so embarrassed and angry that she pushed Parker away, gathered her skirts, and stomped out of the stall, Parker's continued bellows echoing behind her.

"Tell you what, kitten. I'll be sure to let Cooper know how concerned you are of his sleeping arrangements!" He barely had time to duck before the brush came flying past his head.

"You just hush up Captain Sloane, I'll handle things in my own way," McKenna shouted as she walked straight out of the barn and up the walk, not even noticing Cooper coming across the veranda on his way to the barn.

Mere minutes passed before Cooper entered the barn and interrupted Parker's laughter.

"What bee got into McKenna's bonnet? I just saw her and she was all red in the face and steaming mad!" Cooper asked Parker as he leaned against the stall gate.

"Oh, she was mad all right. She thinks that you and Zadie should have a romantic dinner so you can ask Zadie to marry you. She's got it in her head that you two should be hitched. When I told her that I wouldn't help her scheming, well, you know McKenna, she didn't like being told 'no.'"

When there was no answer from Cooper, Parker stopped brushing and slowly turned around, facing his friend. "Coop, you have nothing to say?"

"Well, I got plenty to say, but I don't know how to say it," he said, scratching his beard.

"Cooper, what the hell is on your mind? Tell me," Parker ordered as he walked toward his friend leaning on the gate.

"Well, what's wrong with me havin' a dinner with Zadie? I don't think that sounds so bad." Cooper shifted his weight and hung both arms over the gate before speaking again. "You see, I have been itchin' to ask Zadie to marry me, but I never seem to find the right time. With everything that has happened around here, I just ain't asked her yet."

"Well, I'll be damned. Cooper, do you love her?" Parker asked gently.

"I sure do. I loved her when I saw her all those years ago, but I knew she was goin' back to the States and I was stayin' here. Hell, I couldn't ask her to stay with me and marry me after just seein' each other for a couple of weeks. I hardly knew her, and besides, we both had jobs to do."

"Have you talked about marriage with Zadie at all?" Parker asked cautiously.

"Well, no. I haven't asked her, if that's what you mean."

"Cooper, first you have to ask the woman before you get married. You know that!" Parker chuckled.

"Hell yes, I know that. I just haven't got the nerve to do it yet." Cooper stomped around in the dirt, then placed his hand on Parker's forearm. "I ain't never asked you for much, but I am askin' now. I need a little help." The look in Cooper's eyes warmed Parker's heart. He couldn't help but smile and ask, "How can I help?"

"Would you and McKenna fix that dinner up for Zadie and me? Then, I will ask her to marry me." Parker paused and looked at his old friend with warm approval.

"You son of a gun, you do love her, don't you?"

"I already told you I did," Cooper grunted, tilted his head, and backed away from the gate. "Just never mind. Forget I asked." The picture in front of Parker reminded him of a small child who had just dropped his favorite treat upon the floor.

"Cooper, come on now, you cantankerous old goat. I will be glad to arrange a dinner for the two of you. I didn't mean to embarrass you; if I did, I apologize for that. You are my friend and I would do anything for you. I was just shocked, that's all. Please forgive me if you felt I was making light of your question. I will speak to McKenna and together, we will work out a plan."

"You mean it?" asked Cooper with a grin.

"You bet I do. All I have to do now is approach McKenna. That means I have to walk into the house with my tail between my legs and tell her that she was right all along. You know how painful that is going to be?" Parker asked with a sigh. "Then, she will make me grovel for a bit, and then she will agree to arrange this whole dinner for you and Zadie. Trust me, little McKenna is not going to make this easy for me. But come hell or high water, we will make the arrangements for you and Zadie." Parker extended his hand to Cooper, who nodded a silent thank you to Parker before he turned and headed out the main barn doors. Parker watched his friend leave and shook his head in disbelief. He knew all along that something was happening between Zadie and Coop, but he never thought he would be involved. Parker's thoughts returned to the present long enough to toss a scoop of grain into Midnight's bucket before he closed and secured his horse's stall.

Well, no time like the present. I might as well confront my little kitten. She sure as hell is not going to make this easy. Maybe I'll pick a few flowers along the way to soften her up a bit.

"You know what you can do with your flowers, Parker Sloane!" McKenna exclaimed as she continued swinging on the veranda, avoiding eye contact with the handsome devil.

"Kitten, I am sorry that I spoke to you so harshly a while ago. I have reconsidered and I believe you are right. I will help you arrange a candlelight dinner for Zadie and Cooper." Parker walked toward McKenna and plopped down upon the swing next to her, laying his freshly picked flowers on her lap.

"So, now you are going to help me? What changed your mind?" she asked suspiciously, eyeing her flowers.

"I just had time to rethink your words and came to the conclusion that you were on to something," Parker answered while keeping in sync with McKenna's swing.

"You came to the conclusion? Uh huh... you had time to rethink? I smell a rat, Parker Sloane. Something made you change your mind. Out with it!"

Just at that moment, Cooper stuck his head around the corner with a grin from ear to ear. "Well, have you two come up with a plan, yet?"

"A plan? Parker, you talked with Cooper, didn't you? You dirty, rotten, son of a bi—" McKenna wasn't able to finish her last word properly because Parker had placed hip lips upon hers in a most lavish and provocative kiss. She desperately broke his embrace and stood up from the swing, breasts heaving and face reddening.

"Of all the low things to do. You told Cooper my idea, didn't you! You dirty, rotten cad! You took the credit for my idea after you, in no uncertain terms, told me to mind my own business! You snake, take your flowers and leave me alone! I don't need your help," she shouted loudly, causing Patches to jump from the swing and seek shelter. McKenna turned so abruptly that she nearly knocked over the fern stand. In an attempt to catch her from tripping over her entangled feet, Parker encircled her waist with his massive hands and lifted her completely off the tiled floor.

"I didn't take your idea, you little hellcat! If you had stayed in the barn a few more minutes, you could have talked to Cooper himself. He came in right after you threw your temper tantrum and marched away!" he shouted, trying to hold on to her squirming body and kicking feet.

"Put me down this instant!" McKenna shouted while trying to wriggle free of his hold.

"Gladly." Parker dropped McKenna onto the nearby settee. He then placed his booted foot beside McKenna's thigh, preventing any type of escape to her left. Cooper came to stand on her right, hanging his head in dismay.

"For the love of God, you two fight like cats and dogs quicker than anyone else I know. McKenna, now you simmer down and listen to me, young lady. Parker told me about your idea of a dinner and I liked it. I asked him to help me. Christ almighty, if you would just give him a chance to explain, you wouldn't have had to work yourself up." Cooper just stared at McKenna, gathered his breath, and continued, "I been thinkin' about askin' Zadie to marry me. I just ain't worked up the nerve to do it. I would like to have a nice dinner and all, but I need both of your help and I sure as hell don't need you two scrapin' at each other! If this is how you are gonna act, then just forget the whole damn thing!" Cooper kicked the leg of the settee, turned, and started to head off.

"Cooper, wait!" McKenna pleaded. "Cooper, I am so sorry. I thought that Parker, being the devil that he is, took my idea and offered it to you."

"Well, he didn't, and now you owe us both an apology!" Cooper said as he turned and crossed his arms. "You know, for someone as smart as you are, you sure don't know how to find out all the facts before you go and get all riled up!"

McKenna took a deep breath and folded her hands in her lap with her flowers. "You are right, I don't. And you are right about an apology. I am sorry, Cooper, that I made a mess out of what is supposed to be a happy idea.

"And I am sorry, Parker, that I called you names and didn't trust what you were telling me. Although, had Cooper not walked in when he did, I would imagine that you would have dallied a bit more until the entire truth came out."

"You are right, kitten. In fact, I told Coop that you would make me grovel, did I not?" he asked as he looked at his old friend.

"He did and you both have groveled and hollered long enough. Now, are we gonna plan this dinner or not? Stop bellyachin' around. You said your sorries. Let's get down to business; there's a woman that I want to marry and I need your blasted help!"

McKenna stood up and placed her flowers on the swing. She straightened her hair and patted down her bodice and skirts. "Parker, I am sorry. Once again, I let my temper get the best of me. Will you forgive me?" she asked sweetly.

"Forgiven," he said huskily. "Will you forgive me for beating around the bush with my explanation?"

"Forgiven," McKenna said softly, extending her arms to offer Parker a hug.

"All right, then, let's get down to business. Zadie ain't here, so let's get a cup of coffee and sit down at the table and talk." Cooper turned quickly toward the kitchen, knowing Parker and McKenna would follow.

"Thank you for my daisies; they are my favorite," whispered McKenna as she embraced her handsome beau.

"I know they are," Parker whispered back with a grin.

Chapter 54

"Cooper, what on earth are you doin?" Zadie asked as she followed Cooper on to the back porch. Ahead of her, she saw a small table set for two adorned with lit candles, fresh linens, polished silver, fine china, and a fresh red rose tucked into a small bud vase.

"Well, you just hush and sit down." Cooper scooted Zadie's chair out for her and eloquently scooted her back toward the table, just as McKenna had taught him.

"Cooper, who did this all this?" she asked with tears in her eyes.

"I did, with a little help," he murmured.

"Oh, you did, did you? And who helped you? Because this is not your normal table that you sit down to. This is all the fancy stuff in the house!" she said with raised brows.

"Yep, it is the fancy stuff, and I wanted to use it, so McKenna and Pia helped me. Do you like it?" Cooper scooted himself to the table and put his napkin on his lap, just like Parker had taught him. "Go on now, lift the lid off your plate. Your dinner is ready, my dear," he said with a nod of his head and a smile as he poured each of them a glass of wine.

"Well, I'll be," she said with surprise as she looked at her plate.

"Zadie, I have all your favorite foods. Now, I didn't cook any of this, but I told Pia and McKenna what to make."

"Oh, did ya now? Well then, I thank you." Zadie reached across the table and patted Cooper's hand. "What is the occasion? Why are we out here eatin'?" she asked.

Cooper took a big breath and scooted himself away from the table. He picked up the bud vase, walked to Zadie's side and knelt down on one knee.

"Oh, my Lord in heaven," she whispered.

"Zadie, I love you and I know that you love me. We ain't getting' any younger and I don't want to wake up without you in my life. I need you, Zadie,

310

do you hear me? I ain't got a lot of fancy words to say to you, but I can tell you that I don't want to spend another day without you in my life, from sunrise to sunset. So, Zadie, would you marry me? It would make me the happiest man on earth if you say yes."

Zadie was awestruck. She wasn't even sure what to do. She cleared her throat, grasped at her lace collar, pulled on her sleeve cuffs and finally looked down into Cooper's eyes.

"Zadie, the question ain't that hard. Would you marry me?" Cooper asked again.

"Yes, yes, I will. I never thought you would ask." Zadie warmly brushed Cooper's cheek with her hand, resting it against his stubbled beard.

"Well then, go on now and untie this ribbon." Cooper held the rose bud vase closely to Zadie's hand. She glanced at the vase and looked at the tiny bow that had been tied around the bottom leaf on the rose. There, in its magical splendor, was a golden wedding band with a small diamond in the middle.

"It was my mother's ring. And I know she would want it to be on your hand when we marry. My mother was a wonderful woman, and I can think of no other lady that would come close to her, other than you. If you'll have me, Zadie, I would like us to become man and wife."

"Oh, Cooper, I don't know what to say. This is so perfect, and to think you did this all for me," Zadie said as she began to cry.

"Zadie, say yes," he murmured calmly.

"Yes, yes, yes. I will marry you, Cooper, and I thank you for askin' me!" Cooper stood up and placed both hands on Zadie's shoulders, lifting her to stand before him. "You have just made me a very happy man!"

"And you have just made me a very happy woman!" she whispered back before Cooper enveloped her in a lengthy and passionate kiss. He nuzzled her neck and ear a bit before he was interrupted with Zadie's question.

"Cooper?"

"What?"

"Will we kiss like this when we get hitched?" Zadie asked softly.

"Every day and every night and in between," he answered with a mischievous grin. "And woman, we will do a helluva lot more than kiss."

***

Excitement was in the air, and there was no denying that Zadie and Cooper's euphoric feelings had affected everyone in the house. They had both decided to have a private ceremony with Judge McCain, then host a 'small' reception back at Aunt Olympia's home.

That was an understatement, thought McKenna. *Nothing Aunt Pia did was ever small.*

There were two days left before the wedding, and plans were being carried out methodically and smoothly. Zadie was making the final changes to her wedding gown when McKenna overheard her singing *Amazing Grace* to herself. She quietly stepped into the sewing room to listen.

Zadie has a beautiful singing voice, McKenna thought contently. *She could lull a baby to sleep within moments. Perhaps one day, she would sing to my baby—Parker's baby—our baby.*

"Zadie, try this dress on, and let me see you in it. I will adjust the hem for you," offered McKenna as she approached Zadie, smiling inside about her most recent thoughts.

"Oh, baby girl, I was hopin' you'd be helpin' ol' Zadie with this dress. Your Aunt Olympia was so kind and gracious, and allowed me to buy this here beautiful satin material. Lookee here, baby girl, it even has little pearls along the edge."

McKenna helped Zadie into her dress, and before she could stop herself, she began to weep.

"Baby girl, why you cryin'?" Zadie exclaimed.

"Oh, Zadie, you look beautiful. I just want you to know how happy I am for you. I guess I am a little selfish, though."

"Now, why would you be sayin' such a thing?"

"I don't want you to forget me when you go and get married. I still want to be your baby girl." With tears in her eyes, McKenna looked up at Zadie.

"Now you listen to me, child. Just because I am gittin' married does not mean I will forget you. I am way past the birthin' age, and Cooper don't have no babies. So, as far as we are concerned, you are our child. Do you understand me?"

"Yes, Zadie, oh yes, I do. Please forgive me for crying when you are so excited. I just didn't want to lose you."

"You ain't losin' me, child; you are gainin' another father, so to speak. Lord's sake, girl, you will have so many people who love you, you won't know what to do. Speakin' of love, when are you and the Captain gonna get married?"

"We have discussed it, Zadie. I can't get married until I can be back home, and Papa can walk me down the aisle. Parker is in full agreement, and he knows how much it would mean to me to have my father at my wedding."

"Child, you may have to get married here. There may not be a home to go back to." Zadie held McKenna's face between her leathered fingers and calloused thumb.

"I know, Zadie, I know. Let's not worry about that right now. Let's concentrate on you and your day, and let's get this dress hemmed. But before I begin pinning the hem, I need you to step down here, turn around, and close your eyes."

"Child, what are you up to? I don't have time for games right now."

"Zadie, this is no game. Hush up and turn around."

Zadie turned around and closed her eyes tightly. McKenna took out the string of pearls that had belonged to her mother from the drawstring bag she had tucked in her pocket. She unclasped the hook and gently placed the pearls around Zadie's neck.

"Zadie, open your eyes."

She complied and hushed her trembling lips with her hands. "McKenna, what have you done? I can't wear these. These belonged to your mother."

"Now, you listen to me, Zadie. Yes, they did belong to my mother, but you are my mother now. You always have been. I will wear them at my wedding, as well. These pearls represent the love I have for you. My mother would be so proud, knowing that a person such as yourself raised me. Papa agreed with me in allowing you to borrow these pearls to wear on your wedding day. Now, you will wear them with pride and love because they were given out of pride and love."

"Baby girl, you humble me with your kindness."

"No, Zadie, you humble me with yours. I love you."

"I love you, too, baby girl."

"Well, all right then, hop up on the stand, and I will hem this dress for you. You are truly a remarkable sight. I need to ask you a question though, because I do not know the answer."

"Go on, child, ask."

"If Zadie is your first name, what is your last name? When Judge McCain says your name, he will need your last name."

"Olympia said I could use Wells. That is the closest thing to a last name I will ever know. My momma never told me my full name."

"Then, Wells it is. It will soon be Carson! Mrs. Zadie Carson—it has a nice ring to it. Cooper and Zadie Carson," she said happily. "Zadie, do you know what Cooper's real name is?"

"Yes, but he would skin me alive if I told you."

"Come now, Zadie, he would never harm you and you know it. You can tell me."

"Well, all right, baby girl, but don't you ever tell him you know. And don't tell him I told you."

"Cross my heart," McKenna replied making the sign of the cross upon her chest.

"August," Zadie whispered.

"What?"

"Cooper's real name is August. Since he was born in the month of August, his mama named him August."

"I didn't know his birthday was in August. Why didn't you ever say something? All these years here, we could have had a birthday party for him."

"He didn't want no one to know. Besides, he hates the name."

"Well, I can understand that!"

"Lordy child, don't ever call him that. Hard tellin' what he would do to you! Even though he favors you somethin' fierce, I ain't so sure what he'd up and do if you called him that!"

"Well, one day, Zadie, when he is being grumpy and cantankerous to me, I just may say his name aloud." Together, they giggled like two school girls, working long into the evening hours, preparing Zadie's dress for her wedding.

Chapter 55

"McKenna, come on up here. Hurry and finish your horse brushing. You got a letter from your papa," screamed Zadie from the yard. "Hurry up, baby girl!"

McKenna dropped Solomon's brush and ran as fast as she could. Maybe this letter would contain an answer to her question about coming to England for Christmas. *Oh, my Lord, of all days to wear oversized boots.* McKenna could barely climb the front steps without slipping due to the early November rains.

"Where are you going in such a hurry, kitten?" asked Parker on his way to the barn.

"Parker, gather everyone together. I just got a letter from Papa. He may tell us if he can attend the wedding. Hurry, and I'll meet you at the house."

"Be right up. I'll get Coop, Pepper, and the boys."

McKenna ran into the kitchen, kicked off her boots, and washed her hands and face. Zadie had gathered everyone around the dining table by the time McKenna entered. Shortly after, Parker and the others joined her.

"McKenna, please read it aloud, dear," Aunt Pia said.

"I will, as soon as I get this opened," McKenna replied, her hands shaking so badly that she couldn't tear the envelope.

"Kitten, allow me," Parker said, plucking the letter from her hand and deftly ripping the side. He handed it back with a calming smile. "Here you are, my dear. Please continue."

McKenna took a deep breath and began reading.

"My dearest McKenna,

I am writing from a place that you have never heard of, nor have those sitting in your company while you share the contents of this letter. But let it be known that from the third of July until the finites of history, this little town of Gettysburg, Pennsylvania, will never be forgotten.

By the time you receive this letter, the sound of cannon fire, rifle jams, and musket pillage will be hushed. The screams of wounded fourteen-year-old soldiers will be terminated. The cries for help and the tearing of horseflesh upon bloodied soil will have ceased. All that remains will be the eerie sound of stillness dissipating through what was once wheat fields and peach orchards.

Baby girl, I write this with a heavy heart. I was asked to travel to this little unknown town in the heart of Pennsylvania to assist in surgery and healing. However, I assisted a great deal more with burials, amputations, and letter writing for the terminal to the mothers of the dead. The grief and despair in this town is incomprehensible.

I want you to understand what this war has done to every soldier in the States, no matter the color of uniform he has chosen to wear.

General Lee's victory at Chancellorsville boosted our boys' spirits in May. Robert E. Lee was just plain tired of fighting in his beloved Virginia and sought to take the war out of that state. He needed a good right-hand man, though, to replace Jackson, and he knew that James Longstreet would fill those shoes. Longstreet wanted to meet up and fight against his one-time best friend, Sam Grant. Imagine that: the two leaders—one in blue and one in gray—were once best friends.

On July 1, the Confederates were strong and overtook the Union General Buford on the northwest side of the town.

On July 2, the Union army was stretched out into the shape of a fishhook. General Lee gave orders to attack the Union, starting out in a wheat field. Well, after a while, the middle of the fishhook had a hole in it.

If success is measured in winning a single skirmish, then I guess we were successful. If success is measured in death counts that day, then both sides lost. There were thirty-seven thousand men killed, according to the newspapers.

On July 3, Lee was getting angrier. He wanted this victory, and so, mid-morning, he decided to make his move. He decided to make a charge over a one-mile field, and he asked General Pickett to take the charge. General Longstreet strongly advised against it because he felt it would be suicide. You see, the field was on a slope, and that meant our boys would be running uphill toward the Yanks. There were no trees to hide behind—nothing but an open field.

We didn't stand a chance, McKenna. Longstreet knew it and tried to stop it. He had to obey his orders from Lee, no matter what. We had twelve thousand five hundred boys charging through the field that day. Most of those soldiers were young boys—no older than Caleb. For every soldier who lived that day, twelve died.

On July 4, Lee wanted to counterattack but decided against it and marched back into Virginia. The citizens of Gettysburg were horrified. I was horrified. I walked the streets of what was probably once a nice little town. Bodies, horses, bloodied uniforms, and mounds of boots lined the street. Some thought the reason this whole battle started was because a Rebel soldier was trying to steal a pair of boots from a Yankee supply wagon. That will probably be argued long into the future. The citizens also felt that the soldiers needed to be buried in a cemetery, rather than in a hole where they had fallen. So, they did build a cemetery and named it the National Cemetery. By November 19, President Lincoln came to Gettysburg and talked to the crowds. His speech only lasted two minutes, but it was powerful, daughter. I stood, I listened, I wept, and I prayed for this damn war to end.

I would imagine everyone who was there did the same. Lincoln told us that this war needed to continue to its end. The Union had to be preserved, and for this very reason, it would give purpose to the loss of thousands of lives. My God, McKenna, over fifty thousand soldiers died or were wounded in those three days. I thought I had seen the entire spectrum of death in my medical career. Never have I seen the carnage that I saw in Gettysburg—not even in Antietam.

The newspapers are relentless. They state the heroes in uniform but forget to mention the real heroes—those who perished.

I render my apologies if this letter is filled with despair. Unfortunately, the facts being shared with you are as they happened.

What will happen next? I do not know. Where will I travel to next? I do not know. I can't anticipate the future, but I can pray that the past is never repeated. None of us ever thought this godforsaken war would last this long. Charleston has been desecrated, my dear. I have not been home in over three years. I don't even know if I have a home to return to. What remains standing is by pure luck. There was a fire two years ago, and most of the city was destroyed. Fort Sumter is nothing more than burned rock, or so I have been told.

I will be leaving Gettysburg shortly—I am awaiting orders for my next location. I received your letter, my dear. I understand it is your intent to marry at Christmastime. I would like nothing more than to be there for you and to walk you down the aisle. But I am now under Federal employ. I will ask if I can be released to attend my daughter's wedding. I feel I am long overdue a leave of absence. I will try my very best to attend your wedding, McKenna; you know that. Can I promise you so? No, it saddens me to say. I cannot ask you to postpone your plans for me, either. I simply do not know when or if I will be granted leave.

Now, I do have a question for you. Because I have such high requirements for the man who will take my daughter in marriage, I must know that you are in love with him and he you. I must also know if he is secure financially to provide for you and any children you may have. I wish I could talk with Captain Sloane in person, but this war prevents me from doing so. I must admit that the man who wins your heart must know how to capture it and, to a certain extent, control it.

This man must be able to outride you, outshoot you, and win most verbal battles with you. Any less of a man would bore you. Please give my love and hugs to Pia and Pepper. I know I have much to catch up on; hopefully, we will do this at your wedding at Christmas, if I am able. That would be a glorious ending to such a somber year.

I love you with all my heart,
Papa

P.S. Under no circumstance will those damn animals of yours be in your wedding, in the church, or anywhere near the food table! Maribelle had her mangy mutt and hawk at our wedding, and together they knocked over every food and drink table they could maneuver!"

"Well, that is the extent of Papa's letter," said McKenna as she refolded it and tucked it back into the envelope.

"We must all be thankful that we are across the ocean and safe from that horrid war," Aunt Olympia muttered.

"You are right," whispered McKenna, "but it doesn't make it any easier for me to read Papa's letters. My imagination runs wild with fear for him, and there are so many evenings when I can't go to sleep."

"McKenna, your father is as safe as he can be," her aunt tried to reassure her. "We must all continue to pray that this war ends, and that things will go back to normal."

"Normal? Aunt Pia, I don't know if things will ever go back to normal. Papa is right. President Lincoln's worst battle is yet to come." McKenna released a heavy sigh.

"McKenna, what is that battle?" asked Cooper.

"Mending a broken country, mending broken families, and mending broken hearts. If you will all excuse me, I am going to take Papa's letter and reread it again by myself."

McKenna rose from the table and clutched her father's letter close to her heart. *Dear Lord, please bring Papa to England, if only for a little while. Allow him to see happiness and to share time with us. Are you listening, Lord? Please, answer this prayer of mine*, she prayed silently as she climbed the stairs to her room.

Chapter 56

Thanksgiving preparations were underway at the manor house. Olympia had decided that this Thanksgiving would include a special guest. After hearing Harper's letter, Pia and Pepper had agreed to invite their father. There was enough fighting in this world, and Pia and Pepper agreed not to contribute to any more fighting within their family. In fact, the siblings decided to ride out to Thaddeus's home and personally invite him.

The very next morning, Pepper saddled two horses, and he and Pia rode to their childhood home. Halfway there, Pepper suddenly reined in his horse in to a jerking halt. Pia turned around in her saddle to look at him. "What is wrong, dear brother?"

"I can't do this," Pepper muttered. "We owe that man nothing. It is not our responsibility to reach out and make amends. I thought I was ready, but I'm not."

"Pepper," Pia said gently. She reached a hand back to him, and he reluctantly allowed his horse to trot a few a few steps forward until he was close enough to take it. "I know it will be difficult, but we agreed that this was the right thing to do, for McKenna, and for the healing of the rest of our family. I will be with you."

Pepper stared at their two hands clasped together, then nodded and kicked his mount to continue forward. When they reached the house, they silently dismounted and together, they walked the steps to the main entrance.

Pepper knocked on the door softly. "I never thought I would knock on this door again," he whispered to Pia.

"I know, but it's the right thing to do." Through the glass, she could almost see herself as a young girl, sitting on her father's overstuffed chair, pretending to read the newspaper with him. Her heart was aching; it was like the window was a portal to the distant past.

The door creaked open, and there before them stood their father with a smile upon his face. Thaddeus opened the door wide and warmly welcomed them inside.

"How are you, son?" he asked timidly.

"Fine," Pepper replied shortly.

"And you, daughter?"

"Just as well."

"Good." Thaddeus replied and then went silent. The room buzzed with awkward tension, the only pervading sound supplied by the ticking of the grandfather clock.

"We thought—" Pepper finally said, and then stopped.

"We thought that we would ask if you would…" They looked at each other in trepidation, both cutting their own sentences short. They had practiced this may times at home, but there was something about being here, in this house, that made getting the words out difficult and frightening.

Pia swallowed, raised her chin, and looked directly at her father. "We are having a Thanksgiving feast on Thursday. We thought you might like to join."

Thaddeus's eyebrows rose straight into his bushy grey hair.

"It is late notice, only the day after tomorrow, you don't have to," Pepper rushed to interject, observing his father's hesitance, "if you have your own plans or would prefer not to, I assure you that we will—"

"No, no," Thaddeus shook his head, and Pepper was surprised to see that his eyes were warm and glistening. "I would be honored to attend. I can't remember the last time I was invited to sit at a table with others for Thanksgiving."

"Well, Father, it is time to make up for those lost meals," said Pia with a small smile.

"I am truly humbled to accept your invitation. I know this was a difficult visit for you both, especially for you, Pepper. That last time you were here, I said some nasty things to you. I am sorry, son. If you will allow me to call you son, I surely would be grateful."

"That will take time. For now, just come to dinner on Thursday," said Pepper with a hint of harshness in his voice.

"I understand. Well, thank you for your invitation, and I will be there. I do have one more question for you both. Reverend Jones passed away six weeks ago. I have been checking in on his wife from time to time and helping her with things around her home—mostly repair jobs. I know this is a lot to ask, but she has no family here. Would it be too much to ask if she came to Thanksgiving Dinner, too? She would be all alone otherwise."

Pepper and Pia looked at each other, startled their father would ask such a *kind* question.

"Father, I think it would very nice of you to bring Mrs. Jones to our dinner table on Thursday, don't you, Pepper?" Pia asked while nudging her brother in the ribs.

"I'm sure that would be fine. The Widow Jones is welcome to come. We can always set another chair at the table."

"Thank you both, then, I truly mean that. You come all this way to invite me and I am truly thankful. I mean it." Thaddeus's eyes were filling with tears and all three of them knew it was a humbling moment for their father. Thaddeus cleared his throat and wiped his eyes as though he had a piece of dirt in them before asking, "Am I to bring anything to share? I don't want to come empty-handed."

"Well, I remember that you could make a very delicious cornbread, Papa. Why don't you bring that? Remember his cornbread, Pepper?" Pia asked nervously, hoping that Pepper would support her suggestion.

Pepper flinched involuntarily, the memories of countless Thanksgivings concluded with his father's delicious cornbread washing over him. "I do. Cornbread would be good. Bring that." Pepper nodded, turned, and walked through the front door without looking back. "Come on, Pia. Half the day is over, and I have work to do," hollered Pepper over his shoulder.

"So, we'll see you Thursday, then. I'm glad you are coming." Pia grabbed her father's hand in an awkward attempt at a hug. She quickly turned and opened the creaky front door that Pepper had just walked through, catching it so as not to slam it shut. Neither of the two chanced a last look at their father as they descended down the front steps.

Pepper and Pia quickly mounted their horses and trotted toward home. About a mile down the road, they stopped to water their horses at the familiar childhood stream.

As soon as they dismounted, Pia's pent-up feelings exploded. "I can't believe he asked if he could bring the Widow Jones! Reverend Jones would probably toss in his grave if he knew his former wife would be keeping company with Thaddeus Wells."

"Well, sister, I think Reverend Jones would be happy that his wife will be with a family on the holiday. Mrs. Jones knows the struggles our father has had, and she is aware of his willingness to strengthen his faith, so to speak. Reverend Jones has been there for him for the past five years, through thick and thin. Perhaps this is our father's destiny. Who knows? She may be able to teach him a thing or two about kindness." He chuckled for the first time that morning. "Speaking of bringing someone to the table, when are you going to concentrate on finding someone for yourself? You need companionship in your life, Pia."

"Pepper, you just mind your business. I will concentrate on my future soulmate after you marry yours. If I were you, I would be making plans to marry pretty Jenny McTavish real soon."

"You would?"

"Certainly, I would. For heaven's sake, Pepper, what are you waiting for?" she asked as she picked up her hair and rearranged her hat.

"If truth be told, I am afraid she will say no," Pepper answered so softly, Pia could barely hear him.

"Pepper, for cryin' out loud, ask her. I promise she will not say no. She's waiting for that question. But don't wait too long. A woman doesn't want to wait forever," Pia said with a fair amount of sarcasm.

Pepper grunted, reined his horse around, and began the ride back home.

He is right, Pia thought as she fell in canter behind her brother. *Maybe I should start focusing on falling in love again. Oh, nonsense—who would want to fall in love with a tall, curly-haired woman who smells of horses more often than French perfume? Then again, someone is out there—I am sure of it. Maybe I will begin thinking about finding a man for myself.* She soon caught up with Pepper, and together, they rode toward home in silence. They had just entered the lane to the house when they saw Parker riding up to meet them on his stallion, Midnight, and he didn't look happy.

"Good day, Captain Sloane! I trust you had an enjoyable ride today," said Pia with a smile.

"No, I did not," Parker replied irritably. "I didn't get my ride at all. I need to talk to Cooper. Do you know where he is? He's not in the stables."

"No, I don't know where he is. Most likely, he's in the garden with Zadie, gathering pumpkins. Is something wrong?" asked Pia nervously.

"I am not sure. I have a hunch there will be something wrong before the day is over, though," replied Parker darkly.

"Would you care to explain a bit more?" Pepper asked as he nudged his horse toward Parker.

"The bridles have all been cut to within a quarter-inch. Most of them had burrs on the underside of the leather straps."

"You think someone put the burrs there on purpose? Who would do such a thing? They are pretty obvious to notice!" asked Pia.

"I am not sure, but maybe Cooper knows if anyone strange was in the barn this morning. I aim to find out," muttered Parker as he trotted his horse toward the garden with Pepper and Pia following behind.

Cooper was indeed in the garden, gathering pumpkins with Zadie. Parker brought his horse to a stop next to Cooper's bent form and asked about the burrs.

"Burrs? Who the hell would be puttin' burrs on the bridles?" Cooper demanded as he stood and stretched his aching back.

"I have yet to find that answer." Parker spotted the boys in the garden with Jenny and motioned for them to come over. They quickly complied and ran, jumping over the pumpkin vines.

"Boys, do you know anything about putting burrs on the backside of the leather bridles? I found quite a few of them laden with the prickly things this morning. You weren't playing tricks on each other, now, were you?" asked Parker with raised brows.

"No, I don't know anything about burrs," answered Livingston. "McKenna and Quaid would have noticed, though. When they get back, you ought to ask them."

"What do you mean?" asked Parker as he leaned forward in the saddle with a serious look upon his face.

"Well, McKenna and Quaid left this morning to ride into town and purchase some corn mash and wheat," Livingston replied.

"What time did they leave?" asked Pepper.

"Right after breakfast; Quaid wanted to get there and back before noon," Caleb replied.

"Something isn't right, here. They should have been back by now." Parker looked down the empty lane before he spoke again. "I am going to go into town and make sure everything is alright. I just have a hunch that someone is up to no good."

"Parker, wait for me to saddle up a fresh horse, and I will come with you. No sense in worrying yet; they may be fine right where they are," said Pepper with a cautionary voice. "Caleb, fetch me a fresh horse and saddle him up."

"Sure thing, Uncle Pepper," replied Caleb as he skipped off to the barn.

"I hope you are right, but something in my gut tells me otherwise." Parker examined his bridle one more time, taking notice of the lone burr he hadn't seen still entrapped in the leather.

"I will come, too. Livingston, saddle up a horse for me, will you?" asked Cooper as he gave Zadie a quick hug good-bye.

"Sure thing, on my way." Livingston ran after Caleb and in no time, all three men were cantering down the road toward town.

Chapter 57

Luck was not on McKenna and Quaid's side. Both of their horses had been jittery on the ride to town. No sooner would McKenna get Solomon quieted then Quaid's horse would rear up. This continued for most of their ride until both horses changed speed into a quick canter. McKenna noticed Solomon twitching his head to the left a bit more frequently than when she had first ridden out. "What's the matter, boy? Are the flies bothering you today? Is that it? Why are you so jumpy today?" McKenna patted Solomon's neck and felt a prick brush across her fingertip. Instinctively, she pulled her finger back, then resumed feeling for the source of the unexpected poke on her finger. The closer she rubbed to his chin strap, the more Solomon stomped his hooves. "What in the world?" she asked out loud as she leaned over Solomon's neck, now feeling under the chin strap toward his jaw. No sooner had she realized there were small burrs taped under the strap, she heard Quaid's loud voice booming down upon her.

"So help me, McKenna, if you put burrs under this bridle to beat me at another race, I will tan your hide! I don't care if you are a girl and my cousin!"

"Quaid, you hush up. You know better than that. I would sooner put burrs in your bedsheets! I would never harm or injure my horses. For God's sake, you need to believe me."

"Oh, cousin, calm yourself. I do believe you, but I don't like this one bit. I truly do not believe that anyone at home would have done this."

McKenna huffed in annoyance. "Well, I suppose we'd better ride back, just in case, then. Who would put burrs on the reins like this? I don't—"

"McKenna," Quaid interjected quietly, staring at a point somewhere off behind her head. "Forget the burrs. Kick your horse, right now."

"What? Why?"

"There is someone in the trees. He has a gun." Quaid lifted his leg to kick his own horse into a canter. "We have to—"

326

A shot rang out, and Quaid's mount reared. He fell from his horse and thudded hard upon the creek bed stones below. McKenna scanned the horizon, heart pounding, but she could see no gun, nothing that resembled a gun, or even a reflection from the sun. She leapt off of Solomon with her rifle in hand as she knelt beside Quaid, checking for a pulse. Satisfied that he was still breathing, she glanced for any type of cover before her attacker shot again.

Dear God, she thought as she trembled, *what should I do? Ride for help or stay here with Quaid?*

"Get up, girl, and put that rifle back into your saddlebag. Your friend ain't dead."

McKenna turned so quickly that she almost lost her footing. She scanned her surroundings, stopping and shielding her eyesight from the sun. As McKenna's eyes focused, she saw the shape of a man sitting astride a large black stallion about fifty paces away.

"Who are you, and why did you fire off a shot at us? And why are you pointing a gun at my cousin and me?" asked McKenna. She could tell that the man before her was quite tall and large. He was dirty and looked like he had been in a saddle for days. The tell-tale signs of a sweat-encrusted, dirty neck, wind-burnt face, and filthy gloves were familiar indications to McKenna. His boots were caked in an inch or so of mud, suggesting that he had ridden or walked his horse in a rainstorm. The poor horse's nostrils were flaring, almost red in color. The stallion hung his head very low, telling McKenna that this horse was exhausted. This rider had been on this horse for a long time, too long, to the point of causing this stallion to fatigue.

"Did you hear me, missy? I said I ain't pointing my gun at him; this gun is pointed squarely at you. Now, put that rifle back into your saddle bag. Nice and slow." McKenna refocused and saw the muzzleloader aimed at her. She also saw that the man was balancing the butt of the gun on his thigh. Tiredness meant loss of aim. Maybe she could make a run for it and take her chances of not getting shot. Solomon could easily outrun his horse at this point.

I can't leave Quaid here alone.

The man's deep voice brought McKenna back to her current situation. She straightened her back and slowly put her rifle into its holster. She looked up at her predator, who was sitting motionless in his saddle. He had an intense gaze and McKenna didn't like it one bit.

"Do I know you? You don't look familiar to me," McKenna shouted back while taking a few steps toward Solomon.

The man tilted his head before answering, leaning over a bit. "I know you. You are Thaddeus Wells' granddaughter, aren't you?"

"I am. Who the hell are you?" McKenna took a step closer to her saddle, hoping to get in arm's reach of the pistol she hid under her saddle blanket.

"Now, that ain't no way for a fancy lady such as yourself to talk. You need to clean up that language of yours," the stranger growled. "I am an acquaintance of your grandfather. I can't say I'm a friend, though. That bastard doesn't have any friends."

"State your business and move on. I need to tend to my cousin's head injury. He is going to have a large bump, thanks to you."

The man laughed, showing a smile with missing teeth. "No, you ain't gonna help that boy. Lead your horse over here. You and I are goin' for a ride."

McKenna grabbed his reins in her left hand as she pulled her pistol from under the blanket with her right. She cocked her gun quickly and turned, aiming at her intruder's chest. "No, I don't believe I will ride with you. I have other plans today."

***

"Jenny, damn it all, turn your horse around and go on back home; do you hear me?" Parker hollered at her when she had finally caught up with the three of them while they stopped to water their horses.

"Oh, I hear you just fine, Pepper Wells, but my mind is made up. If you are all going out to check on McKenna and Quaid, then I am coming, as well."

"Jenny, for Christ's sake, turn your horse around, and go back to the barn. This could be dangerous, and you know it. I mean it, now, go on home." Pepper was in no mood for an argument from Jenny.

"Pepper, what happens if my father is truly behind these happenings? What if you have all been right, all along? What if he is the one who took a shot at Parker and nearly got McKenna raped? I need to know, Pepper; I need to know that my father is innocent or that he is the mastermind behind these shenanigans to our family. Please, Pepper, I must come."

"All right, then. But you stay behind me; do you understand?"

"Yes, I understand. You will never know that I am here," Jenny muttered under her breath.

Chapter 58

"I am only gonna say it one more time. Get on your horse before I shoot your friend over there," said the stranger, with his gun still aimed at McKenna.

The next sound caused McKenna to duck. She turned and saw the smoke still lingering in the air from Quaid's revolver. His bloodied forehead told her that he needed to get help and he needed it soon. She turned and began shuffling down the creek bed to where Quaid was laying.

"Missy, you are makin' me mad, and I am not nice when I get mad," the stranger hollered as he nudged his edgy horse forward. "Your friend doesn't have anything left in him to take a shot at me again. But I do. Now, you walk yourself on over here, or I will shoot him right now, right here!"

"People who get mad get distracted easily, mister. Now, get off *your* horse," Parker said as he aimed his gun and brought his horse to stop behind the man.

McKenna anxiously watched as Pepper and Cooper reined in their horses on each side of the stranger, hands on their pistols, ready to fire. There was another rider, but with that hat on, McKenna couldn't see the rider's face. He appeared too small to be one of the boys and Pepper would never have allowed Maggie to tag along... As McKenna began to edge toward the shade of the trees, the rider's features came into focus.

Oh, my Lord, what is Jenny doing here?

Parker's voice brought McKenna's attention back. "Drop your weapon. Raise your hands slowly and dismount. If you give me reason to think you are going to use that gun of yours, I will shoot you dead," stated Parker without a facial flinch.

The man on the horse dropped his gun and slowly dismounted. Parker, Cooper, and Pepper inched their horses closer to the man standing before them.

"Who the hell are you?" the man asked as he spit upon the ground, narrowly missing Parker's boot as he dismounted.

"I have a better question. Who the hell are you?" Parker asked as he stood before the man, spitting with accuracy on the toe of the man's boot. *Parker is intimidating*, thought McKenna. His height alone should have scared this imbecile, and if his height didn't scare him, his size should have. Parker was twice the size of this stranger, and this stranger was not small by any stretch of the imagination.

Jenny slowly rode her horse toward the man, trying to get a good look at him through the bright sunlight radiating down upon the both of them.

The man watched the woman coming toward him. There was something familiar about this slip of a girl. He lifted his hand to pull the brim of his hat down to shield the sun from his eyes.

"Keep your hands where I can see them." Parker knew the type of man that stood before him. He was no better than a bounty hunter. Men like him were driven by the almighty dollar. Self-worth had no meaning for him. The lives of those he took mattered not. He was told who to collect and he collected them—dead or alive. Thank God he and Pepper and Cooper arrived when they did. If not for Cooper spotting a third set of tracks, things may have turned out differently. Parker was so deep in thought that he didn't hear Jenny trot up beside him and dismount. He heard the fear in Pepper's voice and that startled him.

"Jenny, get the hell away from him," Pepper shouted as he strode toward her with a grimace on his face. Jenny didn't respond to Pepper. In fact, she walked closer to the man with a blank stare upon her face, almost as though she were in a trance. Pepper reached her and shook her shoulders. "Jenny, get back over to your horse and stay there." Jenny turned and collapsed into Pepper's arms, crying and heaving, fighting hard for her next breath.

"It's true—dear God in heaven, it's true, Pepper. It is my father!" Jenny clasped her hand to her mouth in an attempt to hold back tears. "I didn't want to believe that my father could have possibly been behind these horrible happenings. I kept thinking that the assumptions that had been made would be wrong. I prayed at night that Father was not involved. But he is, isn't he?" Jenny slowly regained her balance, stood, and turned so quickly that Pepper could not prevent her next move. Jenny marched up to her father and slapped him hard across his face, bracing through the pain it created in her hand. "How could you? How could you do the things that you have done?" Jenny began to tremble uncontrollably, all the while fighting off Pepper's hands as they tried to embrace her and silence her sobs.

Time stood still. The locusts pierced the stillness of the woods. The sway of the leaves provided the only cushion to Jenny's gut-wrenching cries. Time passed before anyone spoke.

"Christ's sake," uttered the man. "What the hell are you doing here, daughter?"

"I might ask you the same thing, *Father*." Jenny stood still and swallowed hard. She was not about to let her father see her as a weak-kneed schoolgirl.

Pepper moved to put himself between Jenny and her father.

"Pepper, is that you?" asked the stranger, now identified as Ian McTavish.

"In the flesh, Mr. McTavish. Now, why don't you answer your daughter's question? Why are you here and why did you have a gun pointed at McKenna? We all take offense to this outlandish behavior on your part."

"You do, do ya?" McTavish snarled. "Well, I take offense to a lot of things that have gone on within your family. Jenny, what in hell are you doin' here... on this land?"

Jenny lifted her chin. "I live here, Father... with Pepper. We are soon to be married. There have been strange occurrences of late, and Pepper was afraid for me being all alone, so he brought me to Olympia's home."

"Afraid? So, help me, God, if that son-of-a-bitch Wells hurt you, I will shoot him in his sleep."

"I believe you have had many unsuccessful attempts at hurting people in our home," Parker growled, touching McTavish's chest with the tip of his rifle as he pushed him backward a few steps.

McTavish looked at the gun and the broad man holding it as though seeing them both for the first time. "Who the hell are you?"

"Your worst nightmare. You see, when one of my friends is injured or threatened in any way, I take it personally."

"Enough," Pepper said sharply. "There have been attempts on Miss Reed's life, and we would like to know what you have to do with it and why. I would encourage you not to lie, especially in front of your own daughter."

"You, of all people, Pepper, ought to know that I harbor a sea of hatred for your father. Don't tell me you have forgotten the hurt and pain he caused you and Jenny, not to mention the embarrassment and humiliation he brought to Jenny's mama and me."

"Oh, I remember more than you know." Pepper turned his neck from left to right in an attempt to alleviate the crick that had formed. "McKenna, where is Quaid? Is he alright?"

"He will be fine. He is sitting over by the tree nursing that goose egg-size lump that this man caused," McKenna replied, still holding her pistol in a tight grasp. Parker realized that McKenna was on the edge of collapse and gently took her gun from her hand and handed it to Cooper. McKenna looked up into Parker's eyes, half-smiling and half-crying.

"Kitten, are you alright? Did he hurt you?" whispered Parker into McKenna's ear.

"No, you got here in time. I was scared, Parker," McKenna said with trembling lips.

"I know, kitten. It is over now, it is finally over. We can finally put an end to this and find out the truth. Stay strong, little one. Jenny is going to need you more than you know. She is about to unravel the mystery that may take her to hell and back."

"I will be here for her, I promise." McKenna reached up and kissed Parker on his cheek, swaying toward his chest for a glimpse of warmth and comfort before separating herself and turning toward the conversation between Jenny and her father.

"Father, have you been masterminding all these mishaps involving McKenna? Tell me it isn't true." Jenny looked at her father in despair.

"I hate that man for what he did to you, child. The only way I could get back at him was to hurt him and those he loved, like he hurt those I loved. I planned my actions for a long time."

"Why, Papa? You are not the type to hurt an innocent person. McKenna has never met you or done anything to harm you."

"No, but she was kin to Thaddeus."

"McTavish, you are a fool. She didn't even know she had a grandfather until two years ago. Harper never told her about him, and he never told her about me. Hell, she just met me on the ship sailing from America," spat Pepper.

"You are lying, Pepper."

"No, I am not lying. These folks here will attest to that. In fact, we went as far as to blame Thaddeus for the mishaps to McKenna. We had no idea it could have been you."

"Papa, you nearly had McKenna raped and killed. Is that the kind of father I now have?" Jenny asked.

To her surprise, his reaction was one of startled shock. "I don't know nothing about no rape or killing. The men I hired were only supposed to scare her enough to go back to America. I had no knowledge of anything else. That is the truth."

McKenna could tolerate no more. She took her rifle from her saddlebag and walked up to Ian McTavish—pushing him backwards with the butt of her weapon until he fell down to the ground. She slowly bent down and faced Jenny's father with a stern but determined look upon her face. She stared at him showing no emotion before she spoke.

"I have been attacked, shot at, mauled, mishandled, groped, assaulted, kissed without permission, and nearly raped. Now, I don't know what your orders were, but they certainly were not carried out. You hired river scum from the docks to carry out your threats because you are too much of a coward to scare me yourself. If any of the things that happened to me had happened to Jenny, you would have killed without a second thought.

"You threatened Reney and cost him his life, not to mention your direct or indirect involvement in the miscarriages of his unborn children. You have interfered with people's lives for the last time. You belong in jail, and you need to stay there and rot, for all I care. Your daughter is happy now, and you do not deserve her. In fact, you have no business calling her your daughter. What would have happened if your paid thugs had hurt your own child? What then, Mr. McTavish? Would you have stopped your maliciousness?

"What Thaddeus did was wrong, but those actions have been accounted for and apologized for. His life with his children is his business. Your business with Thaddeus dealt with hurt from long ago. Unfortunately, you are so filled with hate that you can't see straight. I have never met you nor had any previous affiliation with Jenny or Uncle Pepper, yet you took it upon yourself to harm me and those who love me. You are a scared old man, so filled with revenge that it has misguided your heart.

"I thought the Scots were a proud people and completely loyal to their own. I was overwhelmingly wrong, wasn't I? When you were busy planning the ruination of Thaddeus Wells, you let the one blessing in your family slip from your grasp. If I were Jenny, I would take you to jail myself and throw away the key. Of course, God says we are supposed to forgive, but I think God will understand if I don't forgive you for a long while. You, sir, are a conniving pig. Be glad that I didn't shoot you myself. I don't miss."

As McKenna finished her speech, the silence once again hung within the air. The leaves rustled in the wind. There was no need to speak or to offer a rebuttal. McKenna had said all that needed to be said, and said it well.

Minutes passed before Jenny broke the silence. "Father, does Mama know what you have done? For if she did, she would be as ashamed of you as I am."

"Jenny, please don't say that to me. I did it for you. I loved you, and you loved Pepper. That man hurt you intentionally for no good reason. In my eyes, child, that is wrong. And then, when he sent his man out to the house and tried to pay your Mamma off, well, things turned from bad to worse and… and …"

"And what? What aren't you telling me? What man? Who tried to pay off Mama?" Jenny shouted with the little strength she had left.

"Wells knew that you didn't take the money he had given you to leave. So, he sent another man out to the house—this one had some money as well and he tried to make your mama take it. When she refused to take the money, the man got rough with her and started to slap her around. She ran away from the house and he chased her. She slipped and fell down the stairs to the spring house." Ian McTavish's voice cracked and his eyes looked into his daughter's with such grief that Jenny knelt and grabbed her father's hand into hers.

"Go on, what have you not told me yet? Go on, finish your story!" Jenny could barely keep her breathing in control. She was aching from her toes to her fingertips, not wanting to hear the remainder of this story for fear of more hurt.

"Jenny, your mama was pregnant. We were told that she wouldn't have no more children. Well, the Lord changed his mind after all those years. That scum that Wells hired caused her to slip and fall and lose your baby brother."

Jenny abruptly released her father's hand from hers. She looked into his eyes, then into Pepper's. She didn't move, she didn't breathe, she didn't speak. She simply swallowed and looked up into the heavens. She closed her eyes and let out a big breath before speaking.

"This is irony in its purest form. In my eyes, you are no different than Thaddeus Wells. You hurt McKenna intentionally, for no good reason. In my eyes, that is wrong. Thaddeus had no idea that Mama was carrying a child. You know that. After all these years, he probably knows that he sent a man out to pay off Mama, nothing more. Just like you wanted to scared McKenna, nothing more."

Father looked at daughter with pronounced shame. Daughter looked at father with bitterness and disgust.

"Seems to me we have our answers," Parker announced. "Now then, the matter lies upon McKenna's decision."

"What do you mean by that?" asked a startled McKenna.

"I mean, you now know who planned your attacks. The question you need to answer is this: what do you intend to do about it?"

"I don't know." McKenna walked back to the tree and slumped into a sitting position. "I need time to think."

"Cooper, why don't you escort Mr. McTavish to town and lock him up in jail? At least we know McKenna will be safe until a decision has been made. Jenny, do you understand that this will be for his own good?" Parker asked with authority.

Parker saw the hurt and struggle within Jenny's eyes. He knew she was wishing the man in question was not her father.

"I understand, Parker," she finally whispered. "Pepper, will you take me home now?"

"I'm sorry, love, but I will need to ride into town and talk to the constable, and get the doctor to look at the bump on Quaid's head. I will be home shortly. It will be all right, Jenny; I promise." Pepper leaned down and kissed Jenny's forehead.

"Well then, I am coming with you," Jenny insisted.

Pepper sighed. "Are you sure you are up to it? You look pale, love."

"I am up to it. It is something I need to do and the ride there will clear my head," Jenny replied with a solemn look upon her face.

"Very well, my dear, go get your horse and mount up."

"I will ride with you, as well," said McKenna as she turned toward Solomon.

Parker was quick to shut her down by grabbing her upper arm. "No, kitten. You will ride with me. You have been through enough today."

"Now Parker, I am quite capable of riding Solomon on my own all the way back home. Truly, I am," McKenna said as she softly pried Parker's grip from her arm. Parker slowly turned McKenna in his arms and peered into her eyes. He cupped her face within his calloused hands as he softly moved his thumb over her parted lips.

"I would never question your ability to ride, kitten. But you have been through a lot today and you have been a very brave woman. I insist that you ride with me back home. I need to hold you and feel you against my body. I was scared out of my mind when I realized that you were in potential danger. When I saw Quaid with a bloodied forehead, my heart almost stopped. It was all I could do not to beat McTavish to death with my bare hands."

"Parker, I was scared, too. I was scared because I couldn't see my attacker. I felt vulnerable and I never want to feel like that again." Parker lowered his head and kissed McKenna with every ounce of passion that had built up within him from his morning ride. He knew her lips would be swollen, but he didn't care. He moved his hands down her sides, picked her up by the waist, and placed her astride his saddle. Then, he mounted behind her and enveloped her within his strong, muscular arms. Parker softly pulled McKenna's hair from her ear and gently kissed her lobe. He whispered so lightly that McKenna had to turn her head into his voice to hear his words.

"As God as my witness, as long as I have breath in me, you will never have to feel vulnerable or frightened again. I love you, kitten, and I am here to protect you. Let's be glad that this threat has now been ridden from our lives." McKenna rested against Parker's chest all the way home, knowing that this nightmare that had plagued her for so long was now over. She smiled and silently thanked God for her family and the man who was taking her home. She was truly blessed.

Chapter 59

The Thanksgiving table of 1863 was set to autumn perfection. The guests sitting around the table had bowed their heads as they were prepared to say their prayers and offer their thanks. There were four new guests seated at the table: Thaddeus and the widow Jones, and Ian and Molly McTavish.

McKenna had called a meeting two days before Thanksgiving Day, putting Thaddeus and Ian in a room with Parker, Pepper, Pia, Jenny and herself. McKenna had given both Thaddeus and Ian two options. For option one, they would put the past to rest by working together for two years and rebuilding a brand-new facility and school for the Widows and Orphans—plus a new veterinarian clinic for horses. Option two would see the both of them thrown together for a period of two years working hard labor down at the docks. They would share a supervised room and board together on the ship—one year for Ian's revengeful planning, and one year for Thaddeus's biased intervening. Both men were given twenty-four hours to come to a mutual agreement. Now, McKenna had hoped they would select her first option, ultimately forcing them to get past their prejudices and put their heads and hearts together, forcing them to produce hearty benefits to their community. Of course, both men were to be in church every Sunday for the next two years, come hell or high water.

Heads bowed and hands clasped together as Pepper stood and offered the prayer for dinner. "If there is any more repenting to do within these walls," stated Pepper, "then let it be known now. From this day forward, the Wells family and friends who live on this land will follow the law of God and his writings within the Holy Scripture. We will say the Lord's Prayer and live to its meaning. There has been enough hurt over the years, and now, on this day of Thanksgiving, we are gathered to give our thanks to those who sit beside and across from us. There will be no more deceit or conniving. There will be love, and that love will be shared by all. Thank you, Lord, for bringing us all together. We need to be here...all of us. Thank you for allowing us to forgive and to live our lives for you. Thank you for forgiving our misdeeds, and help us to be better Christians. In your Holy Name, we pray. Amen. And Lord, please make sure Ian and Thaddeus do not kill each other during the next two years. Amen."

Food, drink, and conversation were shared throughout the meal. Knox and Lyla curled up underneath the table beside McKenna and Parker, enjoying the turkey that was secretly fed to them. The November chill had been expunged by the burning wood in the old, marble fireplace, and the aromas of the meal permeated the entire dwelling.

This is a good day—a day to be thankful, a day to forgive and forget the past, thought McKenna as she looked at those seated around the table. It was a day to forge into the future and prepare for the unknown.

It was a time to be thankful for every soul in England and the Americas. It was truly a time to give thanks for one another. Hate would not be invited at this table. Hate would no longer prevail in this family; not if McKenna could help it.

I hope Papa can have a moment of peace, as well. I pray that the soldiers can find a safe bit of time to think of their loved ones. Perhaps the memories of their families and traditions will get them through this day. I hope that President Lincoln can see an end to this nightmare of war as he gives his own personal thanks on this holiday.

The weeks following Thanksgiving were filled with apprehensiveness and unease for McKenna. She had not received a letter from her father and this had caused her to become quite irritable. Zadie, Pia, and Parker had already begun their breakfast when McKenna quickly walked to the table and sat beside Parker with a heavy look of concern upon her pretty face.

"Parker, what are we to do? Papa said he would send a letter to me, and he hasn't! There are only three more weeks until Christmas!" exclaimed McKenna as she threw her open napkin on the table.

Parker glanced at McKenna. He could not bear seeing such despair in her eyes. *Poor kitten*, he thought, *if you only knew.*

"Kitten, give it a day or two. Let's see what the mail brings," replied Parker as he sipped his morning coffee.

"I hope the mail brings me good news, Parker. I just don't know how much longer I can wait." McKenna rose from the table, arms folded tightly, and quietly excused herself to the outdoor porch.

"McKenna, git back in here and eat your breakfast!" shouted Zadie. McKenna slammed the door as she left the dining room, not even turning around to answer her beloved Zadie.

Pia rose from her chair and stood behind Parker, softly placing a hand upon his shoulder. "I know it is hard to watch her sadness, but tomorrow, she will be a different young lady. See it through, dear. Your plan is brilliant."

"It sure is, Captain. Little Miss McKenna will be real surprised!" chuckled Zadie. "Lord help us all though—we got to git through this whole day with her testiness."

Parker shook his head with a wry smile. "Thank you, ladies, for sharing in my little secret. Now, if you will both excuse me, I need to get to the docks for last-minute preparations. Thank you again for the delicious breakfast."

Parker politely excused himself from the room. Not a minute had gone by before Pia began her round of questions for Zadie.

"Zadie, how are the food preparations coming along? Is there anything that still needs to be done?"

"I have it all under control, Pia, you just need to calm yourself," answered Zadie.

"Zadie is right," said Jenny as she entered the dining room with a half-eaten muffin in her hand.

Pia smiled warmly at her friend. "Good morning to you, dear! Jenny, what about the dress? How is that coming? And Maggie's dress and yours—are they finished?"

"Oh, Pia, everything is coming along nicely. You are working yourself up for nothing. Truly, everything is working as planned. Just take a breath and relax; Zadie and I will make sure things are perfect for the big day. Now, I do have a surprise, and I will just burst if I don't share it with you both."

"Lord's sake, girl, another surprise in this house? What on earth could it be?" Zadie demanded.

"Well, do you suppose we could use some of that leftover silk ribbon for another wedding?" Jenny's eyes lit up the room with a magical aura.

"And whose wedding would that be, child?" asked Zadie, a smile forming on her face.

"I have a secret." She beamed as she put her hands to her heart before continuing. "Pepper asked me to marry him!"

The two women clapped their hands and rushed to Jenny with outstretched arms. The three of them hugged and cried until Zadie stepped back, wiping her nose with her apron.

"Well, did you answer him?" she asked in an excited huff.

"Of course, I did. I said yes! And the best part is, Pepper wants to be married on the first day of the new year. Isn't that grand? A new day and a new beginning—January 1, 1864. What do you think?"

"I think we'd better get busy with round two of wedding plans. This old house hasn't seen this much fuss in years! We are so happy for you, dear! Where is that brother of mine? I need to congratulate him!" exclaimed Pia. She glided across the room in a flurry of swishing skirts, intending to burst through the doors, find her brother, and express her jubilance that he would finally marry the love of his life. But as she passed the front window, she happened to catch McKenna swinging on the porch out of the corner of her eye. Her head was hung low, and her shoulders drooped. Even Knox was not getting hugged today. *Hang on, child; one more day and then your little heart will be bursting with joy.* Pia turned from the window and gently asked, "Jenny, may I make a small request?"

"Of course, Olympia. What is it?" she asked as she ate the last of her muffin.

"Can we announce your wedding day at supper tomorrow night? If McKenna hears of your good news today, I am afraid she will succumb to melancholy more than she already has. Harper is supposed to arrive here tomorrow. Once he is here, she will welcome your wedding news with overwhelming happiness."

"Of course, we can. I understand, Pia—I would feel the same if I were McKenna. We will keep my secret just a little longer. Now, if you will both excuse me, I need to finish some sewing." Jenny grabbed one more muffin before she turned and skipped all the way to the stairs.

"Now, Pia, you don't think McKenna will get mad, do you?" Zadie asked as she began to gather the breakfast dishes from the table.

"Zadie, I imagine McKenna will be very upset with Parker when she finds out that most of us were in on his little secret. But then, Parker has a way of cooling that temper of hers."

"Oh, my, he sure does. That man could cool the embers of a fire just by lookin' at them," whispered Zadie, fanning herself with a smile.

Chapter 60

The following day brought December winds and dangerous temperatures. Every walk made to the stable was done in haste. Every member of the household layered coats, hats, and scarfs upon their shivering bodies in a futile effort to stave off the bone-chilling gusts of wind. McKenna was bundling up after breakfast with full intent to do her daily chores in the barn when Zadie stopped her.

"McKenna-girl, why don't you stay in here today? One of the boys will clean the stalls for you."

"No, thank you, Zadie. I look forward to seeing Solomon, and besides, a bit of fresh air and hard work never hurt anyone."

"All right, baby girl, have it your way. I just don't want you to catch cold."

"Oh, I won't, Zadie. The barn isn't that warm, but I have enough layers on to keep out the cold."

"McKenna, you only have on a riding habit, boots, and your wool shawl. Child, put on another layer of clothes, please!"

"Zadie, I am fine. I will be back in a while. Come, Knox, let's go see Solomon."

Zadie watched the two of them trudge out the door shaking her head, thinking that she should have insisted McKenna put on another coat.

***

It is bitterly cold today, thought McKenna as she walked. *Maybe Zadie is right; maybe I should have layered on more clothing.* Knox began to sniff and linger behind.

"Come on, boy, we don't have time to sniff for mice. It's too cold out here," McKenna called. Knox continued to sniff, his curiosity taking him farther away from McKenna.

"All right, boy, if you want to explore, do it on your own. You have a much warmer coat than I do."

The dog paid no mind to McKenna and continued to walk down the back path toward the south pond.

What is wrong with him? thought McKenna irritably. *It's not like Knox to disobey and stray away from my commands.*

"Knox, come."

The dog began sniffing even more forcefully.

Oh, dear, she thought, *what is he after? Something is wrong.*

"All right, boy, I'm coming. You'd better be scenting out something worthwhile."

McKenna followed her dog. She knew he was searching, but for what? Around the bend lay the frozen pond. *What was that ahead?* As she stepped closer, she recognized Maggie's red scarf lying on the ground. McKenna scanned the area until her eyes focused on the pond.

Dear God, McKenna thought as she approached the shore. She gasped as she recognized the small form striking a sharp vibrancy of color in contrast to the translucent ice. What was Maggie doing there, lying so far out on the ice-covered pond? McKenna's heart seemed to skip a step when she realized that Maggie's boot appeared to be stuck beneath the surface of the ice.

"Maggie?" She cupped her hands around her frozen mouth and desperately wished for the sound to carry. "Maggie!"

"Cousin McKenna, oh, thank goodness," Maggie cried. "My boot is stuck in the ice, and I can't get out."

"Maggie, don't move, do you hear me? Do not move. I'm coming to get you." McKenna quickly picked up the scarf and tied it around Knox's neck. "Knox, go get help! Go to the barn!"

Knox yelped once and did as he was commanded.

"Maggie, I am going to come to the pond and release your boot." McKenna's words were calm and even, revealing none of the terror she felt. "Don't move, honey. Can you stay still for me? The ice is thin, and we have to be very quick."

"I won't move, McKenna," Maggie whimpered. "Hurry, I'm scared."

"I know, sweeting. I am hurrying as fast as I dare."

The shore of the pond had frozen, but the layer of ice was still thin. McKenna knew that another ten yards out, the water would be bitterly cold. *What had caused Maggie to carelessly walk on a half-frozen pond?*

She crept along the surface of the pond, looking for the best pathway toward the center. "I am almost there, dear. Do not move."

Slowly, McKenna bent down and began to crawl upon the ice toward Maggie. One step at a time, she inched forward. The ice cracked beneath her weight.

Dear Lord, she thought, *if this ice cracks, both Maggie and I will go under. Hurry, Knox, do your job and get help.*

***

"Cooper, it is cold enough in this barn to freeze water," said Parker, tightening his collar.

"Yes, I know, but these horses have to be tended nonetheless."

Pepper chuckled. "You two need to stop griping and hurry up, so we can all get back into that kitchen and enjoy Zadie's coffee and rolls. And Parker, how are you going to deliver Harper in this cold?"

"Same way I would in the heat. Purposefully and carefully."

"What the hell?" Out of the corner of his eye, Pepper saw Knox running toward them. "Easy, boy, what do you have here? What is this tied around you?"

Pepper pulled the red material off and gasped. "Coop, Parker, this is Maggie's scarf. Something isn't right here. She's in trouble."

"How do you know that?" demanded Parker as he filled the last bucket with mash.

"This dog didn't tie this scarf around his neck by himself. Go on, boy, show us. Come on, let's go." The dog turned and ran back the way he had come, with all three men giving close chase behind him, temporarily forgetting how bitterly cold the temperature was.

Chapter 61

"There!" Parker shouted as soon as the three men caught up with the excitable dog. He pointed to their right, out toward the frozen lake. "It's Maggie! What on earth is she doing out there?"

"What the hell is that? What is crawling out there toward her?" asked Cooper, trying to shield his eyes from the snow's glare.

"That would be your niece and your student, McKenna Reed. Of all the stupid things in the world to do, she is crawling out there to help. If that damn ice breaks, they both go under." Parker hid his panic and concern under a familiar layer of disapproval and fury. "Pepper, go get help and rope," he ordered, while he and Cooper sprinted to the edge of the pond.

"McKenna, stay where you are," Parker called. "Do not move any more, sweet. The ice is too thin, and you will both go under."

McKenna whimpered, but stopped where she was. "Parker, help me, please. My hands are very cold, and I am not sure if I can pull Maggie free. Please, hurry," she shouted back knowing that her voice would carry across the stillness of the pond.

"I know, honey. Do not move. Maggie, you either. I want both of you to stay put until we get to you."

Time felt as if it had stopped for McKenna. The ice around her knee was cracking. She was a hand's length from Maggie's collar, but if she reached for Maggie, McKenna was afraid the ice would break. If she didn't reach for Maggie, she would eventually go under. What was she to do?

"Maggie, stay there," McKenna commanded, trying to keep her teeth from chattering. "I am almost to your knee. I am going to try to tug your foot out of your boot. Do you understand me? Do not move. Let me do the work."

"McKenna, I'm scared." Maggie's face was pale, her words breathless and brimming with fear.

"I know, honey; so am I."

"Damn it, McKenna, do not move," hollered Parker.

"I must try to get her foot out. I know what I am doing!" McKenna hollered back.

The hell you do—you'll get yourself killed! Parker thought to himself with silent disbelief.

Pepper had finally returned with the boys in tow, and together they knotted a long length of rope for Parker to hang onto as he crawled onto the ice.

McKenna continued to tug on Maggie's knee, and, finally, her foot gave way of the boot. Unfortunately, the effort proved to be the final straw for the weak ice. With a cry, Maggie fell waist-deep through the surface. McKenna immediately gripped her collar as tightly and quickly as she could.

"McKenna," Maggie screamed, "help me!"

"Grab on to my arm," McKenna ordered. "Do it now, and don't let go."

McKenna tugged with all her might as she backed up on the ice. With one final tug, Maggie came up out of the water and sprawled upon the ice. McKenna scooted back with Maggie, inch by inch.

"Maggie, crawl back to the shore slowly. Do it now. Stay on your belly."

"McKenna, the ice won't hold both of us—look, it's starting to crack more!"

"Go, Maggie, go now."

Maggie crawled slowly, as instructed. Carefully, McKenna turned to follow her back to shore. But then she heard the ice crack, and felt herself slipping into the water. *Dear God*, she thought, *I don't want to die. Not now, not like this.* There was nothing to hold on to. *Cold, oh my Lord, the water is cold. Pull yourself up, McKenna Reed*, she said to herself, *now is not the time to be afraid. Pull yourself up. Pull yourself up.* The words kept repeating in her mind, but she didn't have the strength to do so. Her hands were slipping, and she couldn't feel anything but the cold water engulfing her head. She saw a figure coming toward her, but she couldn't see who it was.

Oh, Lord, let it be Parker, was her last thought before unconsciousness claimed her.

Chapter 62

Harper remained by his daughter's bedside, catching small naps whenever his eyes could no longer remain open. He was mentally exhausted and physically depleted. His arrival to England was not the sort he had anticipated. Parker had met him at the dock and promptly escorted him to Pia's home, explaining every detail of McKenna's condition along the way. Initially, he was overjoyed to leave the constant battles back at in the States, only to be filled with the terror of McKenna's battle to survive here in England.

Dear God in heaven, please do not let me lose her before I even get to surprise her with my presence.

His bedside vigil continued. He read to his baby girl, he told stories to her about her childhood days, he even sang songs that they use to sing together. He tried anything to bring her out of her unconscious state, hoping that a familiar tune or story would trigger her back to him. Harper was busy preparing another round of tea when Parker knocked lightly upon the door to announce his presence.

"How is she?" Parker asked with trepidation.

"No change, I'm afraid." In that instant, Parker viewed McKenna's father as the epitome of despair and the embodiment of hellish anguish. McKenna was his last remaining family member. It would be Harper's undoing if he lost his daughter. Parker looked to the sky and remembered how he had felt when he had lost his parents. He would rather have died with them than deal with the gut-wrenching turmoil of deprivation, or so he thought at the time. Now, Harper was facing the loss of his daughter, and being a trained medical man made it worse, for there wasn't a damn thing he could do. Helplessness was the emotional enemy for this family. Parker turned from the window and strode to McKenna's bedside, placing a gentle kiss upon her feverish forehead. The quiet was soon interrupted by the harshness of Pia's voice.

"Harper, what is that wretched smell?" asked Pia as she entered McKenna's room with fresh linens.

"You are smelling glycerin, vinegar, herbs, gum arabic, and whiskey, all mixed together."

"What is that used for?"

"To subdue the coughing."

"Why am I giving her this stench-ridden black tea, then?" Zadie asked.

"You know as well as I do, Zadie. Don't pretend you don't see the signs—hot and cold chills, mucus, chest pain?"

"Dear God, no, Harper. Don't let it be pneumonia." Zadie looked at the others in the room.

Harper nodded, confirming their worst fear.

"Zadie, keep the blankets on her, and do not allow her to kick them off, no matter what she says. She goes in and out of delirium and won't remember anything. Pia, keep putting that medicine down her throat every two hours. We will need to take shifts and rest in between."

"That won't be necessary, Harper," Parker said immediately. "I will stay with her until her fever breaks."

Harper shook his head with a sigh. "Parker, you don't know what you're saying. It could be minutes or days. You need to rest as well."

"I will rest once she breaks her fever," Parker insisted. "Go on, now, all of you out of here. I will stay with her. Take this chance and get some sleep, Harper. You need to be rested in case her condition worsens, or improves for that matter. You don't want your daughter to wake up to a tired old man, now, do you?" Parker asked with a glimpse of humor attached to a weak smile.

No one argued. No one dared. The rest of the family left, leaving Harper and Parker standing side by side. Harper sighed, but nodded approvingly at Parker. "You know," he said, "I always knew that McKenna would make the right choice for herself in matters of the heart. How lucky you both are that she chose you." Parker could have sworn he saw a slight tear forming in his tired eyes before he slowly turned and left the room, closing the door ever so gently.

Chapter 63

Minutes turned into hours, and hours into days. On the third day following the rescue, Harper walked into McKenna's bedroom and asked Parker, "Has the fever gone down any?"

"I believe it has. She's gone from warm too hot too cold with her body temperature. Should I open the windows and get fresh air in here?"

"That will always be a dispute in the medical world, son. I would say yes. We need to clean the air in here, and rid this room of germs."

"There has to be something more that we can do. Think, Harper, what else haven't we done?"

Parker was exhausted; he looked like hell and hadn't shaved in three days. His exhausted eyes said more than any words could.

Harper was quick to notice Parker's state. "Let me have some time alone with McKenna," he said, putting a firm hand on his shoulder and guiding him out of the room. "Go on, now, clean up and shave. When she does wake up, I don't want her seeing you in your condition. Get something to eat and drink, and get some sleep. Go on, now."

Parker knew the man was right. He could barely stand. "I will be back shortly."

Parker nodded, left the room, and slowly slid down to his knees in the hall. He put his hands to his head and rubbed his temples, trying to erase the pain from his headache. She looked so fragile lying on that big bed. McKenna was the only woman he knew that would have willingly, without hesitation, risked her life to save the life of a child. Selflessness was a characteristic that defined McKenna Reed, and he loved her for it, but in this case, it may have cost her life.

Maggie had not suffered as badly as McKenna had. Where in hell had his kitten gotten the strength to pull Maggie from the pond? Thank God, he'd reached McKenna when he did. She had already gone under, slipping into the pond's freezing water. Her little hand was the only thing left he could grab onto before she completely submerged. Aside from the fever, coughing, and the current threat of pneumonia, she suffered only bruises and no broken bones.

The swish of skirts and the sound of heels clicking upon the floor interrupted his thoughts. When he looked up, he saw the hand extended to him. He gratefully placed Zadie's hand into his while she helped pull him up.

"Captain Sloane, ol' Zadie will take care of you now. You have had your time to bawl, or maybe you ain't. But I knows this: your little kitten will come out of this. You just wait and see. You hear me?"

Parker smiled, which turned out to be a gargantuan effort in his condition. "I hear you. Harper is with her now."

"Yes, Captain, and now you need to take care of yourself. Take a hot bath and shave. While you are doin' that, I will fix you a plate of food. Go on, now. When McKenna wakes up, you want to look presentable and handsome, and I knows how handsome you can be when you get all fancied up. And, if you don't mind me sayin', you smell somethin' terrible. Go on now, git yourself cleaned up. I'll sit with my baby girl." Zadie clasped his hand in both of hers before she turned and entered McKenna's room.

Parker offered a weak nod and began walking toward his room, stopping along the way to smell his own shirt and chest. Zadie was right, he did smell.

***

Harper had fallen asleep with his head resting on McKenna's hand. An open Bible was laid across McKenna's stomach, a testament to the reading and praying he had done. With a startled twitch, Harper sprung up from his slumber and continued his reading.

"May the Lord bless you and keep you. May the Lord smile on you and be gracious to you." Harper laid his head down a second time and closed his weary eyes. He had made a strong show to Parker, but he, too was fighting sleep.

"You didn't finish it. Papa, there is one more sentence in Numbers—'May the Lord show you his favor and give you his peace.'"

Harper sat up and looked at the tired yet still startlingly blue eyes of his baby girl. "Dear God in heaven, you have brought her back to me. Thank you, Lord!"

"Papa?" McKenna whispered as he embraced her fragile body in a tight, desperate hug. "Is this a dream? Oh, tell me I'm not still dreaming. Tell me you're really here."

"I'm here, baby girl. I will always be here for you when you need me."

McKenna sobbed as she lifted her arms and hugged her father back.

Chapter 64

Ten days. Ten days until her wedding. McKenna had regained most of her strength over the past week and she was feeling much better, but the pneumonia had taken its toll on her, still leaving her tired at times.

McKenna was gazing at the morning sunrise from her window when Maggie entered her bedroom with tears in her eyes. "McKenna?" she asked.

McKenna's attention fell from the window immediately. "Maggie, sweeting, what is it? What's wrong, dear?" She shifted in the nest of blankets covering her bed and patted the open spot next to her. "Come here, pretty girl, and sit beside me."

"I am sorry you got sick," cried Maggie as she snuggled into McKenna's arms.

"Hush, Maggie, it was not your fault. You were in trouble, and I am glad I was there to help you. In fact, the real hero is Knox. You know he is the one who saved you. He ran and got help."

Maggie emitted a wan smile through her tears. "I know; I gave him extra muffins from Zadie. But I need to tell you something, Cousin McKenna."

"Certainly. Now, what could be so bad as to have tears in those beautiful blue eyes of yours?"

"I was following a bird with a broken wing. He ran onto the ice, and I was trying to catch him and bring him back home, so Mama could fix his wing. I didn't think about the ice, and I am sorry you fell through. It was all my fault."

"Now listen to me, child. It isn't your fault. You followed something to help it. I followed you to help you. So, you see, we both were helping. We were not damaging or destroying anything. We should have used better judgment, but nonetheless, we survived. Next time, we will think twice before we walk on a frozen pond again, won't we?"

"Oh, McKenna, I was so scared when you had your fever. I was afraid you would die, and everybody would be mad at me, and then they would never forgive me. I even thought about running away."

McKenna sucked in a breath but willed herself to remain calm and soothing. "Maggie, you must not ever be afraid of your own family. And you especially must not ever fear that we won't forgive you. If there's one thing I've learned…" McKenna smiled to herself as she thought of Thaddeus Wells, and even of her own experiences with Parker. "…this is an exceptionally forgiving family."

"I promise." Maggie nodded. "I am so glad you didn't die."

"Well, I am too because if I did…" The corner of McKenna's mouth turned up into a sly smirk. "…who in the world would marry Captain Sloane? Besides, I need you to walk down the aisle before me, and drop beautiful rose petals. Now, if you weren't here, my wedding would not be the same."

"Oh, McKenna, I love you," Maggie breathed as she snuggled closer to her cousin.

"And I you, sweeting. Let's watch the sun finish its rising, and the beauty of the day begin." The two of them continued to sit side by side, enjoying the quiet until the door burst open.

"Well now, if you two are done weepin' and sayin' your sorries to each other, do you think you might help me sew on these last few pieces of pearls on your weddin' dress? If it ain't too much to ask, I mean. McKenna, you can stay right here in bed and I will bring my sewin' box to you," hollered Zadie in a swirl of her skirts. The woman was on a mission and no one better git in her way. McKenna knew it and even young Maggie knew it. Together, they winked at each other before responding to Zadie's orders.

"Nonsense, Zadie, I am feeling stronger each day. How about I get out of this bed, get dressed, and sit at the table with you both? Then, we can all sew on the pearls?"

"Well, I guess it ain't gonna hurt none, I just don't want to tire you out, 'specially when you are tryin' to heal up for the weddin'.'"

Maggie and McKenna rolled their eyes and once again, exchanged a smile. It was nearly impossible to get upset at Zadie, even if she did interrupt their quiet time.

"Never you mind, Zadie. This would do me good. Besides, I need to put some work into my own wedding dress!"

The three of them were just putting the finish touches on McKenna's dress when Parker entered through the double doors.

"Parker Sloane, you get out of here this instant," McKenna cried immediately. "You can't see my dress. Go on, now, shoo!"

"Kitten, allow me to ask you a simple question," said Parker, an exuberant smile spreading across his face.

"Well, then turn around and ask your question."

Parker sighed with exasperation, but complied.

Once his eyes were safely directed at the wall, McKenna said, "All right, Parker Sloane, what is your question that caused you to stomp in here and rile me up?"

"Would you like to go for a ride and walk with me?"

The response surprised and delighted McKenna, who had been expecting something far more serious.

"Shall I repeat the question, kitten? Or have you lost your voice?" Parker chuckled mischievously.

"Oh, Parker, yes, I would. I would enjoy getting out of this house and being in the sunshine. When can we go?" she asked like a small child getting a treat.

"Now, kitten."

McKenna looked at Zadie, who nodded. "It will do you good to get some fresh air and put some pink back into those cheeks. Go on, baby girl. But Captain Sloane, don't keep her out too long. Her lungs ain't healed yet."

"You bet, Zadie. I will bring her back shortly, I promise," Parker replied as he turned and escorted McKenna through the door.

"Kitten?"

"Yes, Captain?" she replied with one of the loveliest smiles he had seen since her illness.

"I am glad you came." Parker placed a kiss upon the top of her head as the two walked hand and hand out the kitchen door and down the pathway to the barn. McKenna suddenly realized that she had forgotten to do something and looked up at Parker with complete sincerity.

"Thank you for taking care of me all those days, Parker. Thank you for rescuing me—again. I don't know how I will be able to repay you." She reached up and kissed his lips slowly and passionately.

Parker grinned impishly through the kiss. "I can think of a few ways, love."

"Well, why don't you tell me on the way to the barn? I will race you—first to the barn gets a kiss from the other person." McKenna skipped down the pathway steps as if she had never been sick.

"Careful, kitten. If you fall, Zadie will have my head!" shouted Parker as he watched her. *This is one race I will purposely lose,* he laughed to himself as he followed her down the pathway to the barn. McKenna was healthy, and she was almost back to her old self. *Ah, yes, my kitten has her claws back, and soon, I will have my kitten in my arms—to be mine, forever.*

McKenna's laughter lingered in the crisp air. He smiled and gave a throaty sigh. Ten days ago, he had prayed like he had never prayed before, asking the Good Lord to return his only true love back to him. God had answered his prayers. He was truly the happiest man in England right now—aside from Pepper. His wedding day would be perfect, and the wedding night… well, that would be magical.

Chapter 65

Christmas Eve was upon them. Parker stood at the front of the church in his magnificent English Royal Navy uniform. The wedding ceremony was about to begin. Parker waited anxiously for his beautiful bride to appear, noticing the pews embellished in white and pink streamers tied with bits of ivy. Parker cleared his throat and straightened his ascot as he watched the doors at the back of the church open. The ceremony was about to begin.

Maggie took her cue to walk down the aisle and toss the tiny flower petals. She looked like a fairy nymph—tendrils of hair and ribbon flowing about her head. She was a little beauty, no doubt, and Maggie's eyes—an unusual color of turquoise and green, quite stunning on an already angelic face. Maggie was smiling from head to toe and when she approached Parker, she blew him a kiss. Parker immediately caught the kiss and blew one back while the child took a prearranged spot at the front of the church.

Harper and McKenna remained behind, waiting for their own entrance cue. McKenna looked at her father and smiled with pure, undisguised happiness. Harper swallowed as he gazed down at his radiant daughter. "If your mother could see you now," he whispered with tears forming.

"She can see me, Papa. She is watching from heaven."

Harper looked down at the tendrils of golden hair twisting around the pearl necklace McKenna wore—the one his dear Maribelle had worn so many years ago. "You look just like her," he said quietly.

"Thank you, Papa, and thank you for being here, and thank you for taking care of me when I was so sick. I am sorry if I frightened you."

"Hush, now, it is all over, and the only tears I want to see you shed today are those of happiness. You truly look beautiful, daughter. Your dress and your hair are magnificent."

"I can't take credit for either, Papa. My hair and my dress belong to the talents of Zadie, Pia, Jenny, and Maggie."

The ladies had prepared McKenna all morning for this moment. They had fixed her hair in double rolls lying neatly along each temple. They had then braided her long golden locks into three double loops. Zadie had made McKenna's headpiece out of point lace with roses, cornflowers, and wheat-ears. Tucked in between were Christmas flowers and greenery, interspersed with wispy tendrils of uncooperative blonde curls. It was truly a masterpiece. But the dress—the dress was a work of art. McKenna had chosen to wear white silk with brocaded pink flowers and an overskirt stitched with yellow roses and ivy. The bodice was cut low, but not too low, exposing the tops of her breasts. The puffed sleeves reached her elbows, showing narrow, gloved hands.

Pia had fastened a pink silk scarf trimmed in white pearls to McKenna's right shoulder with a brooch—a gift from Jenny. The scarf then passed over to the bodice on the left side, falling in inverted pleats. The dress was one-of-a-kind, and truly extraordinary.

"It is time, my dear. Take a breath, baby girl; you are about to walk down this aisle and get married."

McKenna looked into her father's eyes and nodded.

"I love you, Papa. Thank you for being here with me."

"I love you too, baby girl. The pleasure is all mine. I wouldn't miss this event for anything. This day belongs to you, love."

The processional began, and McKenna and her father made their entrance into the church and gracefully proceeded down the aisle.

Whispers, smiles, and small noises of approval echoed throughout the congregation. McKenna couldn't feel her feet, and she couldn't remember walking toward Parker until her father finally stopped moving forward.

Parker took her hand in his and whispered, "Hello, kitten. I could not believe that you would be more beautiful than you already were. You are enchanting."

McKenna blushed, at a loss for words for once due to Parker's sincerity. "You enchant me as well, dear captain."

Chapter 66

McKenna and Parker swirled on air that Christmas Eve in 1864. No one could have ruined their day—even if someone had tried. Every member of the family and their many guests were all attired in wedding finery. McKenna had handwritten each family member a special note, thanking them for making her past four years in England memorable. She also asked them to meet her and Parker on the front porch at the stroke of twelve.

The harpist and violinist harmonized melodies with ease and grace while the guests avidly danced away the hours amidst the lighted Christmas trees and festive decorations. Pia's home had been turned into a scene from a storybook; it was truly breathtaking.

When the clock approached midnight, the family gathered on the porch as McKenna had asked. When everyone was present, Parker held his glass high and spoke with confidence.

"We would like to welcome Christmas Day, 1864, with a toast. We would like to express how much we love you. We thank you for gathering at our wedding today and for all your hard work and efforts to prepare such a beautiful day for us. Merry Christmas to you all."

The stroke of midnight chimed as the first sips of the toast were swallowed. Tears filled McKenna's eyes, and she knew in her heart that this moment would always be recorded in her mind as the most magical and perfect day of her life.

"Well, now, let's welcome Christmas morning with a Wells tradition," Pia interrupted, placing her glass down on the window sill and clapping her hands together. "Let us all sing our favorite song. I do believe we have a violin accompanist to assist. Jonathon, will you do the honors?"

"Certainly, madam."

Jonathon began to play a few bars of *Silent Night*, and soon the entire family was holding hands together, singing the beloved Christmas hymn.

McKenna bowed her head and silently prayed that the soldiers back home would find a moment of concord to sing a song. She prayed that the fighting and the hatred would subside for Christmas Eve.

"Merry Christmas, kitten," Parker whispered, breaking her reverie with a light touch on her shoulder.

McKenna smiled up at him. "Merry Christmas, husband."

"It is time for you and me to leave this celebration and attend to our own."

"Why, Parker Sloane, what type of celebration do you have in mind?" McKenna asked coquettishly, feigning innocence.

"Come with me, Mrs. Sloane, and you shall find out."

Parker scooped McKenna up into his arms and walked toward the front walk.

"Parker, where are we going?"

"We are going to spend our wedding night in the hunting cottage. The women have prepared it especially for us."

McKenna sighed and relaxed into her husband's arms. "Oh, Parker, this day has been magical. I can't begin to thank them for what they have done for us."

"We will, my dear, in time. Tonight, is our night, and I intend to make this evening magical as well."

Chapter 67

Parker carried her to the hunting cottage, and upon arrival, they opened the door and saw the entire room had been lit in candlelight. The ladies had outdone themselves. It was magical, mystical, and romantic. The fire was blazing, adding warmth and a passionate ambience to the room. The sweet smell of cinnamon and cloves filled the air. Oils, perfumes, and lotions had been left on the bedside tables. The pillows and linens had been freshly washed. Even the rugs on the floor had been placed strategically in front of the fireplace. It looked magical.

"Parker, this is beautiful," McKenna breathed.

"Yes, it is, kitten, but not as beautiful as you are."

McKenna's heart pounded, and before she could stop herself, she blurted out, "Parker, I am frightened. I have never been with a man in an intimate way. I do not want to disappoint you tonight."

Parker cupped McKenna's face between his large hands. "McKenna Sloane, there is nothing you could do to disappoint me."

"Please be gentle with me, Parker. I am nervous."

"Kitten, there will be a moment of pain for you. But only a moment. The pain will escape, and then the pleasure will seep in and overtake you. I promise. Now then, let's get you out of this beautiful wedding gown. I want to see what my wife looks like without clothes on. I have waited too damn long for this moment."

Parker smiled as he turned McKenna around by her shoulders and began to unbutton the long length of tiny pearls that ran from her nape to her waist. McKenna could almost feel his heartbeat as she leaned in toward his chest. His fingers tingled her skin as they unbuttoned her gown, and she liked the sensation. When he had finished, he gently slid the gown from McKenna's shoulders and began to kiss the top of her shoulders from behind. There was something different in Parker's kisses, she thought. Tonight, they were gentle yet demanding. She could hear him inhaling, relishing in the sensual pleasure that he was consuming from his kisses. McKenna took a few steps forward, stepped out of her gown, and slowly turned to face her husband. She placed her hands upon his corded neck and pulled him down to meet her lips. She closed her eyes and kissed him hard upon his mouth. She was immediately lifted off her feet, carried across the room, and placed upon the edge of the bed.

"You are just as soft as I imagined you would be," he whispered as he untied the ribbons of her shift and pushed it from her body. "My God you are beautiful, kitten." He looked at every inch of McKenna, from her flushing face to her tiny feet, losing himself to the need to seek her willing lips. He kissed her back with such fervor that he nearly lost his balance; he was consumed by the hunger he possessed for his new bride.

His hands touched every inch of her body, leaving no skin of her sweet form ignored. Parker's desire grew stronger as he cupped her breasts, pinching her nipples before reaching up and tugging the ribbons of her braided hair, freeing the masses of golden curls, allowing them to flow freely across his fingers. He carefully untangled his hands and scooted her forward upon the bed so that she was completely underneath him. His hands returned to her scalp, massaging from her temples to the top of her head, causing McKenna to close her eyes and welcome his motions. Once again, he pressed his mouth down upon hers, forcing her lips apart and allowing his tongue to slide across the top of her mouth. The sounds that she uttered caused Parker's nostrils to flare. He straddled McKenna and began to kiss her neck, moving down her body and stopping to suckle her breasts. His hands spread wide, caressing the softness of each mound in slow, circular motions. She was exquisite, with her small waist and full breasts. She was perfect—she was his—and his desire for her was starting to erase any reasonable thought process he still had. He wanted her now.

McKenna's gasp brought his attention to her blushing face. "Have I hurt you, kitten?" he asked with an intense look, withdrawing his hands from her chest.

"No, my sweet husband. I have feelings in my body that I haven't had before. I am scared and curious all at the same time! Oh Parker, please don't stop," she urged as she clung to his muscled forearms with her tiny fingers. She scooted up, using Parker's shoulders to pull herself to a sitting position. She unbuttoned his shirt, pushing it open and off of his shoulders. Her movements were quick and filled with a need that she had never felt before. She slid her hands over his shoulders and the dark hair covering his muscled chest. "My God, Parker, you have the body of a Greek God... how on earth did you get such a muscled body?" she asked, sliding her hands up and down his sides, inching her way to his buckled belt.

"Years of working on a ship, love," Parker muttered as he leaned forward and kissed the back of her ear. Her fingertips brushed near his lower abdomen, twisting the dark curls in her fingers, attempting to unleash the leather belt from his trousers. She hesitated and looked into Parker's eyes before she spoke.

"Show me what to do," she whispered.

"Have you ever seen a man's body? Do you know what happens during lovemaking?" Parker asked as he pushed himself off the bed and shed his clothing.

"McKenna, did you hear me? Do you know what happens, love?" he asked softly, grabbing the back of her knees and pulling her toward the edge of the bed. McKenna was entranced with the vision before her. She had never seen a naked man—not one so close. She looked at his manhood and panicked. She quickly looked away and covered her mouth with a trembling hand.

"Kitten, what is it? What is wrong?" he asked, massaging her calves and working his way up toward her knees.

"Is that... that part... going to fit in me? It is so big," she stated with fright in her eyes.

"Yes, love, it will fit. I am a big man, and a big man has big parts. Lay down and let me relax you. I promise, I will be gentle." McKenna allowed herself to be pushed back on the bed, absorbing the pleasure of Parker's massaging hands on her legs. Her breathing began to slow down and her nerves were settling.

"I want to kiss you, touch you, smell you, and be inside of you, kitten. When I am near you like this, I lose control. It is a magical feeling," he said as his hands moved up her thighs and spread her legs apart.

McKenna's intake of breath caused Parker to smile. He placed his face against her soft curls and breathed in her scent. Ever so slowly, he opened her legs farther apart and pressed his thumbs against the folds of her womanhood, plunging his tongue deep into her softness. Over and over again he pushed his tongue into her depths, causing her hips to respond and move against him. "Parker, I have never felt like this... so warm... I feel like I am ready to burst…" Her explosion caused her to call his name out against her pillow. She arched and threw her body back, beckoning the chills that ran throughout her body to end.

"Dear God in heaven, what did you do to me?" She closed her eyes and grasped her head between her hands. "Never have I felt anything like that before… in all my wildest dreams… I never thought to feel the sensations that you gave to me." McKenna quickly sat up and placed her hands-on Parker's face. "I want to touch you. Show me how."

"Yes, love," he whispered. "But right now, I need to be inside you." In a blink he was there, on top of her with his muscled legs pushing her own tender legs apart. He gently placed his weight upon her, placing his hand against her tender folds. She glanced down to see him holding his swollen part with his hand, trying to guide his member inside her. Bracing himself, he began to thrust his hips, penetrating deep inside her.

"Parker, this isn't comfortable." She tried moving her legs and her feet to accommodate his weight. She felt like she was being crushed. Her breathing was labored and her body was beginning to ache.

"Kitten, almost there… keep moving with me and your pain will be gone, I promise."

"Parker, this hurts…" she screamed as tears formed in her eyes. Then, she began to move with Parker's hips. The former pain was gone and the feeling that she had just experienced with his fingers began to creep through her body again. "Dear God, this feels so warm and so good. Parker, it is going to happen again!"

"Yes, sweet, go with it…"

"Oh, dear God… my body is going to explode again!" McKenna convulsed, using her hands to brace the weight of Parker's body as he moved suddenly with a final, deep thrust. She let out a small whimper as she turned her head. She had felt the pain, but it was a different kind of pain.

Parker lifted his weight from her and lay beside her, stroking circles around her nipples.

"I am sorry, kitten. The hurt is over now, and you will never feel that pain again."

"I am fine, my love. It doesn't hurt anymore," she whispered back, taking his fingers in her mouth and sucking them as she would his member. "Parker, I want to taste you as you tasted me." She gathered her knees under her and edged herself off the bed. "Come and sit on the edge... here by me," she encouraged as she pulled his wrist toward her.

"Kitten, you do not have to do this, you will wear yourself out."

"Hush. I want to see, taste, touch, and smell every inch of you... I want you inside my mouth—remember those words?" she asked while placing her hands on his still swollen member.

"Now then, tell me if you like this..." McKenna put her mouth around Parker's hardened rod and sucked the length of his member, tantalizing the very tip—teasing him as though she was licking a stick of candy. She didn't stop; his body was telling her not to. His breathing was shortened and his body arched back, welcoming each thrust of her mouth on him. "Dear God, kitten, I cannot hold on much longer; come here, and let me release inside you." McKenna did as he asked, feeling his member enter her once again. The friction and contact produced by his excitement brought a strange sensation deep within her core. She began to feel an aching, an unexplained heat surging through her, and the familiar feeling of an explosion began to creep up her body again.

"Parker, I didn't think I would feel this again, so soon, but I do. I want to scream and yet I never want this feeling to end."

"Yes, kitten, almost there, almost..." Together, their bodies exploded, and their passion glazed their eyes. They were joined together in every way as man and wife. They lay facing each other, too tired to pull the blanket over their exhausted bodies. Instead, they held each other, sharing their body heat.

"I love you, Parker Sloane..." McKenna whispered as she drifted off to sleep.

"I love you, too, Mrs. Parker Sloane."

***

McKenna softly unwrapped her body from Parker's sleeping form, then captured a raven curl with her fingers and caressed it.

How was I so lucky as to capture this man's heart? He was gorgeous, but even more appealing without clothing. She smiled to herself. His body was like that of a Greek God; the years of working and sailing had sculpted him into one fine form of muscle.

He is mine, and I am so lucky. Would they repeat what they had done last night? Or would this passion subside in years to come?

McKenna quietly left the bed and wrapped a shawl around her naked body. She walked toward the fireplace and gingerly curled up into the adjacent wing chair. Quiet moments passed as she watched the golden flames of the fire spit and crackle. Her tranquility was soon interrupted when she felt two brawny forearms encircle her shoulders.

"Kitten, you are lost in thought. What is it you are pondering on such a glorious Christmas morn?"

McKenna sighed. "Parker, will our lovemaking always be the way it was last evening? Will our passion always be so strong? Will I ever bore you?"

Parker walked around her chair and knelt on one knee. "McKenna, look at me."

McKenna slowly met his eyes. The shawl she had wrapped herself in began to fall off one shoulder. Parker leaned over and softly placed a kiss upon her bare skin.

"McKenna, we will always have passion, my dear. I can say that being married to you will always provide the unknown. We may have disagreements, and our tempers may unfurl. But we will never, never go to bed angry. You and your tempting body will never be tucked away from me in anger. We will only continue to explore each other's likes and dislikes. We will nurture each other and take care of each other. There is no other who could come close to your beauty and your zest for life. You provide me with more than any man could hope for. Now, to prove just how much passion there is between us, let's shed this shawl and repeat last evening."

"Parker, my God, it is daylight," McKenna gasped, pulling the shawl around her even tighter. "We can't do those things in daylight. It isn't right."

Parker let out a low, throaty chuckle. "The hell it isn't."

With that, he pulled the blanket from McKenna so quickly that she couldn't react, leaving her naked in front of Parker.

"We are husband and wife now, and there is nothing wrong or sinful about a husband and wife enjoying each other, whether it is nighttime or daytime."

McKenna stole a glance at the window, the curtains ringed with the soft glow of the morning light. No one would see. And perhaps there *was* something deliciously wicked about enjoying her husband—*husband*, how she loved that word—while the rest of the household busied about their chores.

She turned her twinkling eyes back to Parker and allowed her arms to slowly fall from where they had been crossed over her bare chest. Parker's lips curved up into a wolfish grin, and he lunged forward.

Chapter 68

"Lord's sake, you would have thought they would have made an appearance by now!" exclaimed Zadie at the breakfast table Christmas morning.

"Woman, it was their wedding night. All bets are off. Need I remind you what time we woke up the morning after our wedding night?" said Cooper with a wink.

"You hush up. You don't need to blab our private business all over the breakfast table. There's children here!"

"Come on over on this side of the table, and I'll show you some private business." Cooper winked as he took a sip of coffee.

"You best hush up this instant," Zadie snapped as she wiped her brow with her apron. Those gathered at the table could not help but chuckle at Zadie's embarrassment, knowing full well that Cooper would have a sound lecture when they found themselves alone.

"Oh, can't we open our presents right now? Just one?" Maggie begged.

"Maggie, dear, eat your breakfast first, and afterwards I promise we will open our gifts," Pia said calmly.

"Oh, Mama, I am too excited to eat! Can't we all just hurry up a bit?"

"Oh, all right," said Pia with childlike energy. "Let's all hurry up and eat. There are *a lot* of presents under the tree to open. Merry Christmas, everyone!"

"Merry Christmas, indeed!" shouted Parker as he entered the dining room with McKenna in tow. McKenna blushed, knowing that everyone knew what had occurred the night before. But her embarrassment soon faded when she received smiles of encouragement from those seated.

"I would like to offer a prayer," announced Pia as she stood. "Merry Christmas to my wonderful family and friends. Thank you, God, for what you have given us this day. May we continue to appreciate your goodness."

"Amen," everyone echoed in unison.

The rest of the day was indeed glorious at the manor house. Gifts were shared and sweets were eaten; church was attended, followed by a grand evening supper. Carols were sung, memories were shared, and new memories were created.

"Parker, come here, there is something you should see," hollered McKenna with an eagerness in her voice from the kitchen.

"What is it, kitten?" asked Parker as he ducked through the doorway to McKenna's side.

"I think there has been another marriage of sorts in this house. Look over in the corner by the fireplace."

Parker followed McKenna's glance and saw Knox and Lyla, snuggled together.

"Well, I'll be damned," sighed Parker as he walked toward the pair and bent down to pet them. "Merry Christmas, you two. I can see that you are not going to get up for me with a customary wag of your tail, huh, girl? How about you, Knox? You going to get up for Mrs. Sloane?" Both canines wagged their tails in response to Parker's words, but that was the extent of their movement.

"Well then, by all means, don't let us interrupt your evening." McKenna joined her husband and knelt down in front of Knox, giving him many kisses behind his ears.

"Merry Christmas, Knox. You are such a good boy. You too, Lyla. Merry Christmas, girl." Parker helped McKenna to her feet and together they turned and blew out the remaining candles, leaving both dogs to bask in the warmth of the fire.

Chapter 69

New Year's Day 1864 was a bitter, frosty, and gelid beginning. However, the weather outside had no bearing on the wedding ceremony taking place inside the Wells' home. Jenny had chosen to wear her mother's wedding dress. The Scottish lace was lovely, with peach-colored blooms appliquéd into the hemline and flounce of the sleeves, making Jenny look like a storybook bride. Her ancestral clan colors were cobalt blue, pale green, and soft peach, and such colors had been incorporated into the floral bouquets for McKenna, Maggie, and herself.

Molly McTavish was quite talented with the art of quilling, and she had taken laborious efforts to gather and dye paper to match the colors that Jenny had chosen. The placemats for each guest had been quilled, with an evergreen laid upon each. Pia had purposely chosen her gold-embossed dinnerware to honor Pepper and Jenny. The entire home was magnificently decorated in gold and blue bows entwined with Christmas greenery. It reminded McKenna of a magical music box from a medieval castle of long ago.

Pepper and Jenny were married in Olympia's parlor by Pia's very dear friend, Reverend Caldwell. The ceremony began at noon with Ian's brothers playing *Amazing Grace* on their bagpipes.

McKenna absorbed everything about this special day as she stood beside Jenny. Just a week ago, she had been saying the same vows that Jenny and Pepper were now professing to each other. As she peered out among those who had gathered to witness this marriage, she thought of the events that had led up to this day. Who would have ever imagined that Pepper and his father would be in the same room? Or that Ian McTavish would be invited to this wedding? Ian and Thaddeus had agreed to begin building the projects that McKenna had arranged, rather than submit to hard labor for the next two years on the shipyard. Both men were working together and so far, neither of the two had caused trouble. McKenna imagined that Ian had faced a much harsher punishment from his wife, Molly, once she had been informed of his machinations and deceptions. Hopefully, the next two years' worth of work would find a way to move on and bury the hurt and anger caused by their grudging hearts. Today was a good day to bury the hatchet, so to speak, she thought to herself.

"McKenna. McKenna, the ring! It is in your pocket. May I have it?"

Jenny's nervous voice brought McKenna back to the present, and she hurriedly reached into her pocket and handed Pepper's wedding band to Jenny. The band had come from Thaddeus. That was in and of itself was a monumental gesture.

"What God hath joined together, let no man put asunder. I now pronounce you husband and wife… Pepper, you may kiss your bride."

Those final words and Pepper's lengthy kiss to his bride sealed the ceremony. Once again, the Wells' home was filled with orchestra music, laughter, joyfulness, and the spirit of love.

This is truly a successful conclusion to such a dreadful year, thought McKenna as she walked toward the dessert table, noticing Quaid selecting a piece of cake for the young lady beside him.

"Quaid, New Year's Day is a new start for 1864. My happiness is going to begin right now!" McKenna winked at her cousin as she dipped her fork into an unusually large slice of white cake. Bending over slightly, she whispered into Quaid's ear, trying not to be overheard and said, "Who is the sweet girl on your right? And here I thought, you had a crush on me this whole time!"

"Well, if truth be told, I did have a mighty bad crush on you cousin, that is, when I *first* arrived. I even thought about tryin' to steal you away from Captain Sloane, but, every time I am near you, I get beat in a horse race, or beat in a target contest, or shot at and thrown from a horse. Hell, I figured it was time for me to look elsewhere and have a safer life. With all due respect, of course!"

"Of course, Quaid, with all due respect, she is a beauty. Be a gentleman, cousin, she looks like a keeper," McKenna whispered back with a smile.

"That is my intention," Quaid replied back with a wink.

"So sorry to interrupt your little talk, my dear and Quaid, but I know something better than that slice of cake you are about to eat." McKenna would know that husky voice anywhere.

"And just what would that be, husband?" she asked without turning around, placing the vanilla confectionary in her mouth.

"Why don't you follow me to the kitchen and find out?" Parker smiled with a wink whispering a silent 'excuse us' to Quaid and his pretty little escorted guest.

"Why, Captain Sloane, we couldn't possibly leave this fine wedding celebration just to try new pastries," McKenna exclaimed as she was being ushered forward through the crowd.

"Pastries? I had something else in mind…" he chuckled as he kissed her forehead.

"Would you like to taste this cake, my love? It is delicious," she asked, raising a dessert fork filled with more frosting than cake to Parker's mouth.

"Is that Zadie's cake?" Parker asked before opening his mouth to McKenna's offer.

"You know it is, and it is divine!" she replied as she gently placed a piece of cake in Parker's mouth.

"Here now, Captain Sloane, what's the matter? Have you stooped to being spoon fed by your lovely wife?" Pepper asked as he slapped his best man on the shoulder.

"No and mind your tongue first mate," Parker replied back, swallowing with a half-choke. "Wedding or no, I'll accept no insubordination from you today!"

"Parker Sloane, behave yourself, and quit teasing Pepper. Today is his day and yes, Uncle, he did allow me to offer him a bite of cake," McKenna managed to say before she stuffed another piece of cake into her husband's mouth.

"If you three are done teasing each other, I would like McKenna to step outside with me and help me readjust my headpiece. I fear it is lopsided," Jenny pleaded as she approached the trio and placed McKenna's hand in hers, putting the uneaten cake on the table. "We will be right back, I promise." The two of them winked at their handsome husbands and made their way through the crowd to the outside veranda doors.

"Oh, McKenna, I just had to get a breath of fresh air," Jenny said as she leaned against the wall seat of the rose garden.

"I understand; the fresh air feels good tonight, and you have had a long day," McKenna answered as she looked up into the night sky and sighed.

"McKenna, I am scared," Jenny whispered with a slight frown, interrupting the calm silence between them.

"Scared? Whatever for?" she asked with a stunned look upon her face.

"You know, for…"

"For what, Jenny?" McKenna asked as she stepped closer to Jenny, noticing how she was fidgeting with her hands.

"You know, tonight? The bedchamber…" Jenny, in that moment, looked like a frightened doe—indecisive and unnerved. "I have not been with a man in such a long time, and I don't want to disappoint Pepper."

"Jenny. There is nothing you could do that would ever disappoint your new husband. He loves you, and remember, he never thought he would see you again. Do you really think that he will be disappointed in you? The very woman that he has dreamed about these past several years?"

"Well, when you say it like that, I suppose not. But…"

"No buts. Let the moment lead you. Your love and your heart will guide you, and beyond that, you will have nothing to worry about. In fact, I will forget that we ever had this conversation, because when you wake up tomorrow morning as Mrs. Jenny Wells, you will be a new bride fully cradled in love." McKenna tipped Jenny's chin up toward her with her index finger. "Trust me, you will not disappoint my uncle. Now, bend down a bit and allow me to pretend that I am fixing your headpiece. And when I finish, skedaddle on back to your reception and enjoy every minute. Remember, everyone here is happy for you both."

"Thank you, McKenna. Thank you from the bottom of my heart."

"For what?"

"For being brave enough to ride out to my facility that day and invite me to Pia's Ball. If you hadn't done that, I wouldn't be here today, standing before you as Mrs. Wells."

"You are most certainly welcome. Now, give me a hug and put a smile on your face and forget about your worry." McKenna helped Jenny stand, turned her toward the ballroom, and pushed her forward.

You are such a sweet person… Uncle Pepper is a lucky man, indeed. And I am lucky to call you Aunt Jenny—it has a nice sound, McKenna thought as she watched Jenny's retreating back.

***

"Thank you, Captain, for being my best man tonight. I couldn't have done this without you. I truly mean that." Pepper looked up into Parker's eyes with kindness, clasping his hand over his friend's forearm.

"Yes, you could have. You and I have been through a lot together over the years, Pepper. Tonight, is your night and your celebration. I am just honored to be a part of it." Together, Parker and Pepper raised their glasses and toasted before scanning the room, taking in the sights and sounds before them.

"Look at the two of them together, standing side by side like they were best friends," Pepper said with a tilt of his head in Thaddeus and Ian's direction.

"Well, they probably are getting to that point. Think about it: they are beside each other all day long, working, eating, and sleeping. They will either learn to like each other or kill one another," Parker chuckled in agreement.

"I have to hand it to McKenna, she probably knew the best punishment would be to put those two together for a long time. That was a clever idea on her part," Pepper stated as he took a drink of champagne.

"Yes, I believe you are right, dear friend. I think little Miss McKenna had their punishment all planed out in that pretty little head of hers. It's funny how things have a way of smoothing their way out, isn't it?" Parker asked while watching Ian and Thaddeus from across the room, chortling over a conversation shared only between them.

"Yes, it is. But just wait until their two years are up and McKenna has the option to renew the contract for another two years. By God, she will have the last laugh on them! Damn it all, I am so glad that I met my niece, that she met you, that she met Jenny, and well… you know the rest. Hell, I am just so damn happy that Jenny is in my life now."

"And I am so damn happy that McKenna is in mine."

Chapter 70

Tears formed in McKenna's eyes as she watched her father's ship set sail for America. His leave was up, and he had to return to the dismal shores of war. McKenna hated to see him go on that blustery March morning; she hated the fact that she had to remain in England. She knew this was best, but she was so homesick.

"Kitten, come along; we need to get home before the cold swallows you up."

"Parker, can I just stay here one more minute?"

"No, sweet, it is too cold out here. Come along," Parker urged as he guided her away from the docks. Together, they walked toward the waiting carriage and headed home. She put her head on Parker's shoulder and wept. It was her right to cry. It was unfair. No one knew how she felt now—*Not even Parker*, she thought as she snuggled against his chest and looked across the traveling landscape.

It is the worst emptiness imaginable. Thank goodness, I have Parker. His strength will get me through. But for how long? How much longer will I be in England? Is this going to be my home forever? Home—what does it look like now? Is it still there? Is there anything of Charleston remaining? What about the neighbors and their homes?

McKenna's thoughts abruptly ceased as the carriage pulled up to Aunt Pia's home. The blustery wind nearly toppled McKenna over as she stepped out.

"Cousin McKenna, Cousin McKenna, come quick. We have to show you a surprise," Maggie exclaimed, running up to McKenna like a small whirlwind.

"Whatever is the matter, Maggie? Is everyone all right?"

"Yes, everyone is wonderful!"

McKenna, Parker, and Maggie ran to the barn as quickly as they could. They opened the heavy doors, and there on the pile of straw were Lyla and Knox and six brand new puppies!

"Oh, my Lord!" exclaimed McKenna. "Parker, look at the puppies!"

"I see them, sweet. All six of them! I can only imagine what my girl went through to bear all six of those!"

"Well, I can assure you that Knox did not go through nearly as much pain as Lyla did. We knew she was carrying puppies, but I never dreamed she would birth six of them!"

"Would you care to explain that, my dear?" Parker asked, smiling.

"Well, you see, you plant your seed inside the woman, and then for all practical purposes, your job is done. You don't have to carry that baby and your body doesn't change. You do not get fatter by the day. In fact, your body doesn't change at all. Your bosom or chest does not increase, and you certainly do not have cravings for certain foods. You do not even get lightheaded in enclosed spaces. And most importantly, you do not have to get bigger clothes made to accommodate your rounding body."

"Aw, my sweet kitten. But only you—and other women, of course—can carry a life within you. You can feel the kick of tiny feet and the movement of another human being within you. That is something, my dear, that we men will never be able to feel. As for a rounding body… a woman is never so beautiful as when she is carrying a child."

"Do you truly feel that way, Parker?"

"Of course, kitten. I say what I mean. You should know that by now."

"Parker, repeat the part about how beautiful a woman is when she is carrying a child. I want to hear it again."

"You, my dear, just want to hear flattery. I need to get you inside the house, and we both need to eat. I am famished."

"Oh, I am famished, as well. Especially now."

"Why are you so hungry today, kitten? We had a hearty breakfast."

McKenna began to walk out the barn door and stopped to look back at Parker. "I don't know, I just am. I wished I could have talked to Papa a bit more, though. I really wanted to tell him something, but I just didn't."

"Kitten, what more could you have said to your father that you didn't already say?" Parker asked as he helped her escorted her up the stairs.

"I would have told him that he was going to be grandfather."

Parker stopped, forcing McKenna to stop. "What did you just say, kitten?"

"You heard me. I would have told him that he was going to be a grandfather, just like you, my love, are going to be a father!" McKenna leaned toward Parker and placed a soft kiss upon his lips.

McKenna giggled as she was suddenly picked up and carried to the kitchen door.

"Parker, I am pregnant, not crippled," laughed McKenna.

"McKenna Sloane, you have just made me the happiest man alive! By God, woman, you will not do anything to risk injury to yourself or our babe."

"Our babe..." McKenna sighed. "That sounds nice. I think she will like her father when she makes her entry into the world this fall."

"I am sure he will! Let's not tell anyone until the evening meal. Shall we?"

"Whatever you wish, my dear Captain."

Chapter 71

March passed into a breezy April and rainy May. June brought some heat to the land, and August was downright sultry. The humidity made McKenna extremely uncomfortable. She knew her time was coming, and she was ready for it. Fortunately, McKenna had had very little discomfort throughout her pregnancy, other than the constant reminders that there would be no horse riding until after the baby was born and then only with the doctor's approval. The few times McKenna had ventured out to the barn were disastrous. Parker had planted spies all over Pia's home.

If McKenna even attempted to mount Solomon early on in her pregnancy, Parker threatened to lock her in her room. When she took her daily walks, she was always escorted. There were a few times that tempers exploded, but no one seemed to remain angry. It was as though Parker had bribed the inhabitants of the manor to patronize her. Today, she had had enough. She was going for a walk without an escort, even if it was only to the pond.

The breakfast dishes had long been cleaned and put away. The women were busy making candles in preparation for the winter season ahead. McKenna needed fresh air, and she needed to be alone. She walked through the rear kitchen, grabbing a biscuit and two bones along the way. *I feel so big and round,* she thought. *I am always hungry and tired.*

The babe was busy kicking, letting her know she wanted out. Deep in her heart of hearts, McKenna knew her baby would be a girl. Zadie thought so too, as did Pia and Maggie. Jenny, however; thought she would be having a boy, and of course, so did Parker and all the rest of the men.

The sun felt so good on her skin. The butterflies flew heavily around her, as though even they had been told to escort her!

Oh, Parker, she thought. *You are so eager for this little baby to be born. What a good father you will be.*

He was doing increasingly more business at the docks now, and leaving the sailing to his most trusted crewmembers. Parker had already built a cradle and a small infant bed and placed them on his side of the bed.

Perhaps he will be willing to get up for the early morning feedings! she laughed to herself.

Knox and Lyla walked with McKenna down to the pond, bribed with biscuits and bones. Since Quaid, Livingston, Caleb, Maggie, Pepper, and Cooper had each taken a puppy, Aunt Pia's home was now bursting full with three new wives, three new husbands, one new dog, and six new puppies. Not to mention four new table settings on Sundays plus Quaid's new beau, Julia. Thank goodness, Aunt Pia's heart was as large as her home.

McKenna sat down on the swing with the two dogs by her feet. She reached into her pocket and gave each protector a ham hock bone.

Oh my, she thought, *the sun feels good.* She noticed that the wind was picking up slightly, but still felt refreshed.

"May I join you, my dear?"

McKenna was startled out of her peaceful reverie by her aunt's voice. "Aunt Pia, you startled me! Of course, you may. What brings you down to the pond today? You always seem to be so busy."

"Well, today is special," she said as she next to McKenna.

"Oh, and why is that?"

"Today, I must decide something, my dear, and this decision is going to be important."

"Well, can I be of help to you?"

"I'm afraid not. Although I am happy to share with you."

"Please do, Aunt Pia."

"I think Reverend Caldwell is going to ask me to marry him."

"Aunt Pia! That is wonderful news. You are going to say yes, aren't you?"

"Oh, McKenna, even being pregnant, you are filled with energy. My dear, the truth of the matter is that I desperately want to say yes."

"Oh, oh, I hear a but…"

"But I am afraid. I am afraid I won't match up to his expectations. I like my life and my independence. I am not sure if I am ready for a man to be in my life, again. It has been a long time since I have been with a man—in that sense. Do you know what I mean? Maggie is approaching twelve. My Lord, twelve years without a man is a very long time."

"I do understand, Aunt Pia. But it has been a long time for the reverend, as well. His wife died nearly ten years ago. I believe it was fate that brought you both together, and fate will direct your lives. He is a good and kind man, and he is ready to live his life with a mate. I truly feel that no one should live life alone. You have befriended the reverend for a very long time now. Perhaps tell him how you feel. You don't have to get married right away. If you need more time, take it."

"Hmm… I also must consider my children. What if they don't like him? Maggie doesn't know what a father truly is. She was an infant when her daddy died."

"I feel that your children would want you to be happy, and you deserve to be happy. The boys are old enough to understand what true love means. Just look at Quaid and his new girl. And, keep an eye on Livvy—he is a hit with all the girls, too. So see, it is a decision you must make based upon what your heart tells you. Rely upon your instinct, and let it guide you. A man of God such as the reverend will allow his faith and trust to the Lord. Perhaps you should leave your faith up to the Lord, as well."

"I feel like a schoolgirl, McKenna. I feel all giddy inside when I see him, and I haven't had those feelings in such a long time."

"Sounds to me as if you are smitten with the reverend. If you did accept his proposal, when do you think this wedding ceremony would take place?"

"Well, Jonathon wants to go to Judge McCain's and get married. We both want a simple ceremony and a celebration with our family. No church wedding, no party, no excitement, no reception with the neighbors… just our family."

"Well, I think that can be arranged. But *first*, he needs to ask you and then you must answer him. Aunt Pia, he can't very well hear your answer from this old swing. Why don't you walk over to the bridge right now?"

"The bridge? Why?" she asked with a questioning tone to her voice.

"Because if my eyes do not deceive me, I see a man of the cloth standing on the bridge staring in your direction. Go on, now, go to him, and tell him how you feel. Just remember one thing. You deserve to be happy and you deserve to share all the joys and the sorrows that may come your way with someone that you love."

"Oh, McKenna, thank you for allowing me to share my thoughts with you. If he asks me, I think I may just say yes! I am so excited I could skip all the way to the bridge." Pia shrugged her shoulders and clapped her hands like a child unwrapping a toy.

"Then, by all means, go skip," McKenna replied with a smile.

Pia rose and placed a kiss upon McKenna's forehead, then hugged her tightly.

"Are you feeling all right? Dare I leave you alone? I know you are ready to have this child, my dear, and I remember how I felt toward the end of my pregnancies. You look rather tired; maybe I should stay with you."

"Oh, for heaven's sake, go. If I need you, I will yell for you. I won't be here much longer. Go on, now; say the magic word 'yes' to your future husband."

Pia nodded and half-skipped all the way to the bridge. When she reached the reverend, they embraced. Somewhere in that moment she must have uttered the word yes, because he picked her up and swirled her in circles.

Ah… this day is a day to remember. Finally, Aunt Pia will be married and fill that emptiness she has harbored for so long! She deserves to be happy and she deserves to share her life with that someone special. Reverend Caldwell will be a fine husband and a wonderful addition to this family. Speaking of additions, if only this baby would stop moving so rapidly. It almost feels as if this babe has four feet pressing on my lower back!

Chapter 72

"Parker Sloane, I hate you for what you did to me!" screamed McKenna. "Oh, my God, this really hurts, Zadie I will never allow him to come near me again. Zadie, go get a knife and cut off his male part. I can't do this, I can't." McKenna writhed in her bed relentlessly.

She had been in labor for ten hours. Her first contraction begun at sunrise, when Parker had run to get Zadie.

"You can do this and you will, baby girl," Zadie insisted for at least the eightieth time. "Now, I see the baby's head, and you are just gonna to have to push when I tell you to. Do you hear me? I want you to push in just a bit."

"Zadie, I do not have any more energy left. I can't push."

"Well, I can't do it for you. Hold on to Pia's and Jenny's hands, and *push, now*!"

McKenna pushed and screamed, and pushed some more. Sweat coated her from her temples to her chest.

"Come on, now, push again, McKenna," encouraged Pia.

McKenna gave everything she had left and made one more push.

"Here it comes. I have your baby, McKenna-girl. I have her!" Zadie cried.

"Her?"

"Yes, child, you have just given birth to a baby girl!" Zadie cut the cord and wrapped the infant carefully and tightly and laid her upon McKenna's chest.

"Oh, my Lord, you took your sweet time in coming out to meet everyone! She is beautiful! She has all her fingers and all her toes. Oh, my goodness, she is so beautiful!" At that moment, McKenna had another terrible contraction. "Oh, my Lord, Zadie, when will these contractions stop? This one hurts worse than before."

Zadie checked between McKenna's spread thighs. "Oh, dear, baby girl, you ain't done yet!"

"What the hell do you mean, I am not done yet? I damn well better be done!"

"Well you ain't," Zadie snapped back.

"Zadie," McKenna sobbed, "please, make the pain go away."

"McKenna-girl, the pain will stop when you finish pushing out the second baby."

"Second baby? What do you mean, second baby?"

"You have twins, McKenna-girl! You are givin' birth to another baby!"

McKenna groaned in agony. "Oh, my God, I will kill Parker Sloane for doing this to me. He will never touch me again. Oh, my God…this hurts…"

"Push one more time for me, child—almost there! Now push as hard as you can. This baby's head is bigger!"

McKenna pushed until she collapsed.

"Well, welcome, Master Sloane, to your new world!" said Zadie with tears in her eyes as she cradled the babe in her hands.

McKenna blinked her tired eyes open. "A boy? I have a boy and a girl?"

"Yes, McKenna-girl, you just gave birth to twins—one boy and one girl!"

"Zadie," McKenna gritted her teeth. "you make damn sure there aren't any more in there. Do you hear me?"

Zadie laughed in spite of herself. "Baby girl, you are done. You did real good. Now, let old Zadie clean you up and stitch you up. That last baby tore you a bit. This will hurt, child."

At that, McKenna collapsed with both babies on her chest. Zadie looked at McKenna as she cuddled her babies. *Well, McKenna-girl, you have just given birth to two beautiful babies. You told me you would name your baby Shannon Maribelle Sloane if it was a girl or Liam Parker Sloane if it was a boy. I sure am glad you picked out a name for both!* she chuckled to herself.

"You sure did enter this world with a good set of lungs," Zadie whispered to Shannon as she began to clean her and Pia began to clean Liam. "Lord's sake, you both took your sweet time comin' into this world. I'd best go and tell your daddy. He is gonna be real surprised!" Zadie handed Shannon to Jenny as she turned and made her way toward the stairs.

"Oh, I think he will be more than surprised!" giggled Pia out loud.

"He may just faint when he hears that he is the father of twins!" added Jenny as she continued washing Shannon's arms.

"Parker, Parker, come quick," Zadie hollered from the hallway. "Come quick and see your babies."

Parker had been in the study with Pepper and Cooper since daybreak. He could not eat, drink, or sleep until he knew his precious kitten was all right. When he heard Zadie's words, he jumped from the wing chair and took two stairs at a time. Suddenly, he stopped at the top landing and looked up into Zadie's eyes.

"Zadie, what did you just say?"

"I said, come quick and see your babies."

"Babies?"

Zadie grinned slyly. "Yes, sir, babies. One boy and one girl. Your kitten just delivered twins."

"Twins?"

"Yes, Captain, you are the proud father of twins. Guess your 'kitten' made sure she had a girl no matter what. Come on, now, McKenna is waitin' to see you. I'm not sure if she wants to kiss you or shoot you after what she's been through. But you are the daddy, and you need to see your babies. Go on, now. Go on in."

***

Parker walked into the birthing room. McKenna sat on the bed, propped up against several pillows and holding two small bundles, one in each arm. She looked like hell, but she still glowed.

"Hello, kitten."

"Hello, captain," McKenna breathed, her face warm and welcoming despite her glistening forehead. "Would you like to meet your children?"

"My God, McKenna, you have made me so damn proud at this very moment. I have a son!"

"And a daughter."

"You know, you are just stubborn enough to have two just to ensure you would have a girl." Parker gave McKenna a passionate yet careful kiss. "What have you decided to call them?"

"How does Shannon Maribelle and Liam Parker sound? Maribelle after my mother, and Liam after your father and yourself?"

"I think it sounds perfect. They are perfect."

"Go on, pick them up, and hold them."

"Kitten, I don't know how; I am afraid I will crush them."

"Never you mind about that, Parker Sloane. You will have plenty of time to get used to them. Oh, by the way…you'll need to build another infant bed."

Parker chuckled, and gazed into his beautiful wife's eyes with uncontrollable bliss. He held his entire small family in his arms until McKenna, comforted by the reassuring strength of his presence, fell asleep.

My kitten has done well, he thought. His little kitten had given him not one but two beautiful babies. A man could ask for nothing more. *Ah, yes,* he thought, *I am truly blessed.*

Chapter 73

Thank goodness, the breakfast table had extensions. Pia's table now included Quaid and his new girl, Julia, Livingston, Caleb, Maggie, Pepper and Jenny, Cooper and Zadie, Parker and McKenna and the twins, and Pia and her new husband Jonathon Caldwell. Every Sunday, the family gained four more: Ian and Molly McTavish, and Thaddeus and his new wife, Mary Jones. Conversation was never at a loss, and as far as that went, neither was the amount of food. Percy and Tierney had finally gotten married, and they also joined the family at every meal. There were no servants or hired hands in this house; every member was a family member with a job to do. Christmas was around the corner again, and the babies were growing every day.

Three months had passed since McKenna had given birth to Shannon and Liam, and in those three months, McKenna had gotten back to her old self, both physically and emotionally. She was blessed with enough hands to help her with the babies when her own hands were occupied. Babies had a way of bringing youthfulness to a home. Even the boys took turns holding and feeding them. McKenna had a difficult time nursing the babies at first, but soon worked her way through the process. Parker continued to work at the docks each day, but made sure he and Pepper were never late in arriving at home. The house was filled with contentment and anticipation for the upcoming holiday, as Pia once again prepared for her Holiday Ball.

"McKenna, there is a letter from your father, dear," said Percy as she handed the letter to McKenna at the table.

"Thank you, Percy!"

McKenna quickly opened it, and a bolt of sadness tore at her heart.

"What is it, kitten? Why did you stop?" Parker asked immediately.

"I have a letter from Papa, and yet he doesn't even know that he is a grandfather of twins. I have yet to write to him. Oh, God, I feel horrible. How could I have forgotten him? Dear Lord, I did. I forgot to tell him."

"McKenna, you hush up about that," Pia admonished firmly. "Harper knows how time-consuming infants can be... let alone two infants at once. You can sit down this evening and compose your letter, and then take it to town tomorrow."

"Do you really think he will understand, Aunt Pia?"

"I do. Now, child, would you please read and update us all with news from the States?"

McKenna opened the letter and began to read.

"Dear baby girl,

By now, you may have had my grandchild! Please write soon, and let me know what you delivered into this world. I know Parker wanted a boy, and you had hoped for a girl, but I simply hoped for a healthy baby.

Things here continue, with battles and fights each day. It appears that both sides are having more than their share of casualties. McKenna, I often sit in my tent at night and reflect over my years as a medical doctor. Perhaps that is what keeps me sane, I suppose. I remember the first time I saw your mother; she was the most gorgeous nurse I had even seen. I admired her gentility to her patients and her compassion. I made it my goal to be like her, and I now hope that I have accomplished that. These young soldiers are broken, and I try my best to provide hope for them while under my care. God willing, this war will end soon and these young men can be reunited with their families.

My darling McKenna, you have asked me in your letters about our home. My best guess is that our home, as we knew it, is no longer there. General Sherman destroyed everything on his march to the sea. My patients have told me how he set fire to military targets, cotton gins, telegraph poles, homes, and railroads, and even freed the slaves along the way who were willing to help him. He has ardently offered to live off the land, eating farmer's turnips, apples, potatoes, and vegetables along the way. Food, weapons, horses, mules, and anything else that can be used has been taken. Most of the injured have dictated their letters to me. The problem is, I have no way to get their letters to their loved ones. The mail delivery is in shambles at this point; only the military messengers ride to and from their posts. But this experience has strengthened me, baby girl. Now, you may think that sounds rather odd, but it has. I have become a better doctor because of this war. This has opened my eyes and has forced me to step out of my comfort zone and face the deprivations this country has endured. My doctoring has strengthened my faith and my resolve in God.

I have stood and prayed over enough soldiers to last a lifetime, and each time I find myself praying, I find myself closer to the Lord. Perhaps this was my destiny—my calling—to be here and help. At least, I find peace in thinking that. You must endure hardship as a good soldier of Jesus Christ. Surprisingly enough an amputee, not much older than you, told me this verse from the Bible before he died. I sat with him through the night, holding his hand. He, too, was from Charleston, and I was hoping that he would survive. Unfortunately, he did not remain with us, but his final words have stuck with me. He was right; we must be good soldiers of God.

So, my sweet girl, I end this letter with hope. My gut tells me that this war will soon end. Both sides are tired and supplies are depleted. It is a matter of time—plain and simple.

Once again, please pass on any news about my grandchild. I only wish that Maribelle could be here to see her grandbaby as well. I suppose she is watching from heaven.

And tell Cooper to keep my grandbaby off his damn horse until he or she is at least six or seven years old, if he knows what's good for him!

All my love,
Papa"

McKenna closed the letter and looked into Parker's eyes. "Well, it sounds like the home I know and love is no more. But you know," she sighed before continuing, "I find it peaceful though that Papa feels that he has grown as a doctor, even through all the hellish things he has seen."

"Sometimes my love, we must all endure hardship in our lives to appreciate the small things that we take for granted," Parker said softly, rubbing McKenna's forearm.

"Here, here," chanted the murmurs around the table.

"I suppose you are right. Well then, if you will all excuse me, I am going to call this a night and write a letter to Papa. I need to tell him that he is the grandfather of two very beautiful babies. And, Cooper, just for the record, I was five when you sat me on my first horse. I think Shannon and Liam can top that. Let's try the age of four. What do you think?" she asked with a wink and nod to Cooper.

"I think I will cross that bridge when I come to it. Go on now, and write your letter to your Pa," he answered back while shaking his head. Cooper waited until McKenna had left the room before he spoke to those seated at the table. "You wait and see, she'll have those babies on ponies before they are out of diapers!"

"Well then, Coop, you'd best be getting some ponies within the next year and a half," answered Pepper with a jolly laugh.

Chapter 74

The holidays were celebrated with ardor, avidity, and vigor. The Christmas and New Year's pageantry was spectacular. Olympia's Ball was a success once again. Those in attendance had the opportunity to gush over the twins. Of course, twins were a rarity, and the neighbors were beguiled by their innocence and purity, especially when they were dressed in holiday green and red velvets. The ladies in attendance simply could not keep their hands off of them, or deprive them of any attention, for that matter. Time passed and it passed slowly for McKenna.

The following months saw Parker spending more time at the docks, ensuring that all supplies were accounted for before exporting them from London. The babies were crawling and became more curious every day. McKenna had fashioned a wagon so she could take her children on walks to the pond and back for fresh air and sunshine. Knox and Lyla accompanied her wherever she ventured, knowing there was always a treat or two tucked into that wagon for them.

But today, she was fidgety and she wanted to ride. She hadn't taken a long ride on Solomon in months. She knew that her anxiety would only get worse by the end of the day. She knew one sure way to resolve her restlessness and agitation, and that was to seek out Solomon. So, she promptly finished her morning dishes, gathered the babies in the wagon, and went to the barn, seeking out her beloved horse.

She'd barely taken a step inside before recognizing a gruff voice behind her. "McKenna, what are you doing in here with those babies? It is dirty in here, and they don't need to breathe in this dust and dirt."

McKenna spun, rolling her eyes at Cooper. "Really, and how many times have we breathed in this dust and dirt? Honestly, you are acting like an overbearing grandfather."

"I am their honorary, overbearing grandfather, and don't you forget it, missy."

McKenna laughed and walked over to Cooper to give him a huge hug.

"I love you, Cooper, and don't you ever forget that!"

"Here, now, stop that huggin' and answer my question. What are you doin' down here?" stepping away from McKenna's outstretched arms.

"Well, I am here to ride Solomon," McKenna said as she straightened the blanket of the twins' laps.

Coop let out a disbelieving snort. "No, you ain't."

"Cooper, please, I need to. If I have to stay in the house one more day, I will burst. I feel perfectly fine and you know that I have been riding Solomon for short rides for a while now. Please Cooper, will you watch the babies for me? I won't be gone long."

He sighed and studied her face, recognizing the pent-up frustration on her features before he continued. "Well, go ahead and saddle him up, but I want you to go no farther than the pond. There is a nasty storm brewing, and I want you close by. Do you understand me?"

"Yes, sir! Will you take the babies into the house for me, and tell Zadie I will be back shortly?"

"Sure, I will, but not before I take my grandbabies for a nice, long walk, as well." Cooper winked at McKenna and began to push the wagon toward the side door.

What a blessing this home is, McKenna thought as she watched Cooper pushing the wagon and talking to her twins. She turned to her horse, brimming with exhilaration. "Come on, boy, let's go for a ride." McKenna saddled up Solomon, trotted out of the barn, and made her way down toward the pond. The wind was picking up but it felt good. She felt a sense of freedom and youthfulness flooding over her. She slid her left leg back and pushed her ankle into Solomon's side as a silent command to canter and the horse responded dutifully and immediately. He was enjoying his exercise as much as McKenna was.

"Okay boy, let's ease up a bit. The wind is worse and I suppose we should be getting back. It is getting a bit chilly out here." McKenna reached down to untie her scarf from her waist and realized that it was no longer there. Now, where had it gone? She looked behind her, but to no avail; she couldn't find it.

All right, she thought, *it must be here somewhere. I must not have tied it very tight and now I've lost it. Damn, that was my favorite scarf, too.*

***

"Cooper, where is the mother of these beautiful babies that you are so willingly pushing in their new wagon?" smiled Parker as he trotted up beside him.

"Oh, she's down at the pond with Solomon," Cooper said, smiling down at the twins.

"Well, do you mind watching the babies a bit longer while I go down and fetch her before the storm blows in?"

"Take your time, Captain. I enjoy spending time with my grandbabies. Go on, now, go kiss that beautiful wife of yours and bring the both of you back before you get drenched. Those clouds are storm clouds."

"Thank you, Cooper. I shall."

"And Parker…"

"Yes?"

"McKenna needed that ride today. She's been feeling mighty cooped up, and I told her to go on and ride. Poor thing, I thought she was damn near gonna cry when she asked me to watch the twins. I felt real bad for her, I did." Cooper looked up at Parker with glossy eyes.

"Coop, I know she's been antsy lately. Thank you for encouraging her to go. But I really need to go bring her back—those clouds spell rain!"

Parker turned his horse and cantered down toward the pond, trying to guess the direction of the approaching storm clouds. The wind had picked up significantly and the sky was starting to rumble with distant thunder. He knew he didn't have much time to get both of them home and dry. When he neared the pond, he saw his beautiful wife bending over the cattails, gathering some flowers.

My God, she is a beauty, he thought as he remained seated and simply stared at his wife before him.

"Hello, kitten," he said in his husky voice behind her.

McKenna straightened quickly. "Do you make it a habit of sneaking up on a person when least expected? Or, do you just enjoy looking at my behind?" she laughed as she blew the Queen Anne's lace into the wind. "I have missed you, husband. Crawl on off that horse, and come and give me a proper hug," she ordered with her hands on her hips and a glorious smile spread upon her face.

"Kitten, your wish is my command," he said as he jumped off his horse. It took no more than a few steps before Parker had gathered McKenna in his arms and kissed her hard and long upon her lips. "As much as I would like to stay here and hug your delicious body, we need to hurry, love. The storm is almost on top of us and we need to get home before we get drenched."

"Oh, alright, I will race you!" McKenna offered back as she slipped from Parker's embrace, gathered her reins, and mounted Solomon. "Come on then, let's see who gets to the barn first."

"You little vixen. Do you think I cannot catch you?" he questioned with a smirk as he mounted his stallion.

"I think it will be fun watching you try," she sassed back before she broke into a canter, leaving Parker inhaling her dust.

Parker smiled as he watched her ride ahead of him, knowing full well his mount would be on top of hers in no time. "Okay, boy, she's had her fun. Let's go get her."

Parker chased McKenna for a mere few yards before he overtook Solomon's gait. With one reach, he leaned over in his saddle and pulled Solomon's reins to a stop.

"Parker, let up on your hold!" McKenna squealed, "I thought time was of the essence and you were in a hurry to get to the barn!"

"I am, my dear. But you, my love, have just been overtaken and I wanted to slip in a quick kiss."

"Parker, as much as I would like to sit here and be kissed by you, it is starting to rain. We will have to resume this another day!" she giggled as she tried to release the reins from his large hands.

"Believe me, kitten, we will resume, although I believe you told Zadie to take a knife and cut off my male part. That would make it difficult to resume any love making you may be thinking about," he snickered as they both trotted up the lane toward the barn.

"Oh, I did say that, didn't I? But that was during my contractions, and of course, I didn't mean it," she said with a sideways glance.

"Well, I am glad to hear that," he replied, looking up at the rolling clouds. "Let's get home."

"Parker," McKenna said hoarsely, almost coming to a complete stop.

"Kitten, we dare not stay—the storm is coming," Parker said, urging his mount to continue.

"Parker, look… who is that up by the fence swing?" she asked with a sudden turn in her saddle.

Parker turned in the saddle and looked the length of the pond. "I don't see anyone, love. It must have been a shadow; it is that time of year when the spring sun casts its glow upon the land. Come on, let's ride home."

"No, Parker, it wasn't a shadow. I saw someone standing there. I swear I did. And look! My blue scarf is on the fence swing. It fell off me on my way here. How on earth did it get all the way over there? I didn't ride by the swing on my way here," she asked, remaining still and looking in the direction of the fence. Her face was pitted with skepticism and for a brief moment, she doubted the direction of her earlier ride.

"I don't know love. If it will make you feel better, I will ride over and get it for you." Parker didn't wait for her answer and quickly cantered over to the fence swing, leaned over, and easily untangled McKenna's blue scarf with his long, muscular arms. He scanned the area, and seeing no one, turned his mount around. He tucked the scarf under his leg and took a final glance back. No one was there; he saw nothing but a lone bouquet of faded pink carnations.

What a shame, he smiled to himself. *A young lady and her beau must have come out here and got caught up in the moment and dropped her bouquet. Young love,* he thought as he smiled all the way back to McKenna.

Chapter 75

Supper smelled delicious that mid-April evening. Biscuits and stew, beans, pudding, and fruit tarts were spread lavishly across the table. McKenna and the boys had been practicing their archery skills in the morning and their target shooting that afternoon, before finishing their barn chores, and now she looked forward to sampling those fresh biscuits with the butter Zadie had churned last week. McKenna was just about to bite into one when an unusually loud banging on the front door began. Parker and Pepper immediately rose from the table and saw their young neighbor, Timothy, on the other side.

"What is it, Timothy? God in heaven, what is all this knocking about?" asked Parker.

"My mother told me I ought to rush over and tell you," said the young boy at the door. "Something about the war in the States being over. Here, it is in the newspaper."

Every mouth in the Wells family dropped open.

The child looked from one awestruck face to the next, then shrugged. "She supposed you'd want to know."

"Thank you, Timothy," said Pia as she came to stand beside the boy. "Go on home, now, and tell your mother that we are grateful for the news."

"Yes, ma'am, I will." The door closed slowly and gently. Time seemed to stand still. The air reverberated young Timothy's words. *It is over, it is finally over.* McKenna had left the table with the other family members to see what the young messenger had to say. When she heard the words "It is over," she fell to her knees and wept.

Oh, my Lord, thought McKenna, *I can go home. I can go home after five long years. But what will I go home to? Do I have a home? Will my children ever get to see the home I grew up in? I will wait for a letter from Papa. He will tell me what to do. I know he will.*

Parker could only imagine the thoughts passing through McKenna's mind. He walked to her, bent, and held her tightly. "It will be all right, kitten. We shall take one day at a time, sweeting. One day at a time."

***

The newspaper article had given very little detail, other than the southern army had surrendered to the northern army in a place called Appomattox. None the less, McKenna waited for any news from her father each day in earnest—barely maintaining her composure and eagerness to go home.

Days passed and finally McKenna received a letter from her father. McKenna's fingers trembled so much that she could barely open it. All the members of the household were called inside and soon gathered around the table to hear McKenna read her father's words aloud.

"Dear McKenna,

The war between the states is over, my sweet daughter. It has finally ended. Lee abandoned Richmond and once the city was abandoned, there was little hope left for the Confederacy. Robert E. Lee retreated to Northern Virginia to a little town called Appomattox, and that is where he surrendered. The documents of surrender were signed in the McLean farmhouse on April 9th, and baby girl, I was there. Myself and a dozen of my colleagues were given the assignment to offer any medical help that may have been needed. My God, I was there to witness the end of this hellish nightmare. I watched Lee leave the McLean house, and when he did, the Union soldiers began to cheer—mockingly so. But then, Sam Grant walked out beside General Lee and he put a stop to their jeering. He told everyone that the rebs were 'now our countrymen, and we did not want to exult over their downfall.' The only sound to be heard were the willow trees blowing in the breeze. Dozens had gathered and yet no one made a sound. General Lee walked his horse right past me; in fact, I could have touched him. The picture of him on that horse will forever be embedded in my mind. He sat stoically, not cracking a hint of relief upon his face. In fact, he had no expression at all; he looked forward with one hand on his thigh and the other on the reins. My God, he looked like a king.

Once news spread of the surrender, other Confederate officers surrendered their armies as well. Johnston surrendered ninety-eight thousand troops to Sherman in North Carolina. Imagine that many men gathered in one place!

President Lincoln and General Grant have imposed rules for the Confederate soldiers. The Southern soldiers will not be imprisoned for treason. They will be allowed to keep their sidearms, horses, and mules. They will be able to return home to their farms and resume their farming. General Grant is a man of honor. Everyone there that day, including me, witnessed Grant and his troops saluting General Lee as he left the McLean farm.

I know you want to come home and see me and the house where you were raised. But my dear, you must not. Charleston is a city of ruin. When Sherman cut off the supplies to the city, it crumbled on its own. McKenna, you have no home left. There are no walls or doors left to rebuild. The entire foundation was decimated with burning and cannon fire. The barns are nothing but charred embers. I am temporarily staying with our neighbors, the McCafferty's.

They were spared brutal damage and have graciously allowed me to stay with them until I can figure out what to do. My initial intent was to clear the land and rebuild the house and barn. My dream is to rebuild my office along the Battery. But for the time being, I must wait. There is nothing left of Charleston as you remember. Food is scarce, medical supplies are non-existent, fresh milk is absent for babies, and poverty, penury, and hardship now fill the muddy, rat-infested streets. This is not a place to bring two babies, my dear. There would be no place for you to live, and certainly no place for two grandchildren to crawl and play.

I am torn. I want to see you and Parker and welcome my beloved grandbabies. It is just not possible to do so with such devastation. I have been asked to reinstate my practice in Washington, D.C. I have considered that and am tempted to do so. I was offered Chief of Surgery at one of the local hospitals. My Yankee coworkers have recommended me and have requested I be placed on staff. It was President Lincoln's intent to help all wounded soldiers, no matter the color of uniform. However, President Lincoln will not be able to see his intentions be carried out.

President Lincoln was assassinated on April 14. This country has been torn apart, and now its leadership has been taken from us. President Andrew Johnson has been thrown into a tumultuous scenario.

So, you see, my sweet McKenna, do not come home to Charleston. There is no Charleston. The land remains, but the cradle of your youth is gone.

I most humbly ask you, Parker, and the twins to consider traveling to Washington, D.C. area and live with me, at least until Charleston is rebuilt enough to go home.

I will warn you; you may be looked upon with disdain and contempt. The ladies of the North may spurn and rebuff you, initially. You may not have an inner circle of friends right away and you may not have young playmates for Shannon and Liam right away. Your Southern accent may be heard with unfair contempt.

Parker, however, will flourish with his shipbuilding. He will be needed— desperately so. It is a catch, my dear. Washington, D.C. would be a new beginning for you and Parker and your family. Time will heal the wounds of this war, but it will take a monumental amount of time.

I ask you and Parker to discuss this, and to decide one way or the other. I am certain I will accept the position in Washington D.C. I have been given a home to reside in close to the hospital. It was the Union's way of offering an olive branch to me and to my medical expertise.

Since I have no other home now, this offer is very hard to refuse. If you and your family would like to live with me, I would be honored. With that, I will end this letter and leave you to your decisions. Please give my love to the family and to your friends who are in Pia's embrace. I thank God every day that you were away from this wreckage of our nation.

President Lincoln stated that a 'house divided cannot stand.' It remains to be seen, doesn't it? I would only hope that President Johnson and his cabinet and administration will work faithfully to restore dignity, self-worth, and pride within this country.

I love you, daughter. I pray that these letters that have traveled so many miles between us are at an end. Please write back, and give me your thoughts and your decisions for moving back to America and living with me in D.C. until you are both settled. I love you, baby girl.

Papa"

McKenna slowly placed the letter upon the table and slid it back into its envelope.

"What are you going to do, cousin?" asked Caleb.

"Before you answer that, granddaughter," Thaddeus interrupted, "I would like to offer you a gift." All eyes around the table focused on Thaddeus as he continued. "As you may or may not know, I have owned property in Washington, D.C. for quite some time now. I would like to give a parcel to you and Parker and your children. I haven't been much of a grandfather; in fact, I haven't been much of anything to my family. But working at the shipyard has given me plenty of time to think about things. Things I shouldn't have done and things I should have done better. Perhaps this will help pave the way toward more forgiveness. I was a selfish old man and I recognize the mistakes I have made. If you do decide to move and live with your father, then perhaps this property could provide you a place to build a home or even a horse hospital and barn. It would mean a lot to me if you would consider my offer."

McKenna was already on the verge of tears from her father's letter, and now, Thaddeus's gesture was simply too much. She tried to speak calmly but her emotions were getting the best of her. "That is very generous, Grandfather Wells," she choked out. "I simply do not know. I must think about this. Parker, would you care to walk with me, and help sort this all out?"

"Certainly, my dear. If you will all excuse us, we need to have some quiet time. There has been a lot of information shared this evening. I am sure you all understand if we leave you now to discuss our future. Zadie, would you watch the babies, please? We won't be gone too long."

"You go on now, Captain. There are enough hands in this room to take care of those sweet babies. You both have a lot of decisions to make. Go on now, your babies will be put to bed."

McKenna and Parker nodded with appreciation and excused themselves from the table, walking hand in hand to the veranda. The cool evening breeze did little to lift the heaviness that enveloped McKenna's mind.

"My God, it is over. What are we going to do, Parker?" asked McKenna with tears forming in her beautiful blue eyes as she looked up to his face.

"What do you want to do, kitten?" Parker sat down on the swing, tenderly pulling McKenna beside him and watched her face in the moonlight.

"I want my children to meet their grandfather. I want to make a new life for our children. I want to go home." Moments passed before she whispered, "What do you want, Parker?"

"I want to see you happy. You have given up five years of your life for the sake of your country's struggles. It is now time for you to have your contentment. I can sail from any port."

McKenna's lips quivered. "Do you mean it? Can we go back and see Papa?"

"Yes, kitten, I mean it. Let's go back to the States and make a new home for Liam and Shannon. I am willing to do this if you are."

"Oh, Parker, let's take Shannon and Liam, and Elizabeth and August back to the States and make a new home with Papa."

"What did you say?" Parker's face showed complete shock as his feet stopped the swing from gliding forward.

"I said, let's take Shannon and Liam and Elizabeth and August back to the States and make a new home with Papa."

"Who, my dear?"

"Elizabeth and August. The doctor does believe I'm carrying twins again, you see. They should be joining us around fall. Remember when we snuck out and returned to the hunting cabin during that miserably cold January afternoon? Well…"

"…Well, my dear kitten, are you telling me that is where we conceived these two new babies?"

"I am, my love." McKenna sealed that statement with an eyelash kiss.

Parker stared at McKenna in dumbfounded amazement for a few moments, then swept her into an embrace upon his lap, laughing joyfully. Suddenly, he pulled away. "What in the hell kind of name is August?"

McKenna's built-up tension broke as she rocked with laughter. "Well, I believe you once asked Pepper what in the hell kind of name McKenna was."

Parker shook his head, a smile tugging at the corner of his mouth. "He told you that, did he?"

"He most certainly did. As far as August goes, why don't you ask Cooper about that name? He could fill you in on that answer. Now, stop talking, and kiss your pregnant wife, or I shall rise up off your lap and leave."

Parker wound his arms tightly about her waist in response. "Rest assured, kitten, you shall never leave my embrace."

CPSIA information can be obtained
at www.ICGtesting.com
Printed in the USA
LVHW080231240321
682303LV00023B/342